# Dead Man's Daughter

Roz Watkins

ONE PLACE. MANY STORIES

HQ
An imprint of HarperCollins*Publishers* Ltd
1 London Bridge Street
London SE1 9GF

This edition 2019

1
First published in Great Britain by
HQ, an imprint of HarperCollins*Publishers* Ltd 2019

Copyright © Roz Watkins 2019

Roz Watkins asserts the moral right to be
identified as the author of this work.
A catalogue record for this book is
available from the British Library.

Hardback: 978-0-00-821465-4
Trade Paperback: 978-0-00-821467-8

MIX
Paper from
responsible sources
FSC
www.fsc.org    FSC™ C007454

This book is produced from independently certified FSC™ paper
to ensure responsible forest management.

For more information visit: www.harpercollins.co.uk/green

Printed and bound in Great Britain by
CPI Group (UK) Ltd, Croydon, CR0 4YY

# Praise for Roz Watkins

'*The Devil's Dice* is a terrific debut by Roz Watkins; it teems with shivery atmosphere and introduces a cop quietly different from most of the women detectives in British crime fiction today.'
**The Times Crime Book of the Month**

'A touch of Agatha Christie, a dash of Ann Cleeves's Vera and a suitably moody setting in the Peaks . . . bring a formidable newcomer to British crime writing.'
*Daily Mail*

'A fascinating debut . . . Watkins brilliantly balances superstition and scepticism in this clever first novel.'
*Sunday Times*

'A fabulous book. I can't wait to meet DI Meg Dalton again.'
**B A Paris**

'An outstanding debut. *The Devil's Dice* had me gripped from the start.'
**Stephen Booth**

'Twisty, creepy, funny, and you may shed a tear too. More DI Meg Dalton please!'
**Caz Frear**

'A page-turning debut featuring a fabulous lead character.'
**Susi Holliday**

'A fascinating debut with a deliciously old school mystery at its heart. I can't wait to see what Watkins does next!'
**Angela Clarke**

'A pacy, twisty read that had me on the edge of my seat . . . what a brilliant debut!'
**K.L. Slater**

'Exceptional debut. Beautifully written and observed crime novel, with such well-rounded maturity it was a pleasure to read from start to finish. Glad it is a series so that we all have a lot more to look forward to.'
**Amanda Robson**

**Roz Watkins** is the author of the DI Meg Dalton crime series, which is set in the Peak District where Roz lives with her partner and a menagerie of demanding animals.

Her first book, *The Devil's Dice*, was shortlisted for the CWA Debut Dagger Award, and has been optioned for TV.

Roz studied engineering at Cambridge University before training in patent law. She was a partner in a firm of patent attorneys in Derby, but this has absolutely nothing to do with there being a dead one in her first novel.

In her spare time, Roz likes to walk in the Peak District, scouting out murder locations.

For Rob.

(I still think we could have got
away with a talking dog.)

# Prologue

She lay on her back, hard metal under her, so cold it felt like being punched. The smell of antiseptic scorched her throat. She couldn't move.

She tried to scream. To tell them not to do it. She was still alive, still conscious, still feeling. It shouldn't be happening. But no sound came.

The man had a knife. He was approaching with a knife. Silver glinted in the cold light. Why could she still see? This was wrong.

With all her will, she tried to shrink from him. He took a step closer.

Another man stood by. Dressed in green. Calm. They were all calm. How could they be so calm? She must be crying, tears streaming down her face, even if her voice and her legs and her arms wouldn't work.

*Please, please, please don't.* Inside her head she was begging. *Please stop. I can feel. I'm still here. I'm still me.* No words came out.

The terror filled her; filled the room.

The knife came closer. She couldn't move. It was happening.

The touch of steel on her skin. Finally a scream. One of the men placed his hand on her mouth. The other man pushed towards her heart.

# 1.

The woman grabbed my hand and pulled me deeper into the woods. Her voice rasped with panic. 'She was running towards the gorge. The place the locals call Dead Girl's Drop.'

That didn't sound good, particularly given the Derbyshire talent for understatement. I shouted over the wind and the cracking of frozen twigs underfoot. 'What exactly did you see?'

'I know what you're thinking, but I didn't imagine it.' Strands of dark hair whipped her face. She must have only been in her forties, but she looked worn, like something that had been washed too many times or left out in the rain. She tugged a similarly faded, speckled greyhound behind her. 'I was expecting proper police,' she added.

'I'm a detective. DI Meg Dalton, remember? We wear plain clothes.' No matter what I wore, I seemed to exude shabbiness. I was clearly a disappointment to Elaine Grant. I sneaked a glance at my watch. I'd had a phone-call from my mum that I should have been returning.

Elaine tripped on a stump and turned to look accusingly at me, her edges unclear in the flat morning light. 'Pale like a ghost. The dog saw her too.'

I glanced down at the dog. He panted and drooled a little.

I wasn't sure I'd rely on his testimony, but I couldn't afford not to check this out. I shivered and pulled my scarf tighter around my neck.

'Wearing white, you mean? But you saw blood?'

'It was a nightdress, I think. Just a young girl. Streaking through the trees like she had the devil at her heels. And yes, there was red all over her.'

Branches rattled above us. Something flickered in the corner of my eye – shining pale in the distance. My breath stopped in my throat and I felt a twitch of anxiety. 'Is there a house in these woods?' I asked. 'Approached down a lane?'

Elaine walked a few steps before answering. 'Yes. Bellhurst House.'

I knew that place. The woman who lived there had kept calling the police, saying she was being watched and followed, but she'd had nothing concrete to report. After the first time, they'd joked that she had an over-active imagination. Possibly a fondness for men in uniform. And we hadn't taken her seriously.

Elaine touched my arm. 'Did you see the girl?'

We waited, eyes wide and ears straining. The dog let out a little affronted half-bark, more of a puff of the cheeks. A twig snapped and something white slipped through the trees.

'That's her,' Elaine shouted. 'Hurry! The gorge is over there. Children have fallen . . . '

I re-ran in my mind the control room's leisurely reaction to this call; our previous lacklustre responses to the woman in the house in these woods. A band of worry tightened around my chest. I pictured a little girl crashing over the side of the gorge into the frothing stream below, covered in blood, fleeing something – something we'd been told about but dismissed.

4

Maybe this was the day the much-cried wolf actually showed up.

I broke into a limping run, cursing my bad ankle and my bad judgement for not passing this to someone else. I couldn't take on anything new this week.

The dog ran alongside me, seeming to enjoy the chase. I glanced over my shoulder. If the girl had been running from someone, where were they?

I arrived at a fence. A sign. *Private property. Dangerous drops.* Elaine came puffing up behind me.

I was already half over the fence, barbed wired snagging my crotch. 'Did you see anyone else?'

'I'm not sure . . . I don't think so.' She stood with arms on knees, panting. She wasn't in good shape. 'I can't climb over that fence,' she said. 'I have a bad knee.'

'You wait here.' I set off towards where I'd seen the flash of white. The dog followed me, pulling his lead from Elaine's hand and performing a spectacular jump over the fence.

The light was brighter ahead where the trees must have thinned out towards the gorge. I could hear the river rushing over rocks far below. My eyes flicked side to side. There was something to my left. Visible through the winter branches. 'Hello,' I shouted. 'Are you alright?' I moved a step closer. A figure in white. I hurried towards her. She was uncannily still.

I blinked. It was a statue, carved in pale stone. Settled into the ground, as if it had been there for centuries. A child, crying, stone tears frozen on grey cheeks. I swore under my breath, but felt my heart rate returning to normal.

Was that something else? It was hard to see in the dappled light.

A glimpse of pale cotton, the flash of an arm, a white figure shooting away. I followed. There in front of me another statue. Whereas the first child had been weeping, this one was screaming, mouth wide below terrified eyes. I shuddered.

I ran towards the noise of the river, imagining a child's body, smashed to pieces by stone and current. I didn't need a dead girl on my conscience. Not another one. I'd been good recently – not checking my ceilings for hanging sisters or hoarding sleeping pills. I wanted to keep it that way.

'Hello,' I shouted again. 'Is there anyone there?'

A face nudged out from behind a tree which grew at the edge of the gorge.

It was a girl of about eight or nine. She was wearing only a white nightdress. Her face was bleached with fear and cold, her hair blonde. The paleness of her clothes, skin, and hair made the deep red stains even more shocking.

I took a step towards the girl. She shuffled back, but stayed facing me, the drop falling away behind her. She must have been freezing. I tried to soften my body to make myself look safe.

The dog was panting dramatically next to me, after his run. He took a couple of slow steps forward. I was about to call him back, but the girl seemed to relax a little.

The dog's whole body wagged. The girl reached and touched him. I held my breath.

The girl shot me a suspicious look. 'I like dogs.' Her voice was rough as if she'd been shouting. 'Not allowed dogs . . . Make me ill . . . '

'Are you running from someone?' I had to get her away from the edge, but I didn't want to risk moving closer. 'I'm with the police. I can help you.'

She stared at me with huge owl eyes, too close to the drop behind.

Heart thumping, I said, 'Shall we take him home for his breakfast?' The dog's tail wagged. 'Is that okay?'

She shifted forward a little and touched the dog softly on the head. A stone splashed into the water below. 'He needs a drink,' she whispered.

Elaine had been right. The girl's nightdress was smeared with blood. A lot of blood.

'Okay,' I said. 'Let's take him back for a drink and some breakfast. Shall we do that?'

The girl nodded and stepped away from the edge. I picked up the end of the lead and handed it to her, hoping the dog would be keen to get home. I wanted the girl inside and warmed up before she got hypothermia or frostbite, but I sensed I couldn't rush it.

I walked slowly away from the gorge, and the dog followed, leading the girl. Her feet were bare, one of her toes bleeding.

'What's your name?' I asked.

I thought she wasn't going to answer. She shuffled along, looking down.

'Abbie,' she said, finally.

'I'm Meg. Were you running from someone?' I shot another look into the trees.

She whispered, 'My dad . . . '

'Were you running from your dad?'

No answer.

I tried to remember the substance of the calls we'd had from the woman in the house in the woods. Someone following her. Nothing definite. Nothing anyone else had seen.

'Are you hurt? Is it okay if I have a look?'

She nodded. I crouched and carefully checked for any wounds. She seemed unharmed, apart from the toe, but there were needle marks on her arms. I was used to seeing them on drug addicts, not on a young girl.

'I have to get injected,' Abbie said.

I wondered what was the matter with her. My panic about her welfare ratcheted up a notch. I grabbed my radio and called for paramedics and back-up.

'There's a stream,' Abbie said. 'He needs a drink.' The dog was still panting hard.

'No, Abbie. Let's – '

She veered off to the right, surprisingly fast.

'Oh, Jesus,' I muttered.

Abbie pulled the dog towards the pale statues, darting over the bone-numbing ground. I chased after her.

There were four statues in total, arranged around the edge of a clearing. They were children of about Abbie's age or a little younger, two weeping and two screaming, glistening white in the winter light. I ran between them, spooked by them and somehow feeling it was disrespectful to race through their apparent torment, but Abbie was getting away from me.

I saw her ahead, stepping into a stream so cold there were icy patches on the banks. 'No, Abbie, come this way!' I ran to catch up, wincing at the sight of her skinny legs plunging into the glacial water.

She called over her shoulder. 'He can drink better at this next bit.' She clutched the dog-lead as if it were the only thing in the world. I was panicking about her feet, about hypothermia, about what the hell had happened to her, and who might still be in the woods with us. But she was determined to get the dog a drink. And I sensed if I did the wrong thing, she'd bolt.

'Abbie, let me carry you to the drinking place, okay? Your feet must be really sore and cold. We'll get him a quick drink, then head back and get warmed up.'

She looked at her feet, then up at me. Worried eyes, blood on her face. She nodded, and shifted towards me.

I reached for her, but she lurched sideways and fell, crashing into the freezing water. She screamed.

Heart pounding, I reached and scooped her up. She was drenched and shivering, teeth clacking together. I pulled her inside my coat, feeling the shock of the water soaking into my clothes. I took off my scarf and wound it loosely around her neck.

I stumbled through the mud, filling my boots with foetid bog water, and finally saw a larger stream ahead, flowing all bright and clear. The dog immersed his face in it, gulped for a few moments, and looked up to show he was done.

'Right, let's go.' I shifted Abbie further up onto my hip and limped back in the direction we'd come, trousers dragging down, feet squelching in leaden boots. The dog pulled ahead, shifting me off-balance even more. Through the boggy bit again, past the cold gaze of the statues, and at last to the fence where Elaine was waiting.

'Oh, thank goodness!' Elaine said. 'She's alright.'

I gasped for breath. 'Could you go on ahead and put your heating on high? It could take a while for the paramedics to get here. We might need to warm her up in your house. She's frozen.'

'Shall I run a bath? Not too hot. Like for a baby.'

'No, it's okay. Just the heating.'

'Like for my baby.' Her eyes seemed to go cloudy. 'My poor baby.'

I touched her lightly on the arm. 'I'll bring the girl back. Just put the heating on high and get some blankets or fleeces or whatever you have, to wrap round her.'

Elaine nodded and helped me lift Abbie over the fence, before heading off at a frustratingly slow walk.

I picked Abbie up again. 'Not far now,' I said, as much to myself as her. 'We'll get you inside and warmed up.'

'Thank you,' she said in a tiny voice. 'Thank you for letting me get a drink for the dog.'

Her ribs moved in and out, too fast. That could be the start of hypothermia. I clasped her to me, enveloping her in my jacket and pulling the scarf more snuggly around her neck.

My feet were throbbing, so I dreaded to think what hers felt like. 'Where do you live, Abbie?' I said.

'In the woods.' She held on to me with skinny arms, trusting in a way which brought a lump to my throat. She rested her head against my shoulder. Her voice was so quiet I could barely hear. 'I'm tired. . . Will you make sure I'm okay?'

I swallowed, thinking of all that blood. I could smell it in her hair. 'Yes,' I whispered into the top of her head, ignoring all the reasons I couldn't make any promises. 'I'll make sure you're okay.'

★

We eventually arrived at the edge of the woods, and crossed the road to reach Elaine's cottage. I hammered on the door and it flew straight open. I wrenched off my muddy boots and sodden socks, followed Elaine through to a faded living room, and lowered Abbie onto the sofa.

'Get some blankets around her,' I said. 'I'll be back.' I dashed barefoot over the road to my car, grabbed some evidence bags, and slipped my feet into the spare trainers I'd shoved in there in a fit of sensibleness. My toes felt as if they'd been dipped in ice, rubbed with a cheese-grater, and held in front of a blow-torch.

Back at the house, Elaine had swaddled Abbie in a couple of towels and about five fleecy blankets that looked like they could be the dog's. I decided it was best not to smell them.

'Do you have anything she could wear?' I asked. 'So we can get that wet nightdress off her?'

Elaine hesitated. 'I still have . . . '

Abbie looked up from her nest of fleeces and mumbled, 'Where's the dog?'

Elaine called him, and Abbie stroked the top of his head gently, her eyelids drooping, while Elaine went to fetch some clothes.

The room was clean and tidy but had a museum feel, as if it had been abandoned years ago and not touched since. Something caught my eye beside the window behind the sofa. A collection of dolls, sitting in rows on a set of shelves. I'd never been a fan of dolls and had dismembered those I'd been given as a child, in the name of scientific and medical research. And there was something odd about these. I took a step towards them and looked more closely.

A floorboard creaked. I jumped and spun round. Elaine stood in the doorway, holding up some soft blue pyjamas. 'These?' They must have belonged to a child a little older than Abbie.

I nodded, walked over and took the pyjamas, then sat on the sofa next to Abbie. I opened my mouth to thank Elaine and ask if she had a child of her own, but I glanced first at her face. It was flat, as if her muscles had been paralysed. I closed my mouth again.

I persuaded Abbie to let me take off the sopping-wet,

blood-soaked nightdress and replace it with the pyjamas. Her teeth chattered, and she clutched my scarf. I put the nightdress in an evidence bag.

'My sister Carrie knitted that for me.' I was better at saying her name now. 'When I was very young. It's the longest scarf I've ever seen.'

Abbie touched the scarf against her cheek, closed her eyes and sank back into the sofa.

I looked up at Elaine. 'Do you know if she lives at Bellhurst House? She said she lived in the woods, but she's pretty confused.'

Elaine stared blankly at me. 'Yes, I suppose she must. They own the land that goes down to the gorge.'

A pitter-patter of my heart. The guilt that was so familiar. Again I tried to remember what the woman from Bellhurst House had reported. Someone in the woods, someone looking into their windows, someone following her. She hadn't lived alone; I remembered that. There was definitely a husband, possibly children.

'Is that your house, Abbie? Bellhurst House?'

She nodded.

'A car went down there,' Elaine said. 'In the night. I couldn't sleep. Down the lane. I didn't think much of it at the time. But now I'm wondering . . .'

'What time?'

'I'm not sure exactly. About three or four, I think.'

'Okay,' I said. 'Police are on their way to the house. What colour was the car?'

'I couldn't see – it was too dark.'

I turned to Abbie. 'Do you remember anything about what happened?' I said. 'Where the blood came from?'

She leant close to the dog and wrapped her arms around him.

He gave me a long-suffering look. Abbie spoke softly into his ear, so I could barely make out the words. 'Everyone always dies. Jess. And Dad . . . '

I looked at her blood-stained hair. 'Who's Jess?'

'My sister.'

I imagined her sister and her father bleeding to death in those dark woods, surrounded by statues of terrified children. 'Where are your sister and your dad, Abbie?'

No answer. She closed her eyes and flopped sideways towards me.

I caught sight of the dolls again.

It felt as if someone had lightly touched the back of my neck with a cold hand.

It was the eyes.

In some of the dolls, the whole eye was white – no iris or pupil. In others, the iris was high, so you just saw the edge of it as if the eyes had rolled up inside the doll's head.

I turned away, feeling Abbie's soft weight against me.

# 2.

I skidded my car to a halt on an icy, stone-flagged courtyard in front of the pillared entrance of Bellhurst House. Back-up hadn't yet arrived and the place was deserted. I'd left Abbie with a PC at Elaine's, but my stomach was knotted with concern for her relatives. They could be lying inside, gasping for breath, blood pouring from their wounds. I jumped from the car.

The house was Victorian Gothic, in the style of a small lunatic asylum. The kind of place where you'd find inexplicable cold corners and notice the cats avoiding certain rooms. It had two spiky-roofed, bay-windowed halves, flanking a tower topped with a witches' cap roof.

I bashed a brass lion-head knocker against the oak door. No answer, but when I shoved the door, it opened into a narrow hallway. A stained-glass window splashed colours onto the carpet. I stopped a moment and listened, aware that I shouldn't go in alone.

I stepped into the hall. 'Police! Is anyone there?'

Nothing. The house was so silent, it hurt my ears.

I checked downstairs. There was evidence of a break-in – a forced window and glass crunching underfoot in a utility room – but I didn't stop to investigate.

The stairs were narrow and all slightly different heights, making it hard not to trip. They led onto a landing which smelt of library books and damp coins. I crossed the creaky-boarded floor and poked my head into the first bedroom. It must have been Abbie's room, or possibly her sister's – decorated in the pink and purple that some little girls seemed to insist on, to the horror of feminist mothers. I gave it a quick glance – no blood – and retreated onto the landing. Another door opened into a larger room.

I froze. A man lay sprawled on his back on a double bed. Blood had sprayed onto the white wall beside him – a jagged line of crimson blobs with tails trailing below. More blood smeared the white duvet, the sheets, and the cream carpet by the bed. It was fresh and vivid, its coppery smell filling my nostrils.

I rushed over and checked his pulse, but I knew he was dead. I felt a wave of despair for Abbie – so strong my knees went weak. Was this her father?

I could never get used to these moments. The visceral shock of someone being dead. The knowledge that his family would have to live forever with this. Abbie would always be the girl whose father was murdered. Possibly the girl who saw her father murdered. This would be with her for the rest of her life.

I took a moment to look at the man's face. To think of him as a person, before he became a job, a problem to be solved, a puzzle to be pored over.

I let myself feel the sadness, then took a deep breath and forced myself into robotic mode.

I scanned the walls. The blood was arterial – you could see the tell-tale pattern produced by the pumping of his heart. I glanced at the man's throat. The carotid had been slit. He lay on his white sheets surrounded by the spectacular crimson display, his head jerked back into the pillow.

I flicked my gaze around the room. A window was open. Drawers had been pulled out and upended, leaving T-shirts and underwear littering the floor. A photo by the bedside showed a couple grinning at the camera, blue sea behind them. It was this man. I pictured little Abbie, wrapped in fleeces, hugging the dog, blood smeared on her face. The room shifted as if I was on a boat. Had she seen this done to her father?

And where was the sister? And what about the mother?

I needed to get out. Get the scene secured. My mind was full of all the things I had to do — gripped by that familiar desperation to get this right. To get it right for the relatives. For little Abbie.

I carefully left the bedroom and checked the rest of the house, pushing each door with tight fingers, praying I wouldn't find a dead sister or mother.

I didn't. The house was empty. I called in what I'd found, spoke to the crime scene manager and media officer, and walked back out to my car.

I jumped. Tyres kicked up gravel. A silver four-wheel drive hurtled along the driveway and skidded sideways onto the paved area, almost hitting my car. A woman leapt out and ran towards me. She looked familiar. The woman from the photo by the bed, minus the sunniness. 'What's going on?' she shouted. 'Where's Abbie? What have you done with her?'

I took a step towards her, trying to block her from going into the house. 'Abbie's fine. Wait a minute.'

She pushed past me.

I reached for her arm. 'You can't go – '

She pulled away. 'Where's Abbie?'

'Stop! You can't go inside.' I shot round her and blocked her path with my body. 'Abbie's fine. She's not in there.'

She tried to shove past me, so hard I was forced to push her away. She caught her heel on a flagstone and fell backwards, landing with a thud. I reached down to her, but she jumped up without my help.

I saw her arm draw back and then my eye exploded. I collapsed onto the icy ground.

★

I opened my eyes. Wow, that hurt. Of course they all chose that moment to arrive. The pathologist, a herd of SOCOs, half of Derbyshire's uniformed PCs, and DS Craig Cooper – the nastiest cop in town. I heaved myself up as quickly as possible and tried to look like someone who hadn't been punched in the face.

Craig jumped out of his car. 'Christ, what happened?'

I gestured into the house. 'Victim's wife's in there. Get her out.'

I touched the skin above my cheekbone. There were types of people you expected to thump you, and she hadn't been one of them. I'd allowed her through, and now she'd have messed up the scene.

I suited up in the shadow of the house. My ankle was throbbing. I'd injured it as a child and it hadn't healed well. A big lump of callus stuck out and restricted movement, making me walk with a slight limp and minimising my chances of ever looking like a glamorous TV detective. I must have bashed it when I'd fallen.

Craig appeared, leading the wife by the arm. Her hair and

clothes were smeared red, and she was hunched over, letting out gulping sobs. Craig gave a little shake of his head and rolled his eyes to the sky.

The woman pulled herself free of Craig and stood breathing heavily and seeming to get control of herself. She raised her head. 'Where's Abbie? Where's my little girl?'

'She's with police at a neighbour's. She's fine.'

The woman sniffed loudly and took a couple more open-mouthed breaths. 'I told the police someone was stalking us. I told you but nobody believed me. Oh God . . . ' She folded forwards again and held her stomach.

'We'll need to ask you about that,' I said gently, ignoring the implied criticism. 'But I have to get a few things started. Then I'll take you to Abbie.'

She leant against one of the pillars by the door.

'Was anyone else in the house?' I asked. 'Abbie mentioned her sister.'

'There's no one else.' The woman swallowed and seemed to shrink into herself. 'Jess died. Years ago.'

I opened my mouth to say something, but nothing emerged. Craig took the woman's arm and led her away.

I made sure inner and outer cordons were in place, and went back in for a careful look around.

The hallway led into a utility room that had an old-house smell of mould and mushrooms. Its window had been smashed, the catch released, and the sash shoved upwards, making a space big enough for someone to climb in. The house still had its original wooden windows, making it an easy target. One thing for hideous PVC double glazing – it did make breaking in a little harder, and prints showed up so much better on plastic than on wood.

The kitchen was terracotta-tiled and rustic, with a central butcher's block fit for dismembering large animals. The room was tidy but lived in, the fridge adorned with magnetic letters and a rather competent drawing of a dog's head. A calendar on the wall showed school trips and ballet lessons. I glanced at today's date – *Rachel back from Mum's*. They were so terribly sad, the calendars of dead people, full of assumptions of an ordinary life continued.

One of a collection of impressive chef's knives was missing from a knife block on the countertop. If they were in order, it was the largest. I looked at the others – all throat-slittingly sharp.

There was no evidence of an intruder in the living room. The TV and a laptop were still there, and the normal clutter of a family. A sketch pad and pencils, a thriller involving submarines, a pile of tedious-looking paperwork, a pair of nasty trainers.

A small study next door had been substantially trashed. All the drawers in an antique-style desk had been emptied, leaving piles of papers strewn over the floor. I scanned the piles, not knowing what I was looking for, wondering what they'd been looking for. Trying to sense the murderer's presence in the room amongst the mess they'd made.

I scrutinised the bookshelves. More man-thrillers, reference books, and a little cluster of self-help, including a book called *You Become What You Believe*, which seemed tragically ironic in the circumstances. A card was propped on a low shelf of a bookcase, a picture of a kitten on its front. I lifted it with a gloved hand and looked inside. *Thank you for getting in touch. We appreciated it. We don't know who you are and we can't tell you who we are, but it is of comfort to us that something good has come out of this terrible tragedy.* I stuck it in a bag.

I noticed a door in the corner. It was hard to picture the layout of this peculiar house. I walked over and pushed it, and found myself in a bright room with a bay window overlooking a garden. Green-tinted light flooded in. The walls were lined with benches, on which drawings lay scattered. I stepped over to look at them. A charcoal heart on cream paper, snakes' heads projecting from it, the muscle of the heart melding seamlessly into the snakes' necks, an optical illusion making the muscle seem to twitch. Another heart shown split in two, blood oozing from its red centre. A third with a single eye which stared out at me and seemed to follow me as I walked along by the bench. I felt goose pimples on my arms, and made a note to get the whole lot bagged up.

Upstairs, nothing was obviously wrong in the pink room. No blood that I could see. Just a normal kid's room – another sketch book, pony pictures on the walls, a globe on a painted desk, a mauve duvet hanging over the side of the bed, a fluffy elephant on the floor. My eyes were drawn to a sparkling amethyst geode on the bedside table, its purple crystalline innards shining from inside a dark egg of stone. I'd loved crystals and minerals too when I was a child.

The air in the main bedroom had a metallic sweetness that touched the back of my throat. The pathologist had arrived. Mary Oliver. We'd bonded over a few corpses since I'd come to the Derbyshire force six months previously – we shared an interest in obscure medical conditions and a guilty *Child Genius* addiction.

A glimpse of bone shone through the dark slash in the man's neck, reminding me of abattoir photographs from animal rights groups. 'So, he was killed by cutting his throat?' I said.

'Almost certainly. The PM will confirm.'

'Is the carotid severed?'

'Yep, cut right through with an inward stabbing motion. Two stabs, by the look of it. That's why we've got some nice spatter.'

'Would someone need a knowledge of anatomy or would random stabbing do it?'

'Random stabbing could do it, although you'd have to be lucky with the location of the knife.' She paused and looked at me. 'Or unlucky, depending on your point of view.'

'Time of death?'

'Can't be accurate on that yet, as you know.'

'But . . .'

'His underarms are cool. From his temperature and the lividity, I'd suggest somewhere between 2 a.m. and 5 a.m. He's not been moved post mortem. This is all provisional, as you know.'

'Okay. And he doesn't seem to have struggled?'

'I'd say he was fast asleep and he never regained consciousness. Unpleasant business.'

Something had to be pretty gruesome for Mary to say it was unpleasant. Her bar was high. 'So, it's a premeditated attack then? Is that what we're saying?'

'There are no defence injuries that I can see at the moment. It's not your typical interrupted-burglar or domestic scenario. Shame the wife got in and messed up the scene though.'

'I know.' I reminded myself I'd done my best to stop her, at some personal cost. Guilt was my specialist subject, which I could perform to Olympic level. 'The child had blood on her as well, so I suppose she must have come in and seen this.' I imagined briefly how Abbie must have felt. I'd been about the same age when I'd found my sister hanging from her bedroom

ceiling. I hoped Abbie wouldn't still be having flashbacks in her mid-thirties. 'She's not saying much.'

Mary frowned at me. 'Have you found a weapon?'

'No. What are we looking for?'

'An extremely sharp knife with a pointed end.'

'Something was missing from a knife block in the kitchen.'

'Could a woman have done it?'

I hadn't heard Craig creeping up behind me. He was quiet, given what a lump he was. I stood back a little to let him see into the room.

'What Craig wants to know,' I said, 'is whether someone with limited upper body strength could have done this.'

'Don't get all uppity,' Craig said. 'Women do have limited upper body strength.'

'Assumptions like that get us into trouble,' I said. 'You need to arm-wrestle my friend Hannah. I suppose at least you're not assuming a man did it.'

'Au contraire,' Craig said, having recently returned from some winter sun. 'It's probably the bloke's wife.'

That probably said more about Craig's relationship with his wife than it did about the murder, but I decided to keep that insight to myself.

'You wouldn't need a great amount of strength,' Mary said. 'Because it was done with an inward stabbing rather than a slicing motion. A feeble little woman could definitely have done it.' She smiled at me to show her solidarity.

I nodded a thank you at Mary, and stood for a moment taking in the room. Something was odd. The chaos of pulled-out drawers and strewn clothes was muted. I couldn't imagine an intruder storming through.

An en-suite bathroom led off the bedroom. From the droplets

of water in the cubicle and on the floor, it looked as if someone had taken a shower within the previous few hours.

Back on the landing, I noticed something on the windowsill, almost hidden behind the curtain. At first I thought it was a vase, but then realised it was a carving in pale wood. I walked over and looked more closely. It was a miniature version of one of the stone statues I'd seen in the clearing – a child screaming. The terrible face was the same, making the hairs on my arms stand on end. But there was one difference. This one was naked, and where the heart should have been, the wood had been gouged out, leaving a hollow in the child's chest.

# 3.

Back outside, I found Craig standing on the paved area staring upwards. His breath puffed dragon-like into the air. 'It looks like a house for freaks.'

Good old Craig. Always ready to empathise with the victim. But he did have a point. I loved these kinds of houses, but wasn't sure I'd want to live in this one, even without a corpse in the bedroom. Not in the middle of the woods, isolated from any other human life. I looked up at the central tower poking into the heavy morning sky. 'You can imagine catching sight of dead children's faces in those top windows,' I said, forgetting for a moment that it was Craig.

'You're not going to have one of your funny turns, are you?'

I pretended I hadn't heard. He knew I'd had time off with stress in my last job in Manchester, a fact which I found excruciating. But I was senior to him. He wasn't supposed to talk to me like that. I just wasn't sure how to stop him without resorting to being a total dick. If I ever had to work closely with him, I'd be forced to take up Zen Buddhism or go to anger management classes. I sucked in a breath of bitterly cold, pine-saturated air and thought about fluffy kittens and not at all about smacking Craig's smug face.

'They brought the kid back,' he said. 'She's in the van with her mum and the paramedics. Victim's name's Philip Thornton. His wife's Rachel Thornton. Wife claims she was with her mother last night, left there at nine this morning to come here. Put petrol in the car in Matlock, and we've confirmed that with the petrol station. When did he die?'

'Mary thinks between two and five.'

'How come you were on the floor? Did you fall over?'

I didn't answer. Decided not to mention the punch. It would give Craig far too much pleasure. 'I think she's the woman who's been phoning about a stalker,' I said.

Craig let out a sigh of theatrical weariness. 'Bloody fantastic. So it'll be our fault the poor bastard's had his throat slit.'

★

I climbed into the paramedic's van. Abbie looked tiny, sitting on a robust green chair, quietly rocking to and fro, her legs pulled to her chest. She was still holding on to my sister's scarf. Her mother sat by her, but there was a space between them, a physical distance that seemed matched by something else – something about the way the woman didn't quite look at her daughter, the way she angled herself away from her a tiny bit.

I couldn't take on this case – I'd have to pass it on to another DI or DCI – but early information was vital, so I needed to talk to the wife. In the horror of the immediate aftermath, the relatives often handed you the answers, fresh and steaming on a plate.

The van smelt of bleach and misery. I had a flash of memory. When I'd found my sister, I'd curled up like Abbie was now, trying to make myself so small I'd disappear. I wanted to put my arms around Abbie and make it all go away. But of course nothing would make it go away.

'Mrs Thornton,' I said. 'I'm sorry. You've had a terrible shock.'

She looked up and gave me a blank stare. 'It's Rachel.' There was a deadness in her eyes as if they'd seen too much.

I sat on the seat next to her. All the earlier agitation seemed to have gone, and she looked flat and resigned.

'I'm DI Meg Dalton,' I said. 'I need to ask you a few questions. I know it's hard but the sooner we get onto it, the better.'

Rachel shifted away from me slightly, but still kept a little distance between herself and Abbie. 'I told you someone was following me.' She sniffed and wiped her face with a tissue.

Abbie leant her head against the side of the van, eyes closed, red-smeared blonde hair spilling over the back of her seat. I wanted to get her cleaned up and warmed up and generally looked after. But I'd been told that sensitive kid-people were on their way to handle this, and to make sure we didn't lose any evidence in the process.

Rachel ran blood-stained fingers through her own dark hair. Mascara seemed to bruise her cheeks.

'Can we talk outside?' I said.

She nodded. We left Abbie in the van, being looked after by the paramedics, and walked along a path leading away from the house and into the woods.

The ground was so cold I could feel it through the thin soles of my trainers, and the air was icy and seemed more solid than usual. I remembered Abbie's feet stepping through the freezing stream and hoped the paramedics had made sure she was okay.

'So, tell me about this person who was following you.'

Rachel breathed in shakily, and swallowed. 'No one took it seriously. I told your people but they didn't care.'

'Do you know who it was?'

We walked slowly, Rachel shuffling as if her feet were numb. 'I never saw them properly. I only caught glimpses and sensed someone looking at me when I went outside or walked in the woods.' She sniffed and wiped her face. 'Once I even thought someone was following us when we went out in the car.'

'Can you remember what type of car they were in?'

She shook her head. 'Sorry.'

'It's okay. You're doing really well.'

She ground to a standstill and looked down at her feet. 'How am I supposed to cope? I don't know how I'm supposed to get through this.'

There was no answer to that. A woman in her forties, with a young child, her husband gone. I didn't know how she was supposed to cope.

'There's a bench,' I said. 'If you're not too cold. Shall we sit a moment?'

'I'm not cold. I don't feel anything. I could walk into a frozen lake and I'd feel nothing.'

We walked to the bench, which was in the clearing with the statues I'd seen earlier.

'Do the woods belong to you?' I asked. 'And the statues?'

She glanced at them and let out her breath. Nodded slowly. 'Horrible things.'

'Are they old?'

'Victorian, I think.'

A plaque was attached to the nearest statue's base. I leant forward to read it. *For the weak and the poor who died for the strong and the rich.* How depressing.

I glanced at Rachel. She was shaky but seemed to be coping. 'Just a few more questions. Is that okay?'

'I suppose so.' She stared ahead, as still as one of the statues. 'I don't think it's sunk in.'

'Thank you. We can go back to Abbie in a moment. But do you remember when you first noticed you were being followed?' I was careful not to say, *When you thought you were being followed*, or anything that implied she might have been mistaken.

'A few months ago. I wondered if it was something to do with Phil's job. He's a social worker, and sometimes the parents of the kids can get nasty. But Phil didn't think it was that.'

I twisted to sit sideways on the bench, so I could look at her. 'Who did he think it was?'

She paused and her eyes went glassy. When she spoke, her throat sounded tight. 'I don't think he even believed me. He thought I was imagining it. Ironically.' She twisted her mouth into an almost-smile, and fiddled with her wedding ring, rotating it on her finger. 'But he's been odd recently. He disappeared a few times and didn't tell me where he was going. And he's been a bit secretive.' She sat up straighter, and some life came back into her, as if thinking about her husband's strange behaviour was dulling her pain. She took a deep breath and turned to look at me. 'I do love him though. I really love him.'

'Okay,' I said. 'Thanks. And I need to know where you were this morning.'

She fished a tissue from her pocket and blew her nose loudly. 'That other detective already asked me. I stayed at Mum's. It had been arranged for ages. Phil and Abbie came home and I stayed on a couple more days to help Mum with sorting out some stuff. Wills and things.'

It was one of the most painful things about these investigations. This woman was sitting next to me on a freezing bench with her life splintering apart. Although I could only sense the jagged edges of it, I knew her pain. And yet a part of me was assessing her. Wondering if she could have done it. If she was the one who'd plunged that knife into her husband's neck.

'So, you were at your mother's last night, but you came home this morning?'

'Yes. When I'm away, Phil and I always talk in the morning. And he didn't answer, and he wasn't responding to texts. So, well, I wasn't exactly panicking because he and Abbie are both on these sleeping pills and he can sleep late, but I had a bad feeling. So I came back. And then when I got back, I found you and . . . '

I waited but she didn't carry on.

'Where does your mother live?'

'A couple of miles past Matlock. Not far.'

'And did you drive straight from your mother's to your house this morning?'

She hesitated. 'I got petrol in Matlock. You can check that.'

That suspicious part of me felt something. Something deep inside that my boss would dismiss as a hunch, but that I knew was based on years of experience and observation. Something my subconscious mind had translated into a twitching in my stomach. Her responses weren't quite right.

'So, when you saw me, had you come straight from your mother's, apart from getting petrol?'

She touched her throat. 'I told you that. It took a while though, with the traffic. Do you think Abbie was there when . . . She's really sleepy. She doesn't remember. She's on these pills for her night terrors. But she must have . . . what? Seen the killer? Or wandered through to our room and found Phil . . . '

'How old's Abbie?'

'Ten. She's small for her age.'

I waited a moment, feeling the cold air in my nostrils. The wind whispered through the trees, and I could hear the river in the distance. 'What pills is she on?'

'Sleeping pills. I can show you.'

A ten-year-old on pills. I knew in the US the drug companies had achieved the holy grail of pills for all – old or young, sick or well. But in this country, sleeping pills for a kid was unusual.

'And . . . why did you realise something was badly wrong?' I said. 'When you saw my car, I mean. You seemed very upset and worried.'

Rachel turned her body away from me and spoke as if to someone sitting on her opposite side. 'I just knew.' She blew her nose again.

All the birdsong and rustling of the trees and the rushing river seemed far away. The woods were quiet around us, as if muted by the presence of the stone girls.

'What's the story behind the statues?' I asked.

'Oh, I don't know. Some ancient folk tale or something. Phil was obsessed with them but he always denied it.'

'I noticed a carving on your landing, similar to one of them.'

'You see. Phil did that. I sometimes thought he only bought the house because of the statues. It's such a money pit, I don't know why else he came here. But he always clammed up if I asked him about them, apart from one time when he was drunk . . .'

'What did he say then?'

'I couldn't get much sense out of him. But something about doing penance, I think.'

My ears twitched. 'Penance? What did he mean by that?'

'He wouldn't say. But it seemed to have something to do with these.' She nodded towards the stone children.

Penance. That was a hot word. When anyone wanted to do penance, there was always a chance someone else wanted revenge. I wondered about the story behind the statues. 'So, any more ideas why you were so worried when you arrived at the house this morning?'

She hesitated. 'I don't know. Because no one answered the phone earlier I suppose. I'm always worried about Abbie's health. I'm sure he probably does know what he's doing, but I always wonder if Phil gets her medication right when I'm not around.'

'What medical problem does Abbie have?'

Rachel rubbed her nose. There was something sticky in the air between us. Something she wasn't saying. She didn't seem numb and shocked any more – there was a new sharpness about her. She huddled into her coat as if suddenly aware of the cold. 'You never think about your heart, do you, until it goes wrong? And then you think about it all the time.'

'Does Abbie have a heart problem?'

'Yes. It's in Phil's family.'

'So, did Abbie have a sister?'

'Jess. She died four years ago. She was only six. Not of the heart problem though. An accident.'

'I'm sorry. Were they twins?'

Rachel shook her head. 'Abbie's Phil's daughter and Jess was mine. I adopted Abbie after Phil's ex-wife died.'

I turned to Rachel and looked at her dead eyes; weighed up whether to say anything; decided I should. 'I lost my older sister when I was ten. She was fifteen.'

Some of the tension left her body. Maybe I shouldn't

have mentioned my sister. It wasn't exactly in the manual of recommended interviewing techniques. But Rachel Thornton was a person too, and I found if you shared with people, they often had a strong urge to share back. Sometimes they'd even share that they'd killed someone. Most murderers didn't intend to kill – it was something that happened in a loose moment that slipped away from them, when they were so furious they weren't really noticing what they were doing. Often it was a relief to explain and justify.

Besides, my story was public now. Google my name and there it was. Poor me. Found my sister hanging from a beam, and I was only ten. Everyone knew. After I'd kept it to myself all those years. I felt like someone who'd fallen asleep drunk and woken up with no clothes on.

We sat together on the freezing bench, touched by our own individual horrors.

I hoped she might say more but she didn't, and I decided not to push it for now. We'd need to get her in for a formal statement anyway.

'Is Abbie's heart okay?' I asked.

'She had a transplant last year.'

'That's why you can't let her have pets?'

'That's right. She has a suppressed immune system.'

I pictured the needle marks on Abbie's arms. Remembered her hugging the dog, then wrapped in his blankets and Carrie's scarf, after nearly freezing to death. Not ideal.

'Is she okay though?'

'Yes, of course.'

'Was there a problem with the transplant? Is that what your husband's artwork's about?'

'Of course not. This has nothing to do with Abbie's heart.'

I turned to look at Rachel's face.

'Do you mean your husband's death?' I asked. 'Why would it have anything to do with Abbie's heart?'

She blinked a couple of times and shook her head. 'It wouldn't. I didn't mean anything. Abbie's heart's fine.'

# 4.

'I can't take on a big case,' I said. 'I spoke to the victim's wife at the scene, but I'll have to hand it over to someone else. It's really bad timing for me.'

DS Jai Sanghera leant against the window in my room and hitched one leg up onto the sill in a bizarre yoga-style move. 'Have you told Richard why you're off next week?'

I took a step towards the door and lowered my voice. 'He wants to see me now. I can't tell him. I said I was spending time with family and catching up on some DIY and stuff.'

'If you don't take it on, he'll ship someone else in. DI Dickhead from Nottingham.'

My stomach tightened at the thought of Abbie being grilled in one of our dispiriting interview rooms. 'Maybe he'll bring that woman in? She's alright.'

Jai shook his head. 'She's tied up on a big case already. Human trafficking. No chance.'

I'd told Abbie I'd make sure she was okay. But I couldn't let my family down. I swallowed. 'I can't delay my time off. You don't know what it's like.'

'I know what it's like to lose a grandparent. Tell him you can't take the case. We'll cope with Dickhead.'

It was only Monday afternoon, but I felt as if I'd had a full week at work. And I still hadn't called Mum back. I shoved open the door to DCI Richard Atkins' lair.

'Ah, Meg.' Richard's customary greeting, whether he was bollocking or praising. 'Sit down.' He indicated his spare chair, famous for its ability to engulf the unwary. I suspected it housed the putrefied remains of previous DIs.

I stayed standing. 'I can't take on this case. I've got time off next week.'

Richard looked at me over piles of papers and the tiny cacti he used as paperweights. He rearranged them each morning and I was always looking for meaning in the arrangements, as if he was sending messages about his mood or the state of the world. He cracked his fingers. 'You let the victim's daughter fall into freezing water,' he said. 'You mustn't be so careless. She could have been seriously hurt, and the evidence on her nightdress is compromised. What on earth were you thinking?'

'It was an accident. She wanted to get the dog a drink, and –'

'The dog? You mustn't let your love of animals affect your actions.'

I opened my mouth, so stunned by the unfairness of this that I didn't know what to say.

Richard had put on weight, and was getting the look of a bulbous-nosed drinker. Did he know he was becoming a walking cliché? Eating unhealthily and turning to the bottle because his God-bothering wife had left him and was no longer providing healthy, vegetable-laden meals?

'I'm very disappointed,' Richard said. 'And what's this about the victim's wife reporting a stalker and us ignoring it?'

'We didn't exactly ignore it, but she didn't give us much to go on. And her phone calls stopped about six weeks ago. She hasn't been in touch recently.'

'It's the last thing we need. Stalking's hot at the moment. Pray to God it wasn't the stalker that did for him.'

This was modern policing. It wasn't so much the brutal throat-slitting that was tragic as the fact that we might get blamed. 'If we're asking any favours from deities,' I said, 'maybe pray we catch whoever did it and that no one else gets hurt.'

'Yes, yes, of course. But the press'll act like we went in with a lynch mob of Derbyshire detectives and cut his damn throat ourselves.' Richard rubbed the slack skin on his neck. 'And you shouldn't have gone in without back-up.'

'I know, but – '

'You could have been killed.'

'I had to check – '

'You need to stick to procedure, Meg. No more doing your own thing. Especially when we're already on the back foot with this bloody stalker fiasco.'

'But someone could have been bleeding to – '

'There's no excuse for putting yourself at risk.'

Christ, was he ever going to let me finish a sentence? I'd noticed that more senior people just talked over him, so they both ended up banging on at the same time, gradually increasing the volume until one of them gave up. I didn't have the energy.

'And I know your last murder case ended in a relatively good outcome. But, as we've discussed, you can't behave like that again. What if you'd been seriously injured? Or killed?'

'I know. It would have looked bad, wouldn't it? But I was

suspended, so it wouldn't have been your fault if I'd drowned in a cave or plunged to my death in an old windmill.'

'I'm not sure that's how the press would have seen it.'

'Good to know it's my welfare you're concerned about.'

Had he even heard me say I couldn't take on this case?

'You have to stick to the rules,' Richard said. 'Follow the evidence. This new case is a good opportunity. Show you can be a team player and do things properly.'

Clearly not.

'I'm off from next Wednesday,' I said. 'It's best I don't take on this one.'

'You're not going away, are you? So you can delay your holiday if necessary.'

'I don't think I can do that.'

Richard narrowed his eyes. He knew how important work was to me, almost to the point of it being pathological. Why in God's name had I not planned a convincing lie about a trip to Africa to save sick lions, or treatment for an obscure and terrifying gynaecological condition? I could feel my pulse quickening at the possibility that he'd work it out.

'I'm trying to be fair here, Meg, but I'm a little confused. We could get Dickinson over from Nottingham, but I'm not sure about your level of commitment to the job if – '

'I'll do it,' I blurted. 'I'll delay my time off if necessary.'

'Good. And I'd like you to work with Craig.'

'Craig?' I said weakly. 'But . . . ' I stopped. There was nothing I could say.

'I'm not telling you you've only got six months to live, Meg. I'm asking you to work with a perfectly competent sergeant.'

'Actually, Richard – '

'Right. Let's do the briefing.'

37

The incident room felt hot and muggy, like somewhere you could catch malaria, despite the fact it looked ready to snow outside. A trace of ill-person's sweat hung in the air, and cops coughed aggressively over one other. But the excitement of dealing with a murder fizzed through the air alongside the winter bugs. I shoved aside my worries about time off and family, and allowed myself to be swept along.

'Are they Jackson Pollocks?' Jai nodded towards a collection of blood-spatter photographs.

I frowned, pretending to disapprove of him.

Richard strode in, took off his jacket, and chucked it at a chair. It missed and fell on the floor. I nearly reached down for it, but realised there were precisely three men nearer to it than me. Why should I dash to pick the damn thing up? Especially given the way he'd just spoken to me. I noticed DC Fiona Redfern twitching too. But neither of us moved.

Jai retrieved the jacket.

'Thank you, Jai.' Richard shifted aside to let me into the hot spot. 'It's a long way down for me these days.'

I took a deep breath of the dubious air and stepped forward. 'Right. The victim is Philip Thornton. Forty-eight-year-old male. Stabbed in the early hours. He was in the house with his ten-year-old daughter. Wife was apparently at her mother's.'

Jai yawned inappropriately.

'Am I boring you?' I said.

Craig leered. 'He's been up late with his new girlfriend.'

I didn't know Jai had a girlfriend. I looked at his open face. Would he not have told me? They were all staring at me. I realised I should say something corpse-related. I spoke too loudly. 'The victim's carotid artery was cut with a very sharp knife. As far as we can tell, he was asleep and didn't put up any fight.'

'So, whoever did it went in with the intention of killing him?' Jai said.

'Looks like it. There was evidence of an intruder in the house.' I pictured the upturned drawers in the study and bedroom – remembered my feeling that something wasn't quite right. 'Possibly.'

'We got into his phone. Very interesting.' Our allocated digital media person, Emily, was the antithesis of every stereotype about sad geeks. As well as obviously being female, she glistened with Hollywood shine – all advert-white teeth and smooth-skinned perfection. Every time I saw her, I did a double-take, especially when she was surrounded by her dowdy colleagues, like a dahlia amongst dandelions.

'Go on, Emily,' I said.

'There were missed phone calls and texts between 4.15 a.m. and 4.30 a.m. from a contact called *Work*. A mobile phone which we're tracing.'

Emily clicked something and a list appeared on a screen behind us.

*Call History:*

*4.15 a.m. – Work.*

*4.16 a.m. – Work*

*4.18 a.m. – Work*

*4.20 a.m. – Text from 'Work': 'Phil, I need to talk.'*

*4.22 a.m. – Text from 'Work': 'Why are you ignoring me? I know Rachel is away. I have to talk to you.'*

*4.30 a.m. – Work*

*4.33 a.m. – Work*

*4.40 a.m. – Work*

'Did he reply to any of this?' I asked.

'Nope. Not at all,' Emily said. 'I'll leave you to it. I'm off to find out who *Work* really is.' She walked off, leaving the room feeling drab in her absence.

I turned away from the screen. 'The victim's wife thought he'd been secretive recently. Which obviously ties in with the calls and texts. And the woman who reported the child in the woods said she saw a car driving up the lane to the house. In the night. The lane doesn't go anywhere else. It's possible this *Work* person could have gone to try and meet Phil.'

'It fits the provisional time of death,' Jai said.

The energy in the room bubbled up at the prospect of a good early lead. 'The wife's also been in touch previously about a stalker,' I said. 'And unfortunately – '

'We in our wisdom ignored her.'

Richard was starting to piss me off. He was obviously riled about me having the audacity to want time off.

I folded my arms and pivoted away from Richard. 'We need to look at the details, obviously. But we didn't have a lot to go on.'

'We'll get the blame for this,' Craig said. 'We need to cover our arses.'

'Mainly we need to find whoever killed him,' I said.

Richard coughed. 'Quite so, Meg. And also cover our arses.'

I glanced at the texts shining guiltily from the screen. 'If it was someone he was having an affair with, they could have faked the intruder. There was something not quite right about that. And we should look at the woman who found the girl in the woods. It's a bit convenient that she saw the car in the middle of the night. And she seemed to know who the girl was. Plus, I had a feeling she might have known the victim too.'

They all nodded sagely except Richard, who scowled at me. 'A *feeling*,' he said. 'You need more than that.'

I ignored him and carried on. 'And, oh I don't know, it's probably not relevant, but . . . ' As soon as that came out of my mouth, I knew it wasn't confident enough. Not *Alpha* enough.

Richard jumped on me. 'Why are you telling us then?'

I felt sweat prickling under my armpits. Maybe it wasn't just about Richard's wife leaving. Maybe he was going through the male menopause. I'd read somewhere that men's moods were more cyclic than women's, contrary to received (male) wisdom.

I raised my voice. 'Okay, I think it might be relevant. There was something strange going on in that family.'

'Other than the bloke having his carotid slashed?' Richard said. 'What do you mean by that?'

'His artwork. Her reaction to it.'

Jai gave me a puzzled look. Craig rolled his eyes and said, 'We've got an absolute corker of a lead with those phone calls and texts and – '

'I saw the photos of that artwork,' Fiona said. 'It's creepy. Hearts doing weird things. Do you think he was on drugs when he did it? It's not normal.'

Craig wouldn't like being interrupted by Fiona. He was tapping his fingers on his knee – that meant he was about to get snide or aggressive. He'd have a dig now.

'Poor bastard's had his throat slit,' he said. 'And you *ladies* are all over the fact he did a bit of screwed-up art in his spare time.' There it was.

I pretended Craig didn't exist. I even managed to do something weird with the focus of my eyes, so I was staring directly through him at the coughing IT guy behind. 'The victim's daughter had a heart transplant last summer. There was a card

I think might have been from the family of the donor. But the art suggests all's not well. And the way the wife talked – it made me think there was something wrong.'

'When you hear hoofbeats,' Richard said. 'Think horses, not zebras.'

'Huh?' Jai said.

'Look at the most likely explanations,' Richard said. 'It's not hard to understand.'

'It could have been the wife. If she found out her husband was having an affair.' Fiona was clearly not interested in the zebras, and was of the opinion that an affair was good grounds for throat-slitting.

'And she was desperate to get back inside the house,' I said. 'I think she may have messed up the scene deliberately. And someone had been in the shower.'

'But her story adds up,' Craig said. 'She was at a petrol station in Matlock at nine in the morning.'

'She could have come to the house earlier and then gone back to Matlock. We need to check. There are no immediate neighbours, and there are ways to the house that avoid CCTV altogether, but we can look at the camera on the main road.' I raised an eyebrow at Richard. 'And the spouse is always a horse, don't you agree?'

'Didn't the little girl see anything?' Fiona asked.

'She was on sleeping pills for night terrors she's been having. We haven't been able to get much sense out of her. It looks like she must have woken up, wandered through to her parents' room, found her father, tried to wake him and got blood all over her, and then run out into the woods.'

'How horrendous,' Fiona said.

'She's a lovely kid too.' I felt that weight again. The

responsibility to solve this, for Abbie. 'You know this area well, don't you, Fiona?'

Craig butted in. 'Her gran does. She's on our Blue Rinse Task Force.'

I smiled at Fiona. 'Do you know about a folk story associated with that house? There are some statues of children in the woods.'

'Really, Meg.' Richard wafted his arm as if he was standing over a decomposing rat. 'What does this have to do with the investigation?'

'His wife said the victim was obsessed with the statues, and something about wanting to do penance. It might be relevant. He'd replicated one of them out of wood, except with its heart ripped out.'

The door bashed open and Emily walked in and stood as if under stage lighting. 'Got the trace on that mobile phone,' she said. 'It's a colleague of Phil Thornton's. Karen Jenkins.'

# 5.

Karen Jenkins shuffled into the interview room, bashed her leg on the drab grey desk, and apologised to it. I smiled. It was the sort of depressingly British thing I'd do.

Craig sorted out the recording apparatus and took her through the formal bits and pieces. Jai was watching from an observation room. It was still only the afternoon of the first day and we had a solid lead. I prayed we could get this one cleared up fast so I could avoid my lie to Richard being exposed. There was no way I could delay my time off, whatever I'd said to him.

Karen was in her mid to late forties, and reminded me of one of those hairy dogs whose eyes you never see. She cleared her throat a couple of times and licked her lips. Glanced at me and quickly looked away. 'Sorry. I'm not used to being questioned by the police.' She gave a high-pitched laugh. 'Can I make notes in my pad? It calms me.'

'Yes, of course.' I leaned back in my deeply uncomfortable chair.

She shook her head so her hair covered her eyes almost completely. 'Right. Yes. No. I can't believe it. Can't believe it happened.' She picked up her pen and tapped it against her pad, but didn't write anything.

I chatted nonsense for a while to relax her and calibrate – noticing what she did with her hands and face when she was talking about the weather and the traffic.

Once I'd got the feel of her, I asked casually, 'Were you close to Phil Thornton?'

She swallowed and looked down, much stiller than before. 'We were colleagues. Not close as such.'

'His wife was concerned someone might have been following him. Do you know anything about that?'

She hesitated. I could see her breathing. Raised voices drifted in from in a nearby room. 'No. Sorry,' she said.

'Anything worrying him that you were aware of?'

'Nothing that would get him killed,' she said, more abruptly. 'He was worried about Abbie. And about his wife, I think. She's a bit odd.' She made a few swoopy doodles on her pad.

There was a smell in the air, familiar but wrong in this context. I looked up sharply and scrutinised her. Had she been *drinking?*

'When was the last time you went to Phil's house?'

Her eyes widened a fraction. 'I don't know. Ages ago.'

'What was the occasion?'

'You should be looking at his wife, not me,' Karen said. 'He was worried about his wife.'

'The occasion you went to his house?'

'They had me and my husband round. I can check the dates and get back to you.'

I glanced at the wedding ring on her hand. 'Look, you need to be totally honest with me. Nobody's judging you. But what kind of relationship did you have with Phil?'

'We were close. Nothing ever happened.' Jagged lines on

the pad, deeper now, solid fingers gripping the pen, her body tense and so different to when she'd been chatting earlier.

'Karen, I don't care if you were having an affair, but you need to tell me the truth.'

Her voice shook, as if she was about to cry. 'We were friends.'

I waited a moment, but she said no more.

'Have you ever watched those TV murder mysteries where the victim's friend is always forging Dutch masters or stealing prize orchids or something like that?' I asked. 'So they lie to the police, and you're screaming at the telly saying, "Just tell them about the sodding orchids" because it never turns out well. Have you watched any of those?'

She nodded and licked her lips again, looking on the verge of tears, the skin beneath her eyes beginning to puff up.

'Where were you on Sunday night?' I asked.

'Me? I was at home. You don't think I did it? I would never . . . ' She was crying now, gulping and wiping her hand over her nose.

Craig dived in. 'You see, we have these texts and phone calls on Phil's phone.'

Karen jumped and looked at him, as if she'd forgotten he was there. 'I don't know what you're talking about. You think I . . . Oh my God.'

'You went there, didn't you,' Craig said. 'To his house.'

Karen flipped her gaze from me to Craig, and to me again, and shoved herself back in her chair as if wanting to put distance between us. She moved her foot in anxious circles over the dismal grey carpet.

'You've nothing to worry about if you tell us the truth,' I said. Which wasn't strictly true.

'No. I wasn't there. I phoned him, that's all. You need to

look at Rachel.' She hunched over her notepad and drew more swoops, then dropped her pen onto the desk. 'She's had mental health problems. Who knows what she'd do?'

'What problems has she had?' I settled in my chair, as if there was all the time in the world.

'She had a psychotic episode. She could be dangerous.'

'What exactly happened?'

'You know Jess died? Rachel's daughter?'

'Yes. Four years ago.'

'Well, that was . . . ' Karen picked her pen up again and fiddled with the end of it. 'Anyway, Rachel had a psychotic episode afterwards.'

'What were you going to say about Jess? You cut yourself short.'

She shook her head. 'No, I didn't. I don't know the full details.'

'Of how Jess died, you mean?'

'Yes. Phil didn't like to talk about it.'

'Just tell me what you know.'

Karen wriggled in her seat. 'She fell out of a window. In that weird house. Not long after Rachel and Jess moved in.'

'From a window?' I was momentarily pitched off course. Why had I thought about dead children at the top window? Maybe I'd seen a news report and then forgotten it.

'The attic window. The girls weren't supposed to go up there.' Karen grabbed her pen and doodled again. Jagged lines this time, like the start of a migraine. There was something she didn't want to say. Something around Jess's death. 'It's a weird house. Out in the middle of the woods. I remember when he bought it. He got obsessed with it. Had to have it.'

'Did you know why?'

She relaxed a little with that question. 'It seemed to be something to do with those weird statues in the woods. He was into art so maybe he liked the idea of owning them. I mean, I suppose they are cool in a creepy sort of way. But he was in a strange state at that time – I think he was in shock about his ex-wife dying.'

'His ex-wife as in Abbie's mother?'

'Yes. She died not long after they separated.'

'How did she die?'

'Laura? In a car crash.'

I pondered the statistically improbable amount of death in this family, and made a note to do a check on the car crash, as well as the daughter's death.

'Rachel got really overprotective about Abbie,' Karen said. 'She adores Abbie, Phil said. As much as if she was her own daughter. And she kept thinking Abbie was ill all the time, even when she wasn't, because she'd been diagnosed with Phil's heart condition.'

'Phil and Abbie had the same condition?'

'Yes. Phil had a heart transplant a few years ago. I think he had to go abroad for it, actually, to China or somewhere. He's fine now, but he has to take medication for the rest of his life. So of course they knew all the issues about waiting lists and how Abbie could die before a suitable heart came up. She got the symptoms younger, obviously. Phil was lucky in a way that it didn't come on till later in life.'

'Okay,' I said. 'So, Rachel didn't cope very well with Abbie's condition?'

'No, I suppose having already lost a child . . . '

'I don't see the relevance of this,' Craig said.

Karen reddened. 'I just thought I should tell you Rachel has some strange beliefs. She could be going psychotic again.'

I gave Craig a *Shut up* look. At this stage anything could be relevant and I didn't want to close Karen down. There'd be time to push her later if we got more evidence against her. 'What beliefs does she have?'

'It was because Abbie was having night terrors. She was screaming that her dad was trying to kill her or something.'

I glanced at Craig. He was very still, staring at Karen.

'Did you say Abbie was dreaming that her father was trying to kill her?' I said.

'That's what Phil told me. He was really upset about it. Obviously. He would never lay a finger on Abbie, so it was awful.'

'It must have been. And he shared all this with you?'

Karen reddened. 'Only because it was so weird and upsetting. Rachel thought some bizarre stuff about Abbie.'

'What did she think?'

This seemed to be getting us off track and was probably a distraction, but I thought we might as well hear her out.

Karen pushed her hair off her face. 'Rachel got it into her head that Abbie was remembering what had happened to her heart donor.'

I looked up sharply from my notes. 'What do you mean?'

Craig stopped fiddling with his pen.

'She thought Abbie was having nightmares because she remembered what had happened to the girl she got her heart from. Rachel had this theory that the donor child had been abused or even killed by her father.'

Nobody said anything for a moment. The room seemed to shrink a little. 'Rachel Thornton thought that was why Abbie was having nightmares?' I said. 'Because of her new heart?'

'Yes. She thought Abbie's dreams were from the donor child's memories. From her death, in fact. That's why she thought Abbie was scared of Phil. She thought Abbie was confusing him in her sleep with the donor child's father.'

This was one of the stranger things I'd heard.

'Thank you,' I said. 'You're right to tell us anything you think could possibly be relevant.'

'I think you're trying to distract us,' Craig said. 'There's no way a kid could remember something that happened to a different child.'

'I didn't say Abbie remembered,' Karen said. 'I said that was what Rachel thought.'

'Thank you, Karen,' I said. 'It could be relevant, so thank you for telling us.'

She smiled and said almost under her breath, 'I just thought it was weird.'

I left it a moment and then said, 'We still need to know if you were having a relationship with Phil.'

She shook her head. 'My husband mustn't know . . . '

'There's no reason your husband need find out.'

'The children. He'd . . . He mustn't know.' She put the pen down. Her hand was shaking.

I waited.

'It's been over with Phil for ages. Please don't tell my husband. He . . . He gets angry sometimes.'

'Did you go to Phil's house last night?'

She blinked several times and licked her lips. She'd be wishing she'd asked for a lawyer, wondering what we had on her. 'No,' she said. 'I know the phone calls look bad. But I didn't go to the house. I didn't kill him.'

★

I sat at my desk, looking sightlessly at piles of paperwork, deep in thought. Karen Jenkins had been right that her phone calls to Phil in the middle of the night looked bad. And she clearly had been having a relationship with him. It was hard to imagine her slitting someone's throat, but if he'd finished the affair and she was furious with him, and maybe panicking that he'd tell her husband . . . She seemed the most likely suspect at the moment.

My mind drifted to her odd comment about Abbie's dreams. I supposed having someone else's heart inside you was potentially quite traumatic. It made sense that Abbie could have imagined what might have happened to the donor, and got scared. She wouldn't actually know how the donor died – I knew that would have been kept confidential, but her imagination could have run away with her. Was she imagining that the donor child's father had had something to do with her death? And then mixing him up with her own father in her dreams? That could have been horrible for Phil Thornton. Was that the reason for his artwork, the obsession with hearts? Intriguing though it was, it was hard to see how it could have had anything to do with his death.

Something slammed down on my desk.

Craig's backside.

'Jesus, Craig, you gave me a shock.'

He shoved some papers out of the way and settled down, angled towards me so I could see his flesh straining against his trousers. I needed to stop being so irritated by him – it was like in a relationship gone sour, where every little move sets your teeth on edge. He twisted to look at me. 'I've spoken to one of Karen Jenkins' colleagues. Karen's sounding guilty as hell.'

'What did her colleague say?'

'He ended the affair. She has debts, and she's terrified her husband will leave her. And she has a drink problem. The colleague's happy to come in and make a statement.'

'Obviously a good friend. I thought I smelt drink on Karen.'

'Her husband might be violent too, this woman said. Maybe Phil threatened to tell him about the affair, and Karen was frightened.'

'You got all the gossip.' I was about to say more, in an attempt to be pleasant, but caught myself. The last time I'd said *Well Done* to Craig he'd asked if I was going to pat him on the head and give him a doggie biscuit for doing his job.

He sniffed. 'Yeah, she was well up for dishing the dirt. And she said some bloke had come to the office to see Phil. The guy was furious, but no one knew who he was.'

'That's promising. Could it have been Karen's husband? Could he have suspected about the affair? Or would her colleagues have recognised him?'

'Not sure. I'm looking into it. And I asked her about the stalker. Phil hadn't said anything about that. Seems likely it was Karen, but there had been an accident with a kid and Thornton got the blame. So the parents could have had a grudge against him. Apparently it happens quite a bit.'

'What was the accident?'

'The social workers took some kids who were in care to the beach, and one of them slipped on a rock and got badly injured. Phil was supervising when it happened. He wasn't blamed officially – it was just an accident – but the parents might not have seen it that way.'

'Karen didn't mention that. She must have known. I agree she's dodgy. But we need to look at Thornton's wife as well. If he was having an affair, she's got a motive.'

'I checked with Rachel's mother.' Craig had been quick to start using Rachel Thornton's first name. I wondered if he'd taken a shine to her. 'She slept late and when she woke, Rachel had already left, but she woke at three thirty in the morning to go to the loo, and she heard Rachel snoring then. It's Karen Jenkins. I'll have a little bet with you.' Craig leant across my desk, shirt stretching, and held out his right hand. 'Fifty quid says it's her.'

I was relieved Craig was being pleasant (ish), although I didn't quite trust it, and I wasn't sure what to do with his outstretched hand. If I shook it, he'd probably tell Richard I'd bet on the outcome of the case. If I didn't shake it, he'd think I was snubbing him. I was sure other people didn't put this much thought into every little interaction. I ignored the hand.

Craig pulled his arm back. The atmosphere stiffened.

'Did you get the name of the parents?' I said. 'Of the child who had the accident on the beach?'

'Of course I did. Mr and Mrs Darren O'Brian.'

'She not have a name then?'

'Don't get all feminist with me – that was what they gave me.'

'Get her name too, please, and check them out. They could have a motive.'

Fiona poked her head through the door. She caught my eye and a trace of a smile flitted across her face. 'Craig, your wife's in reception. With your kids.'

Craig jumped up, his bulk shoving my desk backwards in a persuasive demonstration of Newton's Third Law. 'Oh, Christ.' He glanced at his watch. 'Shit.' He blundered out of the room.

I beckoned Fiona over. 'What are his wife and kids doing here?'

She moved close and spoke quietly. 'I got the impression

he'd promised to be home early, and he must have forgotten, so she's dumping them on him.'

Craig was the kind of father who called it *babysitting* when he looked after his own children, so this was a fun development for Fiona and me. 'Good for her,' I said.

'I suppose a new murder case is quite an excuse for being late though.' Fiona was so damn reasonable.

'But someone's got to take responsibility, haven't they, Fiona, and if it's always women, nothing will ever change. Look at all the female detectives we know – hardly any of them have kids. And then look at the men – they've nearly all got them, but little wifey's there in the background taking responsibility. Even if she has her own job – even if it's a good job – somehow it's always her taking little Johnny to the doctor when he's got a snotty nose. And if it's not kids, it's sick relatives.'

'It does seem to work out that way.'

'Never mind the glass ceiling – there's another ceiling made of nappies, baby sick, and grandparents' corn plasters.' I wondered what it would have been like if I'd had a brother – whether he'd have felt as responsible for Mum and Gran as I did. 'And nobody questions it.'

'Well, you clearly are. And so's Craig's wife.' She gave me a conspiratorial look. 'And luckily us two are better than the men here, so we can afford to spend more time on other things and still do a better job than them. That's why Craig hates you so much.'

That felt like a punch. 'Does he really hate me?'

'Maybe that's putting it a bit strongly. He knows he's not DI material and you clearly are. And he's maybe jealous we're women and yet we can stay late, whereas he's getting stick from his wife.'

'I'm not exactly commitment-free.'

'No, and the less said about my family, the better. It's not exactly a positive thing that I don't have much to do with them.'

Not for the first time, I wondered about Fiona's family. She rarely mentioned them, apart from her gran and a brother who she liked, but who I got the impression wasn't her only sibling. I vowed to get to know her better. But now wasn't the time. Rachel Thornton was waiting to give a statement.

'Have you met Craig's wife?' Fiona asked.

'Yes, at that gruesome barbecue Richard organised, after he'd been on a course about how to make us all bond. I admit I may have made assumptions about her based on the quantity of make-up she was wearing. What's her name again?'

'Tamsyn. I think she's actually alright. And I'm sure she has a point, but Craig needs to pull his weight on the case, doesn't he? Kids or no kids. She can't expect him to act like he's got a nine-to-five job.'

He'd pull his weight alright. His desperation to undermine me would ensure that.

I looked at my watch. 'Right. I'm interviewing Rachel Thornton. Craig was supposed to be doing it with me. Can I give you a shout if he's had to go home?'

'Sure.'

I set off towards the interview room, and as I was passing through the reception area, I saw Craig's wife shooing a child towards the door. She looked up, saw me, and gave a bright smile. 'Meg! Hello.'

Thank God I'd asked Fiona for her name. I smiled awkwardly. 'Tamsyn.'

'I wanted a word actually, if that's okay.'

Oh God. 'I'm just on my way to an interview now. But . . .'

'It'll be quick.' She moved closer. She looked like she'd

recently applied foundation and lipstick. How did these women find time? The child had plonked himself on a seat and was looking at his phone and swinging his legs, in a way which made him appear both engrossed and pissed off at the same time. 'I've said it's okay for Craig to stay late tonight, in the circumstances, but I was going to ask you if you could maybe go a bit easier on him?'

I took a step back. 'Sorry?'

'He's been working late a lot and I need him to do more with the kids, and the pressure seems to be coming from you.'

Had he been working late? I didn't remember much of that. I didn't know what to say.

Tamsyn lowered her voice. 'He wants to impress you.'

Now I was in some kind of parallel universe. 'Right. I don't think I'm putting pressure on him but I'll bear it in mind. I'd better go. Sorry. Nice to see you.'

I smiled at a point above her head and scarpered.

★

The light flickered overhead, emphasising the deep, February blackness outside. We were in our oldest interview room – the only one that had been available – and it was rich with layers of unidentifiable smells which no amount of cherry disinfectant could remove. We couldn't even leave suspects in there because it had too many ligature points.

Rachel Thornton perched on the edge of her chair, bouncing her knee and tapping her fingers on the table. There was a tension in her upper body that seemed set into the bones, as if she'd been anxious for so long it had become part of her structure.

She'd got a lawyer in, as some people always did – mid-range, I guessed. Not super-smug and shiny, and with a rather unfortunate mole on his chin, but not actually downtrodden.

'We have a few more questions for you,' I said. 'And we need to get you to sign a statement for us.'

I had to focus on the interview, but couldn't get Craig's wife out of my head. Was any of what she'd said true, or was Craig making it up for his own reasons? I knew for sure he wasn't trying to impress me.

Rachel's gaze darted between Craig and me. 'Why've you asked me to come in here? Can you not imagine how I feel? And I don't want to leave Abbie for long. She's distraught.' She seemed very different from earlier – as if she'd moved past her initial shock and into defensive mode. When she mentioned Abbie, I saw a lioness protecting her cub.

'It's important for us to move quickly,' I said. 'We realise it's difficult for you, but the first forty-eight hours are vital. We want to find who did this to your – '

The lawyer butted in. 'We're very unhappy about your actions this morning.' He stared aggressively at me.

I jerked upright. 'Sorry?'

'We're considering a claim for police brutality.'

'You're *what?*'

Craig visibly perked up. He looked from me to the lawyer and back again.

'It's clear you used unnecessary force against my client. You pushed her to the ground, causing injury to her arm and hip.'

A wave of anger swept over me. 'Let's get it on record, shall we, that I used reasonable force to attempt to prevent your client compromising a crime scene. In retrospect, I clearly didn't use enough force, because she has indeed compromised the crime scene, making it harder for us to catch the perpetrator. And incidentally, she punched me.'

The mole twitched. He clearly hadn't known about the punch. 'We reserve our position. I'm just putting you on notice.'

I took a breath and turned to Rachel. Was this coming from her or from her overpaid lawyer? I decided to ignore it for now. 'When did you last speak to your husband?'

Her face showed a moment of confusion. Why wasn't I saying more about the brutality accusation? Then, 'Last night, from Mum's phone.'

'And how did he seem?'

'Okay, I think. Maybe not quite himself?'

She seemed almost embarrassed. I assumed the police brutality thing had been the lawyer's idea.

'Not quite himself in what way?'

She was still bouncing and tapping feet and fingers, and had angled herself towards the door as if planning to make a run for it. She looked brittle and light, as if you could push her and she'd topple over. 'I don't know. He's been a bit secretive recently, and angry with me for no reason. Complaining about me working too hard, that sort of thing.'

It sounded like the familiar story of the angry adulterer – finding fault with his wife so he could feel better about his own behaviour.

'What job do you do?' I asked.

'Accountant. It can be busy sometimes but he was being unreasonable.'

Her voice was one-dimensional. She was hiding something, but this wasn't at the heart of it.

'Okay,' I said. 'I noticed a window open in your bedroom. Is that normal?'

'I can't sleep with the window shut. Phil complained at first but now he's the same.'

'And, we were wondering, it looked like someone had taken a shower soon before we arrived at your house this morning. Was that you?' I spoke casually as if it didn't really matter. Of course she knew it did, but sometimes if you got the tone right, they'd subconsciously follow your suggestion, and things would pop out before the conscious mind caught up.

Rachel wasn't falling for it, but she was giving me something anyway. A flash of electricity. She stopped both the leg and finger tapping, and her eyes were wide. 'No. Of course not. I didn't get back until after you arrived. Maybe Abbie had one.'

Abbie had been covered in blood when I'd seen her, including in her hair, which had otherwise been dry. She didn't look like she'd had a shower. Rachel may have been going through a similar thought process. 'Or Phil could have had one late the night before.'

The lawyer sat forward on his seat, eyes flicking to and fro, mouth open ready to intervene if Rachel started to say anything too rash.

'Phil's drawings and sculptures – they were interesting.' I pictured the carved girl with her heart missing. That one had seared its way into my brain. 'They're very . . . well, dark?'

There was something there. A crackle in the air. Something around the artwork. 'Are they? I didn't really think about it.'

The lawyer deflated a little. He hadn't noticed.

'Had Phil always been interested in art?' I asked.

A tiny intake of breath. 'I suppose so. Only as a hobby.'

'And you had some mental health problems a few years ago?'

She relaxed – a slight shifting downwards of her weight, the energy that seemed to spin around her dropping a little.

'After Jess died? I was upset but I wouldn't say I had mental health problems. Who told you that? I had an infection and they couldn't get to the bottom of it. And I was worried about Abbie. How could I not be worried when she could have died too?'

'So, did everything improve once Abbie had the transplant?'

There it was again. She tapped her fingers repeatedly against her knee. Then spoke fast and somewhat mechanically, speedy-robot style. 'Yes. I mean, we're still worried about her, but it's much better.'

'Except for the night terrors? That must have been upsetting for Phil, particularly?'

'Well, for both of us.'

'What was she scared of?'

'I don't know, nothing in particular. She was just getting scared in the night. It happens.' I could hear the dryness of her mouth. She hadn't mentioned the dreams about Phil, or the theory about Abbie's heart. Maybe she was embarrassed. Thought it would sound crazy.

'But she was scared of Phil, wasn't she?' I said.

Rachel stood up. 'I have to get back to Abbie.'

'Why did you think she was having such bad dreams?'

'I don't know! She'd had a heart transplant! It's scary. And Phil stupidly told her a horrible story about our house.'

On the face of it, this had absolutely nothing to do with Phil Thornton's death. But if Karen Jenkins had been telling the truth, then Rachel was covering up the fact that Abbie had been terrified of her father. I decided not to mention what Karen had said, and see what more she came out with. The lawyer narrowed his eyes as if wondering what I was up to. Something was afoot.

'But it was bad enough for you to take her to see a psychiatrist?' I said.

She spun round and looked at her lawyer. My pulse whipped high. This was something.

A sharp knock on the door and Jai poked his head round. 'Can I have a quick word?'

Rachel jumped up. 'Can I go?'

Jai gave a rapid shake of his head.

'No,' I said. 'I'll only be a minute or two.' I stepped outside the interview room and pulled the door closed. 'What have you found?'

Jai kept his voice low. 'We got the ANPR data. She drove towards their house at seven thirty, not nine thirty like she said. Then she left again, and came back when you were there.'

'Did the CCTV actually show that she went to the house?'

'There's no CCTV to the house. But she went along the main road just before the turning to her house.'

'So, in theory she could have driven past and gone somewhere else, and then come back?'

'But why lie about that?' Jai said. 'She told us she came straight from her mother's house.'

'I know, I know. She's dodgy as hell. What about in the night? Have we found her on the CCTV then? Around the time of death.'

'No. She could have avoided it then. Gone round the lane off the main road.'

'But then why not avoid it later?'

'I don't know. Maybe she didn't avoid it deliberately.'

I pushed the door open and walked back into the interview room. Rachel was still standing. I looked towards her chair. 'You'd better sit down.'

She glanced at me and then at her lawyer, who nodded. She sat down.

The room seemed very quiet, its air thick.

'We've got the CCTV footage,' I said. 'You need to tell us the truth now. You went back home earlier this morning, didn't you?'

A muscle below her eye fluttered, and she gripped her hands together. 'What? No. What have you seen on the CCTV?'

'How about you tell us what happened?'

The lawyer shifted as if to put himself between me and Rachel. 'Could we have a moment?' he said.

Rachel spun round to face her lawyer. 'It's fine. I've got nothing to be ashamed of. I must have forgotten. I nipped into Eldercliffe to go to the shops, and then went home.'

'That's not true, is it? You don't appear on the CCTV going into Eldercliffe.'

'We need a moment,' the lawyer said.

'I went to the other shop.' Rachel sounded as if she was about to burst into tears.

'Which one?'

Silence.

I was okay with silence. Rachel wasn't. She picked at a piece of skin on her finger. The lawyer sat looking stressed but seemed to have given up trying to restrain her.

'Okay,' she said finally. 'I did go home first. I couldn't get the landline to work and there's no mobile signal so I drove off to call for help.'

'But you didn't call for help.'

'I couldn't get a signal so I came back.'

'Over an hour later? You're not a great liar. You know we're going to find out. I'm sure you had reasons for what you did. It would be in your interest to tell us now.'

'Oh God,' she said. 'Okay.' She dropped her head forward and a tear splashed onto her jeans-clad leg.

'Thank you, Rachel,' I said quietly. 'It'll be for the best.'

The lawyer was poised like a cat about to pounce.

'I got home and he was there. Already dead.'

'So why didn't you call an ambulance? Or the police?'

'He was definitely dead. There was no point calling an ambulance. And I was worried you'd think I did it. I panicked.'

'And left your child in the house with your dead husband?'

'I know. I'm sorry. She was on sleeping pills. I never thought she'd wake up. Of course I regret now what I did. But I didn't want you to think I did it. We've been having a few problems . . . ' She let out a sob. 'I thought you'd think it was me. It wasn't me. I didn't kill him.'

★

'You took on the case then?' Jai sat briefly on the chair by my desk, then stood up and leant against it. Why would no one sit on that chair? Were they so traumatised by experiences in Richard's chair that they shunned anything remotely similar? It was as if they were playing a strange game with me – counting all the ways they could avoid sitting on the damn thing.

'Richard left me very little choice. If we can make enough progress in the next week, you guys can carry on while I'm away and Richard won't have to ship Dickinson in.'

'Did you tell him you'd delay your time off?'

'Sort of. But I can't.' I folded my arms and shivered. It was freezing. Our work-place had no temperate zone – there were either monkeys swinging from the door frames or polar bears ambling over the eco-carpets.

Jai leant forward to pull a few dead leaves from the spider plant that hovered on the edge of death on my desk. 'Mary managed to do the PM today, but there was nothing too surprising. Throat slit with a sharp, pointed knife, twice in quick succession, using a stabbing motion. He was almost certainly asleep, and he'd taken one of his own sleeping pills. He hadn't fought back, at least not in any way that injured him.'

'Anything under his nails?'

'No. No defence injuries. Everything was pretty much as we'd thought. She said he'd had a heart transplant in the past. It wasn't the neatest of surgeries, but it had been doing its job.'

'Any sign of the knife?'

Jai shook his head. 'We're waiting for fibre analysis and fingerprints. And we've got a warrant to search Karen Jenkins' house. But my money's on the wife now.'

'Yes. Why the hell would she run off and not call anyone if she's innocent? And I'm sure she wanted to get into the house when I was there, and mess up the scene. What was she afraid of us finding? Was Mary sure about the time of death?'

'She was reasonably confident it was between 3 a.m. and 4 a.m.'

'Rachel Thornton could have driven from her mother's house,' I said. 'At three-ish. Then killed him, and driven back, taking the route round the lanes that avoids the CCTV, either deliberately or for some other reason. Her mother could have remembered wrong. Or she could be lying about the loo visit. You know what mothers are like where their children are concerned.'

'But why would Rachel go back there at half seven, and then leave again?'

'Maybe she remembered she'd left some evidence. Or maybe she wanted to check Abbie was okay.'

'I suppose she could have gone off to dispose of the knife and her clothes and then come back to Abbie. But then she left again.'

'She might have realised there was something else she needed to get rid of,' I said. 'We'll have to talk to Abbie. She was covered in blood when I found her so she must have gone into the bedroom and found her father while Rachel was out, poor kid. But she might have seen something. Maybe she remembers now.'

'At least we've got a couple of good leads. Maybe it'll work out okay with your gran.'

I twitched and glanced into the corridor. Nobody was around but I still whispered. 'Richard doesn't know what I'm doing, remember. But yes, fingers crossed.'

Jai leant closer to me and spoke quietly. 'Are you okay? It must be pretty shitty.'

I smiled. 'That's an accurate analysis of the situation.'

He jumped up and pushed my door shut, then came back and actually sat on the spare chair. 'When are you going to Switzerland?'

'Thursday. I'll spend Wednesday helping Mum get ready. And trying to spend some time with Gran.'

Jai looked down and laced his fingers together. 'Craig said something about a brutality accusation? What's that about?'

'Oh, I know. It's all I need, with Richard already on at me about my professionalism.'

Jai examined his fingernails as if they held the answer to the meaning of life. 'But you'd done nothing wrong, had you?'

'Of course not. Bloody woman. If anyone was brutal, it was her. She punched me.'

'Why didn't you report it?'

'Because I'm an idiot. I suppose I didn't want Craig to know she hit me.' I looked at Jai's despairing face. 'I know, I know, he knows now anyway. And I shouldn't let him get to me.'

Jai sighed. 'It's best to ignore him.'

A complaint was bad news for us, even if it had no basis, especially with the worry about us ignoring the stalker. Besides, the thought of someone complaining about me gave me a hollow, depressed feeling inside. I reached into my drawer for my stash of organic chocolate. 'Here.' I broke off a couple of chunks and shoved the rest at Jai.

I could see Jai coveting the whole bar, but he glanced at the price label. 'Jesus.'

'It's cultivated by happy, fairly paid people in far-off lands,' I said. 'That doesn't come cheap.'

Jai took a couple of squares. 'Okay. I won't take much. I'll get an exploitative Yorkie bar from the machine on the way out.' He jumped up. 'Don't work too hard.'

★

After another hour of researching, pondering, chocolate eating, and general fretting, I finally drove myself home and got in around ten, letting myself in to the accompaniment of an extremely loud commentary from Hamlet. He jumped onto the shelf in the hallway, knocked a pile of books and the phone onto the floor, and fell on top of them.

'Jesus, Hamlet, aren't cats supposed to be graceful? *Nature's supreme athlete* or something.'

He righted himself, gave me a contemptuous look, and stalked off in a cloud of black and white fur, as if it had all been part of his plan. He was sulking at my lateness, but I'd arranged for a neighbour to feed him at six, so he hadn't missed out.

I reached to pick up the phone, and saw the answer-phone light flashing.

Mum. I'd forgotten to call her back. With a hollow feeling, I pressed the button. Her voice was shaky and upset. 'Love, I don't know if we're doing this too soon. She seems better today. Can you phone me?'

I dialled Mum's number. She picked straight up. 'Where have you been?'

'At work, Mum. There's been a murder. How's Gran?'

'You're not taking on a big case, are you, Meg? We talked about this.'

'It'll be fine.'

'Because you said you'd definitely take that time off. You specifically said you wouldn't take on any big cases.'

'Don't worry. What's going on?'

'Oh Lord, she's started eating again. Maybe it's because she knows she doesn't have much longer, but she seems to have rallied. Are we doing the right thing?'

I sank onto the stairs.

This was the nightmare of the situation. If we left it too long, Gran could end up in agony, permanently sick, vomiting twenty times a day. And it would be too late – she wouldn't be able to travel. But if we did it too soon, Gran could lose weeks or maybe even months of life.

Hamlet butted his face against my knee. I got up and walked to the kitchen; put Mum on speaker-phone while I fed him.

'What does she want to do?' I asked.

'She says she's had enough. But she doesn't want to get you into trouble.'

'Look, Mum, it's all booked. Let's just see how she is. If we end up not going, it's only money, isn't it? I think it's too late to cancel the plane tickets anyway. I'll get over to see you as soon as I can.'

# 6.

I dreamt of Abbie Thornton. She was running through the woods, blonde hair streaming behind her, hidden by trees, almost out of sight. When I caught up with her, it was Gran who'd been running away, not Abbie.

My alarm shrilled into the dream. The images faded away.

I smacked the clock and lay for a moment listening to the rain pummelling the window. The duvet was twisted round my feet. I kicked it clear and imagined what it would feel like to stab a knife into someone's throat, to feel the resistance of the flesh, the moment when the artery burst and blood exploded into the bedroom. It would be quick. It would be better than the agonising, nauseous decline that was probably in store for Gran, if we didn't get her to Switzerland.

I dressed and breakfasted quickly in my freezing kitchen, Hamlet curling around my ankles and demanding three breakfasts before retreating to his ridiculously indulgent heated bed. Sleet battered the windows that never shut properly, and a small dribble of water had seeped inside and plopped onto the tiled floor.

I donned boots and my best coat, gave Hamlet a backward glance, wondered why I couldn't be a cat, and opened the front door. A blast of sleety air whipped into the hallway, lifting unread bills and flipping the pages of books I'd left on the hall shelf. The weather was so bad, it was almost invigorating, allowing me to feel slightly heroic just by leaving the house. I stepped out and pulled the door firmly shut behind me.

★

Abbie looked even younger than her ten years, skinny in too-baggy clothes, dark shadows under huge eyes. We'd put her in our special interview room – made officially child-friendly through the presence of smaller chairs, a couple of pictures so completely lacking in content that no human could be upset by them, regardless of the traumas they'd suffered, and walls where the shade of puke-yellow had been toned down a notch.

Rachel had fought strenuously to attend the interview, but we couldn't let her, in view of her suspicious behaviour. Instead we'd let Rachel's mother sit in. She was Abbie's only grandparent – a robust-looking woman named Patricia, coiffured to perfection and botoxed into a permanent look of horrified astonishment, which seemed quite appropriate for the circumstances. I was a little concerned about her, since there was a chance she was lying to protect Rachel. But I wanted it to be someone Abbie knew.

Craig was in the room with me, Jai watching again.

Abbie was just about holding it together, shaky but coping. She was sandwiched between her grandmother and a child protection officer from social services, who looked about twelve. I tried to put Abbie at ease and gently shift her focus to the day before, by talking about Elaine's dog.

'You shouldn't let her near pets,' Patricia said. 'She could get an infection.'

'I want Mum.' Abbie called Rachel *Mum* even though she wasn't her biological mother. 'Why can't Mum be here?' I sensed she was in danger of completely falling apart. Understandably.

'Your mum's right outside,' I said. 'You can see her in a minute.'

Abbie turned to Patricia. 'This lady was nice.' She pointed a shaking finger at me. 'The dog was nice.' There was tension between Abbie and her grandmother. The air looked sliceable.

I smiled at Abbie, and said to Patricia, 'I'm sorry. We didn't know about not letting Abbie near pets. But the dog helped us get home safely.'

Patricia sniffed and looked over her reading glasses, down her long nose.

Craig set up the recording apparatus and we gently took Abbie through the questions to find out if she knew the difference between truth and lies. It seemed she did. It was a shame we couldn't do the same with the solicitors.

'Abbie,' I said, 'we need to have a chat with you about what happened yesterday. Is that okay?'

She chewed on a piece of hair and nodded slowly, her eyes damp with tears. She was sitting bolt upright with her arms tight to her ribs, as if she didn't want to spread towards either of her companions.

I focused my attention softly on the whole room, rather than directly on Abbie. 'Can you tell us what you remember?'

A tear crawled down Abbie's cheek. The social worker reached into her pocket and passed her a tissue.

Abbie took the tissue and dragged it across her face. 'I had a dream,' she said. 'It's hard to remember.'

'It's okay. Take your time. Just tell us anything you can think of.'

'There was blood everywhere. Then I was in the shower. And Mum dried my hair. Dad was . . . ' She swallowed.

'It's okay,' I said. 'There's no hurry. You had a shower and your mum dried your hair?'

'In my dream, I think?' She said it as a question.

'What else do you remember?'

She shook her head.

'It's okay. Do you remember waking up?'

'I don't know. Later, I woke up, I went to Mum and Dad's room and . . . '

Patricia popped up in her seat. 'This is too much for her.' She wrapped her arm around Abbie.

Abbie accepted the arm but didn't seem to appreciate it. 'And Dad . . . I couldn't make him wake up. I got blood all on me. He wouldn't wake up. I got scared and ran away.' She gulped a single sob. 'And you found me.'

'Well done, Abbie. Well done for remembering.'

She gave me a tiny smile though her tears.

'And the dream where you had a shower and your mum dried your hair – do you remember anything from before that?'

It was so vital not to lead, especially with children. You could easily implant false memories. I wanted to ask if she was sure this had been a dream, if she'd seen anyone else in the house, if she'd ever seen her dad with another woman, if her parents had fights, if she'd seen her mum slit her dad's throat . . . But I had to keep my questions clean.

She swallowed. 'Blood everywhere . . . I always have horrible dreams.' She shrugged off her grandmother's arm and blew her nose. 'I've been screaming in the night. There's something wrong with me.'

I looked into Abbie's eyes. She had thick, dark lashes. 'What do you mean, something wrong?'

'I went to see a man to make me better, but I got scared.'

'Who did you see?'

'It was appalling,' Patricia said. 'They took her to a psychiatrist because of the night terrors, and he insisted on seeing her alone, and hypnotising her, and Rachel said she started screaming and screaming. It was terrible. I don't know what he did to her.'

'I got scared,' Abbie said. 'You won't make me do it again, will you? Make me go to sleep like that?'

'No. Don't worry, you won't have to do it again. Do you remember anything about why you got scared?'

I flicked a glance at Craig. He was tapping his fingers. Uh oh, I could do without him getting worked up. 'Did the psychiatrist do something to you, Abbie?' he said.

Abbie shook her head.

'I don't know . . . Yes . . . Daddy . . . ' She stared behind us, as if she was looking at something we couldn't see. She shook her head, and shrank back a little in her chair.

The social worker shifted forwards in her seat. 'No more today.'

Abbie wiped her eyes. She was crying properly now. 'It's my heart,' she said.

Patricia touched Abbie's arm. 'Come on now, Abbie, don't get upset. They're not going to ask you any more questions.'

I ignored Patricia and spoke gently. 'What do you mean, Abbie? What about your heart?'

The social worker turned to Abbie. 'It's okay, you don't need to say any more now.' She gave me a hostile look.

Abbie let out a sob, and I felt a wrenching in my chest as if I wanted to cry too. Not a good move for a detective.

'What do you mean about your heart?' I said. Was this something to do with what Karen had said? Did Abbie believe her new heart had affected her too?

Abbie shook her head and cried.

I reached forward and touched her hand. She didn't pull away. 'Okay,' I said. 'That's enough for today.'

Abbie took a big, gulping breath. 'Daddy did a bad thing. That's what I dream about. My heart knows.'

★

'Okay,' I said, plonking myself on a chair in the incident room. 'So, she dreamt about a shower and her mum drying her hair. And then later, she remembered finding her dad dead, and she remembered getting covered in blood and running out. Then I found her. Did you get that too?'

Jai nodded. 'If Rachel Thornton killed him, Abbie could have come through and got covered in blood, and then her mum cleaned her up. She thinks the shower and her hair being dried was a dream but maybe it actually happened.'

Voices drifted through from Richard's room next door. Craig was talking. Jai looked up sharply and glanced in that direction. I could only make out the odd word. *She shoved her.* Was that what Craig had just said?

I felt a twinge of worry. 'What's Craig saying to Richard?'

Jai looked blankly at me. 'Didn't hear properly.'

I paused and listened again, but someone had shut Richard's door. I shook my head as if that could clear it of its paranoid thoughts. 'Craig's wife collared me yesterday,' I said. 'Asked me to go easy on him, can you believe?'

'Go easy on him?'

'Yeah. Said he was working too hard and blamed it on pressure from me.'

'I'd hate to see him when he wasn't working hard.'

'I know. You don't think he's using work as a cover, do you?'

Jai shrugged. 'Don't know him that well. No love lost, as you know.'

I put Craig out of my mind. 'So we're thinking Rachel might have washed Abbie, dried her hair, put her back to bed and gone off to dispose of her clothes?'

'It looks that way. Which would mean Rachel must have had blood all over her at some point, and there must be some clothes somewhere that she wore when she killed him. Because there's no way she could have slit his carotid without getting absolutely covered in the stuff.'

A knock on the door. Fiona.

'We've found a plastic bag,' she said breathlessly. 'With clothes in it. And a knife. And some boots that look like the ones that left the marks outside the door.'

'Fantastic!' I said. 'Exactly what we were talking about.'

'It was dumped in someone's bin on the outskirts of Matlock. It was bin day and they noticed the bag when they put some of their own stuff in, just before the refuse guys arrived. They fished it out because they thought it looked dodgy.'

'Has it got Rachel's clothes in it?'

Fiona rubbed her nose. 'It's a bit . . . strange.'

'What do you mean?'

'There's the men's boots, and a set of clothes which look like Rachel's, which have got blood smears on them. It's all gone off to the blood guys but I thought I should let you know . . .'

'What? Spit it out, Fiona.'

'Okay. There was something else in the bag as well. You

know you can tell if something's actually been spurted on? Arterial spurt. Like whoever was wearing them was standing over the person when they were stabbed. Well, there is something like that, but it's not Rachel's.'

I had a bad feeling, right under my ribs. 'Whose is it?'

'It has embroidered puppies on it. It's a little girl's nightdress.'

★

Sleet rolled down the hills as we drove towards Matlock. A grit lorry chugged along ahead of us. I tried to focus on the icy road, while my mind churned with the new information. Arterial spurt on a little girl's nightdress. Did that mean poor Abbie was there, standing next to her father while his throat was cut? I felt sick at the thought.

'Why are we driving all the way out to see her?' Craig said. 'We've got enough to arrest her.'

'Maybe. But there are a few question marks around her behaviour.'

'You overthink things.'

He certainly didn't act as if he wanted to impress me. I wondered again what he'd been saying to his wife.

'They pay us to think,' I said. 'Why would she kill her husband with her daughter there? So close she got spurted on? Why would she kill him, disappear, come back, and disappear again?'

'We could ask her all this at the Station.'

'I know. But sometimes you learn more this way.'

I leant forward and flipped the radio on, wishing Jai was with me. You could toss ideas around with Jai. He helped me think, even if he'd been a bit distracted recently.

'I suppose you'll have to come off the case anyway.' Craig's tone was pointedly neutral. 'Looks like it's going to be a biggie. And you're on holiday next week.'

I contemplated pretending I hadn't heard, but decided against. Rumours would be started that I suffered from hysterical deafness. 'I'll delay my time off.' I glanced at the sky as if God might smite me for my lie.

'Going anywhere nice?'

'Not really. Was your wife okay the other day? She seemed upset. Is she worried you're working too hard?' Two could play this game.

The sat-nav interrupted us, for which Craig must have silently thanked it. 'At the end of the road, turn left.'

I obeyed and sat-nav man told me we had reached our destination – a modern bungalow, surrounded by more of the same. It couldn't have been more different from Phil and Rachel Thornton's Gothic money-pit in the woods.

The door was answered by Abbie's grandmother, Patricia, and an ancient-looking tortoiseshell cat. Patricia looked upset; the cat didn't.

Patricia lead us into a chintzy front room. She wrenched her botoxed forehead into a frown. 'I hope you're not going to bully Rachel. She's just lost her husband, and she has mental health problems. Did you know that?'

'Maybe we could have a chat with Rachel first,' I said. 'And then we'll have a word with you?'

'As long as you know she's not been well. I'll make tea and ask her to come through.'

I sat on a velour sofa in a strange shade of green and Craig went for the matching armchair. They had doily things where our heads went. I hadn't seen that for a while.

The door eased open and Rachel crept in and sat next to me on the sofa. She picked at a loose thread on her jeans.

'Hi, Rachel,' I said. 'How are you?'

She shrugged. Her look said, *I'm socially conditioned to say I'm fine but I'm quite clearly not.*

'We found the bag,' I said.

Rachel jerked back an inch, as if she'd been hit. She took a sharp in-breath.

I held out some photographs. 'Could you confirm if these are your clothes, and Abbie's nightdress. And if you recognise the knife. We've sent them for analysis, but it would speed things up if you'd just tell us what you know.'

She licked her lips and said nothing. I contemplated all the blood on the nightdress, hoping she'd say *That's not Abbie's nightdress and I've never seen that knife before.* She didn't. She leant back in her seat and sat very still, staring at an ugly standard lamp that squatted on the far side of the room. Even though she was shocked and upset, she looked more composed than she had the day before, and somehow more solid.

'Did you kill your husband?' I said.

She looked surprised, and paused with her mouth open. 'No . . . Er, I . . . ' She frowned and shook her head slightly. 'No. No, I didn't.'

'You'd better tell us what happened then.'

She sighed and said nothing for a moment. Then she leant back into the couch. I did the same.

'I didn't want you to jump to the wrong conclusion,' she said. 'I know it looks bad but it must have been an intruder that killed him. That stalker. The woman he was having the affair with.'

'What happened, Rachel?'

She paused. Licked her lips and took a breath. 'When I got in, I went to our bedroom and . . . '

I nodded encouragement at her.

'And I saw Phil lying there covered in blood, like I've told you. And . . . ' She waited a moment and then blurted it out fast. 'Abbie was there. She was on the floor.'

'With . . . ' I took a moment to picture the scene. 'With your husband?'

She nodded. I sensed she was telling the truth. One of those feelings I got, that Richard found so irritating.

'Lying on the floor by our bed,' Rachel said. 'I was terrified she was hurt. Can you imagine how I felt?'

I nodded slowly.

'So I rushed over and grabbed her. But she was okay. Covered in blood but asleep. And unhurt.'

Where does a mother go first – her husband or her child? It's times like these the truth comes out. They usually go to the child.

'She was absolutely drenched in blood.' Rachel sat forward again and crossed her legs, jiggling her foot. She reached round and grabbed one of the doily things, and rubbed it between her fingers. 'And it was really hard to wake her up. I didn't want you to think . . . I got her up and put her in the shower, washed her hair. I had to dry it – it took ages . . . '

Rachel juddered to a halt. She sat staring into space.

'What happened next?' I said, as gently as I could.

She moved her eyes slowly to me, then raised them as if trying to visualise the scene on that awful morning. Some people claimed that if suspects looked up and to the right, they were making things up, but unfortunately it wasn't that simple. Anyway, Rachel was looking up and left. 'I put Abbie back to bed,' she said, 'and packed our things with blood on them into a Waitrose bag, and then I put some of Phil's boots on and I went round and made it look like a break-in, and messed up the study and our room, and then Abbie was sleeping again, so I drove off to hide our clothes and the boots. I went up to Matlock and went to the petrol station, and then when I came back, you were there.'

'If you thought there'd been an intruder, why did you fake one?'

She hesitated. 'I thought you might not realise.'

'Why did you do this, Rachel? What didn't you want us to think?'

She took an audible breath. Wiped a tear from her cheek.

'I can't . . . '

I waited.

'That she did it,' Rachel said in a tiny voice. 'I didn't want you to think Abbie did it.'

Craig let out his breath with a distinct puff. No finger tapping though.

I felt a coldness creeping through my stomach. 'Did you see something else, Rachel? Why would we think Abbie did it?'

'She didn't do it. She must have walked in or interrupted an intruder.'

I clenched my fists together. Had I contemplated this? The possibility that Abbie killed her father? Walked in and cut his throat? I supposed I had, deep down, when we'd found the nightdress.

'We need to know everything,' I said gently. 'All about Abbie's nightmares, what she was saying about her father . . . everything. So we can try and piece together what happened.'

Rachel eased herself back in the sofa again. Her body was

shaking. She whipped a hand to her face and sharply wiped away tears. 'You know about her nightmares.'

'We've been told she was scared of her father. Screaming about him.'

She took a breath. 'I didn't want you to think it was her. That's why I didn't tell you about the nightmares. She's been screaming and sleepwalking. Screaming about . . . well, yes, she has been screaming about her daddy, but she didn't mean Phil.'

I kept my voice soft, and hoped Craig would keep quiet. 'When did this start?'

Rachel breathed out through her mouth. 'It's all since her heart transplant. Oh God, okay, I'm going to tell you. I kept saying to the psychiatrist, she's changed. Her personality was different. She started drawing all the time – really good drawings, like she never used to do before. I mean, that was fine – the drawings. But not the rest of it. She started having these dreams. She was shouting as if someone was trying to kill her. It was terrifying. She'd run out onto the landing screaming and when we went to her, she'd go all glassy eyed and stare at something behind her. Then she'd swivel her head around and scream that her daddy was trying to kill her. It was horrendous, especially for Phil. It was her new heart. And the drugs they gave her. Oh God, I can't . . . Everything was supposed to be okay once she had her transplant.' She was openly crying now, breathing in big gulps, her shoulders shaking. 'It's not Abbie's fault. I couldn't bear her to go to trial and be locked up. She was asleep.'

'So, in her sleep, Abbie thought her dad was trying to kill her?'

'Yes! Because she was remembering what happened to her heart donor. I've looked it up. It happens. But they won't tell us who the donor was. They only let you write via the transplant coordinator and you can't say who you are. I tried writing but the family never replied after their first card, and no one would tell us anything.' She reached over and grabbed my hand. 'You've got to believe me. It's only since she had the new heart. Screaming that her dad was a murderer. Phil's not a murderer. Something happened to the donor child. The heart made Abbie do it.'

I could feel a muscle twitching below my eye. I pictured Abbie's face. 'You think Abbie killed him? She killed her father in her sleep?'

'She can't have . . . ' Rachel said nothing for a long moment. Then took a deep breath and spoke in a voice I could barely hear. 'It was in her hand. The knife was in Abbie's hand.'

*

I called Fiona. 'Can you set up a meeting with Abbie's psychiatrist. Please. We need to know more about this child.'

Patricia charged into the living room and stood staring at us, her fingers spread as if she was about to attack and claw us. 'Rachel's told me what she said to you. I told you she had problems. Abbie would never have killed Phil.'

I stood and touched her arm. 'Would you sit down?'

Patricia pulled away. 'I can't sit down.' She paced to the window and looked into the garden, then spun round to us. 'You've got it wrong!'

'Your daughter clearly thinks Abbie did it.' That was Craig's contribution, despite having agreed earlier that my *feminine touch* would work best.

Patricia's voice was high and shaky. She was on the verge

of tears. 'Rachel's not been well. Do you know how terrible it's been? We're all having to take sleeping pills each night just to get a drop of sleep. She's in a terrible state. And she felt intimidated by you. You have to understand. She's suffered from delusions. You can't trust what she says!'

I stood and walked over to the window. If you met people halfway when they were agitated, it was so much more effective that trying to stay super-calm. 'Was Rachel diagnosed with a particular disorder?'

Patricia came and stood next to me, pointedly ignoring Craig. She lowered her voice. It was still shaky but she sounded better. 'A few years ago she was. She went through a difficult time. It affects people in different ways.'

'What exactly happened?'

Patricia wiped the windowsill several times with her hand, then leant against it. She smoothed her skirt down over her legs. 'You heard about Rachel's daughter, Jess?'

'A little. Maybe you could tell us again.'

'She died four years ago.' Patricia took a determined breath. 'Abbie was with her, saw it happen. And of course Rachel and Phil . . . Well, they went to pieces. And Abbie too. She felt guilty because she was there.'

'I understand.' I knew what it was like to see a dead sister. And to feel guilty.

'And it all happened not long after they'd had the terrible news about Abbie – you know, when they realised she had the same heart problem Phil had, and was going to need a transplant. So they were trying to come to terms with the possibility of losing Abbie, and then they lost Jess. Rachel became obsessed with Abbie's health. I mean, she couldn't bear to lose another child. I know Abbie's not her biological child but she adopted her and she absolutely adores her. We never knew then if Abbie was really ill or if Rachel was just worrying. And Rachel had a bit of an incident where she imagined things.'

'What did she imagine?'

'She thought she was infected with a parasite, but she wasn't. It was short-lived, but you see she sometimes thinks things that aren't real.' Patricia gave me a beseeching look. 'And then of course Abbie started getting really ill.'

'And she had a transplant last year?'

'September. And everyone thinks that's the end of all the problems, but it's not. We have constant worries about her body rejecting the heart, and about cancer developing. She needs biopsies all the time – her poor arms are always full of needle marks. And she can't have pets because of the risk of infection. I even have to keep her away from Minxy here.' She pointed to the ancient cat, who'd sloped into the room and crawled onto the windowsill between us. 'I mean, for someone like Rachel, who's always struggled with her nerves, it was a recipe for disaster. It made her more and more anxious.'

'And Abbie's nightmares?'

'She did have problems. Apparently it's not uncommon. Phil said he had them after his transplant – he had to go abroad for his and it was hard. But for a child especially, it's a scary thing to have someone else's heart. Anyway, Rachel had this idea that Abbie was remembering things from the heart's past life. So, you see, she's not stable. She may believe Abbie killed Phil, but it's not true.'

'So, what do you think happened on Sunday night?'

'Someone else must have killed him and then poor Abbie must have wandered through. She does sleep-walk. And then Rachel found them and drew the wrong conclusion.'

'Do you have any idea who might have killed him?'

Patricia took a breath right into her stomach and gulped. 'Okay. Right. Phil met someone a few times and wouldn't tell Rachel who it was. Whether he was having an affair or something else, I don't know. But you should look into it. And you should talk to that scientist man. There was something strange going on there.'

'Which scientist man?'

'Michael Ellis, he was called. He was from the company that made the immunosuppressant drugs Abbie's on, only he'd left because he was concerned about their safety.'

'What did he say?'

'Something about a drug Abbie takes. Unusual side effects. But he was worried people were after him, not wanting him to talk. Maybe he told Phil too much, and that got Phil killed.'

# 7.

'Jesus Christ.' Jai sat on the spare chair in my room and didn't fidget. He must have been in a profound state of shock. Craig leant against the door frame.

'So the kid stabbed him to death?' Jai said.

I had a sick feeling in the pit of my stomach. People were going to go nuts over this. An angelic blonde ten-year-old savagely murders her father. The eyes of the world would be on us. 'Her mother seems to think she did.'

'Did you think she was telling the truth?'

'Why would the mother make that up?' Craig said. 'Everyone's told us how much she loves the kid.'

'Rachel Thornton's story does fit the facts as we know them at the moment,' I said. 'I've arranged for the child to be taken to a secure unit, just for now, till we find out what's going on.'

'She was asleep when she did it?' Jai said. 'Is that even possible?'

'Her mother thinks she was possessed by the spirit of her heart donor.' Craig seemed to be enjoying this.

'We don't know,' I said. 'We need more information.'

'Jesus. And if she did it in her sleep, I mean, is it even her fault?'

'It's not our business,' Craig said. 'We only have to show if she did it. It's up to her defence team to excuse it.'

I doodled on a scrap of paper. Looked down and realised I'd drawn a series of hearts. I'd drawn their outlines and then coloured them in, using black pen. Black hearts on a white background.

The door banged open, knocking Craig forwards, and Fiona rushed in. 'Did the little girl do it?'

'Christ, woman, slow down,' Craig said.

Jai spun round in his chair. 'Looks like it.'

'Oh my God.' Fiona walked over to my desk. 'Oh my God.'

'I'm off.' Craig headed for the door. 'Have to leave early.'

Jai smiled. 'Doing anything nice?'

Craig blushed. 'Promised the wife. Kids and whatnot.'

It looked like he'd listened to his wife, which was a relief, although I wondered why he seemed embarrassed.

'Bye, Twinkletoes,' Jai called after him.

'What the . . . ' I said. 'Oh, never mind. Fiona, did you manage to speak to Abbie's psychiatrist?'

'I can't get hold of him,' Fiona said. 'The practice manager says he's on holiday this week and he usually goes off to the Lakes where there's no signal. He's not answering calls or emails.'

'Wonderful.'

The door swung open and Richard charged in. 'What's this about the little girl? Did she kill her father?'

Nobody said anything. Richard looked expectantly at me.

'We don't know,' I said. 'If the victim's wife is telling the truth, then the girl was found with a knife, covered in arterial blood, by the side of the victim's bed. Asleep.'

'Good Lord. The child killed her father in her sleep?'

'We don't know if her mother's telling the truth. And the child seemed really . . . well, really sane.'

'She's not sane if she slit her father's throat in her sleep. She's clearly psychotic.'

'It doesn't make any sense,' I said. 'I don't see her as a dangerous child.'

'You can't always tell, Meg.' Richard wiped his forehead. 'My God. The girl was seeing a psychiatrist, wasn't she? What does he say? Is she capable of this?'

'We can't get hold of him, so we don't know. But I've never heard of anything like this.'

'The time of death fits with the mother's story,' Craig said. 'In fact, all the evidence fits with the mother's story.'

'Seriously,' I said. 'When have you ever heard of a ten-year-old kid slitting her father's throat? Let alone in her sleep.'

Richard rubbed his nose. 'There have been cases of ten-year-olds committing murder. But why would she kill her father?'

'She'd been having nightmares where she was terrified of him,' I said, somewhat unwillingly. 'Thought he was trying to kill her. Her mother thought she was remembering how her heart donor died.'

'Heavens,' Richard said.

'I know,' I said. 'There must be another explanation.'

★

Fiona had pivoted her desk away from its normal spot. After a moment of bafflement, I realised she now didn't see Craig's desk when she faced straight forward. I didn't have time for diplomatic outreach this week, so pretended I hadn't noticed. Craig wasn't around anyway.

'Can you tell me about that folk tale to do with the statues?' I said. 'Rachel said something about it. I'm wondering if that was what triggered Abbie's nightmares. I mean, she can't actually have been remembering her donor's death. It's ridiculous. So it must have come from somewhere else.'

'Do you think she really could have killed her father?' Fiona said.

'I don't know.' I sat on a spare chair by Fiona's desk.

Fiona picked up a paper-clip and started bending it. 'The folk tale. It's not very nice.'

'They rarely are, especially when the place where it happened has *Dead Girl* in its name.'

'No. So, it was a few hundred years ago, and they had this spate of young men doing weird things. Have you heard of a *fugue state*?'

'Where you wander off and forget how you got there?'

'That's it. Young men kept disappearing. They could be gone for days, weeks or even months. Some of them came back, but claimed they had no memory of what had happened to them. Others didn't come back at all.'

'How bizarre.'

'I know. And it seems like this did actually happen. I looked into it. There have been other epidemics of it. There was one in Paris. But it was really bad in Eldercliffe. It was often the oldest son who went. It was causing no end of problems.'

'So, what happened?'

'The local priest said the village had to make a sacrifice. A human sacrifice, to stop the young men going off.'

I looked at Fiona's earnest face. 'Seriously?'

'They had to sacrifice children. He said that was the only way to stop it. The village had to choose four children. Virgins.'

'*Obviously.* It's always bloody virgins.'

Fiona smiled nervously. 'They had to vote which children to sacrifice.' She picked up a couple more paper-clips and looped them through the first.

'My God, they sacrificed children to try to stop young men wandering off on a whim?'

'So my granny says. And of course it was poor and powerless girls who were chosen. Just young children. Eight years old, I think she said.'

My fists tightened. I felt a surge of anger for all the girls down the centuries whose lives weren't considered important. 'What the hell did they do to them?'

'There was an old house in the woods, on the site of where that house is now, the victim's house. They put them in there and set fire to it.'

'Oh for Christ's sake. Is this true, Fiona?'

'I'm not sure, to be honest. But my granny thinks it is. One of them jumped out of a window and ran off through the woods, but the villagers followed her and caught her and threw her into the gorge.'

'Jesus. Abbie ran off towards the gorge yesterday morning. Did the girl die?'

'Yes. She either drowned or was smashed to bits. The others burnt. And the particularly horrible thing is their own fathers went along with it. Their mothers didn't, but their fathers bowed to the pressure from the rest of the village. Or at least that's how the story goes.'

'And Abbie was screaming that her father was trying to kill her. Maybe this was the trigger for her nightmares?' I forced my fingers to relax. My nails were digging into my palms. I wished I had a paper-clip installation to mangle.

'And this story's what the statues are about? When were they put there?'

'Victorian times, I think. They loved that creepy stuff, didn't they?'

I rubbed a sore patch on my palm. 'How does the story end?'

'The young men did stop going off. I'm not sure why, so the villagers thought it had worked. It was worth it. Even though four children lost their lives.'

'If the fugue states were hysterical, it could work. Like a huge placebo.'

'I suppose so.'

'The children were sacrificed. For more important lives.' I remembered the plaque beneath one of the statues. *For the weak and the poor who died for the strong and the rich.*

'Horrible, isn't it? My gran thought there was something more. Something about the girls' mothers getting revenge. The *Destroying Angels*, she called them. She's going to ask her friend.'

'I can imagine that story giving a kid nightmares. But the story seemed to mean something to Phil Thornton as well, according to both his wife and Karen Jenkins. In fact, it sounded like he almost sought that house out because of the statues. And he made a carving the same as one of the statues except that the girl's heart had been removed. It's all very strange.'

Fiona grimaced. 'And the other daughter fell from the window of the house, didn't she? Like the poor girl who was sacrificed.'

Richard appeared as if from nowhere. 'We'll need to talk to a forensic psychiatrist about this kid,' he said.

'Yes,' I agreed, although I didn't know any in the area.

'Give Dr Fen Li a call,' Richard said. 'She's on the list. She's good, and if it comes to it, which in the circumstances I hope to God it doesn't, she's excellent on the witness stand. But she's not cheap, so for the love of all that's holy, keep a tight eye on the budget.'

★

Dr Li ran her psychiatric practice from a small clinic attached to her home, about two miles outside Eldercliffe. The area was rocky and barren, known for its tall, spiky houses, but the clinic was all on ground-level, sitting on a flat site partially hollowed out of a cliff. A bungalow clung to its side, where I assumed Dr Li lived.

I'd taken Jai with me. I couldn't face Craig. I kept running through in my head what I'd overheard him saying to Richard, and I had an unpleasant feeling it had been about me.

We walked up a ramp and came to a wide, automatic door. A light blue plaque announced that we were at the *White Peak Clinic*.

We just needed Dr Li to tell us a ten-year-old couldn't have killed her father like this. Then we'd have to find another explanation, no matter how well this one fitted the evidence.

The door whooshed open and sucked us into a reception area suffused with light and decorated with modern art prints and plants of the non-dying kind. The area was guarded by a plastic-faced receptionist who sat behind an expansive, curvy desk, and sported an American-toothed smile of the utmost symmetry. We showed her our ID and she tapped a keyboard with long, scarlet nails.

I glanced at a panel of images of glum-looking women and their smooth-faced *after-the-procedure* alter-egos. 'It's a cosmetic surgery clinic then?' I said.

The woman looked up and answered with a surprising Derbyshire accent. I'd half expected her to be American, or possibly a robot. 'Cosmetic surgery and psychotherapy,' she said. 'Dr Li Senior always makes sure the patients are suitable for the procedures. If their problems are psychological, we won't operate.'

'Dr Li Senior? Is there another Dr Li?'

'Her son. He works here as a cosmetic surgeon.'

A door to the side of the desk opened, and a young man glided through in a wheelchair.

'This is Dr Li Junior now,' the receptionist said.

The man was in his late twenties or early thirties and was skinny with foppish black hair and clear, almond eyes. He rocked back in his chair and pivoted round to face us. 'Are you here for my mother?' He looked South East Asian but spoke public school English.

We nodded and showed him our ID. He glanced at the receptionist and said, 'She's available. I'll take them through.'

Jai and I followed the man into a bright hallway. A vase of flowers sat on a shelf and the place smelt floral, with a hint of bleachy cleanliness. Not a smell I often experienced.

'The consulting rooms are this way.'

The man paused and listened by a door, then knocked and led us into a softly-lit room which smelt of fresh paint.

A compact woman in her fifties sat behind a desk making notes. She looked up. 'Ah. Yes, of course. Come in. Any chance you could organise some coffee for us, Tom?'

I wondered why the person in the wheelchair was doing all the work here, but he smiled and nodded.

'Thanks for seeing us at such short notice, Dr Li,' I said.

'Oh, it's not a problem. And call me Fen.' She stood and

waved her arm at a collection of chairs in the corner, arranged casually around a coffee table. 'Sit down.'

Jai and I sat, and Fen took a third chair.

'No couches, then?' I said.

Fen smiled. 'I'm not into Freudian analysis. Were you hoping for a lie-down?'

That did sound appealing.

The room had a serene feel as if designed to avoid inflaming the unstable. Fen's desk was clear except for one file and a photo of Tom and a girl with the same eyes. The furniture was old but freshly painted in muted colours, and the walls were one of those heritage shades that have pretentious names like *Giraffes in the Mist* or *Dying Salmon* but are actually just off-white or grey. The larger walls were dominated by abstract prints which could have doubled as ink-blot tests.

'So, you have a cosmetic surgery clinic, as well as doing psychotherapy?' Jai asked.

She nodded. 'That's more Tom's thing than mine. Day cases. Minor procedures. Tom's an excellent surgeon. He used to do major surgery, but since . . . well, he focuses on cosmetic surgery now.'

I wondered what had put Tom in a wheelchair, but it didn't seem appropriate to ask.

The door creaked open and Tom appeared with a tray of coffees and biscuits. 'Ashley's on her break,' he said. 'So I brought you these. I don't have any patients till this afternoon.'

'That's very kind of you,' I said. I couldn't imagine many male doctors bringing coffee for their mothers.

Tom placed the tray on the table.

'Thanks so much,' Jai said, and eyed the biscuits.

'No problem.' Tom smiled and spun his chair around. Its

arm caught the side of the coffee table and knocked it, splashing coffee onto its painted top. 'I'm sorry.' I sensed anxiety in Tom's voice. 'I can be clumsy.'

'You don't need to apologise,' I said.

There was a moment of silence before Tom left and Fen shifted her attention to us.

'Okay,' I said. 'We need some advice on a case. This one's highly confidential.'

'Of course,' Fen said.

'And we need to keep a lid on your costs. You know what it's like.'

Fen sighed. 'I do indeed. How's Richard Atkins? He split with his wife, didn't he?'

'He's fine.' I hoped she wouldn't press me for an opinion on Richard's ex-wife, who was a well-known pain in the backside. 'Put on a bit of weight since they split, but fine.'

We signed a few forms in a solemn manner and then explained the situation to Dr Li.

'So the girl was having nightmares,' she said, 'and sleepwalking?'

'So we've been told. Nightmares where she thought her father was trying to kill her.'

'What sleeping pills was she on?'

'Her mother said Sombunol.'

'Interesting.'

'Why's that interesting?'

'There have been some cases with that particular drug. Where patients have got out of bed and done things while still effectively asleep. The next day they don't remember anything. I've read reports of people eating, having sex, even driving, while they're asleep.'

'Blimey,' I said. 'Why would it even be prescribed?'

'The side effects aren't common, and it is effective. But there have been some homicide cases.'

'People have killed in their sleep whilst on Sombunol?'

'Yes, mainly in America. We can't know for sure what happened but the courts have accepted it as a valid defence to murder.'

'Is it possible?' I said. 'Could the girl have sleepwalked and killed her father? Because unless she's a spectacular actor, I'm sure she doesn't remember anything about her father's death.'

'I'm not aware of any cases involving children but I would say it's theoretically possible. Tell me more about the dreams.'

I glanced at Jai. 'They seem to have started after her heart transplant. She was dreaming about her donor – well, about her donor's death, her parents thought. Her mother seems to have thought there was something really weird going on – that she was actually remembering her heart donor's death. Of course that couldn't happen, but the child might have imagined it.'

'It can be a traumatic thing for a child, the idea of having another child's heart. They can feel very guilty that someone died. It affects them in different ways.'

'She told us her father had done something bad, and her heart knew. We're wondering if it was triggered by a story about their house. Some children died there.'

'Of course children have very vivid imaginations. But the issue here is whether the child could have killed her father in her sleep. Isn't it?'

I hesitated. 'Yes.'

'Well, I would say in principle yes she could have.'

★

A light dusting of snow was forming on the distant Peak District hills as we drove back. I squinted into the low, afternoon light. The roads were icy, and I had to force myself to concentrate on driving.

Jai was unusually quiet for the first couple of miles. Finally, he said, 'What are you thinking?'

'I want to do some research on sleep homicide. And on the drugs Abbie was taking. But we carry on looking into other possibilities, okay? Explore all options. Don't get channelled. You know the score.'

We arrived back at the Station, and I retreated to my room. I sat and let my mind chug over the facts. I kept picturing Abbie, remembering the way she'd held on to me in the woods. I couldn't believe she'd killed her father. A knock on the door made me jump. Fiona.

'Some more stuff's come back,' she said. 'The Luminol showed someone had washed blood off in the shower. So that ties in with Rachel washing Abbie.'

'It wasn't necessarily Rachel washing anyone. Let's not indulge in confirmation bias, Fiona.'

'No, of course. But the knife was the one that killed Thornton. And Abbie's prints were on it.'

'Right.'

'What did the forensic psychiatrist say?' Fiona asked.

'Oh, you know what they're like. Hedging her bets. But we can't rule Abbie out. There have been some cases involving the sleeping pills she's on.'

'What kind of cases?'

'A very, very few cases of people apparently killing in their sleep.'

'Oh my God. We've heard back from the lab, and she'd had an overdose of those sleeping pills.'

I rubbed my eyes and tried to bring my focus onto Fiona. 'How much of an overdose? Who could have given her that?'

'Not much of one, apparently. Do you think that made her sleepwalk and kill her dad?'

'Why did she have an overdose though?'

'Rachel said Phil was a bit rubbish at doing Abbie's pills. She takes all kinds of different ones. It's pretty complicated. And you know what some men are like – they leave these things to their wives, and then they're too embarrassed to admit they've got no clue if they have to take charge. Maybe he gave her two sleeping pills by accident.'

We were silent for a moment.

'Plus, Emily's passed me an email that he sent to Abbie's psychiatrist,' Fiona said. 'Do you want to see?'

I nodded, and she slid a print-out over my desk.

The email was sent from Phil Thornton to Dr Gibson, Abbie Thornton's psychiatrist.

*Dear Dr Gibson,*

*I wanted to email you because I need you to understand properly what has been going on with my daughter, Abbie. I know my wife has had some psychiatric issues in the past and I want you to realise that what has happened with Abbie is real and my wife is not imagining it or making it up.*

*Abbie has been waking up in the night screaming that her daddy is trying to kill her and is a murderer. When she wakes up she is terrified but has no memory of the dream. She also screams that she is drowning. This has been very distressing for us because I have never laid a finger on Abbie and also she has not called me Daddy for years, and she has never had an incident where she thought she was drowning. We have come to the unfortunate conclusion that Abbie is somehow remembering something which happened to her heart donor. I know this sounds strange which is why I am writing you this email because I realise with your scientific training you may not want to believe this, and may think my wife is imagining it.*

*The nightmares only started after Abbie's transplant and have got worse.*

*I am not saying I want to look into what happened to the donor child or anything like that but I want you to do what you can with hypnotism or whatever you can to stop Abbie having these memories which are very distressing for her and actually for me too.*

*Thank you for your help with this terrible problem we are experiencing.*

*Kind regards,*
*Phil Thornton*

I sighed. 'So, it wasn't only Rachel. Phil Thornton believed Abbie was remembering things from the heart donor as well. He didn't think she was imagining it.'

'It's pretty creepy. What's the drowning thing all about?'

The door banged open and Craig appeared. 'I need a word.'

'Hang on a sec, Craig. I'm talking to Fiona.'

'It's about that shrink. I bloody knew something dodgy was going on, with the kiddy screaming when he hypnotised her.'

'I'll be with you in five minutes,' I said.

'Fine. If you want to let a paedo carry on abusing kids.' He slammed the door behind him.

'Jeez,' Fiona said. 'Craig sees paedophiles everywhere. What's his problem?'

I stood and headed for the door. 'I'd better check.'

Fiona looked at me through narrowed eyes.

'What's up?' I said.

'I suppose I don't know how you put up with him.'

I smiled and declined to comment on that.

I found Craig at his desk.

'Abbie Thornton's psychiatrist is a paedo.' He sat back in his chair with his legs too wide apart.

I sank onto a chair next to him. 'Okay, slow down. Tell me what you've found out.'

'His practice manager phoned back. A patient called her about some stuff that's appeared online, about him abusing kids. He's been molesting them when he was supposed to be doing therapy. People are sharing it on Facebook.'

'Oh, Christ.' I pictured Abbie's grandmother telling us how upset Abbie had been when she was hypnotised, and felt a coldness in my stomach. 'When did this come out?'

'In the last day or two.' Craig's jaw jutted forward. 'But this could be why Abbie Thornton was dreaming about Daddy. Maybe Daddy was *him*.'

'Let's keep an open mind.'

Craig let out a soft snort. 'Yeah, well it fits with her screaming blue murder when he was alone with her.'

'Have you managed to get in touch with him?'

'The practice manager reckons he might not be in Scotland after all. She went to his house and his car was there but there was no answer when she knocked.'

I took the practice manager's number from Craig, walked to a quieter corner, and gave her a ring.

'There's no way these accusations are true,' she said. 'That's not Dr Gibson. He didn't even see many children. Honestly, there's no way he's a paedophile. He specialises in identity disorders. You know: body dysmorphia, gender issues, BIID . . . '

'BIID?'

'Body Identity Integrity Disorder. Where people feel like part of their body doesn't really belong to them, and want rid of it. One of his patients went to India and had his leg amputated. Not that Dr Gibson approved of that. It's all illegal of course.'

I leant against a nearby desk. This case was getting more bizarre by the minute. I'd read about that condition – people who didn't want their own limbs; who wanted them amputated even though they were perfectly healthy. 'We'll go over to his house,' I said. 'We need to talk to him.'

★

'This'll be fun,' Craig said. 'Off to see a paedo. Better stick together.'

I accelerated a little and glanced at Craig's bulldoggy profile. 'If he *is* a paedophile – which we have no compelling reason to believe – then we're hardly his target market, are we? Chubby cops in their thirties?'

'Makes me feel dirty even thinking about it. You don't have kids of your own. You don't understand. You don't even like kids.'

'That's not . . . Oh never mind. His practice manager said he doesn't even work much with kids. He specialises in identity disorders.'

Craig gave a non-committal grunt. I felt the need to get his attention.

'One of his clients went to India,' I said. 'And paid to have his leg amputated.'

'Why? What was the matter with it? Why couldn't he get it done here?'

'Nothing was the matter with it. He just didn't want it. Didn't feel like it belonged to him. It's a condition.'

I took my eyes off the road a minute to enjoy Craig's expression. He spun his head round. 'What the . . . '

'It's called Body Integrity Identity Disorder. Interesting, don't you think?'

'Mental. That's what I think.'

'Apparently it happens most in middle-aged white males, and the most common desire is for the left leg to be amputated above the knee.'

Craig let out an exasperated breath. 'Some people . . . '

We drove the rest of the way in silence, and I parked at the address we'd been given – one of a cluster of chalet-style houses on the edge of a small lake on the outskirts of Eldercliffe. The sleet had eased off, being replaced by fog which had settled over the hills like a damp duvet.

The houses were Swiss-styled and had been built by a Victorian megalomaniac who'd taken a shine to the Alps and decided to replicate them in Derbyshire. Today their extreme tweeness was moderated by the fog, but the quiet was almost suffocating.

Harry Gibson's drive contained a car. It also contained a dead bird in a puddle, but was otherwise pristine. We walked up a path between neatly trimmed shrubs and I rang the bell.

No response.

'Hard to imagine a kiddy-fiddler living here,' Craig said. 'There's practically gnomes in the garden.'

Craig's brain worked in mysterious ways. I kept quiet.

I rang the bell again. No response.

'Damn it,' I said. 'He probably thinks we're press.'

I tried the handle. It turned, and I gave the door a little shove. It opened into a dim hallway. I glanced at Craig. Why would a man who was being hounded by packs of enraged paedophile-hunters leave his door unlocked?

I poked my head in and shouted, 'Dr Gibson. Are you okay?'

The air inside felt chilly and un-lived-in, and smelt of hangovers.

Music was coming from the back of the house. Like the soundtrack from an old cartoon. I glanced at Craig. 'He's probably watching some TV with the sound loud.'

A rare look of unease crossed Craig's face. 'Yeah, I expect he is.'

I braced myself for a tasteless joke. We called it *Joke Tourette's*, and it was a common affliction – inappropriate humour, blurted out in times of stress. But Craig stayed silent.

I realised my heart was thudding and I didn't want to go into this chocolate-box house. 'We'd better have a look,' I said.

A door on the left of the hall led into a living room. I peered in and glanced up at the ceiling. Nothing was dangling but a paper lampshade. The clamp around my insides released its grip a little. We walked into the room, which seemed to shrink in response to Craig's bulk. It was decorated in a bachelor-mix of IKEA furniture, nondescript landscape prints, and dust.

A door at the far end of the living room seemed to lead into a conservatory – a bright room which must have been bathed in light reflected off the lake, a room that seemed all wrong for the feeling I now had in my stomach. I noticed the hangover smell again, and the music, louder now. I had a memory of watching cartoons as a kid, sitting on the living room floor, too close to the TV, in the technicolour years before my sister fell ill.

I walked through the door.

At first glance, my brain told me he was okay, although at some level I knew he wasn't. He was almost in a sitting position. Almost normal but obviously not. Too low. A rope stretched tight above him. Face bloated, lips black, purple tongue protruding. Sitting, but not on a chair. The chair was next to him, pushed to the side. He was hanging.

Craig's voice was rough like gravel. 'Oh shit.'

I staggered back a step and reached for my radio.

'Cut him down, Craig. Please.'

I called it in, while Craig cut the rope near its middle, careful to preserve the knots. The coroner would take a dim view if we hadn't cut him down and done our best. Always preserve life ahead of evidence. But there was no life to preserve here. He collapsed onto the floor in the same uncanny sitting position we'd found him in, limbs already rigid. Music blared from a laptop on the floor, filling my brain, making it hard to think.

Despite my obsessive need to check ceilings, not all suicides by hanging were high up. Sometimes the drugs-and-booze-jobs took place low down. Take enough stuff that you know you'll eventually pass out, tie a rope around something rigid – in this case a banister to the side of a set of steps leading to a mezzanine room – loop the other end of the rope around your neck, lean against the banister, and wait until you pass out. In the grand scheme of such things, it was a relatively stress-free method. I'd seen it done this way a few times.

I stood back and took in the room. The lake was visible through patio doors, almost completely still, its surface smooth as marble. A couple of ducks swooped onto it, disrupting the calm and sending ripples across its surface.

A full ashtray sat on a glass coffee table beside a wine glass and a whisky tumbler. Three empty wine bottles and a whisky bottle lay on the floor, spilling dregs onto an open laptop, which was still blaring music into the room. I peered at the screen, which was hard to see in the light reflecting off the lake outside. *Tom and Jerry. Blue Cat Blues.* Playing on a loop, the music too loud. The episode where Tom and Jerry kill themselves.

# 8.

'Ah, Meg. Are you still here?'

That was a hard one to answer without resorting to philosophy. I walked a step closer to Richard's desk and nodded slightly. He looked more stressed than usual, slightly damp and pink-faced. He picked up a cactus, touched it gently, and then drew his finger back sharply. A tiny blob of blood swelled at its end.

I winced. 'Are you okay?'

He wiped his finger on a file. Police files smeared with blood. Very evocative.

'The vultures are flying low overhead,' he said. 'And all the professionally-horrified people on social media are working themselves into a lather about Harry Gibson. *Why aren't the incompetent police catching these vile paedophiles?* You know the kind of stuff.'

'For God's sake. The man's dead, and we don't even know he abused any children.'

'That won't bother the angry mob.' He shook his finger, which had thankfully stopped bleeding. 'Sit down, if you want.'

I eyed Richard's visitor chair and wondered if it was part of a bizarre psychological experiment that he was performing on us. Maybe cacti were involved too. 'I'll stand.'

He nodded. 'What did you want to talk to me about?'

'I wonder if we should look more closely at him,' I said. 'At Harry Gibson.'

'The suicide?'

I hesitated. Wondered again if I should let this one go. It almost certainly was a suicide, and I had no time to look into another possible murder. 'On the face of it, it does look very much like a suicide.'

'And he was accused of being a paedophile online. It's text-book.'

I couldn't do it. This man deserved better. 'I know that. And so would a murderer. We're supposed to *Think Murder* aren't we?'

Richard sounded weary. 'Go on.'

'I mean, if you wanted to kill someone and make it look like a suicide, couldn't you just make accusations on social media?'

'You know the situation. We're desperately short of detectives. Nobody wants to do the job any more. We can't justify the resources to look at this in more detail. Craig's already been on at me to look into any other kids he saw. And homicidal hangings are very rare.'

'But not unheard of. And where did the accusations about him being a paedophile come from? And why now, when we need to talk to him about Abbie Thornton?'

'What are you saying, Meg?'

'I think we should get SOCO in, dust for prints, get the knot expert involved, have a look at the scuff marks around that chair, check if anyone else was there. Not just assume it was a suicide. It's possible he was involved with some illegal activity as well. Helping patients get their perfectly healthy legs amputated abroad because they didn't want them.'

'Excuse me? Did I hear you correctly?'

'Yes. He specialised in identity disorders. There are people who don't feel like their limbs belong to them. They want them amputated. If they're not helped, they do things like lie on railway tracks.'

'Good heavens. But, Meg, we don't have the resources. You know the situation. A suspected paedophile hanged himself. It's straightforward.'

'Can I put the coroner's report together then?'

'We don't need someone at your level doing that. Craig can handle it.'

'But what if he was murdered? Craig just thinks of him as a paedo. He doesn't give a damn about finding out the truth.'

'You shouldn't talk like that about your colleagues, Meg. I thought you'd be happy to get this wrapped up.'

'But don't you think it's a bit of a coincidence that Gibson was Abbie Thornton's psychiatrist? Soon it's going to be too late to go back and get decent forensics. If it does turn out to be relevant to Phil Thornton, the media will be all over us. We'll look like incompetent idiots.'

'Okay, okay, calm down.'

Was there anything in the world less likely to make you feel calm than being told to calm down? 'I am calm. I just don't want us to screw this up.'

'Alright, alright, resistance is futile. Look into it a bit more. To reassure yourself it's a suicide. And, Meg . . . '

'Yes?'

'Remember you're working with Craig on the Thornton case. And you can't afford any more off-piste performances, especially with this police brutality thing hanging over us. Not if you want a future here.'

★

I realised I didn't want to go home. I didn't want to walk into my house with my head still full of Harry Gibson – his uncanny pose, his bulbous face, his protruding tongue. In quiet moments throughout the day, I'd had a shimmering sense in my peripheral vision of something hanging, but of course when I'd snapped my head round, there'd been nothing there. And I'd imagined hearing the *Tom and Jerry* suicide music playing in the distance. When I finally managed to get this image out of my head, all I saw was little Abbie Thornton – asleep but with glassy eyes wide open – plunging a knife into her father's neck.

I texted my friend Hannah and she replied to say it was fine for me to pop in on my way home. I felt a wave of relief, left the Station and set off for Hannah's, via a chocolate stop.

Hannah's estate on the outskirts of Belper had the open lawns and wide driveways of a Florida retirement complex, sadly without the weather to match. I parked and strode up the ramp to her door, seized with a sudden desperation to get inside. Hannah buzzed me in, and I shoved the door shut behind me and almost collapsed onto her smooth tiles.

'Have you been shot?' Hannah wheeled herself over. 'You're not going to bleed on the limestone, are you?'

'Feels like it. But no.'

She spun round and whizzed up the wide corridor and into her ludicrously clean and sparkly kitchen. I followed, probably leaving a trail of cat hair behind me.

I placed my offering of Thorntons chocolates on the table.

I realised I'd bought chocolates with the same name as the victim.

'Oh, hurray! I'll put some coffee on. Sit down.'

'How are you?' I asked.

Hannah spun round to fiddle with her espresso machine. 'Oh, you know. Skint, knackered and on a pointless diet. So same same. And another day dealing with asocial IT dorks, but nothing out of the ordinary.'

Hannah did an inexplicable computer-related job, manipulating her socially inept colleagues with brutal ease.

I flopped into one of the leather kitchen chairs and let my head fall back. 'We had a hanging,' I said. 'Can't tell you too much, but you know I'm not great with hangings.'

'Are you okay?'

'Not too bad. He was low down – one of the booze and drugs jobs where they wait to pass out. So I'm hoping it won't send me nuts and trigger my need to check ceilings again.'

'Have you been feeling anxious? You could always have a chat with the counsellor.'

'I'll be fine. I haven't got time to muck about with that at the moment. I stupidly agreed to take on that murder case.'

'The social worker? I heard it on the news. But I didn't think that was a hanging.'

'No, the hanging was someone else. I can't really talk about it. It's just good to be here and get away from it all, to be honest.'

'Blimey. Two deaths. Who are you mainly working with?'

I sank lower in the chair and grimaced.

'Craig. Oh dear.' Hannah passed me a coffee and took a delicate sip of hers. 'How's your mum?'

'Exhausted from looking after Gran, but okay. She tried to get in touch with Dad, but hasn't heard back.'

'He hasn't got back to her even though her mother's dying?'

'No. He's probably just busy.'

'When will you stop making excuses for him, Meg? He's clearly a shit.'

I opened my mouth. Wasn't it an unwritten rule that you could call your own dad a shit but not someone else's?

'What else have you been up to?' Hannah said, possibly realising she'd crossed a line. 'That you're allowed to talk about?'

'Have you come across BIID? Body Identity Integrity Disorder?' I was feeling a tiny bit spiteful after the shit-dad comment, and I knew this subject would annoy Hannah. People who had perfectly good legs wanting rid of them.

She shoved her cup down. 'The people who want their legs chopped off?'

'Sounds about right.'

'Yes. I have. Some of them go on the disability forums. What I wouldn't give to be able to walk, and they want their legs chopped off. And I read about a woman who blinded herself with sulphuric acid.'

'She wanted to be blind?'

'Apparently.'

'Jesus, that must be most people's worst fear. I can't get my head round that.'

'Me neither. You couldn't make it up.'

'It's got to be an incredibly powerful thing though, hasn't it? To want to do that. I mean, especially in the society we live in, so obsessed with physical perfection. To go against it all to that extent. When most people are so far the other way – banging on about how fat they are the whole time and desperately removing perfectly innocent body hair. Don't you think it's interesting?'

'I suppose so.' She sighed. 'It kind of bothers me though. And it ends up being about resources too. That woman who's now blind, don't tell me she doesn't need some help. I mean, I need some help and you know how independent I am, being an obsessive exerciser with muscles like Arnie, and having *been like it since birth*, as they say.'

'I see what you mean. If there's a limited pot.'

'There's a very bloody limited pot, Meg. You're lucky if you don't have to piss yourself on a train these days, since the bastard Tories have been in charge. It's not as easy for us to just hang on as it is for you. And a lot of people have catheters and . . . take my word for it — it's not easy.'

It struck me again how little insight I had into the brutal realities of Hannah's life with spina bifida, no matter how hard I tried. She did upper body exercises for hours each day, just so she had the strength to do things like get in and out of her car, or go to bed. Things I took completely for granted. Over the years, she'd shown me diagrams of her spine; told me about her pain, the problems with her feet, the details of her paralysis. I was the one she came to her when her parents couldn't handle it, when they were overcome with folic-acid-related guilt. But I knew I still didn't fully get it.

'Oh, don't give me that look,' she said. 'I manage. And there's plenty worse off than me. But you know some people already resent the amount that's spent on ramps and toilets and stuff. Imagine if they thought we'd done it to ourselves? I do try to have some sympathy with them wanting to lose limbs or whatever, because I suppose they can't help the way they feel but . . . well, I don't get it.'

'Is it so shocking because it goes against cultural norms?'

'Jesus, Meg, I prefer you on gin and tonic. Have you OD'd on caffeine or something?'

'I was thinking . . . foot-binding went on for thousands of years. That crippled people, but it was socially acceptable. And what about corsets, or to a lesser extent, what about stupid shoes nowadays?'

'Yeah, when you've got nerve damage in your feet like I have, you don't muck about with high heels, that's for sure. Why don't people value what they've got?'

I was on a roll. It was such a relief not to be thinking about Abbie or Harry Gibson. 'Yeah. And breast enlargements, and always being on a frigging diet so they're knackered and grumpy the whole time . . . All these things disable people to an extent.'

'But if someone wants to chop one little leg off, all hell breaks loose.'

'Okay,' I said. 'I know it's not quite as extreme. But foot-binding was.'

'Funny that the culturally acceptable stuff all seems to be done to women. But . . . ' She raised her hand. 'I do *not* want to start you on a rant about that. So, stop right there.'

I smiled. 'Okay, okay. I'm saying nothing.'

Hannah looked into her coffee mug and swirled the dregs around. 'I just wondered – are you still taking your gran to Switzerland next week?' There was a tightness to her voice.

I hesitated. This was not a good subject for us. 'She's got end-stage stomach cancer,' I said. 'It's not going to get any better for her. What's the point in torturing her?'

'It's not always that simple.'

Something in Hannah's tone irritated me. Possibly because she'd briefly become involved with a group of nutty Christians the year before, and I was worried some of her arguments were coming from them. I respected her views as someone with a disability. But using selected quotes from a two-thousand-year-old piece of fiction to force desperate people to stay alive – well, that pissed me off.

'Come on, Hannah. I'm always tip-toeing around you on this one,' I said. 'And I haven't got the energy today. I've had a hard week and a shit day. You've got the ultimate trump card so I always end up backing off, but it doesn't mean I can't have an opinion. Gran's in a worse state than either of us can possibly imagine.'

'Sorry.' Hannah still wouldn't look at me. 'I know you've had a bad day. We don't have to discuss it today, but . . . '

'What?'

'I don't disagree with how you feel about your gran, honestly.'

'But?'

'Because of you being in the police, and that case last year, the press are going to be on to you, Meg, You won't avoid it. There'll be loads of publicity. Did you know Life Line have been blogging about you?'

Oh joy. The nutty Christians. 'What do you mean?'

'I must still be on their email list, and they sent me a link to some blog posts about you taking your gran to Dignitas.'

'Oh fabulous. That's all I need. Thank goodness Richard's so clueless about the internet. How the hell do they know about Gran?'

'I don't know. But they aren't very nice about you. They even talked about you discovering your sister when she hanged herself.'

I sighed. 'Oh God, I know how they found out about that. Remember the girl from that case last year. She did an interview. Really nice about me, saying I saved her life, but she told the press about Carrie.'

'Ungrateful cow.'

'No, honestly, Hannah. It's fine. She didn't realise I hadn't told anyone. I should have asked her not to share it.'

'It was pretty naïve of her. You're a detective – you don't want all and sundry stalkers and psychopaths out there knowing your business.'

'She's only fifteen – she didn't realise, and they're all over-sharers, aren't they, modern kids? Their brains permanently wired into the net.'

'Well the group must have picked up on that and somehow they've found out about you taking your gran, and they're blogging about you.'

'Jesus. What else have they said?'

'They were on about you taking your gran to Dignitas, and they didn't exactly put a positive slant on it. Talked about people disposing of elderly relatives because they'd become inconvenient. And then they got personal about you. One of them even claimed you were responsible for Carrie's death. They mentioned she had cancer but then they said she committed suicide because you'd bullied her.'

'*Bullied her*? I was ten years old, and she was fifteen. And she was dying of bloody cancer!'

'Sorry. Maybe I shouldn't have said anything.'

'No, it's better to know.'

'I suppose so. Bear in mind that the press are going to find out about your Dignitas trip. You're going to end up getting tons of publicity.'

I felt a fluttering in my stomach. Panic about being exposed. A sinking heaviness that anyone would be so horrible about me, even though I told myself I didn't care what they thought. 'I'll just have to cope, won't I?'

'But you know how I feel about this. You'll end up speaking

out everywhere in favour of assisted dying. And it's getting worse with all the cuts. You just have to believe me – if they brought in an assisted suicide law, it would be bad for disabled people.'

'They're not going to change the law, Hannah. No chance. We've got a government full of God-botherers. And Gran's dying. It's not a disability issue for her.'

'I know this doesn't apply to your gran, but it applies to lots of other people. The reasons they give for ending their lives mostly aren't about unbearable suffering – they're about dignity and loss of autonomy. Those are disability issues. We should be helping people live full lives, not helping them die. It perpetuates this idea that our lives aren't worth living. That it's not "dignified" – whatever that even means – to need help.'

'I get what you're saying, Hannah. I just want to make sure Gran doesn't suffer too much at the end. If I end up having to talk to the press, I won't talk about it as a general issue. I'll only talk about Gran, okay?' I so wanted this conversation to end. I'd already tortured myself enough about this decision.

'Imagine if when you felt suicidal, someone had helped you kill yourself. Because they thought it was justified. But actually it was depression, and you recovered. You'd be dead now.'

Well, that was a hard-hitter. 'Thanks for that, Hannah. Nice to be reminded.'

'If you were disabled, everyone would have thought you were justified in wanting to kill yourself but in reality most disabled people have good levels of happiness. Able-bodied people think they'd rather be dead than disabled, just like they think they'd be happy if they were suddenly rich.'

'I get what you're saying.' I sucked the dregs from my coffee cup, wishing it was a gin. 'Wasn't there that famous research?

Lottery winners and paralysed people ending up with similar happiness levels. Mind you, didn't they get a hot young female student to interview the young, male paralysis victims? I think that might have affected the outcomes.'

Hannah laughed. I was relieved we were just about keeping this friendly. 'Would you think about it?' she said. 'Whether you want to end up as a poster girl for assisted dying when your best friend's asking you sincerely not to. There must be ways your gran can have a decent death here.'

★

I arrived home to be greeted by a pile of bills so hefty the door didn't want to open. Since I'd been paying for Gran's carer, and saving for Switzerland, things had got a little out of control. I gave the door a firm shove, kicked the bills aside, and walked into the freezing hallway.

I kept my coat on and took my laptop to the kitchen. I was itching to look at the blog posts about me, but decided not to. I knew they'd be unfair and probably incoherent, and what was the point of letting that into my head? I didn't have a good track-history of coping with that kind of thing. Besides, I needed to put my own troubles aside and research homicidal sleepwalking.

Hamlet bellowed until I gave in and fed him a second supper. I supposed I should eat too. I peered into the fridge, but nothing looked very edible.

I sorted myself out tea and toast.

No wonder it was freezing. The kitchen window wasn't shut properly. I stood and shoved the ancient wooden casement back into place, trying unsuccessfully to get it to latch. I gave up, stuck the fan heater on, and settled at the table with the laptop.

It seemed there had been around seventy reported cases of people killing in their sleep. Most of them had been taking sleeping pills at the time, and in some of the cases the courts had accepted being asleep as a valid defence to murder. Someone (usually a man) would dream they were being attacked, fight back, and then wake to find they'd killed someone (usually their wife). It seemed just about plausible. In a more bizarre case, a man had driven fourteen miles and killed his mother-in-law, apparently in his sleep. That sounded less plausible.

I'd never sleepwalked, although I'd had the opposite experience – waking up paralysed and terrified, heart pounding, my brain awake but my body not. I had shared a house with a guy who sometimes sleepwalked when he was drunk. Once we'd had to intervene to stop him sleep-peeing in the laundry basket. He'd been amenable and not in the slightest bit violent, but there'd still been something chilling about the whole episode.

I tried to picture Abbie throwing the duvet off her bed in her girly-pink room, walking robotically downstairs, her eyes seeing but her brain unaware, taking the biggest knife from the kitchen, walking back up the stairs and into her parents' room, and stabbing her father in the neck. Twice. Could she have done that, if she thought her dad was trying to kill her?

# 9.

I woke in a sweat, heart pounding, fragments of a dream remaining. I'd been in a Victorian house like the Thorntons', creeping from room to room, sure someone was after me. In the final room I'd entered – a huge bedroom – a person had been hanging from the ceiling.

I lay for a moment, forcing my breath to slow, then reached to switch on the reassuring tones of Radio Derby. I wasn't giving in to it.

I stumbled out of bed and peered through my tiny leaded window. It was raining again, and windy. The cold rattled around my ancient cottage, through rafters and between floorboards. I dressed quickly, shivering and still feeling spooked from my dream.

Downstairs, Hamlet was in the kitchen welded to his heated pad. I fed him, drunk a huge mug of tea, and set off for work.

Everyone had gathered in the incident room, which was stuffed with information – photos, maps, random bits of paper, whiteboards scrawled with notes and the odd obscenity. The tedious official operation name for the Thornton case had been replaced informally with *Operation Sweeney Todd*, a fact which I was not supposed to know.

The air in the room crackled. Two corpses in two days was probably a record for our area, and the second had a few benefits. Usually the cops would hide their enthusiasm about a death – it wasn't quite appropriate when some poor sod had been knifed in the colon or trussed himself from a tree. But with Harry Gibson, there was blatant lack of concern. I found it unsettling and it made me all the more determined to look into it properly.

Everyone was speaking at once. *Is it true the kid killed her father? Are we charging her? Was it something to do with her heart? Was it the drugs?*

'Okay!' I raised my voice over the din. 'We have some interesting new leads on Phil Thornton, but we need more evidence.'

Richard butted in. 'We have to manage the media very carefully. For now, we're saying nothing about the heart or the drugs. Alright?'

Much earnest nodding, but more Abbie questions from the team. *Did she remember her donor's death? Did she think her father was the donor's father? Is that why she killed him? What did Dr Gibson know?*

I answered as best I could. *No, it was highly unlikely Abbie Thornton's heart had anything to do with her father's murder. Keep investigating other avenues. No, she did not remember her heart donor's death. Had they been watching too much* Walking Dead?

They eventually simmered down.

'Don't assume it was the child,' I said. 'Continue to investigate all leads. What about his finances? Wills? Anything there?'

'He was quite well-off,' Jai said. 'Parents both died young-ish – nothing suspicious – and left him money. There's chunks of it in various unsurprising places. But a few weeks ago, he transferred twenty grand from savings into his current account and then withdrew it in cash. Five grand a day over four days.'

'And I assume we don't know what he did with it?'

'No. And there's no sign of it in the house. Obviously we're looking into it. The will looks uncontroversial – mostly goes to his wife and into a trust for his daughter. Plus a few charities.'

'What about the ex-wife's death?'

'Clearly a traffic accident. Nothing at all suspicious.'

'And Abbie's step sister? Rachel Thornton's daughter, I mean. What about her death? Anything dodgy?'

'Nothing in the file. Fell out of a window. Tragic accident. And her father – Rachel Thornton's first husband – is safely in Vancouver, so I think we can discount him.'

Emily said, 'We've got some more from his phone. Until a month or so ago, lots of texts between Phil Thornton and Karen Jenkins, the work-place affair woman. Not terribly discreet affair-stuff. Then it looks like he ended it. And recently, increasingly desperate texts from Karen saying she needs to talk, and that he mustn't say anything.'

'Talk about what?'

'Not clear. But there was something she didn't want him to say. Maybe she just didn't want him blabbing about the affair to her husband.'

'She had money problems and a drink problem,' I said. 'She's not going to want that affair to come out.'

Jai spun on his chair. A full three-sixty. 'So she's still a possible.'

'Keep an open mind,' I said. 'Keep going with the door-to-door, and all the usual victimology. Now let's talk about Dr Harry Gibson.'

'It was a straightforward suicide,' Craig said, with the

authority of the cutter-downer. 'Nothing to indicate otherwise. And the motivation's pretty damn obvious.'

'We're not making that assumption,' I said. 'It's most likely a suicide but technically, it could have been a murder. Did you notice he was on a chair on castors, and the floor was hard? And he was hanging very low. So, theoretically someone could have drugged his drink, waited for him to pass out, wheeled him over to the edge of the room, tied him to the banister, and pushed the chair out from under him. That would be hard to differentiate from him doing something very similar himself.'

'It would be pretty unprofessional of us not to look into it properly.' Fiona glanced at Craig. 'If he did it to himself, he'd have stood until he passed out, wouldn't he? So, he'd have fallen further?'

Craig yawned loudly. He didn't like the Fiona who was emerging as she found her feet, the Fiona who stood up to him.

'Yes,' I said. 'I'm hoping the marks on his neck or the analysis from the knot expert, or maybe the scuff marks, will shed some light. And we need to find who started the rumour. There were no official complaints about Gibson.'

Craig sighed. 'Doesn't mean he wasn't a paedo. Abbie screamed her guts out with him when he hypnotised her. And look how the Catholic church covered up what they did.'

'I'm not denying that. But I don't want us to make any assumptions. SOCO are taking a look round the house and we're still waiting on his bloods. I want us to look at CCTV as well – did anyone visit him that evening?'

'There's ways to his house that avoid CCTV,' Fiona said. 'I sometimes think it would be easier if we worked in a city.'

'Oh, it's not,' I said, remembering my experiences in Manchester. 'Look at what we've got. And he had an unusual speciality in his psychiatry practice. He helped people with a disorder that makes them feel parts of their body don't belong to them. Sometimes they want to chop a limb off . . . '

General mutterings of disbelief around the room.

I raised my voice. 'At least one man went to India to get it done. It's not legal. Was Gibson mixed up in anything dodgy? Check it out. And he has a sister and his parents are still alive. So, we need to talk to them. Fiona, can you sort that?'

Fiona said, 'Yes,' simultaneously with Craig saying, 'It's a waste of time.'

'Craig,' I said. 'This man deserves our time as much as anyone else. We don't know it was a suicide, we don't know he was a paedophile, and we don't know it was unconnected to Phil Thornton.'

'I'm more worried about the kids he abused,' Craig said. 'Who's looking out for them?'

'We're all worried about children, Craig.' I projected my voice over the rumble. 'Doing a decent job finding out what happened to this poor man doesn't mean we're not worried about children.'

'But if he did abuse her,' Jai said. 'Could that have triggered her violence towards her father?'

★

Jai strode into my room a couple of hours later. 'Enjoying working with the lumphead?'

'God, how did he make it to sergeant?'

Jai plonked himself on the side of my desk. 'Plenty of senior people think like he does, you know. Not like you newfangled, namby-pamby, politically correct wimmin who picked up dodgy, modern ideas in Manchester. But yes, he's an idiot. I've told him he would never have got the inspector gig anyway, so there's no point resenting you.'

'I'm sure that was a huge step forward for amicable relations. Thanks so much, Jai. He'll hate me a whole lot less after that. And Richard's being weird with me at the moment as well. One minute he's nicey-nicey, the next he's being a bugger. He hasn't worked out what I'm doing next week, has he?'

'Oh, I don't think so. That would have registered on the Richter scale.' Jai twisted round, scrunching paperwork underneath him. 'But I think Craig might have told him you pushed Rachel Thornton on that first day.'

'What? He wasn't even there! He turned up after the bloody woman punched me.'

'I know. Hopefully, Richard will ignore him. It's best you pay no attention to it. Maybe I shouldn't have said anything.'

'No, I'd rather know.' I felt so out of my depth with the Craig situation, unsure what his agenda was, baffled by his wife's comments, depressed that he seemed to dislike me so much. I sighed. 'Okay. Let's forget it for now. You'd better get your bottom off my filing system.'

'Is that what you call it? I've seen more filing in my recycling bin.' He shifted slightly to avoid my files and suddenly looked serious. 'But are you alright? With that hanging yesterday, on top of your gran and everything?'

The siren went off inside me. *Panic, panic, don't appear vulnerable. Show no weakness.* I was fully aware of how ridiculous this was with Jai. He wasn't one of the macho morons who'd use any tiny chink in my armour against me. But old habits die hard. 'I'm fine,' I said.

'Of course you are.' Jai grimaced. 'But it's not going to be easy with your gran next week.'

I still couldn't picture us getting Gran on a plane and all the way to Switzerland. It was hard enough getting her down the hall and into the kitchen. I'd worked it all out in military detail, but had avoided picturing the brutal reality of what it would be like. And I'd been putting Hannah out of my mind too. Was she going to loathe me if I still took Gran, after she'd asked me to reconsider?

'I know,' I said. 'But for God's sake, don't tell anyone about it.'

Jai seemed to accept that the Dignitas trip was best for Gran, but I suspected he had some deep-rooted religious doubts bubbling under the surface, despite having supposedly flung all that off with his turban.

'So,' I said. 'Did I hear Emily had come back with some stuff from Harry Gibson's laptop?'

'Yes. They can't find any actual child sex images. I mean, this is only an initial look, but assuming he's not massively techie, he doesn't have porn on his laptop. However . . . ' Jai jumped up from my desk and started pacing up and down by the window.

'For God's sake, Jai, sit down. My chair won't eat you. It's not like Richard's.'

Jai walked back and perched himself unwillingly on my spare chair, knees crossed, one leg bouncing. 'He was googling about whether it was wrong to look at virtual child pornography, or simulated child pornography. You know, where they use cartoon characters or adults made to look younger or weird shit like that.'

I sighed. 'Oh God, he was a paedophile. Maybe Craig's right for once.'

'There wasn't any actual pornography on the laptop.'

'So, he was exploring whether this other stuff was morally wrong or not. He could have been looking into it for a patient.'

'He's also been on websites for these so-called *virtuous paedophiles*.' Jai uncrossed his legs and fiddled with the chair, raising it higher, then lowering it again. 'They admit they're attracted to kids but they swear to do nothing about it.'

'I've seen. What a horrible predicament. People think paedophiles automatically abuse children, but of course they don't. If Harry Gibson was attracted to kids, the poor sod could have actually been working really hard not to offend.'

'We've had no complaints about him,' Jai said.

'And you know what it's like these days – pretty much anyone who casts an askew glance at a kid is going to get a complaint at some point. But his profession bothers me. Why put yourself in that position?'

'We don't know he's innocent. He could have another computer. No smoke without fire.'

'Jai, would you stop trying to break that chair. You know I won't get another one, with all the cuts.' I folded my arms. 'And maybe there is no smoke without fire. But who started the fire? It might not be Gibson. And why did they start a fire? Someone started posting about him, for some reason.'

'He could have groped a kid or something, couldn't he? And the parents didn't want to go to the hassle of reporting it. So they stuck it online to alert others. I know it's cowardly, but it does happen.'

'Who was the first person to post?'

Jai wrinkled his nose. 'Ah, well, that's proving more difficult. We're bringing in some people who fanned the flames, but the techies can't locate Patient Zero right now. Do you really think he was murdered?'

That was too many metaphors. 'I admit it looks like a suicide.'

'Homicidal hangings are extremely rare.'

'Everyone keeps saying that. Maybe they only seem rare because we don't look for them.'

'SOCO should pick up some evidence if there was anyone with him.'

'Yeah,' I said. 'It just seems a bit of a coincidence. He was treating Abbie Thornton and now she's in the frame for murder. We get told bizarre stories about her heart. We need this man to tell us what was going on, and then he turns up dead. And if Gibson was a vile child abuser, why would he have been searching about the ethics of that simulated stuff?'

A voice came from the doorway. 'I've heard it all now.'

Craig.

'Defending paedophiles.' His lip curled. 'I'm sure it's totally fine for them to work with children. What's the problem?'

I wanted to scream at him. *You bastard! Why did you lie to Richard about me?* But I took a breath and held myself in. 'Thanks for your contribution, Craig. We're not saying it was okay, but we're trying not to jump to conclusions. Even if he was attracted to children, it doesn't mean he was an abuser. He might have had feelings but not acted on them.'

Craig marched over and stood too close to Jai. 'Yeah. Right. And Abbie was terrified for no reason at all.'

I could smell Craig's cheap aftershave. 'She might have been terrified because he was trying to deal with her nightmares, and – '

'Don't bother, Meg.' Jai turned away from Craig. 'You're wasting your time with him.'

I wasn't ready to give up, springing to the defence of paedophiles in my desire to argue with Craig. 'We don't know he was abusive. Assuming he is – that's like saying all heterosexual men are rapists. Or like those morons who say they wouldn't want a gay doctor.'

'I wouldn't want a gay doctor,' Craig said, with absolutely no sense of irony.

I sighed. 'Yeah, those morons.'

I looked up and saw that Fiona was standing near us. I hadn't noticed her approaching. Her eyes flitted back and forth between us. Finally, she said, 'Did you know my brother's gay?'

Craig nudged his chair backwards. 'So?' His tone was defensive, but I sensed he didn't actually want to upset Fiona.

'So,' I said, 'let's ditch the homophobic comments and move on. I only said the thing about the gay doctor as an example of something self-evidently absurd. I never expected anyone to agree with it.'

'Don't worry, Craig,' Fiona said. 'You should be safe. I don't think a gay doctor would be interested in a pasty, podgy, straight man.'

A few moments of stunned silence. Fiona was normally so quiet and professional, so careful not to upset anyone.

Finally, Jai let out a sharp laugh. 'Brilliant,' he said.

Craig got up, giving my chair a belligerent shove in the process, and stormed out.

Fiona bit her lower lip. I should have probably said something about her attack on Craig but no words came. I pulled a chair out for her. 'Have you come to tell us about that Michael Ellis guy I called you about?'

'Yes.' She sat down and seemed to gather herself together. 'I have actually. Okay. Right. Abbie Thornton was on a new anti-rejection drug made by quite a small pharmaceutical company. The company was set up by this Michael Ellis and another man. Apparently the drug's super-effective. But there are some questions over it.'

'What questions?'

'Michael Ellis seems to be keeping a really low profile but I found a blog post about it from October last year, on the Wayback Machine thing that has deleted web pages on it. I printed it off in case it disappears. It doesn't say a huge amount but Michael Ellis had concerns about one of the drugs – the one Abbie's on. So many concerns he left the company.'

'What's he saying?'

'You'll have to read it. It might not be relevant but it's a bit odd. Shall I find it for you?'

I nodded and she leant over my desk and tapped a few keys. Jai scooted his chair round and we both peered at the screen.

The blog post had been on an 'NHS Whistleblower' website, and the author wasn't named.

*Concerns have been raised about a new drug that is being used within the NHS.*

*IMMUNOXIFAN is an immunosuppressant which has been used with success in transplant patients. Rejection of the transplanted organ by the recipient's immune system is the main reason why transplants fail, so effective immunosuppressant drugs are a vital part of the transplant process.*

*But does this drug have terrible side effects?*

*Michael Ellis was one of the founders of Pharmimmune Ltd, the company which makes the drug. He left the company recently, amidst rumours of a dispute with his former colleagues. Ellis had safety concerns about IMMUNOXIFAN, and believed his concerns were not being taken seriously.*

*Ellis is not speaking to anyone, claiming he has been threatened by his ex-colleagues. But we have found out that the side-effects concern the behaviour and mental state of the transplant recipient, rather than any strictly physical problem, and they are potentially very severe. For now, we cannot find out any more. But Michael Ellis was so concerned that he left the company he founded and sold all his shares, and that leaves us wanting answers.*

★

I left the Station late, and drove slowly, knowing I was distracted. The dark had the thick quality it developed in Derbyshire winters – as if even headlights couldn't penetrate it. And I couldn't banish the images of Abbie from my mind – her unseeing eyes, her blood-stained hair, her tiny hands gripping the handle of the knife. What was the phrase used in the article? The side effects concerned *the behaviour and mental state of the transplant recipient, and were potentially very severe.* 'Potentially' was a hedging word, like the annoying use of 'up to' in adverts. But the article suggested that something pretty worrying was going on. Could a combination of the new immunosuppressant and Sombunol have turned Abbie into a sleep-murderer? I let it all swirl around, but my mind was abruptly sliced by a pang of guilt so strong I nearly swerved off the road. Why was I spending all this time working? Abbie wasn't family. Abbie didn't have only a week to live.

Everyone I knew who'd lost someone regretted not spending enough time with them – tortured themselves over those moments when they'd chosen to watch TV instead of talking, when they'd spoken harshly, not knowing it would be their last exchange. *If only I'd been nicer to her. If only I'd taken the time to be with her.* It didn't have to be like that with Gran. We knew how long we'd got.

I took the road to Eldercliffe and headed for Mum's house.

I parked under the street-light on Mum's privet-hedged road, noticing the curtains twitching opposite. Mum's neighbour regarded me with deep suspicion due to my lack of interest in marrying her son who, whilst passable to look at, still lived with his mother and had never read a book.

The man next door was out salting his driveway in the light from the streetlamp, inexplicably wearing hi-viz. He shouted gleefully at me as I climbed from the car and headed up towards the house. 'We're in for a cold snap!'

I nodded weakly and wondered if I should be putting salt down for Mum. She'd been taking Gran out in her wheelchair each day. What if she slipped and fell?

I let myself in and Mum appeared in the hallway. 'Oh. I was watching my *Downton* DVD.'

'Lovely to see you too, Mum.'

'Don't be touchy. I didn't mean it like that. I'm glad you came.' She gestured to the kitchen. 'Come on, I'll put the kettle on. Will you have something to eat.' This was not a question; it was an order.

'No, I'm fine.'

'I'll pop some soup on the hob.'

I followed her though and Mum bustled around, fishing home-made soup out of the fridge and cleaning her already-clean work-surfaces. This clearly wasn't a genetic thing.

'I'll make the tea,' I said. 'You sit down. I don't need soup. Do you ever sit down? How can there be so much to do in a three-bed semi?'

'If you actually tried cleaning your house, love, you'd be surprised.' But she sat, and I made tea.

I put a mug in front of her and plonked myself opposite. I noticed Mum's skin was rough, as if she needed a light sanding. 'You look knackered,' I said.

'Thank you so much, Meg. It's always a great comfort to be told how awful I look. We're in for a cold snap, they say.'

'So I gather. Shall I put some grit down for you?'

'Oh, don't worry, next door said he'd do it. He takes it from the council grit bin.'

'You're not allowed to do that, Mum.'

'Well, I know, strictly speaking. But it's okay if you wear hi-viz.'

'I don't think . . . ' But I decided I had more important things to get stressed about. 'How's Gran? Still doing a Lazarus act?'

'She's worried about us getting into trouble. Especially you. With your job.'

'Oh, for God's sake.' A flush of anger rose in me. 'I feel so helpless. It's not right that we can't give her a decent death here.'

'And she seems to have taken a turn for the better.'

I had a stab of hope that we could postpone it. That I could carry on with the Thornton case. Delay falling out with my best friend. 'You think we should leave it a bit longer?'

'If we leave it any longer, they won't let her on the plane.' Mum's tone was sharp. 'You're thinking about work, aren't you?'

'Only about how I'll manage things. I'm definitely taking the time off if she wants to go.'

'And Richard's okay about it?' She stood and poured some of the soup into a pan; stuck the gas on high.

'Kind of,' I said.

'You're not fooling me. He wasn't even happy about the Yulin dog meat demo, and this is on a different level.'

I shrugged. 'Turns out Fiona was there too, not that I knew her then. I'm not the only one with these radical ideas.'

'Thinking it's wrong to torture dogs and cats? It's hardly radical.'

My mind filled with images from the placards on the march. Dogs being skinned alive, thrown into cauldrons of boiling water. A little girl sobbing over her pet who'd been stolen and killed for meat. I'd had to stop looking, just to get through the day, which was of course what we all did on a larger scale, about all kinds of things, all the time. I shook my head to clear it. 'I think it was the scuffle with the uniforms outside the Chinese Embassy Richard wasn't so keen on.'

'He's not going to like this then, is he?' She turned away from the soup pan, and leant against the cooker, too close to the open flame. 'There's no point getting sacked, Meg. We can't afford to take her if you're going to lose your job. It's already costing more money than we have. You know the police will investigate, don't you?'

'I haven't exactly told Richard what we're doing.'

'Oh for goodness' sake, Meg!'

'Well, we can't pay someone else to help, can we? They'd get into trouble. And Richard's not the one who's going to end up dying in agony if we don't go, is he?' I banged my mug down.

'Okay, love, no need to get all melodramatic about it.'

'Hannah's upset about it though,' I said.

'About us taking Gran?'

'It's about assisted dying in general, more than Gran. She says most people want to die because they're scared of losing dignity or autonomy, not because they're in terrible pain, and it sends the message that being disabled is worse than being dead.'

'That's not the case with your gran though. She's dying. If people knew they could be helped to die when they were ready, they wouldn't be so terrified of losing autonomy. At the moment, they're terrified because they know once they get past a certain point, they won't be able to kill themselves and nobody's allowed to help them.'

'I suppose so. But we don't know what it's like to be Hannah. I don't want to upset her. She thinks I'm going to end up being the poster-child for assisted dying.'

'I'd be surprised if we got that much attention.'

I stood and walked to the window. Looked into Mum's garden. A neighbour's security light cast a pale glow over the tree branches, which swayed in the breeze. 'Mum,' I said. 'Have you told anyone about us taking Gran?'

Mum hesitated. 'I don't think . . . Oh, well I said something to Sheila next door, of course. Because the house is going to be empty. She'd have worried. Why?'

'She doesn't know anyone from that Life Line group, does she?'

Mum flushed. 'Oh Lord, I forgot. I think she knows the receptionist at the health centre. Vivian, is it?'

'Oh God. She must have told her. They've been blogging about us. Slagging us off for taking Gran.'

'Oh dear. But I don't suppose anyone sane reads their blog, do they?'

I laughed. 'That's a good attitude.' Sometimes Mum could be very Zen. Why hadn't I learnt to be the same?

I made a cup of tea for Gran and took it through to her new quarters. She'd moved to the downstairs front room after an unfortunate incident with a gas leak, in which we'd struggled to get her out of the house. Now we could just fling her out of the window onto the front lawn if it came to it.

She was propped on pillows watching a soap in which women with permed hair berated one other. She flipped the remote to switch it off. She didn't look too bad.

I sat on the side of her bed. 'How are you doing?'

Gran took the tea, her hand shaking and spilling it into the saucer. 'I don't want you to go killing me off if it'll get you into trouble, Meg, with your job.'

'Blimey, Gran, can we approach this a bit more euphemistically?'

'Oh, this damn tea. I've spilt it on the sheets again. I'm good for nothing now.'

'Don't worry, Gran. No one minds.'

She steadied her hand. 'How's that job of yours?'

'Okay. They're making me work with Craig though. You know, the one I told you about?'

'Don't you let him get the better of you. You're a clever wee thing. He'll be no match for you.'

I glanced up and saw Mum in the doorway. I gave her a helpless *I-see-what-you-mean* look.

'Yes, a clever wee thing,' Gran said. 'You get it from your father.'

'Oh, thanks,' Mum said. 'I thought you didn't even like him.'

'Can't abide the man but there's no denying he had brains.'

'He's not dead, Gran,' I said. 'Just in Scotland.'

Gran made a *Hmmph* noise to express her feelings about Dad. Mum rolled her eyes.

'Mum, the soup,' I said.

Mum jumped. 'Okay.' She took a step away, then said over

her shoulder. 'I emailed your father again but he didn't reply. You'd think at a time like this . . . I'm done with him.'

She headed off back to the kitchen.

'Do you still want to go, Gran?' I said. 'Next week? You seem really well today.'

I looked at her hand lying on the white sheet and felt tears welling up. How could we do this?

She sighed and all the energy seemed to leave her. 'I'm fed up of feeling poorly.' She lifted her hand, with its paper-thin skin, and put it on mine. 'This is no life. Lying here, staring at the wall and trying not to be sick. Having to be waited on by your mother.'

'You're not a burden, Gran. You do know that, don't you? We'd rather have you for longer if we can.'

'I'm done.' She shuffled down into her pillows. 'I'm going to meet Carrie. She'll be there. It'll be lovely.'

I smiled at her, and for a moment I pictured a heaven-type place – fluffy clouds and green fields and little birdies. Yeah, right.

'I know it's a load of nonsense,' Gran said. 'Heaven. But I meant what I said. I'm done. And I'm proud of you. Catching criminals. You women now, look at you. Not relying on a man. I always said you shouldn't rely on a man. It's alright to have a boyfriend, but don't let them tie you down.'

I coughed. 'Really, Gran? I'm not sure that's in the official book of authorised grandmotherly advice.'

Gran had never spoken to me about her husband. I knew he'd been violent – a drunk and a gambler. She hadn't had an easy life. And now it was ending.

Her eyes closed, their blue-tinged lids fluttering. I carefully lifted myself from the bed and crept out.

Mum was stirring the soup, trying to scrape burnt bits off the bottom of the pan. 'It's ruined.'

I swallowed. My words stuck in my throat. 'Mum, can we actually do this? Is she absolutely sure?'

Mum looked up. Her face was white and traced with deep lines I didn't remember seeing before. 'I've thought some more about it since I called you. I know she seems good at the moment, but she goes to bed every night praying this will be the one she doesn't wake from. Every night. She doesn't believe in heaven but she's talking about meeting Carrie. She wants to go.'

'Enough to go all the way to Switzerland?'

'Do you know what the end might be like if we let it take its course?'

'Of course I do. I've tortured myself on the internet. They can help with the pain but not necessarily the sickness, and morphine makes her vomit so they won't even be able to overdose her on that to end it. I know it all. Is there nothing we can do here? Without having to take her away?'

'Do you want to be the one to put the pillow over her head?'

# 10.

The next morning, Craig and I drove to the juvenile secure unit where Abbie Thornton was being held. The threats of snow hadn't yet materialised, but instead we were blessed with bone-chilling horizontal rain.

The unit looked like a low-budget motel in red-brick. It had recently been the subject of historic sexual abuse allegations from the 1980s – glorious, care-free years when children taken into care because they'd been abused by their siblings were housed with children who'd abused their siblings. Now, in contrast, levels of paranoid arse-covering had reached critical levels, and Abbie was apparently causing the staff Defcon 1 levels of stress due to her extreme medical requirements and the potential liability if anything happened to her.

We showed our ID to several cynical-looking staff members, no doubt ground down by years of pay-freezes, and settled ourselves into a small interview room. It was painted in depression-green, and smelt inexplicably of cat pee. The rain battered a tiny window laced with anti-smash chicken wire. I'd asked Craig to let me handle the questioning. Child suspects were treated as victims, whatever they might have done, and

I knew Craig would struggle with that. I hadn't mentioned what he'd said to Richard, but it was gnawing away at me.

Rachel's lawyer and the teenage-looking social worker sat on either side of Abbie like lions at the entrance to a country mansion. Whereas most of us aged with stress, the social worker looked even younger than before, as if the trauma of the case was forcing her to revert to childhood. She caressed a spot on her forehead.

Craig's sinusy breathing filled my left ear.

'Abbie,' I said. 'We need to know if you've remembered anything more from the other night.'

Abbie wiped her eyes with the flat of her hand. 'I had a knife.'

I spoke calmly, but my insides were squirming as if I was about to vomit something slithery onto the floor. 'When did you have a knife?'

'It wasn't a dream. I remember now. When I had a shower and Mum dried my hair. It was real. I woke up and I had a knife. Did I kill him? Did I kill Dad?'

I felt tears well up in my own eyes. Even if she had killed him, it had been in her sleep. She had no memory of it. How could we hold her responsible for that? 'We don't know,' I said. 'You need to tell us everything you remember.'

She looked so tiny. She took a gulp of air and swallowed. 'Since I got the new heart, it's been . . . ' She tailed off.

'It's been?'

'Mum said I've been screaming in the night. Screaming about Dad.'

So much of this seemed to be coming from Rachel. Could she have implanted these ideas into her daughter's head?

'Do you remember what you were dreaming?'

'I was scared. Scared of Daddy. He did something bad.'

'What do you mean, Abbie, what did he do?'

She shook her head.

I tried to keep myself as un-threatening as possible. 'Do you remember anything more about that night?'

'My heart isn't right and it's made me do this.'

The lawyer and the social worker twitched in unison, as if choreographed. The lawyer's face was pink. 'She doesn't necessarily know what she's saying here.'

Abbie turned and spoke to him. 'I'm not going to lie. I'm telling her the truth. If I killed my dad . . . ' She paused and took a deep breath, looking agonisingly young. 'If I did it, then I didn't mean it. But I'm not lying. And I don't care what you say.'

I felt a wave of affection for Abbie. She was being so brave. She didn't know what had happened, but she wasn't going to lie or try to cover it up. I had a sudden flash of memory. Me discovering my sister, Carrie. Getting home from school and rushing up to her room to apologise for saying a terrible thing to her that morning. Seeing her feet. Hanging where feet shouldn't be. Blaming myself. But I'd kept it secret that it was my fault. I hadn't told Mum or Dad what I'd said to her. What I'd done was too appalling. I hadn't wanted them to hate me, so I'd carried the secret with me for twenty-five years.

How much worse to believe you'd actually killed your own father, who loved you dearly. To think you'd taken a knife and cut his throat, without even realising what you were doing. To wake up bathed in blood, a knife in your hand. I could hardly bear to think about it. But Abbie wasn't trying to cover it up. She was being honest with us. My chest felt tight.

'Thank you, Abbie,' I said. 'I promise if you tell the truth, we'll do our absolute best to . . . ' I hesitated, not sure what I could promise her. 'We'll find out what really happened.'

Her mouth twisted and a tear dropped onto the table. 'I want a different heart. I don't want this heart inside of me any more.'

'Does the heart feel different, Abbie, or is it just because of what your mum and dad said?'

A moment of confusion. 'I'm different. I can draw really well now. I never used to be any good at drawing. But I have nightmares too.'

'Do you remember anything from the nightmares?'

'Not much. Daddy was bad.'

'What made you think he was bad?' I said.

'Daddy was a murderer.' She blinked. 'Dad . . . No, I can't remember any more.'

I could feel my heart pounding. Even the lawyer and the social worker shut up.

'What do you mean, Abbie?' I said. 'How was your daddy a murderer?'

She shook her head. 'I don't know, I don't know. I can't remember. I was scared.'

'Can you tell us any more about what you dreamed?'

'I must have got confused.' She raked her hands through her tangled hair. 'Daddy did a terrible thing, I must have got confused.'

'Okay.' The social worker had sprung back into life. 'She's getting upset.'

Abbie clenched her small hands into fists. 'I'm alright,' she said.

'Thank you, Abbie,' I said. 'Can you remember anything else?'

She shook her head, and whispered, 'He was bad.'

The room was silent. My thoughts swirled, desperately trying to make sense of this. Had Phil Thornton done something, or was it to do with the folk tales, or Abbie's imagination about her heart donor?

'Okay,' I said. 'Thanks, Abbie. A few more questions before we finish.'

'Alright.' She pushed her fists against one another, her arms tense.

'Can you remember going to bed the night before this happened?'

'I'm sorry,' she whispered. 'Dad, I'm sorry. I must have got confused.'

'Sometimes you call him *dad* and sometimes *daddy*,' I said. 'Why's that, Abbie?'

The lawyer shoved his arm half in front of Abbie. 'I think that's enough for today.'

'It's all my fault,' Abbie grabbed a handful of her hair and yanked at it, as if she wanted to pull it from her scalp. 'My sister died too. It's me. People keep dying. If you get a new heart, someone has to die. It's the way it works.'

'Oh, Abbie,' I said. 'It's not your fault.' I'd got so used to saying that to myself, it just popped out. But was it true?

The social worker turned to Abbie. 'You don't need to say anything else.'

Abbie ignored her and looked straight at me. 'The last thing I remember, Dad gave me my pills and I read my book for a bit and that's all I know.'

'How were you feeling about your dad?'

'I was scared in my dreams. Not in real life. I never meant to do anything. I never meant to kill him.'

We ran across the waterlogged car park, Craig splashing through the puddles and spraying me, like a large vehicle drenching pedestrians.

He squeezed himself into my car and dragged the seatbelt over his gut. I slid into the driver's seat and pulled away. There was something about his presence that always made me drive badly, as if I had to fulfil his expectations about women. It was pathetic.

The rain had turned into a fine sleet which drifted over the valley as we headed back towards the Station. The hills seemed to have hunkered down like hibernating animals. My windscreen wipers smeared a thin sheet of ice over the outside of the screen for extra danger points. I should have replaced them months ago.

'What do you think?' I asked in a neutral tone.

'I've seen it all now. Little kiddy like that taking out her dad with a carving knife. And she looks like a friggin' angel.'

'Do you think she did it then?'

'Don't see who else could have done it. You've not got a loony theory, have you?'

I braked a little too hard, throwing Craig forward. 'Oops.'

'Bloody hell.' Craig shuffled his belly back into place. 'Watch it. The roads are icy.'

'We haven't exactly explored all the options, have we?'

'If that paedo abused her, it could have caused the bad dreams and made her violent.'

'I don't want to rule anything out at the moment, but she was having the bad dreams before they went to see Dr Gibson. I'd like you to look, please, for anything in Abbie's past that could have made her think her dad was a murderer, or was trying to hurt her, or anyone else for that matter. Rachel might not know – it could have been from before she and Phil got together. And look into the death of Rachel's daughter again. Is there any suggestion it wasn't an accident? And check out Phil Thornton's ex-wife's death. There's too much death in that family, and now his daughter's calling him a murderer. Maybe it's nothing to do with her heart.'

'We looked at his ex-wife. Definitely an accident. Head-on collision with another car on the A515 south of Ashbourne. No organ donation, by the way. And the kid admits she killed her dad.'

'Didn't that all seem to come from her parents? She doesn't remember anything. She has no idea if she did it or not. She's relying on what her mother told her.'

'Yeah, but the blood splatter was all over the kiddy.'

'Blood spatter, Craig. Spatter.'

Craig pointedly wiped condensation off the inside of the windscreen in front of him. I turned the blowers up, and the screen instantly misted up more. How did that happen? I slowed the car, and leaned forward to rub it with my sleeve.

'Your heating system's screwed,' Craig said. 'Why do women never maintain their cars? Or clean them?'

'Because we have a life?'

I could feel a headache coming on. I couldn't conduct a high-profile investigation like this with the assistance of the lump of meat that was Craig. I drove in silence for the rest of the journey.

★

Back at the Station, I hid in my room with a cup of tea, mulling over what Abbie had said. She couldn't really remember her donor's death. It made no sense. But I couldn't get it out of my head.

My fingers seemed to act of their own volition – creeping towards the keyboard and googling 'remember memories of heart donor'. There were plenty of results. I wasn't the only person wondering about this. Most of the websites had an air of fruit-loopery about them. I clicked on the least mad-looking.

*Cellular memory. It sounds bizarre – the idea that your emotions and memories could be stored in organs other than the brain. But there is mounting evidence that it could be true, with some very strange consequences.*

*Here are some examples from heart transplant patients:*

*A woman in her forties suddenly starts craving beer and junk food, despite never having eaten it before, and dreams the name of her donor (who turned out to be a junk food and beer addict).*

*A five-year-old girl runs up to her donor's parents and calls them Mummy and Daddy.*

*A confirmed meat eater can no longer touch meat after being given a vegetarian's heart.*

*A man not only starts craving his donor's favourite foods, but marries the donor's widow and then shoots himself in the head just as the donor had.*

*A white man receives a young black man's heart and worries he'll start liking rap music. Instead he's strongly drawn to classical music, and only later discovers that the black man played classical violin.*

*A nine-year-old girl dreams of being murdered, and helps the police catch the murderer of her donor.*

The last one touched a nerve, but there were no references. I sat back in my chair and closed my eyes. These people had to be kidding themselves. It couldn't be possible for a heart to have its own food tastes, let alone memories of a murder. I pictured Abbie, so small and innocent-looking, thinking her heart had made her kill her father.

A knock on the door and I jumped so violently I spilt my tea. Jai appeared. I hurriedly closed my browser.

'More forensics on Phil Thornton,' he said. 'There's evidence that Karen Jenkins has been in his bedroom. Other than that, family only.'

'Oh.' It hit me how much I wanted there to be another explanation – anything other than Abbie. I wiped tea off my desk with my sleeve.

Jai strolled over and leant against the back of my spare chair. 'Fiona put Craig in his place yesterday, didn't she?'

I smiled. 'Have you met her brother?'

Jai shook his head. 'She gets on well with him, but he lives in London.'

'Doesn't she get on with the rest of her family?'

'They seem to be a bit of a non-subject. Not sure why.' Jai didn't seem to trouble himself about this kind of thing, whereas I found myself wondering if something bad had happened in Fiona's past. Why would she not want to talk about her family? Maybe she was just being professional and I was projecting my crap onto her.

'Okay,' I said. 'Have we ruled Karen Jenkins out? We know she was having an affair with him, so the fact she's been in his bedroom doesn't mean much.'

'No trace of anything at her house. No sign of her on CCTV near Bellhurst House that day. And it's not her clothes that have arterial blood all over them. It was Phil Thornton's blood on the nightdress. Abbie's nightdress. And Abbie's prints on the knife.'

I sighed. 'Right.'

'Did you and your lovely assistant speak to Abbie?' Jai said.

146

'Yes. She thinks she did it, but she can't actually remember. And she's blaming the new heart.'

Jai sank onto my spare chair. 'God, this is going to be crazy when it gets out. Do you reckon the new heart did affect her?'

I wheeled myself away from the computer and rubbed my eyes. 'Seems highly unlikely. Did you find out any more about the immunosuppressant?'

'Not much. Fiona searched and searched, and she couldn't find any more info online. She's trying to track down Michael Ellis from the details on Thornton's phone.'

I stood and stretched. Abbie was just a little girl. How could a ten-year-old girl kill someone? And could she even be held responsible if she was asleep?

'I was wondering . . . ' Jai said. 'Do you think you could hypnotise a person to make them kill someone? I think Derren Brown did something like that.'

'Really?'

'I think so. What if Harry Gibson hypnotised Abbie into killing her father?'

'Why though?'

'Maybe someone blackmailed him. Found out he liked children, threatened to expose him if he didn't do as they asked.'

'Oh God, Jai, I just can't see it – that someone could control your mind like that. To make you kill someone in your sleep, I mean. There has to be a different explanation.'

# 11.

Richard was in his room, leaning forward in his chair, squinting at his computer screen, shoulders somewhere around his ears.

I gave him an abridged summary of the situation, including what Abbie had said about her heart. He took a tissue from a pack on his desk and wiped his face. 'My God, what have you got us into?'

As if it was my fault.

'Did they pursue that complaint about me?' I asked.

'Not as yet.'

I waited for something positive or reassuring.

Waited a bit longer.

Oh well.

Richard coughed. 'It was clearly a little awkward for him, which is why he didn't say anything at first, but Craig saw what happened.'

A sick feeling inside. I'd so hoped Jai had been wrong. 'What? You mean with Rachel Thornton on that first day? He wasn't even there.'

'He said as he drove up he saw you push her quite hard, and she fell on the floor.'

I took a step back. 'I don't believe this. He wasn't there. She actually got up and punched me before he turned up.'

'She punched you? Why didn't you say anything? None of this looks good, Meg. You need to be more careful.'

I felt a flush rising up into my face. 'What's Craig's problem with me? He's making this up.'

'It seems they're not pursuing it, so let's leave it for now. But be more careful in future. What did you want to say?'

I leant against Richard's dodgy guest chair, my mind full of Craig. I was furious but also upset that he seemed to hate me so much. I took a breath and tried to compose myself.

'Are we ready to charge the child?' Richard said.

'No, I wouldn't say so. If she did it, she was asleep at the time. And the only motive we have is that her drugs made her homicidal or she remembers the death of her heart donor. It's not exactly CPS-friendly stuff.'

Richard reached round to the back of his neck and massaged his shoulder blades. 'Isn't it pretty apparent that she killed him though? As I understand it, everything points to that. She was found on the floor covered in arterial blood, with a knife in her hand, and she's confessed. What more do you want, Meg?'

'You want to charge her now? She hasn't really confessed. She doesn't remember what happened.'

'We've got enough. Don't you think?'

'No. I don't think we have. Abbie's memories are very unclear. Her mother could have put it into her head that she was holding the knife or even put the knife into her hand. Rachel has a motive to kill her husband if she found out he was having an affair. And we haven't eliminated Karen Jenkins either.'

'But there's arterial blood on the girl's nightdress,' Richard said.

'You know that's not conclusive. We haven't even had the full blood-spatter analysis back. And the girl has no history of violence. It's completely out of character. And she's cute. It would be damn hard to persuade a jury she did it, unless there's a reason.'

'Maybe we need to consider whether her new heart did have an effect on her. Or the medication.'

'There are rumours about the medication she was on,' I said. 'That it might cause some weird side effects. But nothing concrete.'

Richard sighed. 'You've spoken to Dr Li, haven't you?'

I nodded. 'The forensic psychiatrist.'

'Talk to her in more detail. See what she thinks about the drugs, and this heart memory business. She's very knowledgeable and down to earth – I've been impressed with her in the past. If this is all fanciful rubbish, she'll make it clear.'

★

I wanted nothing more than to confront that slimy toad, Craig, but I knew I'd end up shouting at him and possibly resorting to violence. He was in the incident room surrounded by other cops and I could just imagine how he'd play it up to make me look like the maniac. And deep down I knew yelling at him wasn't the answer. I needed to be more strategic. For now, I was too consumed with fury for strategy, and Jai wasn't around to talk to either. So I decided to put it out of my mind and see if I could get some more information from Dr Li. On my own.

I drove through brutal sleet to Eldercliffe, trying to keep Craig's squat face out of my mind, and pulled into the parking area outside the White Peak Clinic. There were a couple of other cars, each worth more than a small house. I half expected a security guard to rush out and tell me I couldn't park my old heap next to them, but all was quiet.

Tom Li was sitting behind the desk in the sparkly reception area. 'Ashley's off this afternoon,' he said, 'so I'm doing *Meet and Greet,* although I'm not sure I have the nails or teeth for it.'

I laughed. Obviously I wasn't the only one who'd noticed Ashley's inhuman levels of personal grooming.

'Do you need to see my mother?' Tom asked.

'Yes please. I called her and she said it was okay.'

'No problem. Come through.'

Tom wheeled himself off in the direction of the consulting rooms, and I followed.

'I don't normally chase around after my mother,' he said. 'What must you think of me?'

'You run a small clinic,' I said. 'Everyone mucks in. It makes sense.'

He gestured towards a small waiting area outside Dr Li's room, and I settled myself on a chair in the corner, partially hidden behind a plant.

'I didn't want to do cosmetic surgery at first,' Tom said. 'Let alone live with my mother. But it's . . . complicated.'

I wondered why he felt the need to justify his position to me. But then it hit me how I'd feel if I'd done major surgery in the past and was now doing cosmetic peels. I felt a pang of sympathy, and remembered how he'd seemed anxious around his mother. If she owned the clinic and the bungalow, he probably couldn't afford to upset her.

'I'm sure cosmetic surgery can be very rewarding.' I hoped he couldn't smell my fakery. I supposed it was true if you were working with burns victims or other worthy causes, but judging by the cars outside, he wasn't.

'Of course it can be.' He blinked and glanced down at his immobile legs. 'It's not so easy for me to get another position now. But it's best to focus on what you can do, isn't it? Not what you can't.'

I made a non-committal noise, realising it was odds-on I was about to say the wrong thing. It was bad enough having to talk to Hannah about this stuff, never mind a man I didn't even know. As someone with almost full use of my body parts, I always seemed to say the wrong thing.

Tom showed me into Dr Li's office. 'Doing my receptionist bit,' he said to his mother. 'Maybe I should do this permanently.' I couldn't work out if this was a genuine suggestion, a dig, or something more complicated.

Fen looked up. 'Don't put yourself down, Tom, it doesn't help you.' She turned to me. 'He pretends he's no good at anything, but he's an excellent surgeon, he's great with the patients, he does all our publicity, he does all the IT for the practice, he even sorts out the webinars for the psychiatrists I supervise – '

Tom butted in. His tone was sharp but he was smiling. 'Okay, Mum, that's enough.'

I had no idea how to respond to all this. What did Dr Li want me to say? *Look, Tom, I'm a detective and I'm telling you to stop putting yourself down right now!* Tom reversed out of the room and saved me the trouble.

Dr Li gestured towards her little chair collection. 'Nice to see you again.'

'Sorry to take more of your time.' I sat down in the corner chair. 'Something's come up and we were wondering if you could help.'

'Of course,' Fen said.

I passed her my print-out of the blog post about the immunosuppressant medication. She read it at impressive speed, sat back and said. 'Oh.'

I took my notepad out. 'Is it possible the immunosuppressant could have affected Abbie? Maybe in combination with Sombunol?'

'It's certainly possible that the drugs could affect her behaviour. I'm not sure what exactly the article implies. It's not clear what the side effects were.'

'I know. We're trying to find out more information. Does it ring true that the company would suppress details of side effects?'

'I'm afraid it doesn't surprise me too much. Although the article is a little histrionic.'

'I need to talk to Michael Ellis, if only we could find the man.'

'Is he not available to talk?'

'He's not an easy person to get hold of.'

'Right. Well, if you want an opinion once you've spoken to him, let me know.'

'Thank you.' I swallowed. 'And then there's this issue about the memories from the heart donor. Abbie Thornton's parents both seemed to believe she was remembering her donor's death, but I can't see how that could possibly be. Have you ever come across this before?'

Fen narrowed her eyes. 'Not personally. Some doctors do believe in cellular memory. There's anecdotal evidence. I wouldn't say it's mainstream though.'

'Right. What's your view?'

'I think there are other more likely psychological reasons for most of the observations.'

I was relieved. Of course she wouldn't believe in that nonsense. 'Okay. Thank you. And just one other question. I'm sorry to hit you with all this bizarre stuff, but this is a really odd case. Er . . . is there any way Abbie could have been hypnotised to make her feel violent towards her father?'

'Why in heaven's name would anyone do that?'

'We're just exploring all the possibilities.'

'I suppose it would be possible to give post-hypnotic suggestions to someone that they be afraid of their father, but no more than that. It's quite wrong, this idea that you can turn someone into a mind-controlled zombie through hypnosis.'

My phone rang. Fiona.

'Sorry. I'd better get that.' I accepted the call and walked out of Fen's office.

'I finally got in touch with that Michael Ellis guy.' Fiona's voice was clear, and I could hear the low rumble of cop-talk in the background. I pictured Craig bitching about me. 'He sounds a bit paranoid, to be honest,' Fiona said. He wasn't the only one. 'He refused to come in to the Station unless we arrest him. Says he's worried about being followed. I don't know if he's genuinely in danger or not.'

'Oh, great.'

'He said if you want to talk to him, he's at Eldercliffe Gorge now, but he won't be there long.'

'Eldercliffe Gorge? What the hell's he doing there?'

'He said it's safe. He sounded scared, actually. I knew you were in Eldercliffe but you probably shouldn't meet him on your own.'

'That's as maybe, but how long's he going to hang around for?'

She hesitated. I heard a laugh in the background. 'I don't know. Not long by the sound of him.'

'I'll go and take a look,' I said. 'I've got my radio and my phone's fully charged. I'll go now.'

'Be careful. And call me when you've seen him, okay? He said he's by the Destroying Angels. They're rocks, I think.'

'I'll find him.'

I pushed open the door and walked back into Fen's consulting room.

'I'm sorry. I need to go and see the man from the immunosuppressant company,' I said. 'They finally got hold of him and he's in the gorge near Phil Thornton's house. He seems to think people are after him. Of course if he's paranoid, the accusations about the drug may not be true at all.'

'Would you like me to come with you? It would be useful for me to meet him, if you need an opinion on his mental state. And I know that area.'

'Oh . . . No, we need to keep our consultancy costs under control.'

'I'll only charge you for this meeting. I have no patients this afternoon, and I often take a walk anyway, to clear my head. Sometimes I even go to the gorge.'

I thought for a moment. 'Do you know what the Destroying Angels are?'

'I do. They're rock formations. I can show you where they are.'

'Okay then, if you're sure. We don't know if he's paranoid – thinking he's being followed by his ex-colleagues – or if he really is in danger. So it would be useful to get a doctor's take on it. I'll run it past Richard but I'm sure it'll be fine. Thank you.'

Fen laughed. 'It'll be fine with Richard Atkins if you tell him I'm not charging for it. Obviously if you end up needing a formal opinion on the man's mental state, there will be a charge.'

'Of course. I understand.' I gathered my papers and we headed out.

'There's a fascinating story behind the Destroying Angels,' Fen said. 'They're more than just rocks.'

# 12.

The lane sloped perilously down from the centre of Eldercliffe, and was lined with cars jammed so tightly they looked as if they'd been slotted in from above by a crane.

The village thinned into rocky countryside, and we finally pulled into a stony lay-by. I yanked the handbrake on hard and left the car in reverse.

We got out and I took a breath of freezing air. At least it had stopped sleeting.

'So you often walk in this area?' I said.

'Yes. I became interested in local myths when we moved to Derbyshire,' Fen said. 'Do you know the story about the children who were sacrificed to stop the young men going off?'

I glanced sharply at her, picturing the statues in the woods high above us. 'Yes. The children were burned in the house. And one went into the gorge. One of our DC's told me. That was the story I thought might have triggered Abbie Thornton's nightmares. But my colleague said there was something about the children's mothers getting revenge.'

'Ah, that's the best bit. I can tell you about that.' Fen headed for a path between trees. 'It's along here. You haven't seen the Destroying Angels then?'

'Aren't they mushrooms?' I didn't admit that my botanical knowledge stemmed from an episode of *Midsomer Murders*.

'Yes. The mothers of the girls who were sacrificed used mushrooms in getting their revenge. Well, that was part of it. They were determined to avenge the children's deaths.'

We headed down into the valley. The track was strewn with stones, and I was forced to focus on the ground rather than looking at Fen.

'They were angry with their husbands,' Fen said. 'But they were most angry with the priest.'

'The man who told the village to sacrifice the girls?'

'Yes.'

'Fair enough. What did they do to him?'

'They gathered wild mushrooms that are found in the woods around Eldercliffe.'

We passed between moss-covered slabs of rock and emerged into the gorge. Limestone sides shadowed the river in its base. I peered up into the light, to where I'd been with Abbie at the edge of the woods. The opposite side of the gorge was even higher – right up in the clouds. 'Wow,' I said. 'I've never been to the bottom before.'

'Beautiful, isn't it?' Fen swung her gaze side to side. 'I think it's as beautiful as Dovedale – maybe a touch more ominous. This section's not well known. We've always had the place to ourselves when I've come here with Tom.'

I looked along the valley. It was deserted, the only sound the gushing of the river and the cry of a buzzard high above. No sign of Michael Ellis. 'So they gathered Destroying Angel mushrooms . . .'

'They cause a slow and painful death. But they didn't give them to him immediately.'

158

We took a path by the river and walked between the cathedral-esque sides of the gorge. After a few minutes, we reached a collection of rock spires jutting from the ground like huge stalagmites.

'Carboniferous limestone,' Fen said.

I couldn't take my eyes off them. 'Are they the Destroying Angels?'

Each spire was about the height of a person, and they huddled in a group as if they were whispering to one another. I walked over and stood in the still space between them. I tried to imagine them as the vengeful mothers of the poor, sacrificed children. Wondered what I'd be prepared to do to if someone had been to blame for Carrie. Someone other than myself.

Fen stood outside the small group. As if she was reading my mind, she said, 'Have you ever wanted revenge?' She looked at me with clear, dark eyes, seeming to gaze right into me.

I opened my mouth to answer, but didn't know what to say. It was myself I blamed, not others. Had I tried to get revenge against myself? Was that even possible? I shook my head. 'Not really.' The last thing I wanted was a psychiatrist knowing what was going on in my head. She'd probably get me certified on the spot and shipped off to somewhere high-security. 'What did they do to the priest?'

'See there? It's called Priest's Hole.'

Near the spires, an area of cliff was fenced off. I pulled my coat tight, stepped over to the fence, and leant over, peering into a hole that plunged vertically downwards, so black it made my eyes hurt. A smell of bats and damp wafted out. As my eyes adjusted, I could still see no bottom to it. My stomach lightened as if I was in a lift going down. I shifted back, and took a deep breath.

'They dragged him all the way down here,' Fen said, 'and threw him in. It's quite deep but there's a good chance he survived the fall. So there was always the possibility someone would come with a rope and rescue him.'

'Did anyone come?'

'Not in time. And the women threw mushrooms in with him, and a sheep's stomach filled with water, so he wouldn't die of thirst. If he survived the fall, he'd have had to choose – either starve to death or eat the mushrooms. If he ate the mushrooms, he'd die in agony.'

'Wow.'

Fen stood beside me and looked into the darkness.

I imagined the priest dropping into the hole, crashing onto the rocks at its base, possibly surviving. Eventually going mad with hunger and facing that terrible decision. I wondered if it had made the mothers feel better. Planning revenge must have been distracting. When the priest smashed onto the rocks below, did it hit the mothers that their daughters were still dead? That their friends, neighbours and husbands were still complicit?

'The story goes that the priest ate the mushrooms and while he was dying in excruciating pain at the bottom of the hole, he asked God to turn the four women to stone.'

I reached and touched one of the spires. In this strange place, I could almost believe it had once been a woman. 'And you come here with Tom? Can you get here in a wheelchair?'

She hesitated. 'You can. It's not so easy. We usually go to the top over there and look down.' I followed her gaze up to the cloudy heights at the far side of the gorge. 'There's a car park.'

'Must be an incredible view.'

'When it's clear. Tom likes to sit up there and look down at the Destroying Angels.'

I peered up into the light, picturing the car park high above. 'How did Tom become paralysed?' I asked.

'Car accident. Not his fault.'

I wondered if that was why she was interested in revenge. Did she know who'd been responsible for Tom's terrible accident? For him no longer being a proper surgeon, but instead stuck in his mother's clinic botoxing rich, middle-aged women into attitudes of permanent astonishment. My dad used to drive too fast and I knew I'd never have forgiven him if I'd been in an accident and ended up injured. I imagined him unhurt, and me paralysed and suffused with fury that it was his fault – that his recklessness had ruined my life.

'It must be hard for Tom,' I said.

Fen let out a small, weary breath. 'He gets a little depressed sometimes. He got into a type of Chinese Buddhism and that helped for a while, but – ' Her eyes flicked up.

I looked along the valley. A man was heading for us, but his attention seemed to be all over the place, his head twitching up and down, side to side. It made me feel anxious just looking at him.

As he neared us, I tried a reassuring smile. His lips flickered an acknowledgement.

I stood and showed him my ID. 'Mr Ellis?'

'It's Dr but call me Michael.' His gaze flitted around the stones, the fence, the cliff behind. 'Here's okay.' He walked a few steps towards the cliff. 'We can't be seen here.'

'This is Dr Fen Li,' I said. 'She's working with CID as our consultant forensic psychologist.'

Michael looked at Fen through narrowed eyes. 'Do you work with any drug companies?'

'No. No, of course not.'

A muscle twitched below Michael's eye. Fen and I moved closer to him, so we were all standing near the cliff, out of sight of someone walking along the path by the river.

'Are you okay?' I asked.

'I wanted to check I hadn't been followed. Were you followed?'

'No, I'm pretty sure we weren't.' A breeze rustled the branches of a tree which grew bizarrely out of the cliff above us. 'No, we weren't followed.'

Michael gave an unconvinced nod. 'It's good here. We can't be seen but we can check for people approaching. And I thought you'd know the place, what with Phil Thornton being killed up there in the woods. You probably think I'm paranoid. But I've made myself some enemies, and . . . '

I wanted to ask who his enemies were and what they would do, but for now I decided the best approach would be to listen and see what he came out with.

'I'll probably end up dead at some point.'

I scrutinised his face. That was a dramatic accusation. I wondered if he could be psychotic. I was glad I'd brought Fen with me. Hopefully she'd be able to tell.

'Who might kill you?' I asked.

Something rustled above us. I started and looked up. What was the matter with me? There was no way down from the top of the cliff.

Michael lowered his voice. 'Andrew Bond and his cronies. If I turn up dead, it'll be them.'

'Who's Andrew Bond?'

'I used to work with him. But he won't face the truth. Wants me silenced.'

'If you have concerns like this,' I said. 'You need to let us help you. If he's been threatening you . . . '

'It won't do any good. Please . . . ' He wiped his face with a dirty hand. 'Please keep my details confidential.'

'We'll keep your details confidential.'

'Okay. I hope I won't regret this.'

'We appreciate it. Would you be able to tell us about Immunoxifan? We read a blog post that suggested it had some bad side effects.'

'This is because Abbie Thornton killed her father, I assume?' Michael jiggled his leg up and down as he stood, and his gaze continued to dart around.

There was an uncomfortable silence. 'I'm afraid I can't talk about it,' I said.

'But you want me to talk? You want me to put myself in danger?' He rubbed his temple as if trying to get rid of a headache. 'I already know what was going on with Abbie. I've spoken to the Thorntons. They contacted me, remember? I know all about the girl's dreams. You got my number from his phone didn't you?'

A moment of silence. 'Yes, we did,' I said. 'We'll do our utmost not to put you in danger.'

'I'm not even surprised about what happened. I should have been stronger in my warnings.'

'You weren't surprised that . . . '

'That Abbie killed her father. No I wasn't.'

I looked at his face, earnest and scared. 'You think this is linked to the drug she was on? Immunoxifan?'

'Yes.' Michael seemed to settle a little, to still himself. He gave a hollow laugh. 'You could say that.'

'Why? What's going on with the drug? Have there been other cases where it's caused problems?'

He nodded and then spoke fast. 'It's a superb

immunosuppressant, of course. It's been rigorously tested in animal models and in human trials.'

'But are there side effects?'

'It appears so. There didn't seem to be any at first. It was hailed a wonder drug. We cracked open the champagne. Andrew was thrilled, I was thrilled, everything was wonderful.'

'Sounds good,' I said.

The leg tapped again. 'We were finally given regulatory approval, and we released the drug onto the market. It was well received. As I said, it's an excellent immunosuppressant.'

Fen shifted her weight and glanced up. A crow landed on one of the Destroying Angels.

'I only realised because I talked with one of our lab technicians. He said we'd had a batch of dodgy mice and he was going to discuss it with the supplier.'

I nodded at him to continue, cringing inside at the use of the words *batch* and *supplier* about sentient animals.

'With some mice, he'd had problems with their behaviour. He didn't think it was anything to do with the drugs, or the heart transplants. Physically the mice did well, you see . . . '

Both Fen and I were intently focused on Michael. 'What did they do?' I said.

The air between us felt still. Michael hesitated, then exhaled. 'It happened at night. They attacked and killed their cage mates.'

A small gust of wind swished through the valley. Michael jumped.

'You think the drug made them do it?' I said. 'Made them aggressive?'

'To an extent. I looked deeper into the situation. I almost wish I hadn't. Everyone else was very happy to ignore it, or to blame it on a bad batch of mice. No one else was looking for patterns as to which mice behaved strangely. But that's my training – to look for patterns.'

'What was the pattern?' Fen said.

'It was only the heart transplant mice, but not all of them. I don't even know how I noticed. It's not something we would normally pay attention to . . . '

A rustle of leaves. Michael's head shot round. 'Is someone there?'

'I think it's the wind,' I said. 'What pattern did you notice with the mice?'

Michael stepped forward and flung his attention up and down the valley.

'There's someone there,' he said. 'Sorry. I can't tell you now. We'll have to speak another time.'

He darted away from us.

I ran forward a few steps. 'Hang on. Just tell us what the pattern . . . '

Michael turned and shouted over his shoulder. 'This is about cellular memory. Speak to Gaynor Harvey. She takes the drug.'

He sprinted away.

★

It was early evening by the time we left the gorge. The roads were icy, and my car warned me with a fretful beep that it was less than three degrees outside.

'Do you think he's sane?' I asked.

'He certainly seems scared, but there's nothing definitive to suggest he's paranoid. He said nothing that absolutely couldn't be true.'

'What do you mean?'

'He didn't say people were communicating with him through his television, or sending messages along the water pipes, that kind of thing. Paranoid schizophrenics or those in the throes of psychosis often believe things which are self-evidently untrue. Although so do supposedly sane people.'

Like that there's a bloke with a beard watching over us from the sky, I thought. Luckily it didn't come out of my mouth. I glanced at Fen, wondering what she'd meant. 'He seems to absolutely believe that Abbie killed her father. And that the drug had something to do with it.'

'I have no idea whether he's correct, but I have no particular reason to believe he's delusional.'

'I wish he'd told us exactly what was going on with those mice.'

'It was a little frustrating. I don't know how you'd see a cellular memory effect in mice.'

'Here we are.' I pulled up outside her house. 'If you have any more thoughts about Michael Ellis or Abbie Thornton, would you let me know?'

'Do you have a mobile number I can have?'

I fished a card from my pocket and handed it to her.

She examined my card. 'I didn't get the impression that man was delusional. I'd take what he says seriously.'

★

I headed back to the Station. There was no sign of Craig or Jai, although I didn't carry out a thorough search. I needed to address the Craig situation but not now. I cleared a space on my desk, and typed 'Gaynor Harvey' into our system. We had no record of her. I googled the name.

A recent *Derby Telegraph* article came up in the search results.

It was about transplant patients who'd taken on characteristics of their donors and I found Gaynor Harvey: *Woman craves mushrooms and listens to Radio 1 after receiving young person's heart.* It wasn't the grabbiest anecdote, but she lived only a few miles away.

An email notification popped onto my screen. I was about to ignore it when I realised it was from Emily.

She'd managed to get into Harry Gibson's client files. She'd sent me a copy of Abbie Thornton's case notes.

I felt a spike of adrenaline as I opened the file.

*10 y.o. girl, presenting with night terrors. Screaming. Scared of father? Started after heart transplant. Prior to heart transplant, no recent nightmares.*

*4 years ago, stepsister died falling from window. Some nightmares after this but recovered. Seems normal reaction to traumatic event.*

*Mother – believes new heart affecting patient. Possibly delusional. Previous mental health issues with somatic delusions. Depression/anxiety. See child w/o mother. Danger of child picking up on mother's delusion.*

*Father?*

*Treatment: light trance – relaxation, positive view of new heart, posthypnotic suggestions for calm night's sleep.*

The notes from the next few sessions were brief, confirming continued treatment along the same lines. There was also a copy of Phil Thornton's email saying he thought the heart had affected Abbie. Things didn't seem to be getting any better.

*Night terrors not improving. Screaming, 'Daddy did it. Daddy's a murderer.' Significantly impacting life.*

A few more sessions, then:

*Night terrors worsened. Both parents convinced patient remembering things from donor child's life (or death.) Prescribed Sombunol.*

*Can I regress? Ethical?*

Then the next session:

*Drew picture (attached) while in light trance. No memories when not in trance. No relation to events in life acc. to mother and father. Still saying Daddy's a murderer. Scared of him. Agreed to regress. Keep high above timeline. All precautions in place.*

*Took back to the event she drew. 'Daddy. . . Why didn't Mum and Ben and Buddy(??) come with us? I don't like it here . . . the water's black . . . Daddy, don't!' (Upset — told her to float high above the event and look down.) 'Daddy . . . I'm scared . . . No!' (Upset. Brought her back to now, with usual safety measures.)*

*Fine when came round. No memory.*

That was the last entry in the file.

An image file was also attached to Dr Gibson's notes. I clicked on it and zoomed in. Leant forward to look at the screen. A child's drawing filled it. A lake, the water black. A man — big, with red eyes and prominent teeth. Dressed in khaki, with a dark beard. The man was dragging a child towards the lake by her long blonde hair. The child wore a pink and white spotty swimming costume. Her mouth was open wide in a scream.

Heart thumping, I saw there was another attachment named 'Donor'. I opened it. A scanned letter on Great Ormond Street headed paper, stamped STRICTLY PRIVATE AND CONFIDENTIAL. It was dated 8 February — just two days before Harry Gibson had died.

*. . . providing this information strictly for your use . . . Must be kept absolutely confidential . . . Used therapeutically but not revealed to patient . . . Donor details – Scarlett Norwood. 9 y.o. girl. Drowned. Resuscitated but brain-dead. Kept on life support pre-transplant.*

I knew that name. A child who'd drowned the previous autumn, in a small, remote lake over towards Leek. We'd had it down as an accident, and she'd been with her father.

There was a handwritten scribble on the bottom of the letter. *Donor child killed by father???*

★

I leant back in my chair. I noticed goose pimples on my arms, and felt a tingling of fear, like the feeling you get when you've watched a horror film and then have to go for a glass of water. When you know you're not in any danger, but some animal part of you is not convinced. The picture Abbie had drawn sent those feelings straight to my ancient lizard-brain.

I heard a chair scraping and realised Jai had walked up and sat next to me, without me even noticing.

'Jesus Christ.' Jai dragged his chair closer to my table and squinted at the screen. 'Can you enlarge it a bit?' I zoomed in on the picture. My eyes were drawn to the man's teeth, his wild eyes.

I tore my gaze away, and looked at Jai's face. It was the colour of something I'd find rotting in my fridge. So it wasn't just me. 'Are you okay?'

He hesitated. 'Yeah . . . ' He wiped his face. 'She drew that picture? In a therapy session?'

'Looks like it.'

My heart was pounding. 'Dr Gibson seems to have believed Abbie was remembering her donor's death.'

'And the donor child drowned?' Jai pushed himself away from the screen. 'Abbie was scared of being drowned. We need to find out what happened. Was the donor child drowned by her father?'

I felt panicky. This wasn't right. All the normal rules seemed to be dissolving in front of me. How could we conduct an investigation when the suspect's motive was that her heart's previous father drowned her? I shook my head. 'I don't know. It makes no sense.'

'The donor was the kid who drowned at Mermaid's Pond wasn't she? Last year. Is this evidence it wasn't an accident?'

★

Freezing fog had settled over the hills, making my drive home seem muffled and unreal. I flipped on the radio and listened to a BBC-English voice assuring me we were definitely in for a cold snap, something Derbyshire generally did in style. The sleet had presumably eased off so that snow could be prepared and dispensed later with maximum shock value.

I couldn't get Abbie's drawing out of my head. If that was what she'd been dreaming, no wonder she'd been terrified. I remembered her clinging on to me after falling into that icy stream, and felt a dreadful weight in my chest. Something inexplicable and horrifying was going on, and whichever way I looked at it, Abbie was a victim.

I'd had a quick check for details about the child who'd died at Mermaid's Pond, but there was very little publicly available. I'd be able to get hold of more information the next day from our police records.

I slowed as the fog thickened to the point where my headlights bounced off it and back into my face. I killed the full beam and crawled along, concentrating so hard I felt sick.

My sister Carrie hadn't been able to donate any of her organs because of the cancer. I wondered if I'd have felt any different if she had. If someone was walking around with her heart. Would I want to meet them? Would I search for some essence of Carrie in them? Before I'd even considered this, I imagined Dad looking at me with that critical eye. *Of course you wouldn't – her personality wasn't in her heart.*

The fog thinned and was almost non-existent by the time I arrived at my house and parked on the cobbles outside. I felt anxious walking across my tiny front courtyard, and as soon as I stepped into the hallway, I had the urge to rush upstairs and check the rooms. I told myself to stop being pathetic. I'd been so much better recently. I'd been unsettled by finding Harry Gibson, but I'd coped. I couldn't go back to manically checking ceilings for hanging things.

There was no sign of Hamlet, which was unusual – maybe that was why the house felt so creepy. There was a hint of a sweet smell in the hallway. Lilies. We'd had lilies at Carrie's funeral.

I turned and pushed the front door closed behind me. I seemed to feel it before I saw it.

I glanced down.

Something was dangling through the letter-box.

I stepped back, crashing into the hall shelf and knocking the phone onto the floor.

My heart thudded. I stood frozen.

# 13.

I wanted to run into the kitchen away from it, but a part of me refused to do that. Refused to give in.

I reached forward and grabbed it.

A small rag doll, about Barbie sized. Buttons for eyes, yellow wool for hair. The hair had been hacked short.

A noose was tight around the doll's neck, and a piece of thin rope suspended it from the letter-box.

I yanked the thing forwards, and it popped free. The end of the rope was knotted, so when it had been pushed through the letter-box, the knot had snagged and left it suspended. Hanging. I guessed that wasn't an accident.

I wanted to throw it to the ground, but there was enough of Carrie in it that I couldn't. Someone had cut the hair to make it look like hers when it had just started growing back, once they stopped the chemo. I couldn't hate the doll.

I clutched it to me, shuffled up the hallway and sank onto the base of the stairs.

I sat holding the doll. She smelt of lilies.

I wiped a tear from my cheek and examined her more closely. She had a cloth satchel, and something was poking out of it.

A piece of paper. I swallowed and fished it out. There were words, so tiny I had to squint to read them.

'*You will be punished.*'

My fingers tensed to scrunch the paper, but I stopped. This was evidence.

I stood, laid the doll gently on the hall step, stooped to pick up the phone, and dialled Mum.

'Hello, love. Are you alright?'

I sat back down on the step. 'I'm fine. I just got in.'

'Oh, Meg. You mustn't work so hard. Have you eaten?'

Mum lived in perpetual fear that I would starve, despite my physical appearance providing persuasive evidence to the contrary.

'I'm not going to die of hunger or over-work, Mum. But I wanted to check you were okay. Something a bit weird's happened. And I vowed I wouldn't keep stuff from you again.'

'Tell me. What is it?'

'Someone's shoved a doll through my letter-box. Made to look like Carrie.'

Silence for a moment. 'Oh good lord. How awful.'

'Yeah. There are people out there who don't like me.'

'The Life Liners?'

'I suppose so. I wanted to check you were okay.'

'I'm fine. They've done nothing here. Do you want to come round? You shouldn't be on your own.'

'I might pop over to Hannah's – she always stays up late. Lock your doors and windows, Mum.'

The cat flap slammed open and Hamlet came charging into the hallway. I was so pleased to see him, I realised I must have been worried.

'Hamlet's here, Mum. Better go.'

'Oh, well, get your priorities right, love.'

'Be careful, Mum. Let me know if you see anything odd. Any time. Okay?'

★

Hannah whipped the door open. 'Oh my God, Meg, come in. Are you alright?'

I leant and gave her a quick kiss. 'I'm fine. I just didn't fancy being alone. Thanks for letting me stay over. And would you mind having him? For a day or two?'

She peered into Hamlet's basket. 'Of course not. If there are nasty people hanging around your house, he should stay here. Bring him through.' Hannah wasn't generally fond of cats but for some reason adored Hamlet, even though his black and white fur was capable of destroying any outfit and adding an unwanted garnish to her cuisine.

I leant and peered into his basket. 'You won't let him outside, will you? He'll get lost.'

'I won't let him out.'

I followed her to the kitchen and placed Hamlet down carefully. 'I'm probably being over-protective but he's such a dope, and he'll go up to anyone. And if they hate me that much . . . '

'It's fine,' Hannah said. 'You know I love fat little Hammy. Did you bring it with you? The horrible doll?'

'No. It's evidence. I took a photo though.' I sat down and released Hamlet from his carrier, then fished out my phone and showed her the image. 'Someone had dangled it through the letter-box so it looked like it had been hanged.'

'Oh my God. This requires gin. Can you sort lemons and ice?'

I sliced lemons and grappled with a recalcitrant ice-tray while Hannah grabbed two large glasses and poured about four measures of gin and a bit of tonic into each. 'Is it the Life Line people?' she said.

'I guess so.'

'Jesus. I can't believe I ever got involved with them. How did they know what Carrie's hair looked like?'

'It's public knowledge she'd had cancer. After that girl did her over-share. It was a safe bet her hair would be short.'

'Bloody hell, Meg. This is horrendous.'

'Yeah.' I gulped about half the G and T. 'I'm trying not to be too affected by it. They're losers. Why should I let it get to me?'

Even I wasn't convinced by that.

'They should be locked up.'

'I don't want to spend my whole life defined by this.' I swallowed. 'I'm not just that woman who found her sister hanging.'

'Of course you're not. And you've been fine recently, haven't you?'

'I still have a flashback every now and then.'

'Meg . . . That's not right. You should see a counsellor.'

'I can hardly remember her face any more, Hannah. The flashbacks . . . they're the only time I see her clearly.'

'Seriously. Have a chat with the counsellor.'

'Oh maybe, once this case is out of the way. And . . . ' I didn't say it. I couldn't face talking about Gran today, and I sensed Hannah knew that. But I'd thought it. Once Switzerland was out of the way. I felt a sick churning in my stomach. Part of me was looking forward to it being over. Which meant I was looking forward to Gran being dead. Maybe I was a monster.

'You're assuming it's the religious maniacs,' Hannah said.

'But anyone could have read their insane blog posts. It could be someone else. Someone to do with the murder you're on at the moment.'

'I guess so . . . '

'Could you be in danger?'

'I don't think so. This was pretty cowardly. I don't suppose they'll confront me. Let's talk about something else.'

Hannah looked at me, wide-eyed. 'Is it true the little girl killed her father?'

'Of course not. Where do you get all this stuff from?'

'People are tweeting about it. It's all over the place. Do you know who did it then? Should we be barricading the doors?'

'You'll be okay with your five-lever mortice locks. Think of me in my ramshackle old hovel with un-lockable windows the landlord keeps saying he'll fix.' I had a spasm of worry. Not about Phil Thornton's killer, but about whoever thought it was a nice idea to post Carrie through my letter-box.

'Do you think he'll kill someone else?'

'What? My landlord?'

Hannah tutted.

I wondered how much genuine concern was behind this. Hannah tried to make light of her disability, but how must it feel to know you couldn't kick someone or even run away? Hannah was so far from being a victim, and I'd never told her about my particular terror of paralysis – about waking up sweating and gasping after dreaming I'd been in that car accident with Dad. 'Seriously, Hannah, there's no reason to think anyone's going to kill anyone else, and I came here to get away from all that, and you know very well I can't talk about it anyway.'

'Do you think it's something to do with the paedophile?'

'Anyway . . . How are you?'

'Made the mistake of trying on some of my *thin-clothes*. Maybe I should give up and take them to a charity shop.'

'Life's a lot easier when you stop caring how you look.'

'So you tell me. And when you stop cleaning your car and your house . . . '

'Yep, that too. Accept that you'll share your life with spiders.'

'Ugh. What a disgusting thought. I can't think of anything I'd less like to share my life with.'

'I don't know, Hannah. I'm remembering some of those blokes you've tried to hook me up with on the dating site.'

I so wanted to chat dating and silly, irrelevant stuff with Hannah, but there was too much crap in my head. Gran, the Carrie-doll, Craig . . . Although in a surprise development, the thing with Craig seemed less important now. I could distance myself from it. 'Craig's been lying about me to Richard,' I said.

'The little shit. What's he been saying.'

I laughed. It did almost seem comical now. 'The victim's wife in this murder case had a fairly half-assed go at me for police brutality, and . . . '

'What? You never told me that.'

'It was preposterous. Her lawyer's attempt to distract us. Even she didn't take it seriously. I tried to stop her getting to the crime scene, and she fell, but then she got up and punched me.'

'Christ, Meg, you do have a time of it.'

'I know. Craig turned up after she punched me, but now he's lying and saying he saw me push her. I don't know why he hates me so much. His wife said he was desperate to impress me, but that's clearly not the case.'

'He hates you because you're better than him. He can't stand that. Did Richard believe him?'

'I'm not sure. Richard kind of left it hanging, but I feel I should talk to Craig about it, preferably without resorting to violence.'

'You know what I think you should do? Totally ignore it. Have you told anyone else? Jai? Fiona?'

'Jai seems to know. I don't think Fiona does.'

'Okay, don't mention it to anyone. Don't confront Craig. Be super-nice to him. He'll bloody hate that. He won't know if Richard said anything to you. He'll suspect he didn't and then he'll wonder if Richard didn't believe him, or just thinks you're more important than him. He won't want to ask you about it.'

'What if he does?'

'Be really vague, as if Richard might have said something but you've forgotten what it was because it was a matter of such supreme indifference to you. Seriously, Meg, this is the way to go. Don't reward the behaviour by giving it attention. Basic training principles.'

I smiled. Hannah had read a book called *Don't Shoot the Dog* many years ago, and had been applying dog-training principles to managing her colleagues ever since, although possibly with fewer food-based rewards.

'Okay.' I raised my glass and clinked it against Hannah's. 'I solemnly vow. No attention for Craig. I will rise above it all.'

# 14.

I breakfasted in the reassuring company of Hannah and Hamlet, feeling surprisingly relaxed. Something about Hannah's company did that to me. And her calm, spacious kitchen and neatly bordered garden helped too. It was good to be away from my place, where everywhere I looked there were reminders of things I should have done.

Once at the Station, my calm evaporated. It was the morning briefing for Operation Sweeney Todd. Abbie's drawing was projected onto a screen at the front of the room. I stared at the black lake, the man with the huge teeth, the girl being dragged by her blonde hair. It still gave me goose pimples.

I took myself to the front of the room and tried to look as if I was in control. The excited chatter died down.

'We need to find out if there's anything in Abbie's life to justify her dreaming about a girl being pulled towards a lake,' I said. 'Or thinking her father's a murderer. It must have come from somewhere.'

'Other than from the donor child?' Jai said, and the chatter kicked off again.

I raised my voice. 'Yes, other than from the donor child! It's not possible she remembers something that happened to the donor child. Okay?'

'Could Harry Gibson have inadvertently given Abbie some details about the donor child?' Fiona said.

'That would make sense,' I said. 'Except that the letter giving him the information about the donor child was dated after all his meetings with Abbie.'

'It doesn't matter why she did it,' Craig said. 'If we can show she did.'

I was following Hannah's advice and pretending I knew nothing about Craig's blatant lies to Richard. It didn't mean I had to respond to the guy though.

'Have we got any more from the blood spatter?' I asked.

Jai nodded. 'Got the report back from the Dexters. But it's not conclusive. Unfortunately, there wasn't a person-shaped hole in the spatter on the wall, so they can't actually tell the size of whoever did it.'

'What did Michael Ellis say about the drugs?' Fiona said.

I filled them in briefly about Ellis's odd claims and behaviour.

Craig folded his arms pointedly. 'Paranoid his colleagues are after him? Claiming a drug could make a kid kill someone? He's mad as a box of frogs. Why are we even following it up?'

Fiona shot an irritated glance at Craig. 'Did he seem like he might be mentally ill?'

'Not on the face of it.' I pictured Ellis standing by the Destroying Angels, his gaze darting to and fro, his leg tapping. 'Our forensic psychiatrist said he was clearly scared but didn't seem obviously mentally ill.'

'What about Dr Gibson?' Fiona said. 'Did he know too much about the bad heart or the drugs? Was he murdered as well?'

The energy in the room was bubbling up again. 'We don't know that,' I said.

'No, he wasn't.' Craig's tone was smug. 'His blood was full of booze and his own prescription tranquillisers. His sister and parents were shocked, horrified, didn't believe he was a paedophile, desperate for us to catch the bastards that put his name online. He'd had problems with depression and it was believable that he'd kill himself after reading those lies on the internet.'

'Prints in the house?'

'His and his sister's.'

'There's more to it,' I said. 'He was wondering if the donor child was murdered. There's more to this than a simple suicide.'

★

I eased myself into the car. 'We're meeting her at Black Mere.'

Jai paused half way into my passenger seat. 'At the place where her daughter drowned?'

I nodded. 'I was surprised. But maybe she wants us to see what it was like.'

'Shouldn't you be taking Craig with you?'

'I don't have to take him everywhere I go like a little puppy-dog.' I opened my mouth to say something about Craig's lies to Richard, but then remembered Hannah's advice.

'You'd be upset if you asked for a puppy for Christmas and that turned up.'

'Are you getting in or have you got a more pressing engagement?'

Jai brushed the seat pointedly and plonked himself next to me.

I pulled out of the car park. 'Why did you call Craig Twinkletoes the other day?'

'Ah, now, that's a state secret.'

I looked round at his impassive face. 'Come on, Jai. What's going on?'

'His wife's bullied him into doing salsa classes with her.'

I laughed. Too loudly. 'Oh my God. I love it.'

'To try to re-build their crappy relationship. But you mustn't tell him I blabbed.'

'I won't. It's enough just to know. That's made my day. Like a hippo doing ballet. How fabulous.'

We drove in companionable silence for a while. It was ridiculous how much the salsa revelation had cheered me up.

Jai coughed. 'You think there might be something in this heart business? If you want to talk to the donor child's mother?'

'Something damn peculiar is going on and I want to know what. But hopefully the child's mother can tell us the details of the girl's death, and it'll be nothing like Abbie's picture or her dreams, and we can put this ludicrous theory to rest once and for all.'

'Well, I found out the girl was with her father when she drowned. There are no details of her swimming costume or hair colour or whether her dad had a black beard or anything.' Jai looked at the sky. It was white and low, seeming to sink onto the tree-tops. 'They're saying it's going to snow. If it does, it'll be bad up there.'

'They've been saying that for days.' I had a peculiarly English confidence that it wouldn't snow, and that if it did, I'd be fine. 'This car's not too bad in the snow actually,' I said, further .adding to my ridiculous position on the matter. 'Front wheel drive and narrow tyres.'

'Yeah,' Jai said. 'Sure it is. Old heaps are famously good in the snow.'

'I told the donor child's mother we were doing some research on drownings,' I said, ignoring the dig at my poor car. 'She was happy to help. Seemed keen to talk.'

'Sort of true,' Jai said. 'Did you know there've been a few drownings at the pool? The locals blame an evil mermaid.'

'Of course they do. We're only seventy miles from the sea. Why ever would it not be the fault of a mermaid?'

As I took the road past Carsington Water, I could feel the wind getting up, buffeting the side of the car. But there was no sign of any snow.

'Someone fell in love with her,' Jai said. 'But she spurned his advances so he accused her of being a witch and persuaded the townspeople to drown her in the pool.'

'Some men need to learn how to handle rejection.'

'Don't worry, she sorted it. She cursed him with her dying breath and later he was found dead by the pool with his face covered in claw marks.'

'Seems reasonable.'

'And now she lures single men to her and drowns them in the bottomless depths.'

I glanced sideways at him. 'Does that include you then, Jai? Or not any more? Are you safe?'

An uncomfortable thickness filled the car. 'Er, no, yes, I did meet someone recently.'

'That's great.' The words felt lumpy as they rose up and out through my mouth. 'It'll help you get over your divorce. Anyway, what else do you know about this pool?'

Jai gave me a quick, relieved smile. 'It's supposed to be linked to the sea by an underground passage. They pumped a load of water out of it once, to put a fire out, and the level didn't change. And they say cattle won't drink out of it and birds won't fly over it. The water's supposed to be black.'

'Like Abbie's drawing.'

We were silent for a moment. I pictured the drawing.

We made our way through Ashbourne and on towards Leek. Still no snow but it was bitterly cold. The pool was near the side of the A53 heading north. 'Keep your eyes peeled,' I said. 'We should be nearly there by now.'

'I think I know where it is. I'll tell you.'

The warmth of the car must have loosened me up. I found myself telling Jai about the doll I'd found hanging through my door.

'Holy crap,' he said. 'Are you okay?'

'I'm fine. It freaked me out a bit at first but it's nothing.'

'Have you reported it? And did you get your dodgy windows fixed?'

'Yes, and the landlord's going to do it.'

I noticed a dark patch of water, like a blob of black ink sinking into the hillside. 'Is that it?'

Jai looked over. 'Oh yes. You can park opposite.'

I pulled the car into a small lay-by. 'It's a bit grim.'

'It might be nice in the summer.' Jai eased the car door open an inch. The wind grabbed it and slammed it wide, snatching at the pages of a map on my back seat.

'Christ, shut the door a minute.'

'Okay, okay.' Jai fought with the door, and finally clunked it shut.

A car pulled up in front of us. A woman forced her door open.

We bundled ourselves into coats, battled with the car doors, and emerged into the windswept landscape.

The woman confirmed she was Vanessa Norwood, mother of the girl who'd drowned. She looked drained of life, as if exhausted by tragedy. Everything about her was hesitant, as if any large movement could provoke even worse things to happen in her life.

'If at any point you want to leave,' I said. 'Just say. I know it must be hard to come here.'

'Nick and I split up over it,' she said. 'He's living in our old house up in the hills. I can't bear it there any more. Not many marriages survive the loss of a child. I suppose you know that.'

'Yes. I'm sorry.' The wind took my words and whipped them away.

'Of course I blamed him.'

We crossed the road and followed an unclear path towards the pool. As we neared the dark water, the wind dropped and the air fell still. The blackness of the pool was overwhelming, as if it was sucking the light from the sky. It smelt of peat and something oddly sweet I couldn't place. The first flakes of snow fell onto its smooth surface.

I took a step nearer and felt my foot sink into swampy sludge. I leaped back before it engulfed me.

'What a stupid place to bring her,' Vanessa said. 'He knew there'd been drownings here in the past. She wasn't a good swimmer, and . . . '

I gazed into the pool and imagined a young girl thrashing around, being dragged into the bottomless depths.

'She wasn't his. She never knew, but *he* did. I knew he didn't like her as much as Ben. Ben was his, of course.'

I exchanged a glance with Jai. Ben. Ben had been mentioned in Harry Gibson's report of Abbie's hypnosis. *Why didn't Mum and Ben and Buddy come with us?*

'He used to get really angry with Scarlett. Way more than he did with Ben.'

'You don't think he . . . '

'What, did something to hurt her? No, not really. But how did he let her drown? I just don't think he'd have let Ben drown. What did you want to know anyway? Aren't you compiling statistics or something?'

'We're just after details of the circumstances if that's okay.'

She looked towards the pool and nodded.

'Was it just the two of them that day?' I asked.

'Yes. Ben had football. I don't know why I always took him to football, but you know how it is. Mums always seem to do the boring, regular stuff and dads get to choose. And that day Nick decided he wanted to come here. So he took Scarlett. He didn't even take the dog. The dog would never have let her drown.'

'What kind of a dog is he?' I spoke casually, conversationally. I thought asking his name might seem weird.

'Buddy? Oh, he's just a mongrel – something hairy crossed with something greedy.'

Ben and Buddy. It wasn't only the bitter cold giving me goose-pimples.

'So, they went swimming?'

'They must have done. Although how he got her to swim, I don't know. She had her swimmers on but I was only expecting her to sunbathe and paddle, not to swim. She rarely swam, and now this . . . Sorry, maybe it is too much coming here.'

'Let's go back up to the cars.'

She didn't move. 'He never even learnt first aid. Everyone should know first aid. They revived her when the ambulance arrived but it was too late. She'd not had oxygen for . . . '

I took her arm and led her gently up the slope towards the cars. Flakes of snow swirled across the moor and over the black water of the pool.

'I'm sorry. I know this is hard,' I said. 'We really appreciate it. And, I know it seems like an odd question, but what colour swimsuit was she wearing?'

Her words seemed not to want to leave her throat. 'It was so cute with her lovely blonde hair. Pink dots on white.'

# 15.

'This is seriously creeping me out now.' Jai bundled himself into the car, shaking snow onto the seat and onto me. 'How the hell could Abbie have known that stuff about the donor? The pink spotty bathing suit? Ben and Buddy?'

'I don't know.' It was creeping me out too.

'Do you think the girl's father drowned her? And Abbie somehow remembered that?'

'I think that's one of the less likely explanations.' The tyres slipped as I pulled out of the lay-by.

Jai was on a roll. 'And Abbie murdered her dad in her sleep, because she was dreaming about this girl's father killing her?'

'Good luck presenting that to the CPS.'

'So what do you think happened?'

I gripped the wheel tightly, and flicked the wipers on. It was snowing properly now. 'We've got to be really careful here, Jai. What we're talking about – there's no evidence it's even possible. If it gets out that we're pursuing this lead, the media are going to be on us like hyenas on a freshly slaughtered corpse.'

I didn't want to believe Abbie had killed her father, and as for the idea that her donor's heart took her over, *Exorcist*-style? It was ridiculous.

'But that picture Abbie drew when she was hypnotised? It was bloody spot on. It was the donor child's death scene, for God's sake.'

'I want to know who else knew about the circumstances of Scarlett Norwood's death.'

'There were no details online. Not about the swimming costume, or her brother's name, or the dog's name. I checked.'

'What about social media?'

'There's nothing public.'

'It can't have come from the heart, Jai. It's not possible.'

'I know it sounds unlikely but – '

'Michael Ellis said to speak to Gaynor Harvey. About cellular memory. I found an article about her, and she only lives in Bonsall. Maybe I'll go and see her.'

My phone started ringing and buzzing.

'Can you see who it is?' I fished in my pocket and shoved the phone at him. 'I'm not super-safe talking on the hands-free and driving.'

'I'm not sure that's so safe either,' Jai said. 'If you nearly swerve off the road delving around in your pocket. It's Dr Li.'

'Better answer it.'

Jai picked up. A series of shocked *Okays* and *Rights,* and then, 'Call 999. We're on our way . . . Try and find him . . . Keep him talking.'

I looked over at him. 'What the hell?'

'She thinks her son's gone off to try and commit suicide. At the gorge.'

My pulse quickened. 'What? Her son who we met? The doctor?'

'So she says.'

'Why does she think that? Jesus.'

'She said he left a note saying he couldn't live like this any more or something like that. He's been suicidal before, she says. She's already called his primary care team and they're on their way up there, but . . . '

'Oh God. She did say he'd been depressed since his accident. We'd better go up there too. Is it near Dead Girl's Drop again?' I pictured the sheer side of the gorge that I'd seen when I was with Dr Li by the Destroying Angels. The place up in the clouds where she'd said Tom liked to go.

'The top car park. I know where it is. And she said you saw it the other day.'

'Do you know how to get there by road?'

'I'll direct you.'

I accelerated.

The road from Ashbourne snaked through the valleys and past the ominous grey choppiness of Carsington Water. The snow was still light, but I could see it gathering on the hills to our left. The drive felt painfully slow.

Finally, we skirted the edge of Eldercliffe and Jai pointed to a lane which headed steeply towards the rim of the gorge.

'Not that one?' I said. 'It's a goat track, not a road.'

'Yeah, I'm not ecstatic about it either,' Jai said.

I sighed and pulled onto the lane.

We headed up and up, high into the clouds. There was snow here already – on the ground and swirling in the air. I slowed at the sight of a sheer drop on our left, separated from the road by a few feeble-looking bollards. I wished I'd put winter tyres on the car.

Jai sat stiffly, right foot poised over an imaginary brake, glancing nervously out of his window. 'You're quite close to the edge, Meg.'

'I know. I can't get any closer on this side without driving into the snow. And then we'll never get up there.'

I drove on, eyes fixed on the road ahead, praying my little car would make it.

We rolled into the car park and jumped out. There were two cars already there, but no people that we could see, and no sign of the primary care team. The air was bitterly cold and the wind blasted flecks of icy snow into our eyes. I felt disorientated and confused about where Tom would have gone.

'I think it's this way.' Jai spat snowflakes from his mouth. 'There are footprints.'

The snow hid the path, and the air was so thick and white I worried we'd find ourselves on the edge of the gorge without even realising it.

'Dr Li!' I shouted. 'Tom!'

We followed the rapidly disappearing footprints. I sensed an emptiness next to us where the ground fell away into the gorge, but was relieved to see a stone wall running alongside the path.

Jai pointed ahead. 'Is that them?' His voice was muffled as if I had earplugs in.

I peered into the whiteness. A wheelchair, just visible. Empty.

We hurried forward. The snow masked everything. Fen and Tom popped into my vision only when we were almost on top of them. My pulse quickened.

Tom seemed to be draped over the wall. He'd somehow managed to drag one leg up so his shoulders and one foot sat on the top of it. The rest was set to follow. The wall was only around waist height. Easy to climb over, but we hadn't had a big suicide problem – possibly because the drop wasn't enough to reliably kill you.

Fen stood behind Tom, her arms stretched forward helplessly.

191

Tom looked round, his expression unreadable. 'Don't come any closer.'

'Please, Tom . . . ' Fen reached her hand forward.

'Stay back or I'm going over.'

Fen retracted her hand.

I took a breath and forced my brain into calm mode. We'd had training in dealing with jumpers. They were often in the middle of a psychotic episode, screaming and paranoid. The key was to get them talking. Tom on the other hand seemed coldly detached.

'I've decided to do this,' he said. 'It's my decision and it's rational. I choose not to live like this.' His foot was still on the wall. Flakes of snow had gathered on his back.

'No!' Fen reached towards him, but stopped short of touching him. She turned to us. 'He doesn't mean it. He's been like this before. He'll pull out of it. Please . . . '

Although Tom had said he'd decided to do it, I didn't believe he was sure, or he'd have already jumped. But that foot was making me nervous. If we could get it off the wall, he'd really struggle to drag himself over. I could sense Jai looking at the foot too.

'Please, Tom, let's talk about it,' Fen begged. 'We can sort things out. Make your life better.'

I indicated to Fen to move away a little. Relatives were loose cannons – often the accidental trigger that prompted a jumper to go over.

If I could flip the foot off the wall, then Jai could grab his body. I was sure we'd be able to pull him back. I didn't like to force him down but sometimes it was the best way. He probably wouldn't even kill himself if he jumped, but would end up maimed in hospital and even more depressed than before.

Jai inched a little closer to Tom.

'We'll find a way to make things work, Tom.' Fen sounded utterly desperate. 'Just come down and give me a chance. Please.'

Tom turned away. His shoulders tensed. He was going over.

I lunged for his foot and knocked it off the wall. Jai leaped forwards and tried to grab his waist but he twisted round and shoved him in the face. Jai fell back. Tom was slipping away from me. I managed to get my hand into the waist of his trousers and yanked back as hard as I could, but he seemed to be stuck half over the wall. Fen grabbed hold of me from behind.

I saw Jai in the corner of my eye. He jumped up, reached over the wall, grasped Tom round the neck and pulled him back. We all crashed down in a big bundle, my hip smashing onto the freezing ground, my mouth full of snow.

I lay gasping and wiping snow from my face.

I pulled myself to my feet. Tom lay immobile, horribly silent. Had we even done the right thing saving him? We didn't know how hard his life was.

Fen crouched and pulled Tom into a sitting position. 'Come on. Let's get you home and warmed up.'

Jai scraped snow from the seat of the wheelchair, freed up the wheels and pushed it to Tom's side.

'Help me get in.' Tom spoke to his mother, his voice breaking.

Together we helped Tom into the chair, and Fen started pushing him, forcing him through the snow that had gathered on the path. She was strong, despite being small. 'How can you do this to me?' Her words burst out between panting sobs. 'And you're putting other people's lives at risk.'

We followed along behind Fen and Tom, trailing back to

the car like soldiers after a battle. I was cold to my core, and felt strangely depressed, given the relatively good outcome. There was always a part of me that wondered if we should let people jump, if they wanted to. But I knew there had been times I'd been a whisker away from that state myself – when if I'd found myself on the edge of a cliff, I couldn't swear I wouldn't have gone over. And whilst for me, that might have been a blessed escape, the thought of the effect on Mum made me gasp for breath and thank something – whatever I thank that isn't God – that I hadn't done it.

At the car park, the care team were arriving. I took one of them aside – a middle-aged woman who exuded competence – and told her in hushed tones what had happened.

We stayed a while, checking Tom was okay and the care team had it all in hand. Fen stood apart from the group, arms folded.

We got into our car and Fen plodded over. I wound the window down.

'Thanks so much,' she said. 'He goes through these bad patches. I shouldn't have involved you. I panicked, and I had your card to hand.'

'Will you be okay?' I was struck again by the horror of living with someone suicidal. Felt the crashing wave of relief that I was past that point.

'We'll be fine,' she said, switching abruptly to professional and business-like. 'He's done this before and he pulls out of it. Besides, you've got enough on your plate at work. I looked into it – there's more to that cellular memory theory than I'd realised.'

'You mean Abbie Thornton's heart?'

She nodded and gave a sad smile. 'Talk to me again if you

need to. I think in view of today, I won't charge for a further meeting.'

★

Back at the Station, I pulled rank and left Jai sorting out paperwork for Tom's attempted jump, while I headed to my room to see what had come in on Phil Thornton.

After half an hour, I looked up to see Craig looming over me. 'What's that noise?' he said.

I forced my face into a smile, albeit a rather insipid one. 'Sorry, Craig?'

'Oh, I know. It's the PACE clock ticking. It's almost deafening me.' He rubbed his ear and then looked pointedly at his watch. 'Are we charging the kid?'

'I know the clock's ticking. Thank you, Craig.'

A knock and Jai appeared. He saw Craig and rolled his eyes at me.

'We should charge her,' Craig said.

Jai walked to the far side of the room and stood with his back to the window, arms folded. 'Are we charging her?'

I took a breath. 'I don't think we've got enough evidence.'

'But do you think she did it?' Jai said.

I looked out of the sliver of window Jai hadn't blocked. The sky was white again. 'No. I suppose I don't.'

Craig put his face too close to mine. 'She was lying by her father's slaughtered corpse clutching a blood-soaked knife.'

'Thanks, Craig.' I eyed the door. 'I'll speak to you later.'

He took a step towards the door, then hesitated and looked over his shoulder. 'Are you sure you're up to leading a high-profile investigation?'

'What made you like this, Craig?' Jai said. 'Did your daddy not give you enough praise as a child?'

Craig's faced flushed red. He glared briefly at Jai, and walked out of the door.

Something about Craig's expression had unsettled me. Maybe his parents really had been awful. Maybe he'd been bullied at school. Maybe it wasn't about me at all.

'Back to that ticking clock.' Jai was silhouetted against the bright sky. I felt interrogated. Why was I putting my job on the line for Abbie Thornton?

'Her mother has a history of somatic delusions,' I said. 'This heart thing could be another one. The girl is not possessed by the spirit of another child's heart, Jai. She just isn't.'

'But Dr Li said there was more to cellular memory than she'd thought. And even regardless of motive, Abbie doesn't deny doing it.'

'She doesn't remember a thing. Maybe she did have a knife in her hand, but someone could have orchestrated that. They'd tear it apart in court.'

'She had arterial blood on her nightdress.'

'Someone could have stabbed Phil, and Abbie could have run into the room while he was still bleeding.'

'While she was asleep? And you know arterial spurt only lasts about thirty seconds.'

'I know it's unlikely, but every explanation is unlikely.'

'Maybe only if you avoid the obvious one that Abbie did it. Maybe she was hypnotised by Harry Gibson or it was her heart or whatever, but she did do it.'

'Come and sit over here, Jai. I can't see you against the window.'

Jai sat unwillingly in my spare chair. 'I just wonder if maybe you like the kid a bit too much,' he said. 'She lost her sister, didn't she . . . '

'It's not that,' I snapped. 'Someone could have set this up so it looked like she killed her father.'

'Framed her, you mean?'

'Yes.'

'Who'd want to do that?'

'I don't know. Yet.'

'There's no motive.'

'But there's no motive for Abbie to do it. It doesn't happen, Jai. A ten-year-old stabbing her father to death in the middle of the night. No way.'

'What about the heart transplant thing? Why do you keep ignoring that? What about the picture she drew? The things she said – Ben and Buddy . . . Come on, you were there when the donor child's mother said those things. How the hell could Abbie have drawn that picture and said those things in her dreams if it's not come from the heart?'

'I don't know. I can't explain it. I've got the geeks looking at Harry Gibson's laptop again. But you know how long all that takes.'

'You seem to be doing everything to avoid accepting that Abbie Thornton did it.'

'Jai, please don't get channelled down the *Abbie did it* route and ignore all the other possibilities.'

'Seems to me like you're doing the opposite, and avoiding the most obvious solution. I'm actually wondering if we should have another look at that drowning. Fiona agrees with me.'

'It can't be true,' I said. 'I don't believe it. Assuming Richard's okay with it, we'll release her on police bail and I'll have another talk with her and her mother over the weekend. There's something else going on here.'

'And Ben and Buddy and the pink spotty swimsuit?'

'There's another explanation. But I'm going to see that woman tomorrow. Gaynor Harvey. She thinks she's taken on the traits of her donor. I tracked her down.'

'Good,' Jai said. 'Science can't explain everything.'

'Seriously, Jai? We're detectives. We have to rely on science, and evidence, and logic. Otherwise we have nothing.'

I knew I'd find holes in Gaynor Harvey's story, and it might give me a clue about how these ideas could arise. A memory of my dad popped into my head. He was angry; shouting at me. What had I done? It felt important. Something to do with Carrie.

It came back to me. Some silly thing at school. A friend who'd said her mum had cured her cancer with crystals. I'd bounced home and told Carrie, and Dad had been furious. Disappointed in me, calling me stupid for believing something like that, something so unscientific.

The door started edging open whilst simultaneously being knocked. Fiona's head appeared from behind it. 'Managed to get that name from the social workers at last,' she said. 'The first name of the mother who might have had a grievance against Phil Thornton.'

'Oh? What was it?'

'Elaine.'

'Elaine.' I looked up at my memory banks. 'I know that name. Who else is called Elaine?'

'The woman who found Abbie running through the woods,' Fiona said. 'It's the same woman. She's using a different surname. It's Elaine Grant.'

I jumped up. 'Right. I'm going to see her. Can you check if she had any contact with Harry Gibson?'

'Come on, Meg.' Jai reached out his hand as if to pull me back. 'There's no way – '

'See you later.'

I shot out before he had a chance to say any more.

# 16.

Elaine Grant placed a tray on a glass coffee table and sat opposite me in her moribund front room. 'I hope the poor girl's alright?'

'Abbie's fine.' I pondered all the ways in which Abbie was not fine.

'Shocking about her father being killed. And only up the road. I can hardly sleep at night. I might have to find somewhere else to rent.' Elaine's hand shook as she raised her cup to her mouth. Proper cups, like Gran used to use. She looked so unlike a murderer, it was almost comical. But could she have collaborated with someone? Harry Gibson? Rachel maybe? I had a stab of insight into how ridiculous I must seem to Jai — haring around trying to find anyone to blame other than Abbie.

'It's terrible, yes. I just wanted a word with you. You've been seen near Phil Thornton's house a few times. I wondered if you could tell me what you were doing.' This was a little creative, but worth a try.

'Near Bellhurst House? Really? I often walk in the woods.'

I'd taken a chair facing the window, forgetting I'd be confronted with Elaine's *Uncanny-Valley* dolls, full frontal, their white eyes staring sightlessly down at me. Where was the dog? I felt the need for his robust presence.

'But you had some contact with Phil Thornton?' I said.

'Did I?'

'He was a social worker.'

She sighed. 'They took my Ollie away.'

'Took him into care?'

'They said Darren was hurting him. My husband. But he wasn't. Ollie just had a lot of accidents.'

'What happened, Elaine?'

She reached behind her for one of the dolls, placed it on her lap, and gently stroked its hair as she spoke. Its white eyes rolled in its head. 'Darren used to get angry sometimes. He had a temper, but he wasn't a bad man. We all have a temper. Ollie was a difficult child. They can see that now. I suppose that social worker was doing his best. But he was supposed to be watching Ollie at the seaside. Anyway, I have him back now. They gave him back to me. And he's my baby again.'

I remembered the pyjamas, from a child about Abbie's size, the rigid face when I'd been about to ask if she had a child. What had happened to Ollie?

I instinctively glanced around the room, as if he might be wedged behind the sofa or lurking under the TV. 'Is Ollie in the house now?'

'Yes. In the house. Darren's outside.'

'Your husband?'

'The owner of the house put her pets outside. I sprinkled him there when I moved in. He couldn't cope with . . . what happened. Broke him in pieces.' She gestured out of a side window. A grassy area contained several small wooden crosses, surrounded by snowdrops. 'I went back to my maiden name. It made it easier.'

I looked at her expressionless face, all emotion flattened out of it. 'What happened to Ollie?'

'I don't really resent him. It wasn't that man's fault. Ollie was always accident-prone. I just wanted to know more about him. I've stopped now Ollie's back. I still love him as much as I ever did.'

'So you were following Phil Thornton?'

'I wanted to see who he was. . . and his family. See if he still had a family. I meant them no harm. When this house came up, and I saw where it was, it seemed perfect.'

'Did you ever follow the Thorntons' car?'

She swallowed. 'Not deliberately. Maybe by accident.'

It seemed likely that she was the stalker then. Curious about Phil Thornton – the man who she blamed for her child's accident. 'Where were you on Sunday night?'

'Here. I told you. I saw a car go up the lane. Do you think that was the murderer? I'm always here. With Ollie.'

'Can anyone confirm that you didn't leave the house?'

She hit me with the blank face again. 'Only Ollie.'

'Could I see Ollie?' I couldn't imagine a child in this house. It was too silent. Why was the little boy so quiet? I had visions of a *Psycho*-style back room; Ollie in pride of place – embalmed.

Elaine nodded, put the doll back on its shelf, stood slowly like a much older woman, and headed for the door. 'It's easier if you come to him. Come through to his room.'

I followed her, a sense of unease twitching in my stomach.

Elaine pushed a door from the hallway and it creaked open. The smell reminded me of Gran's room. Antiseptic and sickness. I walked in.

A woman sat by a bed. In the bed lay a boy – about ten years old.

Elaine walked to the side of the bed. 'How's my baby?'

The woman looked up. She was blonde with an open, crooked-toothed smile. 'He's not too bad this evening.'

It didn't seem like a boy's room. There were no toys, no posters on the walls, no sounds.

The boy was still, head rolled back, eyes open. He didn't respond to Elaine.

I walked to his bedside. 'Hi, Ollie.'

No response. I didn't think there was ever going to be a response from Ollie.

'What . . . ' How could I phrase it? *What happened to him?* That sounded wrong. Rude.

'Head injury,' the blonde woman said. 'The children's home took the boys on a trip to the seaside. He fell and hit his head on a rock. Ironic, isn't it? He was taken into care for his own safety.'

Elaine stroked Ollie's forehead. 'He's my baby again now.'

The blonde woman stepped away from the bed to prepare some medication on the other side of the room. I edged closer to her and asked, 'When did he get injured?'

'A while ago. I'm not sure exactly.' She lowered her voice and took a step closer to me. 'He was in hospital a long time. He nearly didn't make it. He came home about six weeks ago. But Elaine needs a lot of help. Her husband died after Ollie's accident.'

I spoke quietly so Elaine wouldn't hear. 'Was a particular social worker held responsible for Ollie's accident?'

The woman shuffled from one leg to the other. 'I don't know.'

'Did Elaine get help from a therapist?'

'I think . . . I'm not sure.'

I looked at Ollie's eyes. Rolling up in his head. White and sightless. Like the dolls.

Hamlet trotted up Hannah's hallway, yowling like a something from the seventh circle of Dante's *Inferno*.

I leant to stroke him. 'You haven't been torturing him, have you, Hannah?'

'He's been fine. He's eaten like a huge fat pig all day. Come through to the kitchen.'

'Oh yeah, he will eat all day if you let him. Don't be bullied by him.' I scooped Hamlet into my arms and followed Hannah.

'Tea or coffee? Assuming you're not drinking?'

'Better not . . . '

'You could stay over again? It's not a problem. I'll have to wash the sheets anyway – may as well get another night out of them. Have a drink, stay with your darling cat, and it'd save going back to your house of horrors.'

I put Hamlet on the table and sank into one of Hannah's kitchen chairs. 'I'm not sure one little doll through the door justifies the *House of Horrors* tag.'

'Not everyone wants a cat on the kitchen table, Meg.'

'Really? He's much more appealing than these diet books.' I lifted Hamlet onto the floor and shoved aside a stack of spinach-covered paperbacks.

'I know. I don't know why I waste my money. I should just buy bigger clothes. Anyway, are you staying over? Go back in the light tomorrow.'

It was tempting. It was a Friday, after all. I could forget about work for an evening. Get the image of poor Ollie out of my mind. And a dose of wine would tone down the inner voices that were telling me I shouldn't have released Abbie – that Jai and Craig were right, and we should have charged her and kept her in custody. 'Maybe I could.' I'd be working tomorrow, but hopefully not going in to the Station. I was going to see Gaynor Harvey. 'Okay, that sounds like a good idea.'

'Brilliant.' Hannah stabbed the *Off* button on the espresso machine. 'Screw that. We're on prosecco.'

Hamlet leaped onto my knee. 'Oops,' I said. 'Catted. I'm so glad he stayed here today. He seems really happy.'

'Yep, he's good. I had to pop out though. I didn't stay with him all day. But he was locked in. Triple locked.' Hannah produced a bottle of prosecco and split it between two extremely large glasses. Definitely not prosecco glasses.

I reached for my glass and took a life-enhancing gulp. 'It's okay, I didn't expect you to sit and cuddle him all day. Where did you go?'

'Doctor. They want to do another MRI on my back.'

I grimaced.

'Yeah. *Just lie there still as a statue for an hour, inside a hideous, claustrophobic metal tunnel while we smash hammers against it, right by your head.*'

'It doesn't sound like a bundle of fun. Is it the magnets that make the noise?'

'Apparently. They're so strong that if you take your wheelchair in, they'll whip it off the ground and slam it across the room like you've gone near a black hole. It happens every now and then. Flying wheelchairs, mangled MRI machines, and that's if it doesn't take your head off.'

'Jesus.'

'Meg . . . ' Hannah sipped her prosecco. 'I saw something on Facebook about the little girl killing her father because she remembered something from her heart donor's death . . . '

'Oh fabulous.'

'Is it true?'

'Of course it's not true, Hannah. People make this shit up all the time.'

'Did she have dreams about her donor being murdered though? I read a book about that. Apparently it can happen.' Hannah shuffled closer to me. 'It's really interesting. Lucky you, being involved in this.'

'It's not quite like that, Hannah.' I felt crushed suddenly by the pressure of the investigation. The need to get everything right, knowing you were being watched and analysed, and that it would all be picked apart afterwards. Always hanging over us the nightmare of not getting a conviction because we mucked up some minor detail that a defence lawyer would spring on. And in this case . . . I could picture the barrister's glee over this donor heart business. Field day coming. 'No,' I said. 'I don't get to enjoy the excitement of this.'

Hannah didn't seem to tune into my mental state. 'I read about this girl,' she said. 'Who dreamt about her donor's death and then the police caught the murderer.'

'If you can locate any actual names or real evidence of that, do let me know, because all I can find is that some psychiatrist in America told some other psychiatrist in America that it had happened. So it doesn't exactly meet the standards of criminal evidence necessary in UK law.'

'Alright, no need to get snippy with me.'

'Sorry, Hannah, it's this stupid heart donor thing. I know it's all very fascinating for everyone not involved, but the kid's actually really nice. It's quite upsetting that she's being accused of killing her father.'

'You don't think she did it?'

I hesitated. 'You know I can't talk about the case.' But I realised I'd shaken my head.

'Oh.' Hannah put her glass down with a thud. 'You'll do it, Meg. You'll find who really did it.'

# 17.

I slept fitfully in Hannah's hotel-standard spare room, and woke early with a nervous tingling in my stomach. If I was so sure Abbie was innocent, why did I keep thinking about her? I kept picturing the pink and white swimming costume, the bearded man, his teeth. Maybe Gaynor Harvey could help me understand what was going on.

I left Hamlet with Hannah and set off for Bonsall, which perched in the hills behind Matlock Bath. If it was going to snow again, it would do it big-time up there. The forecast was inconclusive so I chose to ignore it. I didn't have time to muck around being put off by bad weather.

I parked near the base of some stone steps that had apparently been built by German prisoners of war, with a competence rarely found in the English. The Harveys' cottage was around the corner and up an alleyway. A few random flakes drifted from the sky as I walked between mossy stone walls.

I knocked, and heard a good minute of muffled shouting before the door was flung open by a scowling man.

Bill Harvey must have only been in his sixties, but he looked ravaged, as if something had been eating him from the inside. He showed me into a heavily beamed living room and indicated a chair with its back to a mullioned window. I sat down.

A woman perched opposite on a floral sofa. She looked plump and healthy like a well-fed cat. It seemed wrong that she was the one who'd had the heart transplant.

Bill sat next to his wife and put his hand on her knee in a possessive gesture. 'Is this something to do with a police investigation?' He fixed me with a suspicious gaze. 'Gaynor can't get involved. She mustn't get upset.'

'I'm fine.' Gaynor shoved Bill's hand off her knee. 'I don't mind talking about it. I know you probably can't tell us what it's about.'

'I think we do need to know what it's about.' Bill folded his arms. 'My wife doesn't mind sharing our personal information with all and sundry, but I do. I think I know anyway. It's to do with that man who was killed. His daughter had a transplant. So, what's going on? Why are you here?'

I hadn't anticipated that. I'd only spoken to Gaynor on the phone and she hadn't seemed interested in why I wanted to talk to her – she was just eager to share her story.

'I'm afraid I can't tell you exactly what it's about.' I pulled myself forward on my too-squishy chair. 'It would be helpful for me to know what it feels like to have had a heart transplant. If you'd prefer not to talk to me, that's fine.'

'I'm perfectly happy to talk to you,' Gaynor said.

'Gaynor's not your typical patient.' Bill gave me a hostile look. 'She thinks the heart has a mind of its own.'

Gaynor spoke across the coffee table to me, excluding her husband. 'You can't understand unless you've felt it. Bill hasn't tried to understand what it's been like for me.'

I looked from one to the other. I didn't fancy being the pawn in a huge marital blow-up.

Gaynor shuffled her body to angle it away from Bill. 'In answer to your question, it feels very strange and it's extremely difficult at first. You feel this tremendous guilt. Why should I be alive when the donor's dead? If you believe everyone's equal and has the right to life, why should I have survived at her expense?'

'But, Gaynor, she would have died anyway. It's not as if you killed her.' I guessed from Bill's extravagantly patient tone that this wasn't the first time they'd had this discussion.

'Thank you, Bill. I'm well aware she would have died anyway, but it's still hard. I know it doesn't make much sense to feel guilty for being alive.'

It made a whole lot of sense to me. I wondered if Abbie felt the same.

Bill leant forward and spoke directly to me. I felt like a judge in a courtroom. Were they going to whip out wigs and start calling me *Your Honour*? 'I'm afraid Gaynor had some outlandish ideas about her heart. I think the guilt made her imagine the donor was still alive inside her in some way. It made it easier for her to cope.'

Gaynor shot him a defiant look. 'Maybe you could leave us for a while, Bill.'

Bill stood, gave his wife an exasperated glance, and stalked out of the room.

Gaynor relaxed into the sofa and sighed. 'There, now. Take a cup of tea, my love. And what else would you like to know?'

I hadn't noticed there was a tray on the table containing a teapot, a milk jug and three cups. I obediently poured myself tea. There was no point trying to get information out of anyone in Derbyshire if you didn't enthusiastically drink their tea. 'Thanks so much for this,' I said. 'I understand that you felt . . . well, different after your transplant?'

'Very much so. Bill says it's all in my mind but he doesn't know what it's like. And you grieve for your old heart. Even though it did you no favours, it's a bit like leaving a bad relationship.' She glanced at the door. 'You feel sad, even though you know it was killing you. I went through something of a bad patch. And Bill and I . . . you see, when you're ill, you put off arguing, you brush things under the carpet to deal with later, and I'm not sure either of us really thought there would be a later. We put off all our little disagreements and resentments. But then, after the transplant, you realise actually you may have quite a long life, so . . . we've been quarrelling. I seem to lose my temper a lot more than I used to. Sometimes I feel I could strangle Bill.'

Bill did seem quite strangleable, but it was making me uneasy that she'd felt more aggressive since her transplant. Like the mice. And like Abbie?

'It must have been hard,' I said. 'I suppose everyone thinks you should be incredibly happy simply to be alive, but you still have your own problems.'

'Exactly. But when I started coming out of the initial depression, I had this really strong sense of someone else inside me. And I kept dreaming I was in a car, and something was coming towards me really fast, and I was scared, and it came closer and closer and then, when I couldn't cope with how scared I was, I'd wake up. Then I dreamt I was inside someone else's body, and we were fighting. In the dream, I was her. The donor. I was dreaming it from her perspective. She was stuck inside my body fighting to get out. I had some therapy, and the counsellor said the doctors aren't careful enough about their language. She said all this talk of your body rejecting the heart – it can make you feel this way, as if it's a battle, as if my body was fighting with her. That made me feel better, but I still have this strong sense of someone inside me.'

'That sounds really strange.'

'It is. And then, there were other things. Bill said it was me struggling to adjust and not coping with the guilt. But I felt different. Even my taste in food changed, and music.'

I took a large gulp of now-cold tea. 'You talk as if your donor was a woman. Did you have any information about her?'

'Not at first. But I became desperate to find out who she was. I just knew it was a woman, and I thought she was young, and she'd died in a car crash. They let you send a card but it all has to go via the transplant coordinator and apparently a lot of donor families don't want contact because it's too traumatic. So at first I sent one saying how grateful I was. You can only include your Christian name. Anyhow, they sent one back, and we've exchanged a few letters. They don't want to meet and I respect that. It's still so raw for them.'

'And did you find anything out about her? About the donor?'

'Yes. I was right. She was a young woman who was killed in a car crash. She even loved garlic mushrooms and I have cravings for those now. I never liked them before. And I listen to Radio 1, can you believe? That was her favourite.'

'So the dreams about being in the car. Do you think that was how she died?'

'Yes, it was. It was a head-on collision and the other car was on the wrong side of the road. I felt so scared in the dreams.' She touched her heart. 'I feel bad that she went through that.'

'It's an incredible story,' I said.

'Is there anything more you need to know?' She glanced at the door.

'Do you take a drug called Immunoxifan? An immunosuppressant?'

'Yes, I do. Why? Is there a problem? A man from the drug company already asked me that.'

The door was shoved open. Bill walked in and sat on the sofa next to Gaynor. 'It's in her mind,' he said. 'A young woman who was killed in a car crash. It's not that surprising, is it? It's not as if she told us anything we couldn't have guessed.'

'I don't know why you're being so obnoxious.' Gaynor shifted away from Bill. 'It's not a challenge. I'm not trying to win the Randi Prize. I'm telling the inspector how I felt. That's what she wanted to know. There are doctors who believe in this. I've read up on it. They have theories about how it works. The heart even has its own mini-brain.'

Bill made a spluttering noise.

'Have you noticed any change in your wife?' I asked.

'She's a lot more argumentative,' Bill said. 'I think her real personality must be coming out now she's well. It's nothing to do with the donor, that's for sure.'

'Honestly, Bill, you're very irritating.' Gaynor turned to me. 'All I can tell you is what I've experienced. Why would I lie? I'm sure of it. I dreamt her death. Michael Ellis believed me. Even the mice experienced it.'

'What did you say?'

'I don't know the details. You'll have to ask him about it, but he said the same thing was happening in mice.'

★

I drove a few miles from the Harveys' house, pulled over in a lay-by and sat staring at an odd lump of rock that stuck out

213

of the hillside. It looked like an eagle, a dark smudge forming its eye and a crack in the stone outlining a hooked beak. I pictured Gaynor sitting on her sofa, sharing her story with me so eagerly despite her husband's bad attitude. She was clearly suffering from terrible Survivor's Guilt. Maybe this was her way of coping – to imagine that the donor was still *there* in some way, living inside her. That would probably help you feel better.

After Carrie had died, I sometimes used to feel her in the room with me. I'd turn to say something to her, and then it would hit me like a truck that she was gone. Guilt could do strange things to you.

And Bill had a point about there being nothing particularly unusual in Gaynor's story, and nothing easily verifiable. We didn't know if she'd really craved garlic mushrooms before she found out the donor liked them. In fact, there was no proof she thought any of it before she had the information from the donor family.

I remembered an experience with a supposed clairvoyant, when I'd been in my twenties. A friend had dragged me along for moral support. The *Mystic Meg* character had given me no concrete information, but for a while I'd been seduced by it. She'd told me she was in touch with a dead relative of mine. He was called John but oddly he wasn't willing to share his surname. *He wants you to have more confidence in yourself. You're better than you think you are. Live your life to the full. Stop trying to impress people.* She came out with a fair bit of this before I started to wonder why she wouldn't have picked up on Carrie. A huge, gaping hole in my life where my sister should have been, and no mention of it. Just some random relative called John, who talked in platitudes. But my friends were willing to feed her information and then be stunned when she added a dose of flattery and bounced it back at them. People loved to believe.

This had to be the same. It was Gaynor's way of coping, and I didn't have a problem with that. It made a traumatic experience easier to bear. But it was all in her mind. She was more argumentative because previously she'd been too ill to argue. And it couldn't be true about the dreams. She must have found out how her donor died before she had them. Or made some lucky guesses. That was the only explanation.

I did wonder how Immunoxifan fitted into it all. And the mice. I needed to talk to Michael Ellis again. But first I wanted to see Rachel Thornton. What did she know about Elaine Grant? And poor Ollie?

# 18.

Rachel's voice hardly penetrated the front door of her mother's bungalow. 'Who is it?'

'DI Meg Dalton. Can I have a word?'

The door inched open and butted against a chain. Rachel's eyes appeared, flicking to and fro as if she was searching for someone else behind me. Finally, she looked at me, but stared for a moment as if she didn't know who I was.

'Are you alright?' I asked.

'No.' But the chain slid and unlatched. Rachel pulled the door wide and gestured me in.

She locked the front door behind us, before heading down the hallway.

She led me into a dining room at the front of the house. It was dominated by a dark table and upright wooden chairs with stripy green padded seats. 'We'll have to go in here,' she said. 'I'm sleeping in the living room for now. Abbie's in the guest room. I mean, she's sleeping in the guest room. She's out now with my mother. Tea?'

'Please.' I didn't want more sodding tea but sensed it was necessary.

While Rachel bustled in the kitchen, I looked around the

room. It was gloomy, in the manner of traditional dining rooms, as if the pleasure of food had to be offset by the grimness of the surroundings to avoid the risk of too much fun being had.

A sketch pad lay at the end of the table. Someone had written *Abbie's* on it in marker pen, together with a No-Entry sign. Not taking the hint, I tentatively reached over and lifted the cover. A drawing of a cantering horse, its mane flowing out behind it. Very good for a ten-year-old – she'd got the legs and the feet right, which I remembered from my childhood artistic endeavours wasn't easy. I lifted the page but the next was blank, as was the rest of the note-book. I let the cover drop again.

A shiny-veneered dresser housed a set of photographs. A gilded frame surrounded a formally posed Phil and Rachel at their wedding, both looking as if they'd forgotten to turn the gas off. A more casual shot showed two children on a climbing frame – Abbie and another girl. I leant closer and squinted at the girl's faces. Abbie looked wary – her grin toothy but her eyes nervous. The other girl gazed out confidently, with no sense of her future, reminding me of the photos of Carrie from before the cancer. For years I hadn't been able to look at those photos.

'Half of them are dead now.'

I jumped. Rachel clunked the door shut behind her with a foot, put two mugs on the table, and sat opposite me.

I took one of the mugs. 'How are you doing?'

'Someone's watching me again, but I don't expect you to take it seriously.'

'Of course we take it seriously. What have you seen?'

'I just have a feeling someone's watching me.'

I caught her eye. She must have known we could do nothing with that.

'It doesn't matter,' she said. 'I'm probably imagining it.'

217

'Let me know immediately if you see anything definite. Shall I get someone here to keep an eye on the house?'

She settled in her chair. 'No, no, it's fine. I'll let you know if I see anything.'

'I need to ask you a few more questions.'

'Right.' She folded her arms.

'Phil was involved in a trip to the seaside, where a child had an accident, and the child is brain-damaged. Did he share this with you?'

'What?' She sat up straighter. 'You think this is to do with his murder?'

'Not necessarily. But we were told Phil was supervising the children when it happened.'

'No. That's wrong. He told me there'd been an accident but it wasn't his fault. He was with another social worker and she'd had a drink. It was her fault. She was supposed to be supervising the children when it happened.'

I felt events slotting into place.

'Oh God,' Rachel said. 'It was *her*, wasn't it? It's that Karen woman. That's who he was seeing. And he covered up for her. She would have been sacked if it had come out that she'd been drinking, so he took the rap. The stupid *idiot*. You think this could have got him killed?'

If Phil Thornton had covered for Karen, that could be what he'd been threatening to reveal, after their affair ended. That was quite a motive, if it could cause her to lose her husband and her job, and she was already in a financial mess. I felt a little twinge of hope.

'*She* could have killed him,' Rachel said. 'Phil might even have given her a key to our house. He was stupid like that. She could have set Abbie up. Girlfriends often hate the kids – they're inconvenient.'

Could it have been Karen? I ran through it in my head. But there was so much I couldn't explain. Abbie's dreams, the screaming about her father, the drowning.

'Did anyone else have a key?'

Rachel twisted her lower lip. 'We kept one under the stone cat by the door.'

'Even though you thought someone was stalking you?'

She paused a minute. I couldn't read her. 'I forgot it was there.'

'So, anyone could have let themselves in?'

'Yeah.' She sounded defiant, as if she thought I was going to have a go about her lack of security. 'If they looked under the cat.'

'Okay. I need you to talk me through exactly what happened in relation to Abbie's heart, and the approach from Michael Ellis.'

'Why do you need to know about that?' Rachel dug her finger into a scratch in the wood of the dining table. 'Aren't you going to question *her*? It sounds to me like she had a motive.'

'We're looking into it.' I took out my notepad. 'But I also need to know about Abbie's heart. Something was bad enough that you believed your little girl had killed your husband. Talk me through it.'

'But it's more likely to be this woman he had the affair with. I was wrong about Abbie. She must have set her up.'

'Just talk me through it.'

The dining room had a bay window with a wide padded seat, which overlooked a neat front lawn surrounded by a low hedge. In the centre of the lawn was a stone bird bath. A robin perched on it. I had a fleeting daydream about swapping places with him. Flying away over the snow-topped hills and leaving him to sort out this mess.

Rachel sighed loudly, ending my robin-fantasy. 'Okay. Like I said, soon after the transplant, Abbie started having nightmares. She was screaming, *Daddy's a murderer.* Stuff like that. Severe nightmares. It was terrifying. And totally out of character. At first we thought it would go away in time, but it didn't and I was at the end of my tether. Phil too. It was horribly upsetting for him. So I started wondering about all the drugs she was on and if they could be causing problems, because I know night terrors can be a side effect. I found out what they were and googled them. And I found an article about this drug she takes – an anti-rejection drug – and how it had caused psychological problems in some patients. It gave a name – Michael Ellis – so I got in touch with him.'

'You definitely contacted him, rather than the other way round. And Abbie was already having nightmares before you met him?'

'Definitely. Well, unless he'd been in touch with Phil earlier. I'm realising I had no idea what Phil was up to.'

'Okay, so you contacted Michael Ellis.'

'Yes. He won't talk to people now but he was more open then. He was from the company that made the immunosuppressant drugs. And he started asking us these weird questions about Abbie's behaviour.' She wiped a hand over her forehead. 'Anyway, he gave us the impression that the drug *could* be causing her problems. Which I suppose was a relief in a way. We told him about Abbie screaming all these weird, *awful* things, and he was, well, he didn't want to say at first . . . I didn't tell you all this before because, seriously, everyone already thinks I'm mad.' Rachel's face flushed. She looked less scared, more angry.

'It's okay. I don't think you're mad.'

'Alright. Well, Michael Ellis seemed really worried about Abbie. About the effect of that drug.'

'What exactly did he say?'

'He thought the drug might make her be affected by something that had happened to the donor. I know how it sounds, but with all her nightmares and everything, we listened to him. I mean, calling her dad a murderer. Scared of being killed. There was nothing in Abbie's life that could possibly have caused that. And he told us there have been lots of cases where people took memories from their donor. I googled it and he was right.'

'But could Abbie have been remembering something from early childhood, perhaps? Did she ever nearly drown, for example?'

'I didn't know her when she was very young but Phil racked his brains and he couldn't think of anything. And as for her being terrified of him and calling him a murderer . . . it makes no sense. He'd never laid a finger on her. I'm sure of that. And she only started having the dreams after her transplant. And I started to think, maybe something really did happen to the donor child, and that's why she was scared. Because she'd never been scared of Phil. Anyway, we knew she needed help. So we started going to Dr Gibson. We decided to tell him everything. Obviously at first he didn't think it was anything to do with her heart donor. But the nightmares got worse. She was definitely screaming that her dad was a murderer. And she'd never been scared of Phil before. Never. It was awful.'

'And did she scream anything else?'

'*Don't kill me. Daddy's a murderer.* Awful things like that. And then something about water. About drowning.'

'Did you hear all this yourself or did only Phil hear some of it?'

'I heard most of it. I think Phil heard her mention drowning. Honestly, it was terrible.'

'Did she usually call Phil *Daddy*, or *Dad*?'

'Actually she calls him *Dad*, but in the dreams it was *Daddy*. I wondered if the other child, the donor child, called her father *Daddy*.'

A prickle on the back of my neck. A wave of sympathy for this woman who'd had to listen to her child screaming and terrified, thinking her own father was trying to kill her. This woman who'd lost her child and her husband, and who might lose her remaining child too.

'Did Abbie ever seem scared or worried about anyone else or anything else?'

'I don't think so . . . ' Rachel gave me a sudden, sharp look. 'You're taking this seriously. Have you found the donor child? Does her death fit with Abbie's dreams? Oh God . . . '

I hesitated. 'I'm just trying to find out all the facts. When she talked about her daddy being a murderer, is there anyone else she could have been talking about other than Phil?' Rachel licked her lips nervously. 'I wondered if something could have happened with Dr Gibson. I tried to ask Abbie, really carefully, and she doesn't remember anything. But he hypnotised her, and she absolutely screamed when he regressed her. I assumed she was remembering the donor child's death, but then I wondered. Although he seemed fine, not a weirdo, or I would never have let him be alone with her.'

'Did you see a drawing Abbie did when she was hypnotised?'

'No. They don't show you them. Dr Gibson said it was better not to – if she or I saw them, it could consolidate the memories and make them seem more real.'

'And did Abbie ever say any names when she was screaming?'

'Not that I remember. It was hard to tell. Why are you asking all these questions? Do you believe me about the donor heart?'

'Why were you so sure it was her heart that was causing the bad dreams?'

'It all started after her transplant. And then the stuff Michael Ellis said.'

'Did Abbie ever have nightmares after her sister died?'

Rachel jumped. 'No. Um, not really.'

I pictured the top attic window in that strange house of hers. Rachel's daughter falling from it. 'Tell me about what happened to Jess,' I said. 'How exactly did she die?'

Rachel crossed her legs and her arms and hugged herself as if it was cold. 'Why? That was years ago. It's got nothing to do with this.'

'I'm sorry. I need to know.'

She dragged a strand of dark hair across her mouth and spoke in a monotone, as if she'd said this too many times already. 'The girls were playing upstairs. The attic was locked with a padlock and they knew they weren't supposed to go up there. I was out and Phil was downstairs.'

'Phil didn't realise they were up there?'

Rachel sighed. 'I try not to blame him. It was a bad time for him. We'd recently found out that Abbie was going to need a heart transplant. I mean, Phil had known for a couple of years that she would need one at some point, but she'd started having symptoms, so suddenly it was real. I suppose he was distracted.'

'But it was another few years before Abbie had her transplant?'

'She was quite ill by the time she had it. She wouldn't have lasted much longer.'

'It must have been very hard for you.'

Rachel nodded. She didn't seem keen to carry on telling me about Jess.

'So, the girls were playing upstairs?' I said.

'They must have broken the padlock and gone up. I'm not sure which one of them was responsible. Actually, Jess was probably the one who broke the lock but I'm not sure. The cat went up with them – that would have been Abbie's influence.'

'Could she have pets then?'

'Before she was on the immunosuppressant drugs she could. So, they were playing up there, and it doesn't have safe windows. They're old Victorian ones. I mean, that's why we put the lock on. Jess must have leant too far out. Abbie doesn't remember exactly what happened or what she was doing, but she gets very upset. Jess fell.' Rachel pushed her hair back. A tear shone on her cheek.

'I'm sorry,' I said.

A click from the corridor and Rachel jumped from her chair. The thud of the front door closing. 'Mum and Abbie. Are we done?'

'Yes. I need a word with Abbie though.'

Rachel left the room and I heard low voices in the corridor. I leant back in my chair and closed my eyes.

The door banged open, bumping into the back of one of the chairs. I opened my eyes. 'Hello, Patricia.'

Patricia gripped the back of one of the dining room chairs. 'Abbie was terrified in that place. The secure unit. You're not taking her back there, are you?'

'No, I just need a word with her. You can sit in if you like.'

Minxy crept into the room and twined herself around Patricia's ankles.

'What do you want to say to her?'

I smiled. 'If you sit in, you'll find out.'

Patricia tutted and left the room. I leant and wiggled my fingers at Minxy, the universal language for *Come here and I'll stroke your head*. Minxy was familiar with the lingo and walked over and butted my fingers. I rubbed under her chin. She looked up and jumped onto my knee.

Patricia appeared in the doorway and saw Minxy on my knee. Her whole demeanour changed. I could almost hear her thinking, *Oh well, if my cat likes you, you can accuse my granddaughter of murder, you can think my daughter's psychotic . . . whatever you want is fine*. 'Isn't she a lovely cat?' she said.

Minxy's purr filled the room. I nodded. 'Gorgeous.'

'Come on then, Abbie.' Patricia shuffled Abbie forwards. 'Sit down and answer the detective's questions.'

Abbie sat on a chair opposite me and stared with eyes that looked even bigger than before. 'Did I not do it then? I didn't kill Dad?'

My heart felt squeezed in my chest. 'Have you remembered anything else, Abbie? About that night?'

She shook her head glumly.

'Don't worry,' I said.

Minxy stepped off my knee onto the table, leaving behind a spectacular quantity of hair, and headed for Abbie.

'Keep her away from the child,' Patricia said. 'She mustn't get an infection.'

I wasn't sure I could influence Minxy in any way but she responded to my gentle suggestion to return to my knee.

Abbie frowned. 'Is it not my heart then?'

'Your heart's fine.'

She visibly brightened, then sank into her chair again. 'But Dad's still dead. I don't understand . . . I don't know what happened.'

'Abbie, I'm sorry to ask, but do you remember when Jess fell from the window?'

'Oh, come on.' Patricia's tone was sharp. 'Why are you bringing all that back? It's nothing to do with this.'

Abbie looked up at me through her hair. 'I remember a bit. Not much.'

'Could you tell me what happened?'

She shook her head. 'I can't remember exactly.'

'What's the last thing you do remember?'

'We were in the attic and Jess fell and I can't remember anything else. I can't remember anything else.'

'Come on now,' Patricia said. 'She's getting upset. She can't talk about it.'

'No, I can't talk about it,' Abbie said. 'Dad told me.'

'What do you mean, Abbie? Your dad told you not to talk about it?'

Abbie shook her head. She was saying nothing more.

# 19.

There was a message on my mobile from Fiona. Her voice came through clear and bright, despite the iffy signal. 'Elaine Grant's been seeing Harry Gibson. He's her therapist too. And both Karen Jenkins and her husband are alibied out for Sunday night. A neighbour had a camera which covers their driveway. Caught them arguing outside the house early evening, which the neighbour took a dim view of. And then neither of them went out until the next morning. Hope you're having a good weekend. Cheers. Bye!'

Karen Jenkins was alibied out. I suppressed a stab of disappointment and put the phone away. So that was one less alternative to Abbie.

I started the car and set off into the wintry afternoon gloom. My head felt foggy and not up to the job of untangling all the information. There was definitely something going on with Abbie's sister. Why would her dad tell her not to talk about it? I remembered Karen Jenkins starting to say something about it, but then clamming up. Maybe I could get her to spill the beans with a little more persuasion.

And Elaine Grant had been seeing Dr Gibson. Could she have seen his notes on Abbie? Could she even have blackmailed him? Got him to hypnotise Abbie into killing her father? Dr Li hadn't seemed to think that was likely, but nothing in this case was likely.

I would have loved to talk about the case with Jai but he had the day off. He'd be with his new girlfriend and would hardly be delighted to hear from me. I tried to picture him with her. I didn't even know her name, let alone what she looked like. Maybe he'd pleased his family and gone for a Sikh? She was probably beautiful, with big brown eyes.

I slammed my hand against the steering wheel. 'Oh, for God's sake, stop it!' I realised I'd spoken out loud, to myself. I was becoming that person you avoid on the train.

I knew what Jai would say about the case anyway. I heard his voice in my head. *Everything leads to Abbie. Why are you chasing around after these other people? And why won't you even consider that the heart could have affected her? You heard that Gaynor woman saying she'd had dreams from the heart's perspective. Even Dr Li seems to think it's possible.*

I turned the radio on loud. It was still only late afternoon, although the sky seemed to have collapsed onto the hills, pushing the light from the scene.

I knew where I needed to go. I remembered the address from when we'd looked at the CCTV. A quiet middle-class street – the kind where it was okay to shout at your family as long as you kept the windows shut while you did it. There was a good chance she'd be at home herding children at this time.

I drove there and parked under a cherry tree in the wide suburban road.

Karen Jenkins opened her door, clutching the hand of a toddler. A look of alarm flitted across her face. 'Oh,' she said. 'I've got the kids.'

As if to provide further evidence, a shriek ricocheted down the hallway. Something about *Minecraft*.

'Can I come in?' I said.

Karen glanced up the road. 'You'd better. We'll have the Stasi, aka Neighbourhood Watch, on to us. But we're going out. I only have ten minutes.'

'Okay.' I smiled and walked into the hallway. Lego crunched underfoot.

A child of about eight shot into view. 'Mum, it's my turn!' His face was red and tight like a balloon about to burst.

Karen shouted into a room on our left. 'Give your brother a turn.' Then she bellowed up some stairs on our right. 'Look after the boys. I've got Charlie. I need to talk to . . . ' She glanced at me. 'Just look after them.'

She led me and the toddler into a large kitchen and shut the door firmly behind her. 'I wish you'd warned me you were coming. I hope you're not tied in with environmental health. It's like running a zoo here. I don't know how all my friends seem to keep things under control.' The words spilled out in a nervous stream. She paused and removed a toy helicopter from a wooden chair. 'Sit down anyway. Coffee? Tea?' She released the hand of the toddler, who wandered in the direction of a large window overlooking a garden strewn with dead plastic things.

'Tea please,' I said, somewhat unwillingly. I really didn't need more tea. 'And don't worry, it's fine.' I glanced around. Piles of washing and stacks of papers sat on every surface, and toys littered the floor. 'I'm always suspicious of people whose houses are too tidy. So many hours wasted.'

'I just wish I could be a little more in control. But with them . . . ' She gestured to the door. 'Hopeless.' She stuck the kettle on and turned to face me, leaning against the counter. 'Can you believe I've got two-year-old twins. . .' She nodded in the direction of the toddler. 'At my age? Apparently I had double egg follicles in both ovaries or something ridiculously fertile. Like a closing down sale. Buy one, get one free.'

I laughed. The over-share was a good sign, although I was conscious she'd said she only had ten minutes. Still, I couldn't afford to steam-roller my way in and expect her to answer my difficult questions if I refused to drink her tea and discuss her reproductive prowess.

So I chatted while she boiled water and dunked tea bags in chipped mugs, staying away from the tricky subjects, building rapport via our similarly chaotic lives. The nervous babbling calmed a little.

Once the tea was made, Karen sat opposite me and slotted my mug into a space between some (possibly unwashed) socks and a packet of instant rice. I picked up the mug and took a sip.

'What exactly happened with Ollie?' I asked. 'On the trip to the seaside.'

A range of emotions flitted across her face. 'What do you mean?'

'He was injured. The official record says Phil Thornton was supposed to be supervising. But there was more to it than that, wasn't there?'

I glanced at the toddler. He was sitting down and smacking the floor with his palms.

'What do you mean?' Karen said. 'Phil admitted it. He should have been supervising.'

'You'd been drinking, hadn't you? You'd have been sacked.'

She was silent.

'Did Phil threaten to tell your boss what really happened with Ollie?'

'I didn't . . . Oh my God. Do I need a lawyer?'

'I'll need you to come into the Station and make a statement. You'll be entitled to a lawyer.'

'Oh Christ. You're on the wrong track. You've got it wrong. Yes, Phil was threatening to tell everyone it was my fault about Ollie. But I didn't do anything . . . Oh God, I should have told you before. He made me promise not to say anything. I don't know why I stuck to that promise – he'd been a shit to me, threatening to tell everyone about Ollie after he'd said he'd keep it quiet.' She pushed her hair off her face, and I noticed a tiny muscle in her cheek twitching.

I saw the toddler out of the corner of my eye. He stood and reached up towards the counter-top. There was a glass on the side above him. I didn't want to interrupt Karen's revelation, but . . . I jumped up and shifted the glass. 'What should you have told me?'

She didn't seem to have noticed the near-glassing. I wondered about her suitability as a social worker.

'He made me promise,' she said. 'On my mother's grave. It never occurred to me you might think I killed him, for God's sake.'

'You promised, but now he's dead. I think he'd urge you to go back on that promise.'

'Yes, okay. I was protecting Abbie but . . . '

'Just tell me, Karen.'

We sat looking at each other over the piled-high table, clutching our mugs like weapons.

'I was protecting Abbie,' Karen said again. 'Oh God . . . Okay. She pushed her.'

'Who pushed who?'

Karen put her mug down with a shaking hand. 'Abbie pushed Jess out of that window. He only told me recently.'

My wrist went weak for a moment and I spilt a blob of tea on the table. Karen leant forward and wiped it with one of the socks.

'He didn't tell you at the time?' I said.

'No. But recently he thought Rachel might have found out.'

'You'd better tell me exactly what happened.'

'This is what Phil told me. The girls were both six. Abbie had been diagnosed with the same heart condition as Phil and she'd started developing symptoms. She was going to need a transplant at some point, and she got obsessed with the fact that someone had to die for her to get her new heart.'

The toddler bashed his head against the window. And again. What were you supposed to do when they attempted self-harm? Karen didn't seem to have noticed. I winced as he smacked his head harder. I jumped up and grabbed his hand. Led him back to the table, and looked for something he could safely destroy. 'And this was four years ago?' I said. 'A few years before Abbie actually had her transplant?'

'Yes. They knew she'd need one at some point but it wasn't yet critical. Abbie killed Jess to try and keep her dad happy. She thought he was really upset she was going to die, and she killed Jess to try and make it better.'

'She did it for her dad?'

'It's awful, isn't it? But, you know . . . Do you have kids?'

'No.' That was why I had no clue what to do with hers when it head-butted a pane of glass – hadn't she noticed?

'Well, they can get the wrong idea about things at that age, and have some odd stuff going on in their heads. Phil wondered if it had something to do with that horrible folk tale. But I mean, I'm not saying I can imagine my kids doing that, but . . . I kind of can, at that age. They don't fully understand the consequences.'

'No. Six is pretty young.'

'Yes. I mean, they shouldn't even have been in the attic.'

'So, did Abbie tell Phil she pushed Jess deliberately?'

'I think so. I think she ran down and said something like, *Daddy, I've done it. I can have a new heart now.* Like she was expecting him to be pleased with her.'

My insides felt solid and cold. 'Was Rachel there?'

'No. That's the thing, you see. Obviously Phil rushed to Jess and called an ambulance, but she didn't make it. And he told Abbie to say it was an accident and never tell anyone anything different. When the ambulance arrived, everyone just assumed it was an accident.'

'And they kept it secret ever since?'

'Yes. Abbie might even remember it as an accident. You know how you can manipulate kids' memories.'

I pictured Abbie in her grandmother's dining room. What was it she'd said? *I mustn't talk about it. Dad told me.*

'Phil didn't even tell Rachel?'

'No. Terrible, isn't it?'

'But he thought she'd found out?'

The door banged open. A thickset man was silhouetted against the light from the hallway. He marched in and scooped up the toddler. 'For God's sake, Karen, the babysitter will be here in a minute.' He stormed out again, not waiting for Karen to respond, and completely ignoring me.

Karen stood and shifted towards the door. She spoke quietly. 'Phil wondered if Rachel had started to suspect. It was things

Abbie said when she was hypnotised recently. The therapist mentioned them to Rachel and she started asking questions of Phil. That was when he spoke to me. He was quite upset and worried about it all. It was a terrible thing he'd done, and he didn't know what Rachel would do if she found out.'

★

I drove to Hannah's to pick up Hamlet. She swung the door open. 'Come in. Fatso's having some food.'

I followed the piggy guzzling noises through to the kitchen. 'He's not the most polite eater, I'm afraid. He takes his food out of the bowl so he can eat it off the floor.'

'Thanks, Meg. I discovered that. After I didn't put a tray down for him.'

I sat down to wait for Hamlet to finish chucking food on the shiny white floor.

'I bought him some special stuff,' Hannah said. 'I'll get it for you.' She fished a box from the cupboard and shoved it into my hands.

I examined the box. '*Tender morsels of gourmet-roasted beef in a rich sauce.* Blimey, I wish I ate that well.'

'I did hear about a woman who bought dog food accidentally instead of pie filling,' Hannah said. 'Meaty chunks. Said it made a lovely Cornish pasty. I could whip us up some now if you like. Are you staying for tea?'

'Not if you're going to make me eat Cat Food Pasties.'

'Just a cuppa then?'

'No. If I have to drink any more tea, I'll need a catheter. What are you up to anyway?'

'A night with the girls.' A reminder that she had plenty of

other friends. I needed to make some more for myself. Stop working all the time.

I waited for Hamlet to finish dining, and persuaded him into his carrier. He gave me a look of utter loathing.

Hannah laughed. 'Oh dear. Look at his little face.'

'He's such a prima donna.' It came over me in a wave how much I loved the little sod. I'd become a cliché. *Single-woman-with-cat.* Supposedly this made me very sad, but in reality I wasn't. I certainly wouldn't swap for Karen's suicidal offspring and grumpy husband. It would be nice if I could afford a better house for us, with windows that closed and heating that worked, but I liked Hamlet's company. And if I died alone and he chose to eat me, that was a sensible use of resources as far as I was concerned.

★

It was snowing again on the way home – fat flakes that danced in my headlights like a threat but melted as soon as they hit the tarmac. I glanced at the car's temperature gauge. Two degrees.

I arrived at the cottage and walked into the hallway. I needed to get my life in order. The clutter of books, the cobwebs lacing the corners of the rooms, the unread bills perched on the hall book-case – they reminded me how out-of-control things had become.

I released Hamlet from his carrier, swerved into the living room and put the TV on loud. I didn't care what was on. In fact, the more puerile the better. Bring on Simon Cowell or the dim bloke from Essex.

I went through to the kitchen, turning the thermostat up on the way, more in hope than in expectation.

I hadn't eaten for hours. I pulled open the fridge door. Not good. I wasn't going to do much domestic-goddessing with a few mouldering carrots, a piece of cheese, a bottle of cheap Pinot Grigio, and one can of Pedigree bitter. The milk was fresh though. I sorted myself out some cereal and a glass of wine. All major food groups catered for.

I knew I shouldn't contact Jai. It was his day off.

I paced the kitchen, clutching my bowl of muesli. Sat back down. Pushed the bowl aside. Picked up my phone and stared at the screen.

I sent Jai a text. *Are you busy? No problem if you are but found out something interesting. Would be helpful to talk it through.*

A reply came shooting back. *No. Watching crap. Could pop over to discuss?*

I paused. Went and switched the loud TV off so I could think. I'd only imagined a phone call. I hadn't expected him to come over. It was a Saturday evening. How did this fit in with the new relationship? Surely he should be with her.

Another text from Jai. *Suki is out with the girls so she doesn't care, if that's what you're worried about.*

The name sounded like a Sikh. No doubt gorgeous with perfect skin. Jai obviously thought she'd see me as so little of a threat that that she wouldn't mind.

I typed a reply. *OK, that would be good. Head is spinning with it all. Whenever convenient for you, but don't expect food!*

My finger hovered above the keyboard. I pressed send.

# 20.

Jai brushed snow from his coat and shoved a large pizza box into my hands. 'It's snowing again. Veggie something or other.'

'Brilliant. Amazing. Thanks so much, Jai.'

'Yeah, I've seen inside your fridge.'

I led Jai through to the kitchen. 'Are you okay in here? I think it's warmer.' I gestured towards my table and chairs, still orange pine, and not painted in a sophisticated neutral as per my plan. 'Do you want a drink?'

Jai eased himself onto one of the chairs. 'I suppose I could have one beer. If you're going to make me think about the case.' He opened the pizza box and grabbed a slice.

'I've only got one beer.' I poured the Pedigree into a pint glass with all the finesse of a former (very bad) barmaid.

Jai took the glass and glugged a foamy mouthful. 'Where's the little porker?'

'You mean my sleek and beautiful cat?' I glanced out of the window at the snow, the flakes shining in the light from the kitchen. 'Probably buggered off to get some freedom. He's been trapped inside at Hannah's so he probably hates me.'

'You brute.' Jai gulped more beer. 'So, what have you found out?'

I took a mouthful of pizza, dropping a lump of mushroom on the table and picking it off again, probably with orange varnish attached. 'Did you notice that Rachel, Abbie and Karen the girlfriend all clammed up when they were talking about the dead sister – you know, the one who fell from the window?'

'Clammed up? They never really un-clammed did they?'

'They did a bit. Anyway, I went to talk to Karen again.' I took a sip of wine. It tasted like nectar. 'She told me Abbie pushed her sister out of the window.'

Jai slopped beer onto the table. 'Jesus.' He reached for some kitchen roll and dabbed at his spillage. 'So, Abbie isn't a little angel. She could have killed her father too?'

'That's one interpretation. Don't worry about the beer, it might get some of the varnish off.'

'Oh, don't tell me you're still going to find another explanation?' He gave the table another wipe. 'No, it seems to be making it even oranger. Maybe bright orange pine will come back in?'

'I doubt it. And no, I don't think she's a little angel but assuming it's true, she was only six when she pushed Jess.'

'What the hell happened, and how did Karen know about it?'

I explained what Karen had told me.

'Oh. I get it. Abbie killed Rachel's kid. Phil covered it up. Rachel found out so she killed Phil and framed Abbie.'

I seemed to have finished my wine. 'I wanted to run that past you, at least.' Would it be rude to have another drink when Jai had to drive home? I glanced out of the window again. The snowflakes looked fluffy and weirdly some of them seemed to be drifting up rather than down.

The cat flap banged open. Hamlet charged into the kitchen and stared at me.

I stooped to stroke him, then sorted him out some more of the gourmet cat food Hannah had treated him to. He purred ferociously, his wet hair standing out in comical little tufts as he stuffed it down.

'Funny little bugger, isn't he?' Jai gulped his beer. 'So, if Rachel did it, why did she cover up for Abbie at the start?'

'I'm not sure. Maybe once she'd done it, she regretted it? Or maybe it was a double bluff?'

'She's very clever if she did that.'

'She is clever. She's an accountant, remember. She's capable of strategic thinking. And it's the perfect revenge, isn't it? Abbie gets done for murder, albeit not the murder she committed.'

'How would Dr Gibson fit into this?'

'I don't know. And it doesn't explain Ben and Buddy, and the pink spotty swimming costume.' I chewed the inside of my lip. 'Jai, don't take this the wrong way, but you could stay over if you want? It's snowing badly now, and then you could have a glass of wine and I wouldn't feel so bad about sitting here guzzling the stuff.'

Jai grinned. 'I'd be doing you a big favour?'

'I don't want to cause any trouble with you and Suki though.'

'Why? Should she be worried?'

'No. Of course not. Forget it. Get stranded in the snow and die of hypothermia.'

'Oh, well, if you put it like that. Have you still got those horrendous clothes you lent me after you nearly got me killed in a flooded cave? They'd do as nightwear.'

'Yes. Very fetching they were too. And the spare bed's clear. If you just jump from the landing over the books, you land right on it.'

'Roll over, the Hilton. Crack open another bottle.'

239

'Here, have some of this. I'll stick another one in the freezer to cool down.' I reached for a second glass and poured Jai some of the cheap Pinot. 'So what do you think about Rachel?'

Jai settled more deeply into his chair. I decided we'd stay in the kitchen. It felt more friend-zone. And I'd keep us on the wine and off the gin, even though it was Saturday night. I could be so sensible at times.

'It's possible.' Jai examined a thumbnail intently and then sighed to indicate a major subject change. 'I'm finding it difficult with Suki,' he said. 'I really like her but it's hard.'

'Oh.' I needed more wine if I was going to have this conversation. Or did I need less wine?

Hamlet eased himself out of the cat-flap again. Obviously couldn't cope with the tension.

'She doesn't understand. What it's like being a cop, I mean. And I'm not sure she gets my humour.'

'Your humour is a pretty niche product.' Maybe I shouldn't have said that. 'She might learn to love it. It's probably an acquired taste, like beer or olives. I had to make myself like beer at uni. I'm not sure why I bothered.' Now I was gibbering.

He gave me a wry smile.

I knew I should shut up and leave the subject alone, but I couldn't do it. 'Is she a Sikh?'

'Yes. And my parents like her, so at least that side of things is easy. I'm not sure why, because she's quite modern – plucked and shaved and generally un-devout – but I suppose she puts on a good act for the olds.'

'Are they still bothered about that stuff? I mean, you've cut your hair anyway . . . Is it different standards for women, as usual, or have they not totally given up on you?'

'No, they have. Pretty much. After I married Linda, I dropped the pretence. When I was younger, I didn't have the nerve to fight with them about it. They turned up for an unexpected visit once when I was at uni and my friends had to keep them talking while I hid the beer bottles and put the bloody turban on because I couldn't face the argument. They thought my friends were the most sociable teenagers in England.'

'Oh God, I can imagine.'

'The state of my student house, I was lucky the damn turban hadn't been chewed up by mice and used as a nest. I'm not sure it looked quite right, but they didn't say anything.'

'I can't picture you in a turban.' I took a gulp of wine.

He looked towards the window, now half covered with a precarious film of snow. 'I don't know how we're supposed to make relationships work in our job.'

'Most of us don't.'

'I think she wants the whole marriage and kids thing, you know? I don't want to lose her, but . . . Did I tell you Linda had met someone new? A lawyer, of all things.'

'I'd imagine that would suit her. I never understood why she went for you.'

'Oh, thanks Meg, very good to hear.'

'I don't mean it like that, but she always seemed so status-driven. She needs to be with someone who cruises around in a Porsche and stays in the Dorchester.'

'You're probably right. I'm sure Mr Pretentious Lawyer will suit her fine.' Jai's voice pitched into vulnerable. 'But what if the kids start to think of him as their dad?'

'They won't. He's probably a total nob.'

Jai laughed. 'No doubt. I haven't met him yet. So anyway,

it's already complicated enough. I don't want to be thinking about more kids with Suki.'

'Blimey, Jai, I thought you'd only just met her.'

His expression was glum. 'Women in their thirties like to move fast.'

I knocked back a bit more wine and decided to go *meta*. 'Jai, I'm finding this conversation a bit tricky. Especially after offering you a bed for the night and giving you beer and wine. I don't want you to think I'm trying to get my thirty-something claws into you. Because I'm really not. I have no biological clock – or if I do, it's buried in a kind of concrete bunker like decaying nuclear waste, and it doesn't tick – well, not audibly, especially after experiencing that lemming-like toddler today. And I'm actually happy single, despite Hannah's best efforts to hook me up with reasonably successful but always slightly unhinged men on the internet. Which, incidentally, I've decided she only does to make her life more interesting.'

Jai laughed. 'Okay, we're fine. You're clearly a lesbian.'

'Perfect. I'm happy with that. Talk to me on that basis.'

'I've already got two kids and an obnoxious ex-wife, and I'm not sure I want any more right now.'

'Have you told Suki that? The kids bit, I mean. I'm sure she'd be fine about taking it slowly if she really likes you.'

'Maybe I haven't made it clear enough.'

I fished the now-chilled wine from the freezer and topped our glasses up. It wasn't even the same wine. Classy. 'Sounds like you need a proper chat with her.'

Jai groaned. 'I know. What about you? Any of these unhinged men look promising?'

I waved the thought of them aside. 'In a word, no.' I caught Jai's eye. Looked down into my glass and swirled the wine around. 'I'm taking my gran's advice and staying single and care-free. Well, single anyway.'

'How's your gran doing?'

'She's kind of rallied a bit.' I felt a wave of misery. For just a moment, I wanted to be hugged and told it was okay, even though it clearly wasn't. 'But we have to take her. If we don't do it next week, it's not going to happen, and then she could have the most awful death.'

'I'm sorry. It sounds horrible. I'm not trying to get rid of you but are you sure you don't want to take a few extra days off?'

'It'll be fine. We'll bring Rachel in on Monday. Maybe if we confront her with what we know about Abbie pushing Jess, she'll confess and we can wrap it all up.'

Jai looked at me for a moment, then sighed and took a deep gulp of wine. 'Maybe. Do you think Rachel made up all the heart stuff then? How would she know about the donor child's details?'

'I don't know. There are still lots of questions. And we only have Karen's word for all this, of course. We need to talk to Rachel.'

'It's a bizarre thing for a child to do. Pushing her sister from the window.'

'Not compared to all the other stuff that poor kid's been accused of. And it sounds like she did it to make her dad happy. To make him happy, she needed a new heart.' I wondered what I'd have done as a kid to keep my dad happy. Sometimes it had felt like the most important thing in the world. Might I have pushed someone out of a window if I thought it would please him? I couldn't rule it out.

'But why kill her sister? Why did she think that to be given a new heart, you had to kill someone?'

'I don't know,' I said. 'Maybe that's what we need to find out.'

*

It was one o'clock in the morning, the wine was gone, and fortunately I didn't have another bottle. We'd slipped into the timeshift that happens when you drink. It was ten, then suddenly one. I needed to get to bed before we entered the second phase and found ourselves at three.

'Do you want to use the bathroom first?' I said. 'There's a new toothbrush in the cabinet.'

Jai stood. 'Thanks, Meg.' He brushed into me on his way past. Paused a moment. Shifted slightly towards me. I held my breath.

Hamlet crashed through the cat flap and stood centre-stage. He let out a blood-curdling yowl.

Jai leaped away from me as if he'd stuck his finger in a mains circuit.

'Jesus, Hamlet,' I said, heart pounding. I turned to Jai. 'He fights with the local tomcats. Sorry.'

Jai sighed. 'Don't worry. I'll use the bathroom while you calm him down.'

*

I was at a festival, trying to find a toilet. They were all full, or impossibly filthy. I stumbled around. My phone was ringing. When I tried to answer it, nothing happened. It just kept ringing. I stabbed at the green symbol but it rang louder and louder.

My eyes popped open. The clock said 06.30. I groaned. My

phone was on the bedside table, ringing, vibrating, and flashing a blue light. I reached and pulled it to my ear.

A woman's voice. High-pitched and upset. The words tumbling out on top of one another. 'She's tried to kill her!' Then something incoherent. 'Unconscious . . . ambulance.'

# 21.

I wrenched myself out from under the duvet and sat on the side of the bed. My breath came fast. I felt a sick crunching in my stomach. 'Please,' I said. 'Take it slowly. First, who are you?'

'Patricia! Rachel's mum.' Something buzzed in the distance at her end. I heard a crash that sounded like her dropping the phone, and I was cut off. I called back but it went to voicemail.

I jumped up and rummaged for clothes. Dragged on something that was hanging over the back of the chair. Shouted to Jai while standing on one leg clawing a sock onto my foot. No response.

I ran and bashed on the spare room door. 'Jai! Get up!'

His bleary face appeared. 'What on earth?'

'I've had a phone call from Rachel's mum. She said *She's tried to kill her.*'

'Oh shit.' He retreated and reappeared moments later wearing yesterday's clothes. 'Shit. Does she mean Rachel? Has she tried to kill Abbie?'

'She didn't say. She was very upset.'

I limped downstairs with Jai hot on my tail.

His voice was loud, and close behind. 'Maybe she decided yesterday that you weren't going to arrest Abbie. Her plan hadn't worked. If only we'd done something last night.'

'I know. I know.' I felt ready to throw up at the thought that Abbie had been hurt because of me. How could I have been so slack? *Bring her in on Monday.* Was I mad?

'We'd better get over there,' Jai said. 'Do you need anything to eat?'

'No. I'll puke if I try to eat. We should go in separate cars.' I grabbed my keys from the overflowing bookshelf, and pulled open the front door. 'Oh, fabulous.'

Snow carpeted the road, the cobbles showing through only where cars had driven over them. The world felt muted like a film with the sound turned down. Flakes were drifting from the sky.

'Will your car be okay?' Jai said. 'It wasn't so great yesterday. We should probably go together, you know. If anything happens . . .'

'What if Craig's there?'

'Bugger him. I don't care. We've done nothing wrong.'

'Come on then. Let's go in yours.' Although I was a stalwart defender of my little car, Jai's had functioning windscreen wipers and heating.

Jai drove at a speed which may have risked innocent road users, and I sat in the passenger seat and beat myself up. Poor Abbie. Even if she had pushed her sister, she'd only been six. She couldn't have properly understood the implications. I'd let her down. I squeezed my eyes shut and shook my head rapidly as if to punish my brain for its stupidity and bad judgement.

By the time we arrived, the ambulance had been and gone, and a uniformed PC stood guarding the door. 'They've taken her off in the ambulance,' he said. 'Her mother's gone with her.'

'But she's a suspect.'

'What? The old dear?'

'No. The younger woman.'

What was the matter with me? My brain was chugging at steam-powered speed. I glanced at Jai. 'Oh,' I said. 'Where's the child?'

'She's inside, with another PC.'

★

Abbie sat on one of the stiff-backed dining room chairs and sobbed. A male PC sat opposite her looking desperate. When I walked in, Abbie's head shot up and she shrieked. 'It was in my hand!' She grabbed at her hair, pulling out a few strands. 'In my hand, with blood on it.'

I sat on the chair next to her. 'It's okay, Abbie. Tell me what happened.'

Her voice came out in a high-pitched wail. 'I'm evil. I can't help it.'

'What happened, Abbie?'

She jumped from the chair and ran to the bay window which overlooked the road. She spoke through sobs. 'Where's Mum? Where've they taken her?'

I walked over and stood beside her. 'She's gone to hospital.' I resisted the temptation to say she'd be okay. I didn't know if she'd be okay.

Abbie turned to face me. Gulped down her tears. 'It's me,' she said. 'You didn't think it was me, but it was. In the night. I can't remember.'

The PC spoke in a monotone. 'The victim's mother found a piece of rock, amethyst, next to the child's hand this morning, with blood on it. The victim had been hit on the head with the rock.'

I remembered the purple amethyst by Abbie's bed in the

248

house in the woods. Light enough for a child to carry but solid enough to give someone a nasty thump. 'Is it your crystal, Abbie?'

She nodded, and positioned her skinny body so she was sitting on the wide windowsill, looking out. She'd stopped crying but her face was smeared with tears.

'Do you remember anything?'

She stared out of the window at the snow-covered garden. 'I woke up with it by my hand.'

'Can I see your hand?'

She turned and held it to me, passively. There was a smear of blood on her palm.

She pulled her hand back and looked right into my eyes. 'What's wrong with me?'

★

I left Abbie with the PC and headed for the living room at the back of the house, where Rachel had been sleeping. I bumped into Craig in the hall. 'Oh,' I said. 'Hi, Craig.'

'Hoping I wouldn't turn up?'

He was standing too close. Craig had no concept of personal space. If he'd been a dog, other dogs would have bitten him.

'So,' he said. 'It turns out the kid did it after all?'

We still didn't know that, but I was damned if I was sticking my neck out again. 'She may have done,' I said.

'Is there anything you'd like to say to me?'

'Oh yes, Craig, there's lots I'd like to say to you.' I squeezed past him and into the living room. The velour sofa and chairs had been shoved up against windows overlooking a conifer-hedged back garden, and one of the casements was open.

Rachel always slept with the window open. An air-bed took up most of the remaining floor space.

There wasn't a lot of blood – just a few smears on the pillow case.

I realised Craig was behind me again. 'Why won't you admit you were wrong? You made the wrong call. You let the kid out, and she was dangerous. Everyone knew she'd done it except you. And now she's done it again.'

I spun round. He smelt of cheap aftershave and mouthwash, with a subtle hint of male sweat. 'Did you predict this, Craig, or is this all with the benefit of hindsight? Because I don't remember you saying she posed a threat to anyone else. Can you remind me? No, actually, don't bother – ' I stopped myself. I'd been going to say he'd only lie about that too. But I remembered Hannah's advice.

'It was bloody obvious.' Craig turned and stamped out of the room.

Of course, the sickening truth was that he was right. I'd made the decision and I'd got it wrong. Did he think I didn't know that?

★

Jai drove with exaggerated care, pretending he was concentrating too hard to talk.

'Are you alright if I wind the window down a bit?' I said.

Jai shot me a perplexed look. 'That white stuff's snow.'

'I'm too hot.'

'Okay,' he said warily, as if dealing with someone unstable.

I wound the window down and stuck my arm into the icy air.

'Fuck,' I said.

'We couldn't have predicted she'd attack her mum. It was her dad she was dreaming about.'

How did he manage to stay so balanced? Bad things just slid off him. Perhaps because it was my responsibility, not his.

I retracted my arm and wound the window up a bit, leaving a couple of inches at the top. 'Why do we still say *wind* the window, when it's been all buttons for years?' I said.

'Has your car got automatic windows?' Jai said. 'It barely has windscreen wipers.'

He was being mean again. That was a good sign. 'I didn't even think she'd killed her dad.'

He came straight back at me. 'What do you think now?'

'I suppose she must have done. I cocked up.'

I looked round at Jai's profile. His lips moved as if he was about to say something, but nothing came out.

'What were you going to say?'

He shrugged. 'Doesn't matter.'

'No. Go on.'

'Okay.' His voice was quiet. Almost drowned out by the tyres on the slushy road. 'You're still not convinced it's Abbie, are you?'

The road had become a tree-lined tunnel, the snow sitting on the branches overhead and making it so dark it almost felt like dusk. Was Jai right? Was I still not convinced? I'd thought I was. I'd been doing a solid job of berating myself for getting it wrong. But had I got it wrong? 'There are still some questions in my mind,' I said. 'Anyone could have climbed through the window into the room Rachel was sleeping in. And they were all on sleeping pills.'

'Oh, for God's sake, Meg!' Tendons stood out on Jai's hands as he gripped the wheel. 'And can you shut that bloody window.'

I shut the window. 'Drop me at my house. I'll pick up my car.'

'Okay.' Jai sighed. 'I'm sorry, but I think you're refusing to see what's in front of you. I just think you're a bit too attached to Abbie. Don't you agree?'

I shouldn't have shared so much with Jai. What did I really know about him? Fell out with parents over marrying an English girl; parents proved right when English girl turned out to be crazy cow; interminable custody battles; new relationship with Sikh version of the same. It wasn't that he didn't talk. But nothing deep. Nothing I could hurl in his face and say, *You're not thinking rationally because of your screwed-up childhood.*

'No, Sigmund fucking Freud,' I said. 'I don't think I'm too attached to Abbie.'

# 22.

'Sit down, Meg.' Richard scowled at me.

'No, I – '

'Sit down please.'

I sat down. This had the benefit that as I sank into the chair I could see less and less of Richard, behind his piles of files and cacti.

'Right.' He slammed his elbows onto his desk. 'Can we wrap this one up now? We must have enough evidence that the girl did it. She's attacked her mother as well, for God's sake.'

'I know the evidence points that way. And she doesn't deny it. But I still have some concerns about – '

'Get it to the CPS and get her charged. We're already in a mess about why we let her out. Once the press get hold of this . . . ' He wiped his forehead. 'And it'll be all over Twitter and Insta-bloody-whatever-it-is in no time. Christ almighty.'

'Shouldn't we look into it a bit more? I mean, keep her in custody, yes, but . . . '

'But what, Meg? This has gone far enough. She admits she did it. She was found with a knife in her hand, and now she's been found with a rock in her hand. What more do you want? It's not our problem if the motive's a bit odd.'

I clawed myself out of the lower regions of the chair. 'It is our problem if she didn't do it.'

'We've wasted enough time. Get her charged and get it wrapped up.'

★

Back at my desk, my mobile phone rang. Michael Ellis, the immunosuppressant man.

I snatched it up. 'Hello?'

'Do you want to know what's going on with Abbie Thornton?'

I could see Craig's shadow. He was hovering by my door. I'd thought by coming in on Sunday, I'd at least escape Craig – he'd probably come in specially to watch me suffer. I spoke quietly into the phone. 'Do you know what's going on?'

'I'll meet you if you come alone. No other cops and not that psychiatrist either. I mean it.'

I flipped my eyes to Craig. 'Where do you want to meet?'

'The Cat and Fiddle car park.'

'But, Michael, it's snowing again. My car might not even make it up there.'

'We go in mine then.'

'I can't do that.'

'Deal's off then. I'm not talking. Do you want to know what the pattern was? Which mice turned into killers and what that means for Abbie Thornton? And who else has taken Immunoxifan? I have details. I don't care if you know. I'm past caring if there are other . . . incidents. I'm just trying to keep my head down and not get killed.'

I walked to the far end of my room and put my hand around the microphone as I spoke. 'Michael, you need to let

254

us help you. If you think someone's trying to kill you.' Again I wondered if he was completely deranged. But he was the only person who seemed to have any explanation for what had gone on with Abbie, and he'd originated the theory about her heart. Whether Abbie was the killer or not, Michael Ellis was involved.

'No deal,' he said. 'I'm changing my number. You won't be able to contact me again.'

'Hold on.' I spoke as firmly as I could, whilst keeping my voice down. 'Where are you now?'

'Near the pet cemetery at Harpur Hill.'

I didn't just *want* to know what was going on with Abbie. I was practically bleeding with my desperation to know. I wanted to know like an addict wants heroin. 'Pick me up from the car park by the chip shop in twenty minutes.'

I put the phone down, shocked at what I was planning to do. Richard would go bonkers if he found out. Was I making some stupid attempt to redeem myself? To prove it wasn't really Abbie's fault, even if she had killed her father? To stop other people who'd taken Immunoxifan from doing anything wrong? Would that go some way to offsetting what I'd let Abbie do?

I aborted the amateur psychoanalysis of myself, made sure I had my radio and my phone, both fully charged, and sneaked out.

Once at the chip shop car park, I sat with the engine running and waited for Michael Ellis. I texted Fiona brief details of what I was doing, so they'd stand a chance of finding my decaying corpse if it all went wrong.

Ellis turned up on time, in a Land Rover.

I knew I was being rash, but I had to find out what he knew about Abbie. I climbed into his car. 'Are you sure it's a good idea to go to the second highest pub in England in this weather?'

He made a throat-slitting gesture and whispered, 'Car could be bugged. I'd prefer to talk up on the moors where we can see them coming.'

If he was psychotic, did he pose any threat to me? It seemed unlikely. He didn't think I was out to get him or he wouldn't have agreed to see me. Richard wouldn't see it like that. 'Okay. Let's go.'

We drove in silence through the swirling snow. He was right that we'd have the moors to ourselves. No sane person would be up there in this.

Finally he pulled up in the car park by the Cat and Fiddle.

I glanced at the surroundings and pictured the headline. *Detective Inspector dies of exposure after paranoid schizophrenic leads her onto deserted moor.*

'Can I interest you in talking to me inside the pub rather than on a bleak hillside in a snowstorm?' I said. Actually, it would probably be *Disgraced Detective Inspector. Deluded? Deranged?* There was a rich vein of alliterative headlines to tap.

'They might have followed us,' Michael said. 'I'd rather be in the open where we can see them. And it's stopped snowing.'

I sighed and pulled my hat over my ears. 'Okay.'

Michael led me over the road and onto a bridleway that crossed the moor. The path was invisible in the snow but he seemed to know where he was going. I slipped and my foot plunged into a bog, up to my ankle. I swore under my breath.

'You do know you're putting yourself in danger,' he said. 'Being seen with me.'

I glanced behind me. I was picking up on his paranoia now. 'Do you really think they'd harm you? Surely if there's a genuine problem with their drug, they'd want to know about it.'

His laugh cut through the thick air, loud and humourless. It had an edge of something from a horror film. 'Oh,' he said. 'That's funny. That's genuinely funny.'

'Okay, okay.' I felt a little sulky, like a kid who was being teased. 'What's so funny?'

'You think a drug company automatically wants to know if there's a problem with its drug.'

'Well, I mean, I know they covered up the problems with Thalidomide, but that was decades ago and surely nowadays . . . Even just to avoid getting sued. I'm not saying they'd necessarily do it for ethical reasons.' The bog water had seeped into my boots, my toes squelching in sodden socks.

'Do you know about statins?'

'Anti-cholesterol drugs? They want to put my mum on them.'

'Look them up. Look for any evidence that they help women. Then ask yourself why your mum's being put on them, when they have very significant side effects.'

I wondered if he was against the whole pharmaceutical industry. Maybe he'd been pushed out of his company, and now he wanted revenge. Were the claims about Immunoxifan even true?

'What was the pattern, Michael? Gaynor Harvey said the mice were affected by cellular memory too. What happened? Why did they kill their cage mates?'

Michael looked behind him. Paused a second, and glanced at me. 'Are you sure you want to know? There are people who do *not* want this information out there.'

I couldn't help glancing around at the snow-covered moor. I pulled my coat tight and shivered. 'Just tell me.'

He looked at me through narrowed eyes. 'Okay. I'll tell you. Mice which hadn't had a heart transplant weren't affected. We worked on other transplants and none of these mice became aggressive. And mice which hadn't been given Immunoxifan weren't affected either. But even out of the heart transplant mice which had been given Immunoxifan, not all of those were affected. Only a minority in fact. I eventually realised . . . You probably won't believe me. My colleagues didn't. Although after what's happened with Abbie Thornton . . . '

'Try me,' I said. The wind picked up some snow from the ground and blasted it in our faces.

Michael kept walking. We were quite a way from the pub now. 'Okay,' he said. 'It seemed to depend on what had happened to the donor mice before they were killed.'

I hurried to keep up, slipping into a rut. 'What do you mean?'

'I mean the manner in which the donor mice died was a factor.'

'Didn't they all die the same way?'

'No. Some of the mice had a more traumatic death than others. Not deliberately of course. Although I wonder if in the future, they'll have to add that to the tests . . . '

'Christ, let's hope not for the poor mice's sake.'

The wind dulled Michael's words. 'It's always the case,' he said, 'that certain lab technicians are better with the mice than others. Some are gentle, some less so. I'm afraid some are downright sadistic.'

'Hold on,' I said. 'I have a dodgy ankle.' It was throbbing from running to help Tom the day before.

He didn't slow down. 'We do try to get rid of them – the cruel lab techs – but we had one . . . You know nowadays, you have to give them no end of warnings and so on. This man – I don't know exactly what he did but he always upset and scared the mice.'

I felt a creeping coldness at the back of my neck as if snow had fallen inside my clothes. 'Go on.'

Michael stopped and looked at me. His eyes were bloodshot. 'All the mice that killed their cage-mates had received hearts from mice that were anaesthetised by this man before surgery. So we can assume they had traumatic deaths, or at least traumatic last memories. And they'd also all had Immunoxifan.'

'What does that mean?'

Michael shrugged. 'I'm just telling you what I observed.'

'The mice who turned violent were the ones whose donors had had traumatic deaths. As if something from the traumatic death had been transferred with the heart? Is that what you concluded?'

Michael nodded. 'I'm afraid so. The recipient mice which had turned violent had nothing else in common with each other. And they were all handled by different technicians.'

'So if this applies to people . . . '

'Yes?'

'You're saying that if a heart donor had a traumatic death, it could make the recipient of their heart violent?'

'If they'd taken Immunoxifan, yes.'

'But that's terrifying,' I said. 'Why wasn't it made public?'

'Do you know much about the way drug companies operate?'

'Not really, no.'

'Did you know that about half of all clinical trials aren't even published?'

'I did read something about that.'

'Which ones do you think *are* published?'

259

'I'm guessing the ones that make the drugs look effective.'

'On the whole. I can't believe I was ever part of that racket. It makes me sick now.'

'But if they thought a drug might make people violent? Surely that wouldn't be covered up?'

Michael gave me a pitying look. 'It was only mice that became violent, of course. They didn't know it would apply to humans.'

'But if they think mice are similar enough to people to do the trials on them – surely they couldn't discount side effects?'

'You think that? Oh, how sweet. It's amazing how mice can transform between *similar to humans* and *not similar to humans* depending on what point is to be made.'

'I was always sceptical about animal experiments,' I muttered. 'Weren't they worried something might happen? That a person might . . . do something?'

'They probably thought that a person would be better able to control their behaviour.'

'Hollow laughs all round,' I said.

Michael smiled. 'I know. How ridiculous. And it also doesn't take into account that the person could be a child, or could sleepwalk.'

The snow was disorientating. I had a moment of vertigo and felt the ground shift towards me. Had Abbie really killed her father because of this drug, and her donor heart?

'You believe Abbie was affected by something that happened to her donor? You think the heart was causing her nightmares?'

'I think it's a possibility.'

'Do you really think a heart transplant from a traumatised donor together with Immunoxifan could make someone a murderer?'

'I had hoped not.'

My breath puffed into the cold air. 'Do you have a list of patients who've taken Immunoxifan?'

Michael reached into his pocket. 'You met Gaynor Harvey? She's one, but I'm not concerned about her.'

My phone beeped. A text must have come through in one of the occasional-signal-moments that appeared in this area, just to torment you. 'Hang on,' I turned away to read the text. It was from Fiona.

*Are you OK? I found out Michael Ellis shorted shares in own company after he left.*

I stared at the screen. My financial experience mainly consisted of Mum telling me to improve my pension, but I had watched the film, *The Big Short*. I knew enough to realise that if Michael had shorted shares in his own company, he made money if the company failed. He'd effectively betted on the value of his company declining.

My understanding shifted. If Michael wanted the company to fail, could I believe anything he was saying?

# 23.

I shoved the phone out of sight. I couldn't text back without Michael seeing and I didn't want that. 'Shall we walk back to the car?' I took a step in that direction.

'What was the text?' Michael looked at my pocket. 'Someone's told you something. Trying to discredit me or frame me. I can see it in your face.'

I was on a snow-covered, deserted moor, my only transport Michael's car. My heart pattered unevenly. I reached into my pocket and felt my radio. If I pressed the orange button, a pack of cops would hot-foot it here. I ran my finger over it.

Michael did the same scan I'd done. Deserted moor. 'They'll be watching us,' he said.

I moved my finger to the side of the button, thinking about all the questions I'd have to answer if I summoned help. I was already on a warning.

I shuffled from one freezing foot to the other, eyeing the distance to the pub.

Something grabbed my arm and yanked it from my pocket. The arm that should have been able to reach the orange button, if Michael hadn't been holding it in a limpet grip.

'What is it? What have they told you?'

'Nothing. Let me go.'

He didn't let me go. 'What have they said? You can't trust them.'

'You're not doing yourself any favours here.' My voice sounded calm, but my pulse was racing.

I could stab him in the eyes, kick him in the balls or shins, I could –

He gripped my arm tighter. 'They're trying to discredit me. I'm the innocent one here.'

'Michael, let go of my arm.'

He seemed to be on the edge of a complete melt-down, wild eyes flitting to and fro, fingers stabbing into me, his voice high and shaky. 'Tell me you believe me.'

I cursed myself for being so reckless. I always shouted at the TV when detectives chose to confront the potential homicidal maniac alone on a deserted moor. I certainly wasn't going to challenge him. 'I believe you.' I looked pointedly at his hand on my arm.

'I haven't done anything wrong. I just told the truth.' He stared into my eyes and blinked several times in quick succession. Didn't psychopaths do that? Then he dropped my arm and jumped back.

'That's them.' He looked over the moor towards the car park. A four-wheel drive sat next to Michael's. A Toyota, I thought. I couldn't see the number plate.

Michael's voice was jittery. 'They'll try to make you think I'm mad. They'll do anything.'

I took a step away from him. 'You need to let us protect you then.'

'No. No.' He shook his head fast and muttered under his breath.

I edged further from him and started walking slowly towards the pub, my hand in my pocket over the orange button again.

Michael followed close beside me. 'You do believe me, don't you?'

I hurried to get some more distance between us. 'I believe you.'

My foot caught on something. I lurched forward and fell onto my knee, one hand trapped in my pocket and unable to break my fall. Adrenaline burst into my stomach.

I clawed myself up, my pulse thudding in my ears. Michael grabbed at me again. I gasped; then realised he was only helping me.

I brushed snow off my sodden trousers. The wind whipped at my legs and I realised I was so cold my teeth were chattering. I looked across the hillside. The Toyota was gone.

We walked down to the pub car park, stiffly, like a couple of cats that might fight at any moment.

'I'll just pop to the toilet,' I said.

'You're going to call your colleagues, aren't you?' Michael took a few sheets of A4 from his pocket. 'This is a published paper which confirms what I've told you.' He handed me the paper, which looked like a photocopied excerpt from a scientific journal. I slipped it into my pocket.

Michael looked over his shoulder, then fished a piece of paper from his trousers. 'These are the names of the other patients who took Immunoxifan. I have records because it's such a new drug. You won't be able to get these from anywhere else. You probably think you will, but you're wrong.'

'Are you going to give me the list?'

'I need to go now. I won't see you again. I'll get this list to you once I'm safe.'

I eyed the paper. I couldn't see what was on it.

Michael shoved it back in his pocket. 'You need to give me your word that you'll let me get away.'

'I'll let you get away. Just tell me the names. Or it could be too late. What if there's another death?'

Michael looked over his shoulder. 'I can't do that, I'm afraid. I need to make sure you've stuck to your word first, you see.'

'You should let us help you. You know – '

'You stick to your word and it will be okay. I think you'd better get someone else to give you a lift back. The pub will let you use their phone if you can't get a signal.'

He beeped open his Land Rover, clambered in with snow still caked to his feet, and drove away.

★

I eked out enough signal to call Fiona, and then installed myself in the softest sofa of the Cat and Fiddle.

I started on the scientific paper. The purpose of the experiment hadn't been about the side-effects of course, so I was looking for information buried in the appendices. It did seem to note which technicians had handled the mice, but I was still struggling to work out the connections when Fiona arrived. She rushed over. 'Are you okay? What happened?'

'I'm fine. I'm not sure they'll ever get me out of this sofa though.' I sank deeper into the leather. My feet were sodden and my trousers steamed gently.

'You look a bit cold.' Fiona was never one to exaggerate.

'I'm warming up now. Thanks for coming. Get yourself a drink, and I'll tell all.'

'I struggled to get my car up the road in the snow,' Fiona said.

'Sorry. It's a bit high up here. The sign behind your head says sixteen hundred and ninety feet. Almost Everest.'

She slapped her bag down beside me. 'Are you drinking *gin*?'

'What on earth makes you say that?' It could have been mineral water for all she knew. And I'd only had one.

Fiona fetched herself something sensible and appropriate for the driver, and sank into the sofa beside me.

'I know you like to play everything by the book,' I said, 'but it might be easier if we kept some of this to ourselves.'

Poor Fiona, I was such a bad influence. She nodded.

I told her the gist of what had happened.

'Oh my God. So he's saying the mice remembered something from the hearts they were given? The ones who'd had Immunoxifan?'

'He thought something from the donor heart had affected their behaviour. He's not sure what exactly. Or how.'

'But they killed their cage mates? The mice who'd been given hearts from donor mice who had traumatic deaths?'

'That was what he said. And only the ones who'd had Immunoxifan. We need to check it out.'

'God, Meg, if this gets out . . . '

'He might be delusional. Or lying. I didn't think he was lying, but you can't always tell. You say he shorted the shares.'

'Yes. It looks like if the company goes under, he'll be pretty rich.'

'So he's not exactly objective.'

'And he's in a financial mess if that company doesn't fail. Why did you let him go?'

'Even if I'd called for back-up, it wouldn't have arrived in time.'

'And you didn't want anyone to know you'd gone up there with him.'

'We needed the information, Fiona. About Immunoxifan. What if it did somehow cause Abbie to kill her father? We need to know.'

'Was she really remembering things from her donor's death?'

'That's what Michael Ellis seems to think.'

'Okay. So, does this explain it? I mean, how she knew the names of the donor child's brother and dog, and how she drew that picture – the man by the lake, and the girl in the pink and white spotty swimming costume. Was it the drug that let her remember it all? I'm really starting to think that girl was murdered. We've got to look at the donor child's father.'

★

There was one light on in Dr Li's clinic, but the reception area was in darkness, and the front door was locked. Lights were on in the attached bungalow. I could barely make out its surroundings in the dark, but it sat beneath the cliff, and was enclosed by a little garden and a low hedge that separated it from the clinic car-park. I rang the doorbell. I knew it was a Sunday night and there was a chance Dr Li would charge us double and I'd get more bollockings from Richard, but she had offered another meeting for free. Besides, I was desperate to discuss what Michael Ellis had said, and Dr Li seemed our best bet for someone who might have a clue what was going on.

The door swung open and Tom Li backed his wheelchair away. 'Come in.' He looked embarrassed. 'I assume you want to see my mother?'

'Sorry it's a Sunday evening. If it's a bad time . . . ' I tried to look like someone who hadn't recently plunged into a quagmire.

'No. She's in her office doing paperwork anyway. She'll probably be glad of the interruption. It's her accounts, I think.' There was no trace of the man who'd been intent on throwing himself off a cliff. I wondered if I should pretend it had never happened.

I shook my coat outside and followed him into a wide, show-home-smart hallway, Fiona just behind.

'How are you?' I tried to keep my tone neutral so he could choose whether to take it as a genuine enquiry as to how he was, or a social greeting, depending on how he was feeling.

'I'm not so bad, now.' He hesitated. 'I'm ashamed actually, about the other day. I'm sorry to have put you to all that trouble.'

I felt a flash of pity for his situation. 'There's no need to be ashamed.'

I was surprised he was at home. I supposed they were relying on Fen to keep an eye on him. Budget cuts and all that.

Tom wheeled up the corridor. 'Anyway, come through here – it leads into the clinic.' He pushed a door to the side and ushered us through. I recognised the corridor that led to Dr Li's room.

'Thanks. We can find our way now.'

The clinic was dimly lit and almost sinister in its silence. Tiny red security lights flashed above us, and the before-and-after images stared down at us, their eyes seeming to follow us as we padded up the corridor. I glanced behind and saw I was leaving a trail of wet footprints. 'Oops.'

'They won't invite *you* back,' Fiona said.

I knocked on Dr Li's door, and she shouted for us to come in. I pushed the door open, glancing guiltily down at my wet shoes.

Dr Li looked up from behind a pile of papers. 'Hello, this is a surprise.'

'I'm so sorry to come on a Sunday,' I said. 'If it's not convenient, we'll come back another time.'

'No, it's fine. It's good to have an excuse to ditch this paper-work for a while. I have half an hour before I need to phone someone I supervise. I suppose this is about Abbie Thornton?'

I nodded. 'Yes. But is Tom okay?'

'He'll be fine.' She shook her head as if denying her own assertion. 'It's so sad. I wish I could help him feel better about his life. He doesn't seem to value what he has . . . ' She trailed off and looked at Fiona. 'I don't think we've met.'

I introduced Fiona, and Fen directed us to the casual corner.

'I'm sorry,' I said. 'I'm a bit damp. I hope I don't drip bog-water on your chair. I'll sit on my coat.'

'Don't worry,' Fen eyed my trousers. 'But maybe do put your coat down.'

'We just wanted a word with you again. I've managed to speak to Michael Ellis about the immunosuppressant. And you said the other day that there was more basis to the cellular memory theory than you'd thought.'

I explained what Ellis had said on that freezing hillside, and dug out the paper he'd given me. 'It's quite hard to find the relevant bits.' I passed it over.

'How interesting.' Fen scrutinised the paper. 'The information about the aggressive mice will probably be hidden away under *Side Effects* and dismissed as irrelevant.' She flipped the pages. 'Here. There's a table. Not easy to interpret. But it seems that the information's there if you know where to look. See these initials? They're the technicians who handled the mice. Here are the donors. And here are the notes about the mice which became aggressive.' She stared at the page for a few minutes. We sat in silence.

Dr Li looked up. 'I see it. The recipient mice which became aggressive all had hearts from donor mice handled by this technician NPW.'

'Do you think what Ellis said is possible?' I asked. 'Is there any way the drug could somehow allow memories or emotions to pass with the heart?'

Fiona said, 'It reminds me of a thing I saw about past lives. This little boy knew the complete layout of a house he'd lived in before.'

'Whenever they look into those things properly, they always find holes in the story,' I said. 'We need to look for rational explanations.'

Fiona folded her arms. 'I don't see why it shouldn't at least be possible. And poor Abbie if that's what's happened.'

'But it can't happen, can it?'

'I did some digging,' Fen said. 'You know I'm highly sceptical, but as I said, there is a little more evidence for this than I'd realised.'

'That a heart could have memories, you mean?'

'To a degree. Scientists have found traces of memory in cell nuclei, not only in the synapses. And there does appear to be a sophisticated collection of neurons in the heart, organised into a small nervous system. I'm not saying this means a heart has memories, but it's more complex perhaps than I had thought. It's not something I'd looked into previously.'

'But what about the drug? Immunoxifan. Could that have anything to do with it?'

'I found an article that suggests it's a possibility.'

I felt a heaviness growing inside me. Was she really going

to say this could have happened? That Abbie might have been affected by the donor child's heart? 'What did the article say?'

'It's complicated. But did you know your personality can be affected by what we'd normally regard as purely physical things? Like your gut bacteria, for example?'

'Yes. I read that you can make normal mice anxious by giving them gut bacteria from anxious mice.'

'Indeed. And have you heard about Toxoplasma?'

'The parasite you get from eating raw meat and clearing up after cats?'

'Yes. That can affect your personality too.'

'Doesn't it make you reckless and irrationally fond of cats? I probably have that one.' I turned to Fiona. 'This organism actually makes mice braver and even makes them like cats, so they're more likely to get eaten by a cat and the thing can carry on its life-cycle inside the cat. How about that? And when it gets into humans it seems to have a similar effect.'

Fiona wrinkled her nose.

'Seriously,' I said. 'Regions with high rates of infection have more car crashes.'

Fiona smiled, not sure if I was being serious.

'She's right.' Fen raised an eyebrow at me. 'You take quite an interest in science? I wasn't expecting you to know this.'

'She's a geek,' Fiona said.

'I skim-read New Scientist magazine, if that counts.'

'That's unusual in a detective?'

Fiona again. 'She is pretty unusual.'

'Alright, alright,' I said. 'That's not feeling like a compliment.'

Fen smiled. 'I think you'll understand what I'm saying then. I don't know whether the paper I found has any validity. I've not had time to look into it in detail, but it was in a peer-reviewed journal.'

'What exactly did it say?'

'It suggested there could be something in the heart that affects a person's thoughts or behaviour, perhaps making use of a microbe. Every day we're finding more evidence that our behaviour isn't exclusively governed by our brains.'

'Okay,' I said. Fiona and I both sat forward in our seats, focused intently on Fen.

'The theory is that occasionally this microbe or whatever it is gets transferred when someone has a transplant. Imagine if the donor was infected with Toxoplasma, and this was transferred to the recipient. It could cause the recipient's personality to change after the transplant.'

I glanced at Fiona. She sat wide-eyed. 'Okay,' I said. 'That does make sense.'

'The paper suggests that new, highly effective immunosuppressant drugs make it less likely that the patient's immune system would kill this thing off. Which is why we're seeing more cases of transplant recipients taking on traits of their donors.'

I swallowed. It felt like something was stuck in my throat. 'It seems a step too far to take on their memories though.'

Fen nodded abruptly. 'There's plenty we still don't understand about memory.'

Fiona shifted forward on her seat. 'But to murder someone because of this?'

'That obviously wouldn't happen normally. It would depend on exactly what was transferred from the donor. Like with the mice – only hearts from the ones that had been killed traumatically caused a problem.'

'But surely a lot of donors die traumatically?' I felt cold. I didn't want Abbie to have killed her father. I didn't want Fen to come up with an explanation as to why she might have done it. I wanted her to tell me it was impossible. Ten-year-old girls didn't kill their parents. Ten-year-old girls weren't responsible for people's deaths.

Something passed across Fen's face. Like a memory of something painful that she brushed aside. 'Yes,' she said. 'I suppose they do.'

I shuffled in my chair. 'There's a chance this new immunosuppressant could allow something to survive that's normally killed off? Increase the chance of a recipient taking on something from the donor? That sounds quite a scary prospect.'

'It's quite worrying. But I'd need to know more. Please don't take this as an opinion as to what happened with Abbie Thornton.'

'But do you think we should be looking into other patients who took Immunoxifan?'

'I might be a little concerned in the circumstances.' Fen frowned. 'There is one option, of course, given that we can't discuss this with poor Dr Gibson. A way to discover if Abbie does remember what happened to her donor.'

'Yes?' I said.

'I could hypnotise her.'

I could sense Fiona holding her breath.

I felt a stab of excitement at the possibility of finding the truth. 'But she was terrified when Dr Gibson hypnotised her,' I said. 'I promised she'd never have to do that again.'

'She's up for murder,' Fiona said. 'This might tell us what really happened. If you genuinely don't think she did it, Meg – '

The door swung open. Tom. 'Would you like drinks?'

'We're okay, thanks,' I said. 'We'd better get off. You need to make that phone call.'

Dr Li looked at her watch. 'Yes, I do. Let me know if you'd like to discuss hypnotising the girl.'

We thanked Dr Li profusely and made our way out.

'I think we should ask Dr Li to hypnotise Abbie,' Fiona said. 'She might even remember what happened the night her father died.'

★

Fiona returned me to my car, and I set off for home. The snow wasn't bad in the lower regions – the kind of light dusting that brought London to a standstill but just caused Derbyshire people to stick on their big coats and joke about soft Southerners. I turned the car's blower up high and tried to ignore the dampness which had seeped into my underwear.

At the precise moment that the car had fully de-misted, de-frosted and become relatively pleasant to be in, I arrived home. I sat for a moment, not wanting to move. The damp underwear had reached body temperature and I didn't want to expose it to the freezing air.

Eventually I steeled myself and clambered stiffly from the car. I pushed open my front door, tripped up the step, and glanced back at the letter-box, all in one not-so-graceful manoeuvre. No Carrie-dolls, but I was still spooked at the memory.

My house wasn't warm enough to get rid of the chill that seemed to have solidified my moving parts, and I half-walked, half-crawled up the stairs to check the rooms and then have a bath. Hamlet appeared while I was lying in the glorious warmth, and sat on a corner of the bathtub staring ghoulishly at me, telepathically reminding me that he hadn't been fed for at least an hour or two.

Once out of the bath, I donned a nightshirt, three fleeces, some leggings and a dressing gown, fed Hamlet, grabbed a glass of wine, and retreated to my bed with the laptop. I wanted theories and I wanted evidence, and I wanted to be tucked up in bed where the duvet would protect me from all known dangers.

Not all the people who believed in the memory-transfer theory were on the fringes of medicine – some were highly qualified researchers and doctors. I checked out the possible explanations, hardly believing I was taking it seriously. Whenever I heard my dad's scathing voice in my ear, I blocked it out with a glug of wine.

One of the most plausible explanations seemed to be the *Little brain in the heart* theory. As Dr Li had said, the heart apparently had a nervous system of its own, containing around 40,000 neurons called sensory neurites, which could act independently of the brain and possibly store memories.

I was struggling to visualise a heart having memories, but realised I knew virtually nothing about how memory worked anyway. Why was I so sure it was all in the brain? We felt as if we lived in our brains, but was that because our eyes and ears were on our heads? If our brains were in our hearts, would we even feel any different?

Then there was the Neuropeptide Theory. Pharmacologist Candace Pert had proposed that neuropeptides in every cell were able to store emotions. Neuropeptides had been found in the heart, and could theoretically transfer emotions from donor to recipient. I'd heard of Candace Pert and she was no dummy, although I knew her theories weren't exactly mainstream.

I put the laptop aside and flopped back on my pillows. Had I been too hasty dismissing these ideas? Too influenced by my dad yet again? I closed my eyes and saw Abbie's face. Maybe she had done this after all. I imagined her life if she was found guilty of murder. Held in a secure unit, surrounded by the most brutal children, horrified by what she'd done, terrified of her own heart and what it might make her do next.

# 24.

Monday morning. I sat in my room sifting through the data on our system, looking for links and patterns and anything that didn't involve Abbie slaughtering her father and attacking her mother.

I jumped. Jai was standing over me. 'Jesus,' I said. 'Are you perfecting your ninja stealth skills?'

'No, you're clearly missing some senses this morning.' He shunned the chair, of course, and leant against my desk. 'Still worried Abbie didn't do it?'

'Worried she did; worried she didn't. I am kind of an expert at worrying.'

'As far as Richard's concerned, it's all done and dusted.'

'But, Jai, if she did do it, then what's her motive? That some weird drug caused her to remember her donor's death? If that's true, there are other people out there who could be dangerous.'

'I suppose so.'

'And if she didn't do it . . . '

'Oh, Rachel Thornton's out of hospital. Doesn't remember a thing.'

'So, if it wasn't Abbie, Rachel might be in danger.'

'It was Abbie, Meg. I know you don't want to believe it because she's a kid, but it was.'

Fiona sidled up, looking depressed. 'Richard's taken me off this case. Said it's just tying up loose ends now. But I think there's leads we should be following up. And we should be looking at the donor child's father. What if he drowned his daughter?'

'Tying up loose ends? God, am I the only one who thinks Abbie might not have done it?' I only had two more days before I had to leave them to it. Although I knew it was silly, I felt I was letting Abbie down. 'Let's think about whether we should hypnotise her.'

Fiona's mouth twisted and she pushed herself back a little as if wanting to keep her distance from me. 'It's hit the papers.'

'It's okay, Fiona. I'm perfectly safe to be around.' Of course I hadn't read the papers yet. Maybe I wasn't safe to be around.

Fiona laughed politely, as if humouring a slightly insane and possibly violent relative.

'Do you want to show me?' I said.

'Yeah. I've got it on my computer, if you want to come over.'

I followed Fiona to her desk and pulled up a chair. Her fingers flicked over the keyboard and she brought up an online news article. Jai walked round and stood behind us.

The headline screamed: *Transplanted Heart Turns Young Girl into Evil Murderer*. The byline read, *Derbyshire police in chaos as body-count increases*.

'Fantastic.' I leant forward to read the article.

*'A recent heart transplant has turned a young Derbyshire girl into a devil child, who has killed her father and left her mother in a coma.*

*'Until her transplant, the girl, who cannot be named for legal reasons, was a normal schoolchild who wanted nothing more than to play with her friends, and chat about boys . . .'*

I broke off. 'Chat about boys? *Boys?* She's ten years old, for God's sake.'

Fiona shrugged. *'That's* the bit you're worried about?'

'And her mother's not in a bloody coma.'

I carried on reading.

*'But soon after the girl received her new heart, she started having nightmares, screaming that her father was a murderer and was trying to kill her. Her distraught parents took her to a psychiatrist, but nothing seemed to help. The nightmares became more and more distressing. Finally, last week, the girl left her bed in the middle of the night, apparently asleep, crept into her parents' room, and slit her father's throat with a knife from his own kitchen.*

*'Derbyshire police are in chaos. They inexplicably released the girl and left her in the care of her mother and ageing grandmother. Tragically, she struck again, bludgeoning her mother with a rock, leaving the woman in a coma.*

*'We have reported previously on recipients of heart transplants taking on the donor's personality, but this case adds a horrific twist to the story. Who was the donor child for the girl's heart? Rumours are that the girl dreamed she was drowned by her father. Is that what happened to the donor child? Did the donor child's heart seek revenge? Are the police investigating this?*

*'It is suggested that new immunosuppressant drugs may have allowed the transfer of memories and emotions from the donated heart, according to "cellular memory" theory. There are now calls for these new drugs to be banned.*

*'Questions will be asked about where donor hearts come from. Would you be happy for your loved one to receive the heart of a convicted murderer (as happens in some countries, such as China) or the heart of someone who died a traumatic death?'*

I leant back in my chair. 'Oh God.'

'It's all over social media,' Fiona said.

'How the hell,' I said, 'did this get out? We didn't release any of this? Did we?'

'No,' Jai said.

'I want to know how it got to the media.'

'I meant to tell you,' Fiona said. 'My granny confirmed it – people move into that house to do penance.'

'Sorry?'

'You know the story about the children being sacrificed? There's this thing that if you've done something terrible, then you move into that house with the statues of the children, and something bad happens to you, like in revenge, and then you've done your penance.'

'We know Phil Thornton wanted to do penance. Rachel told us.'

Jai smiled. 'People don't still believe that shit these days, Meg.'

'Maybe Phil did. Both Karen and Rachel said he was desperate to move into that house and the statues were really important to him. What was he paying penance for? Check which charities were in his will, just in case. What had he done that he felt so terrible about?'

I grabbed my bag and headed out. 'I'm going to give Dr Li a ring about hypnotising Abbie. I'm not keen, but if it's what it takes to find the truth . . . '

Craig was in the corridor. I tried to walk past without acknowledging him, but he blocked me. 'For God's sake, Craig. I have a call to make.'

'You're off on holiday on Wednesday, aren't you? Don't worry, I'll be able to sort out charging the kid without your help.'

He was bang in my way. I tried again to skirt round him, but he shifted over. 'I'm surprised you haven't postponed your holiday,' he said. 'Richard thinks it shows a lack of commitment.'

'Richard didn't say that.'

'Only because you lied and said you'd postpone your time off. You haven't even said what you're doing, so it can't be anything that special.'

My teeth and fists clenched with that instinctive readiness to smack him in the face. It would feel so good . . . My breathing came faster. 'You're in my way, Craig.'

We stood for a moment in the corridor, tense and hard as those statues in the woods. Finally, Craig shifted sideways a fraction and I pushed past and towards my room.

A shout from behind. 'Meg!'

I glanced round and saw Fiona. She walked a step down the corridor and then stopped abruptly as if bouncing into the force-field that Craig and I had created. 'Can I just check something with you?' she said. 'I'm not sure if I should go and see . . .'

Craig was heading for me again, Fiona behind him. 'Oh, God, Fiona,' I said. 'Make up your own mind.'

Fiona gave me an astonished look.

'No,' I said. 'Sorry, Fiona, I didn't mean that.' I turned and walked a few paces back up the corridor towards her, even though it took me closer to Craig.

Craig's face spread into a delighted smirk.

'It's absolutely fine.' Fiona strode off, speaking over her shoulder. 'I'll make up my own mind.'

I spun round to face Craig. I was burning with all the pent-up fury I'd been so carefully restraining. 'Leave me alone, you lying shit-head!'

281

An hour later, Jai wandered up to my desk, chomping on a chocolate bar. 'Have you seen Fiona? No one knows where she is.'

A shifting in my stomach. 'She wanted to talk to me earlier.'

'What about?'

'I didn't get a chance to ask.' A flush of shame. 'Craig was being a dick. I snapped at her, and she shot off. Then I called Craig a lying shit-head.'

'Oh dear. Fair enough about Craig though. Seems accurate to me.' Jai finished the chocolate. 'But I hope Fiona's not trying to impress you by doing something stupid. You do know she stuck her neck out for you?'

'No? What do you mean?'

'She told Richard she'd overheard a conversation between Craig and one of his cronies. Where he admitted he didn't see you push Rachel Thornton. That's why Richard didn't follow up on it, and why Craig's pissed off with her.'

'Oh, God.' A wave of mortification. She'd helped me and all I could do was snap at her.

'She'll be okay.' Jai fished out his phone, tapped the screen and waited a moment. 'Straight to answer-phone.'

'She was on about seeing the donor child's father.' I jumped up and headed through to Fiona's desk. Jai followed. No sign of her, and Craig wasn't around either. A fresh-faced DC, Ian something-or-other, was staring intently at his screen.

'Do you know where Fiona is?' I asked.

He looked up and shook his head.

'Or Craig?'

Another head shake.

'Oh, come on, Ian,' Jai said. 'Meg's okay. What's going on?'

His eyes flitted from side to side. 'Craig thought she'd gone to see the kid's father – the donor child's father. She's not supposed to be on the case so she didn't want Richard to know.'

'Oh no,' I said. 'Do we have the guy's address?'

Ian passed us a scrap of paper. An address somewhere up in the hills. 'Craig left it with me. He went after her.'

'Why did Craig go after her?'

'The guy's into guns. Craig got worried when he couldn't get in contact with her.'

'Guns?' I started to feel a little sick.

'Yeah.' Ian scratched his nose. 'He's into running about the countryside shooting grouse and whatnot.'

Jai sighed. 'Craig may be an arse, but he's a loyal arse. He doesn't like to see his colleagues in trouble.'

'Even though she grassed him up to Richard?' Sometimes I felt so confused by the relationships in our team. If Jane Goodall was observing us, I'd be that sad chimp sitting at the edge of the group looking baffled.

I waved the paper in Ian's direction. 'Do you know where this address is?'

'I think it's near the village of Flash.'

'You're kidding. Isn't that the highest village in England?'

Ian nodded. 'The snow'll be seriously bad up there.'

Jai tapped on his phone. He waited a moment and shook his head. 'No answer from Craig either.'

Ian said, 'You won't tell Richard, will you? Craig made me promise.'

I was already half way out of the room. 'Not unless absolutely necessary.'

'You think Nick Norwood drowned his daughter?' Jai said, as we pulled out of the car park. 'Is he dangerous?'

I tried to keep the panic from my voice. Fiona was in danger and it was because I'd snapped at her. And Craig had proved himself to be not-so-bad. 'If I really thought he was a significant risk, we wouldn't be taking off into the wilds of Derbyshire with no back-up, would we?'

'Righto. Just checking.'

I reached to put the address into sat-nav, although I wasn't hugely optimistic it would get us there.

'Looks snowy up in the hills,' Jai said.

'Exactly where we're going.'

The snow was thawing in the lower regions but it would be piling out of the sky and coating the hills and valleys around Flash. We'd taken Jai's car – not four-wheel drive but a better choice than mine. I looked towards the snow-iced peaks in the distance.

The tyres slipped as we pulled onto the main road. Jai gripped the steering wheel with rigid fingers.

We climbed higher. Snow was falling properly now. Big flakes like something from a Christmas film. The fields were thickly coated. 'It's minus five out there,' I said.

Jai reached forward and turned the heating up high. 'I've been thinking. Is there any way something iffy could have happened with Abbie's transplant? Like somehow Phil Thornton persuaded the doctors to take the donor child's heart even though she wasn't properly dead?'

'You do get scandals about brain-dead patients waking up every now and then,' I said. 'I read about a young lad – in

Leicester, I think. Four doctors pronounced him brain-dead and then he sat up. Or something like that. So I'd imagine parents are unwilling to accept a diagnosis of brain death.'

'What if something corrupt was going on? Phil knew Abbie could die while waiting for a transplant, so he bribed the doctors or something . . . I don't know . . . to declare a kid brain-dead when maybe she could recover. What if that happened to the donor child? Maybe Rachel didn't know at the time, but she found out and was really angry, and called Phil a murderer and Abbie overheard the conversation. That could have triggered her nightmares.'

'The donor child wasn't properly dead?'

'It's possible,' Jai said.

'Are you thinking the donor child's parents could have found out what happened?'

'It would be a motive, wouldn't it?'

After a few more miles of climbing, the sat-nav told us to take a right.

'Really? Up there?' Jai pulled onto the side road. It had been cleared by a snow plough and we drove between walls of snow so high we couldn't see the fields. Jai flipped the wipers onto fast – fat flakes were coating the windscreen.

I checked my phone as we travelled deeper into nowhere. 'No mobile signal. Do we even know this is where Fiona went?'

'It's not like her to go charging off like that,' Jai said.

I felt a heaviness in my chest. 'I shouldn't have snapped at her. I can't believe I did that, after she'd stuck up for me. And I shouldn't have shouted at Craig.'

'It was still their decision to go, Meg. Don't beat yourself up.'

We arrived at a surprising hamlet, beyond which the snow plough hadn't ventured. We had no choice but to stop – we'd get no further in the car. The sat-nav told us we'd reached our destination, but there was no sign of the place we were looking for – Coldwater Farm.

'We'd better ask someone,' I said.

'Rather you than me. It's like bloody *Deliverance* up here. If it wasn't so cold they'd be out with banjos.'

I glanced around. The local pub did indeed look like darts might stop in mid-air at the sight of us, but a tiny shop shone a welcoming light.

'I'll ask in there.' I fought the swirling snow and tramped my way to the shop. The door pinged. A saggy-faced woman was lodged behind the counter as if she'd grown there like a mushroom. She gave me a suspicious look.

I smiled at her. 'I'm after Coldwater Farm.'

'What's going on? I've already had one young lassie asking after that place. I told her not to go up there. Is there a problem?'

'Why did you tell her not to go up there?'

'The man that lives there's dangerous. I never liked him. He's been in prison before. And since his wife moved out, well . . . '

'What's he been doing?'

'Talk is he killed his daughter. What's this about?'

'Who said that?'

I could sense the shutters coming down. 'What's this about?'

I flashed my ID. 'We need to talk to him. Who said he killed his daughter?'

She folded her arms and her body seemed to solidify. 'It's just gossip. I can't remember.'

'Did she turn back then, the lassie, do you know?'

'I don't rightly know. I hope so.'

'Where's the house?'

'Up the lane a couple of hundred yards and down the track to the right. You'll have to walk it though. You'll not get any further in the car today.'

'Have you seen a man at all? Looking for Coldwater Farm?'

'No. What's this about? What's going on? You have to tell me. We have children here.'

I headed for the door, calling back, 'Thank you, you've been a great help.'

I could hear her shouting at me as I stomped back to Jai. The wind was getting up and the snow was already piling against the side of the car. I wrenched the door open and climbed in.

'Try Fiona's mobile again, Jai.'

'I can't get a signal. Nothing at all.'

'Shit. The woman in the shop said Nick Norwood's been inside. Did we not find that?'

'We weren't exactly looking at him, were we? He's the donor child's father. Nothing to do with Phil Thornton other than that.'

'We should have picked that up if it's true,' I grumbled. 'And there's rumours in the village he killed his daughter. She told Fiona to go back. I hope to God she did.' I pointed up the lane ahead of us. 'Up the lane and on the right, but we won't get any further now in the car.'

'We'd better go and have a look. I don't know how we're getting out of here now anyway.'

'Not much point calling for back-up either.'

We left the car at the side of the lane and set off towards the farmhouse. Jai brought cuffs, just in case.

A track led off to the right. It looked like the snow had been cleared earlier but had built up again. The farmhouse sat in a small dip.

'Uh oh,' Jai said. 'Craig must have driven down there before the snow piled up again. His car's by the house.'

# 25.

I fished out my phone. Zero signal. Should we radio for back-up? A car wouldn't get there. I imagined Richard's apoplexy if we blew a helicopter-sized hole in his budget on this. And we'd get Fiona into trouble. And Craig who, whilst he clearly was a shit-head, had gone after Fiona even though he must have been angry with her. 'Let's walk down there,' I said. 'Check everything's okay.'

The track was icy and rutted under the snow, which was forming a drift against a dry stone wall to our left.

'Who's idea was this again?' Jai said.

I slipped. 'Shit. Ow. God, I always end up hurting this bloody ankle.'

'Are you okay? Do you want to wait here?'

'No, it's fine. I'll just limp a little worse than usual. Watch that bit though – there's a hole.'

We walked more slowly as we approached the farmhouse. All we could hear was the wind – the usual country sounds were muffled by the snow.

'Can't see any signs of life,' I whispered.

Jai froze. 'What was that? I heard something? Is someone there?'

We stood and listened. A snuffling noise.

'Uh oh,' I said. 'An animal?'

Jai took a step forward. 'Is anyone there?'

Something shot into view and tore towards us, sending snow flying up behind it.

'Don't run,' I said, and grabbed Jai's arm. 'It's a dog. Stand still.'

It was hard to take my own advice as the thing hurtled in our direction, but there was no way we'd outrun it. It was a black Labrador. Not one of the cuddly ones – a huge, thick-necked beast with the muscles of a Rottweiler.

The dog was a foot away from us and had its teeth bared.

A yelp and the dog stopped. It shook its head violently, but didn't move any closer to us.

My heart was pounding. 'I think it's an invisible fence,' I said. 'Electric. Gives the dog a shock if it goes through. Horrible things.'

'I'm kind of liking them.' Jai's breathing was loud beside me. 'So, if we go through the fence, will we get a shock?'

'No. The dog's wearing a special collar. We might get bitten though.'

'We'd better call for back-up.'

'But look at the snow. And if Craig and possibly Fiona are in trouble . . . '

The dog whined and sloped off back towards the house.

'Cross your arms,' I said. 'Don't look at the dog. Come on.'

I held my breath and walked smoothly forwards. The dog snapped its head round, then turned and ran towards me. I stood, ready to leap back through the invisible force field. But the dog sniffed me and wagged its tail. I let out my breath.

'Sometimes I think you're nuts,' Jai said.

'Don't worry. It's like that old joke. If it does get vicious, you don't have to outrun it, you only have to outrun me, which won't be a challenge.'

'Knowing you, it'd take a shine to you and rip me to shreds.' But he followed me towards the house.

I walked closer and peered through a grimy window into a living room. Worn sofas and a patterned carpet. Wood chip on the wall. No people. Six crushed cans of Special Brew and a whisky bottle on its side. A gun cabinet. Open. Empty.

Jai was behind me. 'I'm not keen on that dog,' he said.

'I'm not keen on that gun cabinet.'

We crept through rapidly piling snow at the side of the house, accompanied by the dog. He was giving us the kind of grovelly friendship that can quickly turn to violence.

Jai arrived first at a window at the back. Snow was banked against it, driven over the hills by the sideways wind. 'Can't see anything,' he said. 'The curtains are drawn.'

I kicked my feet forwards into the snow and pressed my ear against the window. 'I can hear voices. Was that Craig?'

Jai shuffled into the snow and flattened his ear against the freezing glass. 'Could be. Can't hear over this bloody wind.'

A hefty oak door sat mid-way along the back of the house. Jai shuffled towards it and gave it a shove. It opened, spilling snow onto the stone floor of a tiny back porch crammed with boots.

I stepped into the porch and listened against a door which I guessed led into a kitchen.

I knocked.

No answer.

I gave the door a push and stood aside.

No shots.

Craig's voice. 'Careful! He's got a gun.'

I inched forwards into a large kitchen which smelt of stale alcohol and wet dog. Plates and food remnants covered the counter-tops – old milk bottles, bean cans that hadn't been washed out, a plastic container full of Chinese take-away, the noodles curling and yellow.

Craig was on the far side of the room. His hands were bound behind his back, and he was slumped in a sitting position, leaning against a cast-iron kitchen range. 'Bloody hell, Craig. Are you okay?' I said. 'Have you seen Fiona?'

Craig shook his head, and gave me a warning look with his eyes.

An aggressive voice. 'Stop right there.'

I spun round. A man stood in a doorway which seemed to lead into a hall. He had a black beard and wore khaki. He looked like the man in Abbie's drawing. He was pointing a shotgun at Craig. He slurred his words. 'Move any closer to him and I'll shoot him. Or you. I might shoot you.'

We didn't even have our protective gear on. Jai was behind me. The man could shoot either of us.

He poked the gun in my direction. 'Step back to the door,' he said.

I stepped back to the door. I was now next to Jai. We were all arranged stiffly around the perimeter of the kitchen, as if we'd been flung apart by centrifugal force.

The dog padded past us into the centre of the room and hesitated, as if unsure whether to approach its owner.

The man waved the gun at Jai and me. 'Who the fuck are you anyway?'

'Mr Norwood?' I spoke as calmly as I could, given that he appeared to be a deranged drunk with a gun. I could hear the shake in my voice. 'I'm Detective Inspector Meg Dalton and this is my colleague DS Jai Sanghera.'

'Bully for you.' Norwood lurched a step towards us, then stopped himself and edged back to the doorway. 'Why have you been saying I killed Scarlett? I didn't kill her. I fucking loved her.'

I could hear our breathing even over the wind outside. My eyes flicked from Craig to Norwood.

'Saying that girl's got her heart. Saying her daddy killed her . . . ' He looked over at me and a spasm of vulnerability flicked across his face. 'Has that girl got Scarlett's heart?'

'We've no reason to think that,' I said.

Norwood raised his gun an inch and pointed it directly at me. 'Cos I fucking need to know. I never thought I wanted to know. People sending cards to each other and all that shit – we never wanted that. But now I need to know. So you'd better tell me.'

'We don't know!' I said. 'We don't know who has Scarlett's heart.'

Norwood lowered the gun a little, but kept it angled so he could flick it up again quickly. 'Tell me or I won't say where your little friend is.'

'Fiona?' I whispered.

'Who's got her heart? Nobody tells me anything. Vanessa craps on to her Facebook friends, telling them every little detail of Scarlett's life, but would she talk to me? Would she fuck.'

'Have you got our colleague?' Jai said.

No response.

The dog glanced at the gun and then walked over to Craig. It lifted its lip into a snarl. Craig struggled to his feet and I saw he was tied to the range behind him. The dog growled, and Craig shifted as if he might kick it.

'Don't you dare.'

My head whirled round. Norwood had raised the gun and was now pointing it directly at Craig. It was remarkably still. He wasn't so drunk after all. 'Kick my dog and you're dead.'

Craig froze. The dog hesitated, then walked a couple of steps forward. It lifted its leg.

'Oh Jesus Christ.' Craig pulled away as much as he could but the range wouldn't let him move far. The dog lifted its leg higher.

'Get off!' Craig kicked out, deliberately missing the dog. He shouted towards Norwood. 'Get your dog off me!'

I watched with horrified detachment as the dog raised its leg higher and peed on Craig's trousers.

'For Christ's sake.' Craig whipped his leg away but it was too late. His trousers were saturated from mid thigh to calf. He shook his leg again and again. 'Bastard thing. Bloody thing.' His voice was frantic. He wasn't coping with this.

'Oh my God,' Norwood let out a single high-pitched note of laughter. He had prominent teeth. Like Abbie's drawing. 'That's disgusting. Oh God, that's horrible.'

Craig shook his leg repeatedly. Desperately.

'Come here, Spike.' Norwood clicked his fingers. The dog hesitated, then sloped towards him, glancing up at the food-strewn counter as it passed.

Norwood stroked the dog's head. 'Take your trousers off,' he said. The laughter was gone and his voice was low and menacing. 'They're revolting.'

Craig's head shot up. 'What?'

'I said, take your trousers off. They stink. I want them out of my kitchen.'

'No!' Craig pulled against the range.

Norwood raised the gun. 'Take them off, or I'll shoot you.'

Jai said, 'Just take your bloody trousers off, Craig.'

'No.' Craig pulled harder. 'No.'

I looked from Craig to Norwood. 'He can't! His hands are tied.'

Norwood laughed again. 'You do it for him then. Go on. His girlfriend can do it.'

'You bastard!' Craig yanked forwards. The range shifted forward a millimetre.

'What's your fucking problem?' Norwood said. 'Have you wet yourself too?'

Craig let out a roar and pulled forwards with such force that the handle of the range broke off. He was free, but his hands were still tied.

'Craig, no!' I shouted.

Craig stopped in the middle of the room, poised as if about to hurl himself at Norwood.

'I mean it.' Norwood pointed his gun at Craig. 'Come any closer I'll shoot you.'

I could feel a vein pulsing beneath my eye. There was nothing we could do. If we lunged for Norwood, he'd shoot Craig. If we didn't lunge for Norwood, it also looked like he'd shoot Craig. I could see his finger tight on the trigger. What the hell was the matter with Craig? Would he rather die than take his trousers off?

Craig leaped towards Norwood, smashing his arms upwards. The gun flew off into a corner of the room. I took a step towards it.

'Stop!' Norwood bellowed. 'One move towards that gun and I'll set the dog on you.'

We all froze. Norwood started backing out of the door.

'Have you got our colleague?' I said.

'Shut up and stay where you are.' Norwood held his palm towards the dog's face, but he wasn't touching it. 'If I give him the command, he'll rip your fucking throats out, one after the other.'

Norwood was backing away. I didn't want to let him go. Not without knowing where Fiona was.

The dog crouched next to him, its lip raised into a snarl. Its eyes were yellow and cold. But it was a Labrador . . . I remembered its ambivalence about going to Norwood, the way it had glanced at the counter top.

I looked into the dog's eyes. My heart thudded.

# 26.

I grabbed the Chinese take-away carton and chucked it on the floor. Vegetables and noodles exploded over the tiles.

The dog lunged forward and started hoovering up the food with a feverish enthusiasm. Craig, Jai and I jumped on Norwood and basically flattened him. Jai handcuffed him.

'Chill the fuck out,' Norwood grunted. 'I haven't got your little mate. I didn't see anyone until Dog Piss Boy here turned up.'

Craig stumbled to his feet and glanced down at his trousers. The dark stain had spread over his whole thigh and half way down his calf. He had a look on his face that I couldn't fathom. There was something seriously deep going on, and even though I didn't like the guy, I was prepared to respect that. I undid his hands, while Jai kept hold of Norwood.

I ran into the hall and up some stairs, and found a man's bedroom. Rummaged in drawers until I located a pair of jeans. Grabbed them, ran down the stairs, chucked them at Craig.

'You shouldn't have done that,' Jai said.

'I don't want us to tell anyone about the dog pee.'

Craig shuffled into the tiny porch and I heard trouser-changing noises.

'But if we have to get forensics here,' Jai said. 'If this guy killed Thornton . . . '

'I don't think he killed Thornton.'

'But . . . '

'Come on, Jai. Cops stick together. Craig didn't hurl himself at a suspect with a gun, and there was no dog pee.'

Once Craig had changed, we bundled Norwood up the snowy lane and into Jai's car, and set off back to the Station. I sat in the back with a silent Norwood, and Jai sat in the front with an equally silent Craig.

When we reached the main road, all our phones started ringing and buzzing. I had a batch of increasingly frenzied messages from Fiona. She was fine. But Richard was after me, and he wasn't happy.

★

Back at the Station, Fiona was waiting for us with mugs of coffee. To my relief, Richard had gone home.

Craig excused himself. He hadn't looked at me since I'd given him Norwood's trousers.

We trailed into my room and I collapsed into my chair. Even Jai sank gratefully into my guest chair and sprawled with arms and legs apart.

Fiona stood by the window, eyes flitting to and fro. 'Oh my God. What happened? I was so worried. I turned back. The weather was awful and then the woman in the shop said Nick Norwood was unstable and liked to wave guns around. But then when I got back, you'd all gone missing.'

We gave her a quick run-down of the situation. Rabid dogs, gun-wielding psychos. No dog pee.

'You did the right thing, Fiona.' I gulped coffee. 'I'm so sorry I snapped at you earlier. I'd had a difficult conversation with Craig.'

'Don't be silly. I know what Craig's like. I'm just grateful you came after me.'

'I hope you're not picking up bad habits from your seniors,' Jai said. 'Stick to the rules, that's what we need to do.'

'Yes,' I said. 'That is true. Really. At least you had the sense not to go to the house. He didn't make a great host.'

'Why was he so furious?'

'He was angry about the rumours that he killed Scarlett,' I said.

'There's even a chance he killed Phil Thornton,' Jai said. 'Something dodgy could have gone on with the heart transplant. What if Norwood's daughter came into the hospital still alive, but was later declared brain-dead? Norwood could have found out something and blamed Phil.'

'We need to look into the circumstances surrounding that transplant,' I said. 'There are so many checks and balances. If something dodgy happened, there must be at least one corrupt doctor. But Phil Thornton had money. He could have paid. And I suppose people will do virtually anything to save their own child, even at the cost of another child.'

'But Dr Gibson's notes?' Fiona said.

'Someone could have faked those notes,' I said. 'Or blackmailed Gibson. Obviously Norwood knew about the circumstances of the drowning, since he was there. Very few people knew about that.' I hugged my coffee mug. 'But it doesn't seem right. It's too intricate – not his style. And why would he frame Abbie?'

Nobody answered.

'Can you check out some other stuff too?' I asked. 'Norwood said a couple of things that made my ears prick.'

Fiona grabbed a notepad.

'Norwood said his wife had shared a lot on Facebook. Can you take another look? We can get permission from Facebook but see if you can charm her into letting us see her private stuff. It'll be much quicker.'

'No problem.'

'Also, Norwood said he and Scarlett's mother hadn't been interested in knowing who the recipient of Scarlett's heart was. They hadn't exchanged cards. But Abbie's family had a card, which we'd assumed was from the donor family. Remember?'

'Yes,' Fiona said. *'We don't know who you are and we can't tell you who we are, but it is of comfort to us that something good has come out of this terrible tragedy.'*

'That's the one. You've got a good memory. If that was from Abbie's donor's family, then her donor wasn't Scarlett Norwood. Which ties in with this whole damn thing being a set-up.'

★

I arrived home feeling as if I could collapse and fall asleep right there in the hallway. One more day and I'd be off the case. One more day to stack up enough questions that they wouldn't just charge Abbie. I was sure now that she hadn't done it. That she'd been framed. But who by?

I wondered if Richard had found out about us taking Gran. Maybe I could avoid him. I could surely keep a low profile for one day, and confront him when I got back from Switzerland. Forgiveness was always easier than permission.

Hamlet was in battle gear, with a fully-fluffed-up coat and bottle-brush tail. He stood stiffly with a leg at each corner and stared accusingly at me.

'Oh God, Hamlet, you haven't been fighting with the local gang-cats or bullying next door's Great Dane again, have you?'

He ignored me. His puffed up winter-woollies made him appear almost spherical. Or possibly that was the amount of food the neighbour had given him. But he definitely looked edgy. I noticed the lily smell again, and turned abruptly to look at the front door. There was nothing protruding through the letter-box. So where was the smell coming from? A slither of anxiety.

I sniffed Hamlet, in case it was the neighbour's perfume sticking to his fur, but he just smelt of wet cat. Something twitched in my stomach.

The boiler was clunking from the kitchen. It had an extensive repertoire of noises but wasn't so good on the heating side of things, and should probably have been condemned years ago. If only I could get round to it, I'd complain to the landlord. He could sort it when he fixed the windows.

I nipped upstairs to the bathroom. Something on the landing made me pause. A bad feeling. A stronger smell of lilies. I wanted to check the rooms. The urge was fiercer than it had been for a long time. I decided to poke my head into my bedroom, with the excuse of getting a warmer jumper.

I looked at the door – old wood with peeling paint – and didn't want to open it. My stomach fluttered again. I was being ridiculous. I nudged it open with my foot and walked in.

Something was there. Something familiar. Dreamt about so many times.

# 27.

The room seemed to go black. I gasped and stepped back, crashing against the wall. Squeezed my eyes shut, clamped my hand over my mouth, tried not to scream. My heart pummelled my ribcage.

I collapsed onto the floor and sat against the wall, eyes still closed. It couldn't be real. I'd imagined it. But I couldn't make myself look again.

I tried to breathe into my stomach. Slow and steady.

I opened my eyes a slit and looked towards the ceiling.

It was real.

It was hanging.

Hanging from the centre of the room.

My gaze crept up to the feet, stalled and then continued to the face.

It was a dummy. A shop-fitter's dummy. A young woman.

Her neck was in a noose, and the noose was tied to the light fitting.

I dragged myself into a standing position. Took a step closer. My breath seemed to tear at my throat.

They'd cut the dummy's hair. Like the doll through the door.

It looked like Carrie when she'd hanged herself.

I touched her. She swung slightly.

I burst into tears, ran from the room, crashed down the stairs, and grabbed my phone.

★

'In there.' I shoved Jai into my bedroom, not wanting to see her again.

'Jesus Christ.' He took a step forward. 'Who in God's name has done that?'

'I don't know.' My voice sounded distant, and weak like a small child's.

'We'll get them, Meg. They won't get away with this.'

Jai touched the dummy. 'There's a note.'

I hovered in the doorway, staring at the floor.

Jai turned to me, his expression full of concern. 'It's tied around her neck.'

'I didn't look that closely. What does it say.'

Jai coughed. 'It's not very nice, Meg. It says *You deserved to lose her.*'

'Oh.' I felt a deep heaviness inside, that someone could despise me this much.

Jai moved away from the dummy and shuffled me towards the stairs. 'Come on, let's call uniform and get some tea.'

'I feel numb,' I said. 'I can't believe someone would do that.'

We walked into the kitchen. It was freezing. The window overlooking the garden was wide open. I nodded towards it. 'I've been on at the bloody landlord about these windows.'

'You sit down,' Jai said. 'I'll call it in and make tea.'

I smiled a thank you and sat at the kitchen table with my head in my hands.

'They really hate me.' I sounded pitiful.

'They're bat-shit crazy, Meg.' Jai handed me tea. 'It's not personal. Go into the other room. There's penguins wandering around in here.'

I went to the living room and sat in a kind of stupor with Hamlet, while Jai organised everything. Uniform turned up, prints were taken, the dummy was removed and taken away, the window was nailed shut, I was asked some questions. I responded to people as best I could, but mainly sat, stared into space, and stroked Hamlet. If they'd wanted to do the worst thing in the world to me without actually hurting anyone, this was it. I felt sick that someone would do it.

I realised I was still scared of having a relapse. My mind flitted back to Manchester two years ago. Walking into the apartment by the river. One of the posh ones, kitted out all New York Industrial style, not the kind of place you expect anything too bad to happen. The phone call had seemed like guilty parents worrying unnecessarily. *Fifteen-year-old daughter home alone, can't seem to get in touch with her or her friends, please could you take a look.* General police grumpiness about rich people expecting us to run around after them, but I was in the area.

And the thing about those apartments is they have good, strong beams.

She was hanging from the central one in the living room. And it was just like Carrie.

And I'd realised I'd never really dealt with finding her.

And everything had gone to shit for a while. Time off, counselling, guilt, suicidal thoughts. But I was over that now. I'd made a new start back in Derbyshire. I would not be pushed back into that.

'I phoned your mum,' Jai said, when it was all under control. 'You're staying with her tonight.'

'No, Jai, I – '

'You're staying there and having the day off tomorrow. Have you seen what time it is?'

'Late?'

I grabbed a few clothes and a sleeping bag, and stuffed an unwilling Hamlet into his carrier. I looked up at Jai, who'd appeared in the doorway. 'This is scaring me now,' I said. 'This isn't sane. What might they do next?'

★

I sat at the kitchen table while Mum bustled around making tea. I couldn't even face going through to see Gran. I was already too close to the edge.

Mum put a mug in front of me and sat opposite. 'What exactly happened? What did they do?'

I saw it again, hanging from the ceiling. 'I told you about the doll the other day . . . That was clearly just a taster. Someone had rigged up a shop-fitter's dummy to look like Carrie and hung it from the light-fitting in my bedroom, with a note around its neck. So I could re-live the joy of finding my dead sister all over again.'

Mum reached and put her hand on my arm. 'Oh my goodness, that's terrible. What did the note say?'

'Something like: *You deserved to lose her.*'

Mum's face was white. 'Do you think it's Life Line?'

'I don't know.'

'Is it about us taking Gran to Switzerland? They know about it, don't they? And it's all my fault for telling Sheila. Oh, how stupid of me!'

'It's not your fault. Nobody would have expected them to do something like this. They're not rational. What kind of person hangs a dummy from the ceiling?'

She touched my arm again. 'How awful for you to come home to that.'

'Yeah. I'd just stopped feeling the need to check my rooms for dead family members hanging from the rafters, and this happens.' I gave her an attempt at a smile. 'How is Gran anyway?'

'Nowhere near as perky. That must have been her final burst of life. I've still been taking her out for a walk every afternoon though. We go along to the shops and she looks at the adverts in the window while I get the paper.'

'That's nice. I like looking at those ads. Random guinea pigs, yoga lessons, old washing machines. I sometimes wonder if it's all code for drugs and strange sexual offerings.'

'Oh, honestly, Meg. Anyway, your gran's very brave, but she's had enough.'

'At least she's getting out a bit.'

Mum nodded. 'I can't quite think about . . . But we do what we can while we can.' She pushed her chair back as if to mark an end to that conversation. 'Is your landlord sorting out your windows?'

'Tomorrow.'

'Are you going to take the day off? Bring your time off forward a day. Spend some time with your gran.'

'I'd better not,' I said. 'This case is really tricky. I have to go in. But keep all your doors locked, won't you? Even when you're inside.'

'Yes, yes, I will. And you be careful too, Meg. You work too hard.'

'I'll be fine. Work helps me forget.'

'And I'm sure someone else could help me take Gran if . . . '

'No. It's not fair to get anyone else involved. It has to be just me, you and Gran. I'll be there.'

I reached to stroke Hamlet. He'd ignored his posh bed and settled himself in a cardboard box which was on its way to the recycling. I noticed something on his collar that I hadn't seen before. A tiny silver barrel. I peered at it. The top was screwed on. I unscrewed it.

A piece of paper was curled up inside. I fished it out and read it.

*I'm such a friendly cat. It would be terrible if something happened to me.*

# 28.

I spent the night in Mum's spare room, clutching Hamlet to me. I slept badly, consumed with fury; Hamlet appeared to sleep very well despite my needy attentions. If anyone hurt Hamlet, I'd probably end up in prison, because I'd hunt them down and assassinate them. Although I was (of course) glad things had changed since the days when the police rammed suspects' heads into walls, it sometimes felt like we were playing a game where only one side stuck to the rules.

I woke early and wondered if I should take an extra day off after all. Not go in. Avoid Richard. Leave them to it and spend the time with Gran. It made sense. What difference would one day make anyway?

But I couldn't bear to let Abbie down. What if they charged her? What if she'd been framed and I was the only one who realised it? I flipped to wondering if we could put Gran's trip back a while. But I couldn't do that either. Whatever I did, I was going to end up feeling guilty, as usual. At least it distracted me from my worry about the threat to Hamlet.

I rose and made tea, and sat in Mum's kitchen with Hamlet on my knee, staring out of the window at Mum's garden. The trees were outlined with frost, making everything look pale and perfect.

Mum appeared in a dressing gown. 'Change your mind and stay here today?'

'Oh God, Mum, I'd like to, but isn't that just giving in to these people? I won't be a victim.'

Hamlet jumped from my knee and sidled up to Mum. She responded to his mind-control by putting down more food.

'I'm sure one extra day off work doesn't give you official victim status, Meg. You've had a nasty shock.'

'But it's a critical time with this case.'

'The young girl whose heart made her kill her father?'

I put my mug down with a thud. 'You actually buy that? Is that what you've read in the papers?'

'They're talking about it everywhere, love. How a heart could make someone do that. People are fascinated. I mean . . . it's terrible for the poor family of course.'

'You'd never have believed something like that when Dad was still around.'

'Well, he's not, is he? Maybe there is an essence of a person in the heart. People have always felt that the heart's where our strong emotions come from. There's more to life than can be explained by science.'

'But it's not been verified, has it?'

'By science, you mean?'

'Yes, by science.' I stood and brushed cat hairs from my knee. 'I have to go in. This is a ten-year-old girl we're talking about. A terrified little girl who's already lost her sister and her father, and who's somehow been made to think her new heart's turned her into a murderer. If there's even a chance someone's done that to her deliberately . . . '

'You don't think she did it? I thought she was found with the knife in her hand. And arterial blood all over her clothes.'

'You're bang up on the case, aren't you Mum?'

'No need to get difficult. I just think you should have a day off. I'm sure your colleagues are well capable of managing without you for a day or two.'

'I have to go in. I won't be bullied. Are you going to be okay?'

'We're fine. I won't let Hamlet out, I'll keep the doors locked, and I'll have a gun trained on the window.'

'Nothing much would surprise me about you any more.' I leant and kissed her, reached and picked up Hamlet and gave him a long hug, which he didn't much appreciate. 'Tell you what – I'll pop back for half an hour, at about four, so we can take Gran out together.'

I took one last look at the pair of them, tucked my guilt into its usual spot, and left the house, locking the door behind me.

★

Richard must have been looking out of his window, ready to pounce. He intercepted me on my way in and beckoned me into his room.

Fear and panic that he might know what I was doing with Gran pushed me onto the offensive. 'You've heard what happened at my house last night.'

He stayed standing but positioned himself behind his desk and the file-barricade, arms folded. He didn't ask me to sit in the chair. 'Yes. I didn't expect you in this morning.'

'What are we doing about them?'

'We're taking it very seriously, Meg. We're – '

'But are we? Because nothing seems to have happened so far. They threatened me the other day by shoving that thing through my letter-box. And it's clear now they think they can do whatever the hell they like. Break into my house, threaten my cat. What next?'

'This gives us something very concrete. We'll get them, Meg. Don't worry.'

'We know who it must be,' I said. 'And telling me to take time off doesn't actually solve the problem. This is not my problem.'

'I'm only thinking of your health.'

'There's nothing wrong with my health.'

'I don't want you to – '

'This is not about me.' Two could play the interruption game.

He paused a moment for maximum impact. 'Especially with what you're planning with your time off.'

Uh oh. He did know something. I hesitated, wondering what he'd discovered. He looked at me through narrowed eyes. 'It's the lying I don't appreciate.'

'I don't remember lying.'

'Faults of omission, I'd say. And you never had any intention of delaying your time off, did you?'

'You put me in a difficult position.'

'I'm going easy on you because of what happened last night. But I do think you should take today off.'

Did that mean he wasn't going to try and stop me taking Gran? Was he okay about it? Did he know what we were doing? If not, what did he mean? He was often baffling, which I suspected was the secret of his success. People didn't want to challenge him for fear of looking stupid.

Richard didn't say anything more. Sometimes it was best not to push things. I'd worry about it when I got back from Switzerland. 'Okay, then,' I said. 'I'll get on.'

I scuttled out before he had a chance to change his mind.

★

I sat at my computer trying to work out who would have wanted to kill Phil Thornton and frame Abbie, and trying not to think about dead sisters hanging from ceilings. I kept coming back to Phil's heart transplant.

I noticed Jai approaching and put on a *Don't Ask Me How I Am* expression.

'How are you?' he said.

I lowered my voice. 'I think Richard might know about me taking Gran. Have you heard anything?'

'Oh shit. Is he trying to stop you going?'

'He doesn't seem to be. But it was one of those cryptic conversations you have with him, where you daren't clarify in case it takes a turn for the worse. So, I'm avoiding him for the rest of the day.'

'Maybe he thinks it's best if he doesn't officially know. Then he can't be accused of condoning it. Anyway, are you alright? After last night, I mean.'

'You know what, Jai, I think they've done me a favour. Instead of seeing my dead sister hanging from the rafters, now I see a stupid dummy.'

Jai bounced from leg to leg. 'Okay. Good.'

'It's like one of those things therapists make you do, not that you'd know, being all sane and that. But they make you do things in your head to turn something traumatic into something silly. I got it for free.' All lies. Why did I feel the need to do this?

Jai smiled. 'Is Hamlet alright?'

'He's with Mum. She just texted and he's in good spirits. A bit narked at being shut in, but not off his food of course. And the landlord is finally putting window-locks on my house, so I'll be fine too.'

I looked up to see Craig flopping down on my spare chair. 'It wasn't Nick Norwood,' he said.

He slid his eyes away before I could catch his gaze. He was thinking about the dog pee incident. I suspected me knowing about it would make him hate me more, even though I'd done all I could to be decent about it, and I had no idea why it had stressed him so much. I wondered again what had happened to him to make him the way he was.

'Is he alibied out?' I asked.

'Rock solid. And he told me what happened with his own kid.'

'Was he being cooperative?'

'Yeah, when the three of us jumped on his head, I think it took the edge off.' Craig gave a little smile.

'What happened with the kid then?'

'They went to the Mermaid place because his friend had told him there were pheasants up there. He's a dodgy bastard – I mean it wasn't even in season, but he went up there with his gun. Saw some birds and got distracted. Left the kiddy by the pool. Came back and she'd drowned. It was too late to save her.'

'Did you believe him?'

'I did, actually. It all rang true.'

'I wouldn't trust him, but we've got no evidence against him, other than Abbie's dreams, which aren't exactly admissible.'

'Yeah. He's in a lot of trouble anyway after his little performance with a shotgun, but he didn't kill Thornton.' Craig stood as if to leave and then hesitated. 'Are you alright?' he said. 'I heard about . . . '

'Thank you, Craig, I'm fine.' I realised that sounded snappy. 'Seriously. Thank you for asking.'

He gave me a self-conscious half-smile. 'They reckon the paedo might not have been a suicide.'

I jerked my head up. 'Oh?'

'Scuff marks on the floor, distance of drop, angle of knots, etc. They reckon he probably passed out at sitting height rather than standing height, and someone pulled the chair out from under him.'

'I knew it. Could you chase Emily again – she's trying to find out when those notes were put on Gibson's computer. What if someone killed Gibson and then hacked into his laptop and edited his notes. Put in Ben and Buddy, and that horrendous picture. What if Scarlett Norwood wasn't even Abbie's donor? What if the whole bloody lot's a set-up?'

# 29.

Jai went off to find Emily, and I closed my eyes and tried to think. I'd only had a few peaceful seconds when I heard someone approaching. The gentle step of Fiona.

I opened my eyes and Fiona sidled up to my desk, looking slightly furtive. She sat in my guest chair and spoke quietly. 'I know I'm supposed to be off the case but . . . '

'Never mind that,' I said. 'What have you found?'

'Are you okay though? It sounded awful. Did you not want to take today off?'

'I'm fine. I'm not giving in to them. What did you want to talk about?'

'It's this Facebook friend,' Fiona said. 'I managed to look at private messages because Vanessa gave us her log-in details. The names of her other child and the dog were available to her friends. But not the spotty swimming costume. So I was trying to find out who knew about that, and she told her friend Helen Key about it in a message. And I checked again what was publicly available about her, about Scarlett. It was in the paper that she was with her father, that she drowned, and that she'd donated her heart. But there was nothing anywhere about Ben and Buddy or the swimsuit, so if the killer knew about them, and it didn't come from Scarlett's memory, then it came from somewhere else, and it looks like it might have come via this Helen Key.'

'Who is she?'

'She only appeared a few months ago, and rapidly friended friends of Vanessa, before sending Vanessa a friend request in December, by which time they had ten mutual friends and lots of hobbies in common, and Vanessa accepted. But I can't find out who she is.'

'Is it fake? A catfish profile?'

'I think so. It's like it was designed specifically to have stuff in common with Vanessa. She said she'd had a daughter who drowned too, but I can't find any proof of that, or even any evidence that she exists.'

I felt a stab of excitement, and hope for Abbie. 'Seriously, Fiona, I think this whole thing was made up. Abbie Thornton's been framed. I don't even think Scarlett Norwood is Abbie's donor. Did we ever find out what Phil Thornton thought he was doing penance for? Why he moved into the house with the statues?'

'I managed to get through to the woman who sold the house to him five years ago.'

'And?'

'Thornton definitely knew about the statues before he viewed the house. The estate agent remembered because they were such an unusual feature and Thornton seemed fascinated by them. And he knew the story behind them, almost as if he wanted the house because of them, like Karen Jenkins said.'

'What was he doing penance for?' I said. 'It was something from years back. I think this might have all started with Phil's transplant, not Abbie's. What if his ex-wife called him a murderer, and Abbie overheard that?'

My internal phone rang. 'Someone to see you. Andrew Bond.'

I blinked and tried to recall where I knew that name from. Michael Ellis's business partner. 'I'm coming.' I turned to Fiona. 'Could you track down someone who knew Phil Thornton's ex-wife? I want to know exactly where his new heart came from.'

*

Andrew Bond was smooth and shiny, in his thirties with a trendy beard and glasses, more salesman that scientist. I supposed Bond was quite a name to live up to.

He looked disdainfully around our grotty interview room. Probably an unpleasant contrast to life in the pharmaceutical industry. 'I'm worried about Michael Ellis,' he said. 'He's mentally ill. And he wants to bring our company down. I don't know what lengths he'd go to.'

'Okay, Mr Bond,' I said. 'Maybe you'd better start from the beginning.'

'Call me Andrew.' He touched his beard as if it was a lucky charm. 'He got this ridiculous idea into his head. About the mice.'

'What was that?'

'It was after he got together with his latest girlfriend. He started going a bit native. Believing a load of pseudo-scientific claptrap.'

'Like what?'

'Oh, she'd done a PhD in psycho-neuro-something-or-other. New Age rubbish.'

'Psychoneuroimmunology?'

He gave me an irritated look. 'Yes. That. Why have you heard about it?'

'I read some articles. I hadn't understood it was New Age rubbish. It's about the interaction between mental processes and physical things like immune response, isn't it? Doesn't your company specialise in the immune response?'

'Not in that rubbish. I realise the brain can affect the immune response. But Michael got it into his head that individual cells had a kind of consciousness. He got carried away. He wouldn't be the first scientist to get sucked onto the woo-woo side.'

Andrew was so annoyingly smug I had to suppress the urge to argue. 'And your point is?'

He sighed aggressively. 'It set him up for what happened with our drug. If he hadn't been so bloody gullible, it would never have happened. And now he's trying to bring the company down. And me personally. He's not amenable to reason.'

'Tell me what you think happened.'

'It's not what I *think* happened. It's what actually happened.'

If I'd had to work with this guy, I might have wanted to bring him down too.

'We had some aggressive mice,' Andrew said. 'Michael decided there must be a reason, and of course he refused to look at the sane, obvious reasons and went straight to the nutty ones.'

'I thought only certain mice were aggressive.'

'Yes, yes. Ones that had been handled by this particular technician. We've got rid of him now. He'd been fabricating records to cover up the fact that he was upsetting the mice. That was a sackable offence.'

'What exactly had he done?'

'He'd changed the notes so it didn't look as if he'd been

handling the mice – the ones that became aggressive. We've just found out what he was doing.'

I could feel things shifting in my mind. 'Go on,' I said.

'So the same technicians handled the donor mice and the recipient mice for the heart transplants. Okay? That's how it had been set up for these experiments. It wasn't normally like that and Michael obviously didn't realise, because the technician covered up the fact he'd handled the recipient mice that became aggressive. He didn't want to get into trouble. But of course he didn't bother covering up the fact that he'd handled the donor mice. It never occurred to him that a nutcase like Michael would come along and decide that the way the *donor* mice were killed had any bearing on the behaviour of the *recipient* mice. Do you see what I'm saying?'

I sighed. 'Yes, I do.' I pictured a house of cards – the construction of the donor heart theory. Andrew had just knocked a card out of its base. 'Ellis saw a connection between the way the donor mice were handled and the recipient mice's behaviour. But actually the recipient mice had been handled by the same technician. The old situation of correlation but not causation.'

'Exactly. So Michael formulated his crazy damn theory that the hearts were carrying their anguish with them or some such rubbish. Because he was desperate to make some sense of it.'

'But in fact all the mice who got aggressive had been handled by this dodgy technician – the donor mice and the recipient mice?'

'Yes. All the recipient mice that Michael thought had picked up on the trauma from their hearts or whatever cobblers he believes – actually it was very simple because they'd all been handled by this guy who we've just sacked. They obviously were a dodgy batch of mice for whatever reason and his handling pushed them over the edge. But he'd covered that up and made it look like they were handled by different technicians, so it wasn't obvious that his bad handling was making the mice aggressive.'

'I understand.' The cards crashed down.

'So Michael's theory is a steaming pile of horse manure. I do hope you didn't take it seriously. He's suddenly against drug companies, going on about how we're only out to make money, not help people, even though he set up the company with me in the first place.'

'Does he know about the technician faking the records?'

'No. He's disappeared. But this has all come out and our shares are plunging like a skydiver with no parachute. Michael's deluded, but he's not stupid. He made sure the data about the experiment and the information about the aggressive mice were formally released. Of course no one drew any particular conclusion from it except him. I'm sure he shorted shares in the company after he left. And because he made the information public, it probably won't count as insider trading because he only based his selling of shares on publicly available information. But now that girl's killed her father and all the nutcases have come out of the woodwork, this is going to ruin us. And get Michael out of his financial mess. You need to release something to say that the kid killing her father had nothing to do with our drug.'

'We didn't release anything to say that it had.'

'Look at this.' He shoved a paper over to me. I glanced at the headline. *Recipients take on the pain of their donors. Will this end transplant tourism?*

'Oh, hang on.' Andrew pulled it back. 'That's a different hysterical article. This one.'

*Immunosuppressant drug implicated in tragic case of possessed schoolgirl.*

I skim-read the article. I could see it wasn't going to be good for Pharmimmune's share price.

'Michael was broke, you know.' Andrew folded his arms. 'This has actually been extremely good for him. I've even been wondering how far he'd go to bring our company down and save himself from bankruptcy.'

'What are you saying?'

'He was desperate. He despises us. And he's clearly not quite sane.'

'Are you suggesting he could have killed Phil Thornton?'

'I'll leave you to draw your own conclusions.'

There was something unnerving about Andrew. I wondered if he really had threatened Michael Ellis. Or was Ellis the dangerous one after all? And I'd let him get away.

★

Fiona intercepted me in the corridor. 'They found something a bit weird, Meg. On Abbie's nightdress.'

I pulled her into a spare interview room. 'What do you mean?'

'They missed it earlier because it had been taped for fibres, so they thought it was just the adhesive from that . . . '

I felt a twitch of hope. 'What did they find, Fiona?'

'Adhesive on the back of her nightdress.'

My heart was pounding. I spoke slowly. 'Somebody stuck it onto something . . . '

Fiona nodded.

I'd been wondering how it could have been done. How the

killer got arterial blood on Abbie's nightdress. Could they have stuck it to themselves? I pictured the scene. Somebody leaning over the sleeping Phil Thornton, Abbie's nightdress taped onto their front. The knife slicing into Thornton's neck, arterial blood jetting out all over the nightdress.

'My God,' I whispered. 'She really was framed. It was set up so it looked like Abbie stabbed him.'

Fiona looked uncomfortable. 'You think the killer stuck it on to himself?'

I ran over it in my mind again. 'It's possible.'

'It does seem like maybe Abbie was framed. Emily came back and said it looks like the notes on Harry Gibson's computer were modified late on the day he died, like you suspected. So they could have been changed after he died.'

My knees suddenly felt wobbly and I sank down onto a chair. We'd been so close to believing Abbie had done it. 'She never dreamt about Ben and Buddy,' I said. 'She didn't produce that hideous drawing of Scarlett Norwood's death.' A flash in my mind of Abbie's cantering-horse picture, and the dog on the fridge. Why hadn't I seen the discrepancy before? What an idiot. She drew better than that now. She didn't draw like a typical kid, and the murderer had overlooked that. 'Yes, she had some nightmares, but she didn't say anything that related to Scarlett Norwood. The killer added all that to Dr Gibson's notes. Found out the information from that poor drowned girl's mother by befriending her on Facebook and put it in the fake notes. It was all made up. The whole heart memory thing. And listen to what I've just found out about those bloody mice.'

Fiona popped down into the chair opposite me, as if she was about to take a statement. I told her about my discussion with Andrew Bond.

'I want someone to look into the animal welfare in that lab, as well as what Michael Ellis got up to with shorting shares.' But in the back of my mind, I was mulling over the first newspaper headline he'd shown me. *Recipients take on the pain of their donors. Will this end transplant tourism?* This tied in with something I'd been thinking. Phil Thornton went to China for his transplant. And something had happened in the past that he felt he should do penance for. Something that made somebody call him a murderer. My mind was chugging away while I explained what Andrew Bond had said.

'Oh my God.' Fiona touched her mouth. 'The whole mice heart theory was based on a mistake because a technician faked the records.'

'So Andrew Bond says. Of course he may not be telling the truth. He's terrified of people blaming his drug.'

'Do you think Michael Ellis believed what he told us?'

'I'm not sure. But it all started with Ellis – the idea that Abbie was remembering the donor child's death. Yes, Abbie was having nightmares, dreaming about her father, but no one thought she was remembering the donor's death until Michael Ellis came along.'

'Could Michael Ellis be the killer then?' Fiona said. 'He was on the verge of bankruptcy, you know. And he shorted those shares.'

'He didn't need to kill anyone though. Surely.'

'No one would have listened to him. Now they're all over it, but only because of Abbie. If she hadn't killed her dad, everyone would have just thought he was a loon.'

'And he wants to bring their company down.'

'But, when you met him on that moor . . . '

'I know. I let him go. But what about Rachel being hit with the rock?'

'Maybe she knew too much? Or he realised she'd keep digging about Abbie until she found out the truth? Without her, who'd be working to get Abbie cleared?'

'Okay, I suppose so. Obviously we need to look into him properly. I'll have to come clean about my meeting on the moor. I'm going to be in the crap over that. I'll ask Jai to look at him. But there's something else I've been thinking about.'

'Yes?'

'You went to the Yulin dog meat demo in London last June, didn't you? Do you remember?'

'How could I forget? Surrounded by horrendous pictures of tortured animals.' She lowered her voice. 'I remember how annoyed Richard was, too.'

'Never mind that. Do you remember opposite the Chinese Embassy, the people who were sitting there, in protest?'

'Vaguely. Hadn't they been there since 2002 or something unbelievable like that? Weren't they a type of Buddhists? Being persecuted by the Chinese Government. Locked up for their beliefs?'

'You know what I remember? They claimed they were being killed for their organs. I could hardly believe it at the time. I was going to check it out, but I got so overwhelmed with the tortured cats and dogs, I never did. And it seemed so unbelievable. I mean, surely even in China, they couldn't imprison you and then kill you for your organs.'

'The rest of the world wouldn't let them do that, would they?'

I gave a hollow laugh. 'I think we both know the truth there.'

'Right.' Fiona gave me an uncomfortable look. 'Phil Thornton had his transplant in China.'

'We've been so busy concentrating on Abbie's heart,' I said.

'We never thought about his. Maybe it wasn't about the donor child at all. Did you find anyone who knew his first wife?'

'I've tracked down a friend. They were close around the time Phil and Laura split up. She said we can go and see her.'

# 30.

Caroline Shepherd, the friend of Phil's ex-wife, lived in one of the tiny cottages that clustered on the hillside above Eldercliffe, leading up to the rim of the quarry. We had to park far below and wind our way on foot up a slushy alley.

'How do they do their shopping?' Fiona puffed.

I could hardly breathe. 'What about when they need a fridge delivered?' I paused a moment and peered over the steep drop to my left. The roofs were spread below, smoke drifting from chimneys. I gave a moment of thanks for the fact that I felt okay about heights again. 'I could imagine buying a house here because I fell in love with it and only thinking about these things after I ordered my washing machine.'

Fiona laughed. 'Me too.'

I wondered if we could be friends, or if it was too complicated, with me in the boss role. I wasn't a natural in the boss role at the best of times.

'I think it's that one.' Fiona pointed at a little stone terraced cottage that huddled between two larger cottages like a young kid standing between older siblings. 'They're not even allowed to paint the woodwork in tasteless colours here,' she said. 'You get reported to the Heritage Committee.'

'Sounds terrifying. Any minute we'll get moved on for being unsightly.' I glanced at Fiona. 'Or at least I will. I need to keep an eye on the time, by the way. I'm helping Mum take Gran out at four.'

We knocked on the French-grey door, and it was flung open by a woman with long hair, in a long skirt and a long, chunky jumper. There was nothing short in sight. We showed her our ID.

'Oh, yes, I'm Caroline. You'd better come in.' She shuffled back and beckoned us into a small living room, enthusiastically decorated with wall-hangings and throws. This woman had been to India and nobody was going to escape the house without knowing it. With a wood-burner in the corner, and a thick rug on the oak-plank floor, it was cosy enough to make me fancy a snooze.

'Sit down.' She waved her arm at an extensively cushioned sofa. 'Herbal tea?'

'Do you have any normal tea? Or coffee perhaps?' No points for rapport-building but I couldn't face a chamomile concoction, and I felt the need for caffeine.

Caroline gave me a disappointed look and took herself off into the kitchen. Fiona and I sat wedged together on the tiny sofa, hemmed in by cushions.

Caroline reappeared with tea. No biscuits here. She settled herself on a chair opposite us and looked concerned. 'You want to talk about Laura?'

'Yes,' I said. 'I know it's a while ago, but we're looking into the death of her ex-husband, Phil Thornton.'

Caroline's face hardened. 'I heard someone killed him. He probably deserved it.'

This was odd. She was the first person who hadn't said he

was a nice, ordinary guy. I sat forward, feeling the throw pull under me. 'What makes you say that?'

'No morals.'

'Can you be more specific?'

Fiona took notes, poking me with her sharp elbow.

'You know he had a heart transplant?'

My pulse quickened. We were onto something here. I nodded.

'They split up over it in the end.' Caroline narrowed her lips. 'We were good people. We marched against the poll tax, demonstrated outside animal testing labs, shouted for *Grants not Loans*.' She shook her head. 'That seems a long time ago now. The way the world's gone in the last few years, the idea of a student grant seems rather quaint. Anyway, I thought Laura had married someone like us. He was a social worker, for goodness' sake, even though his parents were bankers or something hideous. I suppose you don't know someone till they're up against it, do you?'

'What happened?'

'He needed a heart transplant. But the waiting list was long. Lots of people die waiting. Phil didn't want to die waiting. He had a baby on the way.'

'It was when Laura was pregnant with Abbie?'

'Yes. And he heard there was a way round the wait. He had a friend who lived in Taiwan, who told him about it. I think it was a well-known thing there – that you could go to China and get a transplant within weeks, blood type and tissue matched.'

I felt Fiona squirming beside me. We'd both been hoping it wasn't true; that it was propaganda invented by a religious sect.

'So, Phil looked into going to China?'

'Yes. And I mean, at first Laura was excited. It seemed like a brilliant solution. It was spectacularly expensive, but they decided it was worth it. You probably know – Phil had inherited money from the banker parents. And I took it at face value at first. I didn't think it through. This was ten years ago – you didn't automatically google everything the way we do now. But Laura was the sort to research things. It was more the safety for Phil she was thinking about at first. So, she started wondering, where are all these organs coming from? I mean, for any specific donor there's only a few percent chance they'll match you. So, to go over there and get a donor within a week or two, you have to wonder how they're doing that, when it takes years in the UK. And China didn't even have an organ donor register. I mean, with no donor register, where the hell were the hearts coming from?'

With a sinking feeling, I asked, 'What did she find out?'

'The hospital in China admitted the organs came from executed prisoners. Not great, but Laura convinced herself they were murderers so it wasn't so bad. The numbers still didn't add up if you thought about it – there weren't enough genuine criminals. But Phil was keen. He didn't want to know where the heart came from – he just wanted it for himself. He got angry with Laura for even doing the research. It was really upsetting.' Caroline put her mug on a coffee table piled high with paperbacks. 'And then she found the report. About the Falun Gong. Do you know this? Are you just here for confirmation?'

'No, tell us,' I said.

'The Falun Gong are like Buddhists. They're harmless. They do exercises and aim for detachment and spiritual enlightenment

– that kind of thing. But the Chinese government took against them, probably because they thought they were becoming too influential. They started arresting them and locking them up. Trying to get them to renounce their views. I'm guessing you've worked out what this has to do with Phil Thornton's heart transplant.'

'We have some suspicions.'

'Laura couldn't believe it at first, but the numbers the Chinese were giving didn't make sense, so she knew something was wrong. She managed to call the medical centre where Phil was going to have the transplant. And she pretended they were worried about the quality of the heart he'd receive. *Good heart*, the centre told her. *Healthy heart*. They were *selling* it to her. It was appalling. Laura had her suspicions about where that heart might have come from. They're sought-after, you see, because the Falun Gong live a healthy lifestyle – don't smoke, don't drink – and they die healthy, because they're executed.'

'Oh my God,' I said.

I glanced at my watch. It was nearly four. I should have been at Mum's to help her take Gran out. I needed to wrap this up and get over there.

'Laura was absolutely horrified,' Caroline said, 'and she told Phil. And he got really angry. He said he didn't want to know. He said it's like when you eat meat, you don't want to know about the shit life the animal had. You block it off.' She paused. 'I don't agree with that approach either, as it happens, but I'm prepared to acknowledge that it's how most people operate.'

'You're probably right,' I said.

Caroline reached for her mug and cradled it in both hands. 'But I do think most people would draw the line at stealing someone else's heart, even if they were dying. I like to think that.'

Fiona's voice was quiet. 'Me too.'

'So,' I said. 'Phil wanted to go to China to get a heart, even though he knew there was a possibility an innocent prisoner-of-conscience would be killed for it?'

'Yes. I think he used the leather-wearing vegetarian's argument.'

I glanced at my leather boots. 'They were going to kill the person anyway.'

'Yes. But having looked into it some more, I don't even think that's true. They didn't kill all of them by any means. Maybe they took blood samples and picked the ones who were compatible with the people needing organs.'

'It's almost unbelievable,' I said.

'I couldn't get my head round it at first. But when Laura did so much research . . . well, there was a lot of evidence.'

'Did Phil go ahead then, even though Laura was against it?'

'Yes. In the end he just did it. Laura didn't want to lose Phil and she wanted Abbie to have a father, so she accepted it. Well, no, she didn't accept it, but she didn't leave him.'

'Okay, so then what happened?'

'After he got back, they didn't talk about it. It was a non-subject, even though he was having nightmares about it when Abbie was small. But then when Abbie was four, they had her tested for Phil's condition. It's hereditary, you see. And she had it, but she started having symptoms much earlier than Phil. She was going to need a transplant. And then it all kicked off again. Phil said they should take her to China if they could get one there. Laura went ballistic over that – thinking he'd let another child be killed to save his daughter. I mean, I have no idea if they do kill children. But just the fact that Phil would ever consider it . . . '

'Do you think Abbie could have overheard these arguments?'

'Yes. You know what it's like with parents. They always try to keep it away from the kids but when people get angry, they get careless. Laura admitted to me she'd got so angry with Phil, she'd screamed at him that he was a murderer. She knew Abbie must have heard, because Abbie said something to her – something like *Why is Daddy a murderer*? Laura was really upset about it.'

I exchanged a glance with Fiona. 'And she could have overheard them talking about a child being killed to give her a new heart?'

'Yes, she could. And Laura used to go on about how the donors were still alive, some of them weren't even given a proper anaesthetic. It's horrific. Abbie could have heard that. Why are you asking this? Is it something to do with Phil's death?'

'We're not sure. Did they split up over this in the end?'

'Yes. Laura couldn't cope with Phil's attitude any longer. They split when Abbie was five. Then Phil met Rachel really fast. She had a child too.' Caroline put her mug back, fished a well-used tissue from her pocket, and wiped her face. 'I'm sorry. It still upsets me.' She spoke fast, as if trying to get it over with. 'Laura was killed in a car crash not long after she split from Phil. They'd met up and they'd ended up arguing again about the transplant. She texted me to say how angry she was. She crashed on the way home.'

'I'm so sorry,' I said. 'How terrible.'

'I suppose it didn't work out so badly for Abbie in the circumstances. She got a replacement mother and a sister about

332

her age. And then she got a transplant in the UK anyway, so whether Phil even spoke to Rachel about taking her to China, I don't know.' Caroline dragged a cushion onto her knee and picked at a mirrored decoration. 'But I believe in karma. It looks like Phil got what he deserved in the end.'

# 31.

We stepped out into the freezing air.

'My head's spinning,' Fiona said. 'Could that really be true? They kill people and sell their organs?'

I glanced at my watch. Four thirty. A flush of guilt. I should have been at Mum's helping her take Gran to the shop. If we hurried over now, hopefully she'd have waited.

'I need to get over to Mum's,' I said. 'You know, after what happened last night, I don't want her taking Gran out on her own. Shall we just nip over there together and talk on the way? It won't take long.'

Fiona nodded and we headed down the path towards the car, stepping carefully on the frozen pathways.

'Caroline seemed pretty convincing,' Fiona said.

'That's what Phil Thornton was doing penance for.' I clicked the car locks and we climbed in. 'Why he did that artwork, and made the carving of the girl with her heart ripped out. Why he was obsessed with the house and the children who were sacrificed. The weak and the poor sacrificed for the strong and the rich. He knew he'd let someone be killed so he could live. The kind of person who chose social work as a career – he'd probably have been really messed up about it.'

'Do you think all this could have triggered Abbie's nightmares?' Fiona said, as I pulled onto the lane and drove in the direction of Mum's house.

'I don't see why not. If she heard her mum calling her dad a murderer, and heard her parents saying that a child would have to be killed for her to get a new heart. She could have heard all sorts of awful stuff about the heart being taken out while the child was still alive. If she was only four or five, she'd have found it hard to make sense of it.'

'And then when she did get a new heart, it could have all come flooding back.'

'It's common to have dreams from the perspective of the heart,' I said. 'Apparently it's just the way our brains work. But if in Abbie's mind, the heart had been torn out of a live child . . . '

'This could explain Abbie's nightmares, except for the ones that named stuff to do with the donor child. If that's not real, how did she dream it?'

'She didn't dream anything from the donor child, Fiona. That was made up by the killer, and added to Dr Gibson's notes. Abbie dreamt her dad was a murderer, but I don't think she ever dreamt about drowning, or Ben and Buddy or the spotty bloody swimming costume.'

'You think someone killed him because of his transplant? And set up Abbie?'

'What about someone who lost a relative in China?'

'I don't want to target her just because she's Chinese,' Fiona said. 'But did Dr Li ever live in China?'

'I was wondering the same,' I said. 'And I wonder whether she's had any contact with Harry Gibson in the past, with them both being psychiatrists. I'll get Jai to carry out some discreet enquiries.' I dialled his number. He didn't answer, so I left a message.

I called Mum and she didn't answer either. I left a message telling her to wait for us.

We drove in silence for a while. My mind was spinning with this new information about Phil Thornton, going back over all the times I could have picked up on this.

My phone rang. Jai. I pressed the button to answer hands-free.

'Where the hell are you? Richard's on the war path. What's this China connection about?'

'Oh God, I'll talk to Richard some other time. Look, we think we might be on to something here.' I slowed the car so I could concentrate. 'You know Phil Thornton had a heart transplant in China? It looks like he might have had a heart from someone who'd been murdered. Deliberately for their organs, I mean.'

Jai sounded pissed off. 'What are you on about, Meg?'

'It's rumoured that they use the organs of prisoners-of-conscience. Falun Gong practitioners.'

'One of the charities in Phil's will was something to do with that. Falun Gong. He gave them quite a chunk of money.'

'This is it.' My mind suddenly felt sparkly and clear. 'Did you check if Dr Li had had any contact with Harry Gibson?'

I could hear Jai breathing down the phone. 'I found out she was his supervisor.'

'Oh God.'

'I don't have many details but his practice manager checked on their system and he had periodic meetings with her, and joined in webinars. Why didn't she tell us she knew him? And Richard said she'd emailed him her updated CV just as the whole Abbie thing was kicking off. That's why she came to mind when we needed a consultant.'

My heart was racing. 'Bloody hell, she put herself forward deliberately. Why didn't Richard say?'

'I suppose he had no reason to question her motives. But why didn't you tell me you were looking into the China connection? I've checked and Dr Li and her son did live in China for a few months. It looks like she had a daughter too. Why didn't you tell me you'd gone dashing off looking into something to do with China?'

An icy feeling under my ribs. I remembered the photo in Dr Li's office. Tom and a girl with the same eyes. 'Where's the daughter?'

'There are no recent records of her.'

'Oh God.' *What the hell had happened to the daughter?* 'So Dr Li could have had access to Abbie's notes. Have we heard back about the identity of Abbie's heart donor? I'm sure now it's not Scarlett.'

'They're really funny about giving the information out. You have to jump through so many hoops.'

I pictured the scanned letter in Harry Gibson's file. From Great Ormond Street Hospital. Why hadn't I questioned that at the time? It had looked so official, but would have been easy to fake, especially for someone who worked in the medical profession. It now seemed obvious that they wouldn't just give that information to a psychiatrist. I spoke quietly. 'Scarlett Norwood wasn't Abbie's donor.'

'Right.'

'What if Dr Li's daughter was involved in this supposed organ harvesting – and she died? Then Dr Li realised Phil Thornton had got his heart from China. Could she have done all this?'

'I don't – '

'And it's getting people thinking about where organs come from. It's already in the papers – talking about transplant tourism, saying people aren't going to want hearts of convicted murderers. Maybe that's what she wanted as well as revenge. She could have even tipped off the papers. I've been wondering how it got out. And it was her that really convinced us that Abbie could be having memories from her donor. She did it very subtly, but she made the point.'

'Are you saying she killed Harry Gibson?'

'She could have done. He would have trusted her if she called round to support him after the paedophile allegations. She probably knew what tranquillisers he was on. And she's strong. I remember her pushing her son through the snow after he tried to commit suicide. And she would have known Abbie was on Sombunol. She's a doctor, so she could have easily found the carotid artery on Phil Thornton.'

'But Abbie Thornton's at Dr Li's now,' Jai said. 'She's gone for a session to see if she's up to being hypnotised again.'

'Christ, Jai, I didn't know that.'

'I'll get over to Dr Li's clinic,' Jai said. 'But it'll take me a while from here.'

I pictured Mum waiting with Gran for me to come over. She'd be pissed off with me, but Abbie could be in danger.

'Okay, Jai,' I said. 'Take back-up. We're in Eldercliffe. We'll go to the clinic now and check Abbie's okay. If there's any problem, we'll wait for back-up.'

★

I skidded into the health centre's car park, nearly crashing into a black car that was leaving at high speed.

A woman came charging towards us, slipping in the slush. Rachel, wild-haired and frantic. 'She's taken her! Dr Li's taken Abbie!'

Fiona and I jumped out of our car. Rachel grabbed Fiona's arm. 'Come on. We need to follow them.'

I glanced behind me at the black car, which was now disappearing round a corner in the lane. 'What happened?'

'I was in the waiting room . . . ' Rachel spoke in gasping bursts. 'Dr Li saw Abbie on her own. Oh God, why did I let her? Abbie started screaming . . . She took her out the back. We need to follow them! She's taken her in the car.'

My phone rang. I picked up, whilst following Rachel across the car park at a run.

It was Mum. 'Meg! It's your gran!'

'What?' I lurched to a stop, put my hand over the phone, and shouted to Fiona. 'You go with Rachel. Follow Dr Li. But call for back-up!'

I watched Rachel's car accelerate out of the car park. 'Mum. What did you say?'

'I took her to the shop. She wanted to go. She only has a few more days. How could I say *No*? I went inside . . . ' I was losing signal. ' . . . she'd gone . . . '

My knees felt weak as the poisonous guilt flushed through me. Was she saying Gran had disappeared?

I glanced down at my phone. The signal had dropped out. No bars. We were in the shadow of the rock that loomed over the clinic.

There were lights on in the far end of the clinic, the opposite side to where we'd seen Dr Li. They'd have a landline I could use. The main entrance door was locked, so I ran down to the lit end to see if there was another way in. I pushed against what looked like a fire door.

The door swung open, pulling me off balance.

Someone grabbed me and dragged me forwards. Something sharp stabbed into my arm. A voice. 'You will keep interfering.' Then nothing.

# 32.

Where was I? I opened my eyes but couldn't see. My brain wouldn't work. How long had I been unconscious?

I was on my front. On some kind of padded trolley, my face pressing into cold plastic. The smell of antiseptic. I opened my eyes wider and twisted my head around, straining to see into the darkness. My heart thudded in my ears.

I couldn't move. Something held my wrists and ankles. Straps like leather. I tried to wrench my hands free but they were held down tightly.

Panic swelled inside me. I kicked my legs but they were held fast. I kicked harder but nothing shifted.

I yelled, 'Hello? Help!'

My clothes were gone and I was wearing a hospital gown, the type that fastened at the back.

A square of light to my side. A door must have opened. Someone was silhouetted against it. A light flicked on and the door shushed to a close.

The gentle noise of a wheelchair rolling towards me.

My breath tore my throat. I shouted. 'Tom! What the hell's going on?'

He was close now, so close I could have touched him if I hadn't been restrained.

His voice was smooth like oil. 'If you'd only left me alone, everything would have been fine.'

I fought against the restraints. 'What do you mean? What are you doing?' My voice bounced from the walls.

'You'll soon find out,' he said. 'Don't worry.'

I thrashed from side to side, stupidly pulling against the restraints, rubbing my skin raw.

Tom stood and walked around me, leaving his wheelchair behind.

He stood. He walked.

Was I hallucinating? 'What . . . ' I whispered.

And then it began to click into place. 'Oh God.' I twisted my head to see him, squashing my face into the surface of the trolley. 'You're one of those people. You're not paralysed.'

'Soon I will be. I don't have to wait much longer.'

'You want to be paralysed?' My brain wouldn't accept this. How was it possible? That my worst fear could be his dream? My mind whirred, trying to make sense of it all. I was so helpless lying on my front, only able to move my head. I tensed my back muscles and pulled upwards, but only succeeded in wrenching my shoulders.

'You messed it all up, didn't you? You had to come along, all pally with my mother, and rescue me.' He looked straight into my eyes. 'You stupid bitch.'

He switched on another light. We were in a large, spotless white room. My eyes were drawn to the brightly illuminated, shelved wall a few feet from me. Arranged neatly, glistening in the light, were surgical instruments. Something solid welled up in my throat. 'I'm going to be sick. Tom. I need to be sick.'

He glanced round. 'Go ahead.'

I gasped for breath and fought to control myself. I let out a sob. But I wasn't sick.

'And it could have worked, jumping there. The height was perfect and I knew how to jump and what position to land in, if you people hadn't been there getting in the way. I wasn't trying to kill myself. Only to break my back. My mother knew.'

I blinked back helpless tears.

'She still doesn't understand. She was always trying to cure me. Taking me to China to see crazy, alternative therapists; getting me involved with the Falun Gong – I suspect you know how that worked out for us. And sending me to Harry Gibson, as if that would help. Why do you people care? It's my life, my spine, my legs. If you'd all left me alone, none of this would have been necessary.'

My gaze slipped over the shining instruments. My voice croaked in my dry throat. 'What do you want from me?'

He looked straight at me. 'I'm going to operate on myself. I've realised it's the only reliable way. But it's difficult to do. I'll have to come in from behind like for an epidural, and sever the spinal nerves. I need to practise first on another person, to get the feel of it.'

I felt bile rising again in my throat as his words rearranged themselves in my mind. 'What do you mean? You can't practise on me! Let me go!' I pulled at my arm restraints, desperation making me drag skin from my wrists and ankles. 'They'll send someone for me. They're expecting me back.'

He walked closer and stood over me. His voice was cold and emotionless. 'That probably would have been the case. That nice colleague of yours – he'd have realised you were still here. But unfortunately I drove your car, including your bag and your phone, to your mother's house. They'll think you went over there because of your poor grandmother going missing. There was no room to park outside. All those pesky police vans. So it's down the road. They'll probably wonder if you were taken by the people who took your grandmother. It certainly couldn't be me, could it? A poor disabled man.'

I let out a tiny whimper. 'How did you know . . . '

'It's so easy to hitch when you're in a wheelchair. A very polite gentleman gave me a lift back here. He was worried my chair wouldn't fit in the car, but if you take the footplates off, it's fine. And of course I'm unusually good at getting myself from the chair into the front seat.'

'Oh my God.' I was entering a kind of alternative state. As if my brain was shutting down. I'd never been scared of dying. But to be paralysed . . . I wanted to pass out.

'I know they'll want me to go to the police station,' Tom said. 'But it might not prove possible. You see, I'm leaving the country soon. I'd prefer not to go to an English prison if I can avoid it. So I have plans in place. I won't be doing my own operation here, but I really would like to do this practice run. To get the feel of it.'

I looked at his blank, dark eyes. 'Was it you? Did you kill Phil Thornton and Harry Gibson, and attack Rachel Thornton?'

'They deserved it,' he snapped. 'If your sister had been butchered and her organs removed while she was still alive, you'd feel the same way.'

I let my head flop forwards. I'd been right. This had all started with Phil's heart transplant. In China.

I had to keep control of myself. There must be a way out of this.

Maybe if I could express sympathy. Get him talking. The

longer someone talked to you, and the more they told you about their life, the less likely they were to slice you up. Useful fact. 'Yes,' I said. 'I probably would.'

'Phil Thornton didn't care. He didn't even feel guilty that they treated us like animals.'

'But . . . ' I couldn't think properly, tied to this cold table, scalpels glinting next to me. I needed to keep him talking to me. Ask him questions. Act almost as if I admired what he'd done. 'How did you know he went to China?'

Tom flicked his head in a dismissive gesture. 'My mother got me to set up the computer when she did Harry Gibson's online supervisions. I heard about Abbie's dreams. I don't know why my mother didn't realise. But she didn't. Then it was simple enough to find Thornton and get the truth out of him.'

'Was Phil Thornton given your sister's heart?'

'Of course not.' Tom's upper lip twitched and those almond eyes narrowed. 'Some other rich Westerner will have got her organs. But it might as well have been him. My sister wouldn't have died if it wasn't for people like Phil Thornton. And he wasn't even decent enough to help me try to stop it.'

'You asked him to help you?'

'All I wanted was for him to tell his story honestly, so I could publicise what's going on. But he wouldn't do it. Too worried his wife would find out what a monster he was. That's when I knew he had to die. And they thought their daughter was remembering her donor's death – it was too good an opportunity to miss. He did help me in the end, without meaning to, of course. I met him a couple of times. Suggested he encourage his wife to think their daughter had memories from her donor. He even said he'd heard her screaming she was being drowned. He thought it would cover up the truth

345

about what he'd done, of course. If everyone thought it was the donor child's father who was the murderer, it would stop them asking questions about him. Oh I loved that – the way he helped me set it all up to kill him.'

'It's terrible about your sister,' I said. 'I agree with you. I'll help you . . . Help you tell people about this. It has to stop. You planned all this so well – imagine what we could do if I helped you. I could start petitions. I have lots of friends and contacts. Please, Tom.' I could feel myself moving towards complete, abject, grovelling desperation. 'Don't make yourself as bad as them. Let me help you tackle it.'

He spat on the floor. 'People don't want to hear about transplant tourism. Nothing ever changes. But if people think hearts can bring *feelings* with them? Then they'll think twice about having one from someone who's been murdered, won't they?'

'You won't get away with it.' I fought to control my breathing, my face twisted over the smooth plastic. 'They'll find you. You know you won't get away with it.'

I was struggling to keep myself from becoming hysterical. I told myself it must be a dream. Things like this didn't happen in real life. I'd play along and soon I'd wake up, soaked in sweat and tangled in the sheets.

'That's why I had to do it this way,' Tom said. 'It's already making people think. It's in the papers and people are blogging. I did have to give the press a little steer, and write a couple of scientific papers to refer to. I quite enjoyed making that one up about new immunosuppressant drugs allowing hearts to take their feelings with them. Luckily nobody checks their sources these days, including my mother.' He gave a little laugh. 'Suddenly people are asking where the organs come from. Now it might affect them. People are selfish like that.'

'But Harry Gibson?' I said. 'What had he done wrong?'

'I needed access to his notes. And I couldn't have him saying that Abbie didn't really mention Ben and Buddy, could I? He was easy. Delighted to let me in and drown his sorrows with me, when I said I'd found out something about the people who spread those rumours. I was the technical one, of course. He knew that. I'd helped him log in to my mother's webinars. And who'd turn away a man in a wheelchair? And of course I wear gloves – I have to wheel my chair. Nobody's going to challenge that.'

Poor Harry. Like all of us, he'd looked at Tom and seen someone harmless, vulnerable even. And it had all been an act. 'So Gibson wasn't a paedophile?'

'I didn't put real pornography on his laptop.' Tom's tone was defensive. 'I wouldn't have accessed those websites and encouraged the abuse of children. I'm not a monster.'

I could have almost laughed, if I hadn't been about to be butchered. The minds of murderers – they *never* thought they were monsters. It didn't matter what they'd done – they'd always find a way of justifying it.

'And Rachel Thornton didn't care,' Tom said. 'Phil told me. He said Abbie was getting worse and he couldn't carry on the pretence that it was all coming from her heart. He tried to pay me off. Idiot. Then he said he'd told his wife what he did in China and she wasn't bothered.' A hint of doubt crept into his voice. 'She said it wasn't their problem. So she deserved to die. I should have hit her harder with that rock.'

Tom must have been the angry man who visited Phil's work. The reason for Phil getting out twenty thousand from his account. It hadn't gone to Karen. I didn't tell Tom that Phil Thornton had been lying about Rachel knowing. I didn't want to aggravate him.

'And that child,' he said. 'Abbie. She killed her own step-sister. She told Harry Gibson. She'd overheard her parents talking. She knew someone had died for her father, and she wanted a new heart, so she thought someone had to die. She deserves to be locked up.'

I felt a wave of despair. He could twist anything round to his own agenda. If he wanted to practise his operation by severing my spine, he'd find a way to convince himself it was justified.

'She wouldn't back down.' There was a break in Tom's voice. 'I said to her, *Just tell them what they want to hear.* But she wouldn't do it. Wouldn't renounce Falun Gong. And it was my fault. Lily would never have been interested in Falun Gong if it hadn't been for me and my condition. If my mother hadn't insisted on dragging us to China to try and fix me.'

'I lost my sister too. But of course you know that.'

He glanced at me. 'You're nothing like me. I read about you online. You bullied your sister and she killed herself. I hate you for that. You and that Abbie Thornton – you both had sisters and you killed them. I can't forgive you. You should be punished.'

'It's not true. Please, Tom, you have to believe me. My sister had cancer and I didn't bully her. They made that up. But I think about her all the time, just like you think about your sister.'

Tom gave me a wary look. He shook his head rapidly. 'I see what you're trying to do. You're trying to make me like you. I don't trust you. You made your sister kill herself. And you kept interfering. Everyone else was happy Abbie had done it. You

348

never thought she had. Even after her mother was attacked. I heard that colleague of yours say so – the woman. When my mother was talking about hypnotising the child. You still didn't believe she'd done it.'

I released my back muscles and sunk onto the trolley. 'It was you. You hung the dummy in my bedroom. And put the note on my cat.'

'If you'd just had some time off then, it would have all been alright. Why would you go to work after that? Why would you leave your family when they needed you? Your colleagues were happy Abbie did it. But you wouldn't stay away.'

I closed my eyes. Felt the silence of the room. I could die there.

How would Mum cope? What would happen to Gran?

Tom touched me lightly on the back. His hand was cool. 'I'm not saying any more to you. I need to do the operation. But where shall we make the incision? Since you're being nice, I'll try it a little further down than I was thinking. Maybe I'll let you keep bladder and bowel control. You won't be able to use your legs of course.'

'No. Please, Tom . . . ' I was ready to beg, to plead, to give up any semblance of control or dignity and say I'd do anything, *anything* if only he didn't take away the use of my legs.

'There is another option.' He ran his finger up my spine. 'What I planned initially. I thought it was a perfect solution to my problem. An ethical solution under the circumstances, and surely it would have kept you away from work for a while, but you had to come along and offer yourself up instead. I'll give you the choice.'

# 33.

He was gone. I was in darkness again, my face pressing into a pool of my own tears.

What a fool I'd been. Seeing only the poor disabled son, when in fact he'd been orchestrating and plotting and scheming whilst pretending to be depressed and vulnerable.

I pulled more carefully at the restraints, trying not to panic. Jai would come. He'd work out that I hadn't left here. Or Fiona. She'd realise.

I wasn't even convincing myself. They'd think I'd gone to Mum's. They'd come eventually, but it could take them hours if they were distracted with Fen and Abbie.

I pulled my left leg towards me, feeling the strap strain around my ankle. My bad ankle. The ankle which was much thicker than it should be. Pain shot into my foot, reminding me of that day, the day when I'd found my sister hanging, when I'd climbed the ladder to try to save her, and fallen, breaking my ankle, which no one had noticed with so much other horror around, so it had set wrong. But the lump of callus meant my foot was smaller compared to my ankle than in normal people. And my ankle was swollen from falling in the snow the day before. Which meant a strap tightened around my ankle might just not be so tight around my foot after all. I wiggled my foot and repeatedly pulled my leg towards me, lifting my stomach upwards away from the trolley, gasping with the effort but feeling the strap straining. I did that again and again.

Light. The door was open. Something was being wheeled into the room. Another trolley. Someone lying on it. I peered into the brightness, my eyes not focusing.

I gasped and let out a sob.

'No, Tom. No, you can't . . . '

'Can't what? Use her for my experimental surgery?' He was back in the wheelchair. He glided forward a couple of feet and flicked on the light. The one that illuminated the surgical instruments. 'Why not? When I found out about your plans, I thought it could have been designed for this.'

'Please . . . '

I was sniffing and gasping. I needed to blow my nose and wipe my eyes. I couldn't bear this.

'It's much kinder than taking her all the way to Switzerland on an aeroplane,' Tom said. 'You do know she'll be terribly sick, don't you?'

My heard thudded in my chest. 'You haven't killed her?'

'No, no. I need her alive if I'm to practise cutting the spine. I want to work with a live body. I'll have to allow her to wake up a little, so I can check whether she's paralysed, but it won't be too traumatic for her. And of course if I use her I won't have to use you.' He leant forward, looked into my eyes and hit me with a full-on smile, sunny like a friend on a warm day holding out a drink.

A wave of blackness came over me.

'I don't know why you're so concerned,' Tom said. 'It's all about suffering. That's what you think, isn't it?'

'How do you know what the fuck I think?' I wanted to put my arms around his crazy, psychopathic throat and throttle him until he gasped for mercy.

'There's plenty about you online. Taking your grandmother to Dignitas. *There's nothing sacred about human life – it's all about whether someone suffers*, isn't that what you said? You really think there's nothing sacred about human life? That made me angry. But if that's what you think, why are so concerned about my plans for your grandmother?'

There was something missing from him. Something had been taken in that Chinese prison. When his sister's heart stopped beating, Tom's heart had died too.

'Only if they choose to die,' I said quietly. 'It doesn't mean we can just kill them, Tom.'

'Well, hurry up and make your decision. I have plane tickets booked tonight. I don't have forever. I'm confident my mother will take the blame for a while, but eventually she'll blab. If I use your grandmother, I'll obviously have to leave you tied up, but once I'm out of the country, I'll let them know where you are. This is a special area of the clinic – no one uses it but me, but don't worry, I will let them know. And I'll put your grandmother to sleep. I have the right drugs for that. Much better for her than going to Switzerland, I think. Wanting to bring her round now and keep her alive is a little selfish, wouldn't you say? I'll give you a moment to think it over.'

'We haven't said goodbye.' I sniffed and then felt like I was choking. I'd thought I had time. Time to say all those things I'd never said to Gran. To tell her what she meant to me. And now he was taking that time away, and it was all my fault for insisting I carried on with the investigation and then letting

Mum down today. If I'd just taken some time off to be with Gran like a normal person, this would never had happened.

'But saying goodbye is for your benefit, isn't it?' Tom said. 'Not your grandmother's. Don't people say it's much kinder if they just slip away? But don't let me persuade you. If you'd rather I did it on you, and let your grandmother wake up to discover you let yourself be paralysed so she could have another week of feeling sick and flying to Switzerland to be killed, I really don't mind.'

He wheeled himself from the room, leaving Gran lying unconscious on her trolley a couple of feet from me.

I strained my neck and looked over at Gran's face, impossibly old in the light that bounced off the gleaming knives, scissors and tweezers behind her. I so wanted to reach and touch her.

I yanked my ankle against the strap. Then pushed it deep in and yanked it back again. To and fro. Agony. But I thought I felt it loosen. Just a tiny bit.

I tugged my leg towards my torso and felt a definite loosening. I inched it back more slowly. It was coming out. I felt a flush of excited adrenaline, even though this didn't exactly put me in a strong position. I shoved it back into the strap again, knowing if I pulled hard, it would come free.

Maybe he was right about Gran? It probably would be kinder to let her die here. She wouldn't know that this insane man had hacked into her and severed her spine for *practice*. Her last moments would be going to the shops with Mum – surely much better than having to fly to Switzerland and watch me and Mum fall apart around her. So, why couldn't I let that happen? Was I really prepared to risk my own legs for this principle that I couldn't even make sense of?

The door banged open and Tom walked in. 'You'll need to

tell me what you're feeling – where you feel pain or numbness. I'll give you a mild anaesthetic.' He touched my back again. A shudder went through my body. 'Or of course I can use your grandmother instead.'

I wanted to scream. I imagined breaking free and mashing Tom's head into the concrete floor, taking one of his surgical knives and stabbing it into his heart. I pulled against the restraints. 'You sick bastard. Let me go!'

'What's it to be?' he said. 'Shall I use you or your grandmother?'

I fought to control my breathing. In through the nose and out through the mouth. This wasn't a dream. It was real and I had to deal with it.

I thought of all the times I'd talked to Hannah about her spina bifida. When I'd been the sounding board her guilt-stricken parents couldn't be. When she'd shown me diagrams of the spine; told me exactly where she felt pins and needles, where she felt shooting pains, which damaged nerves had messed up which bits of her lower body.

'Use me,' I said. 'Don't use my grandmother. Do it on me.'

# 34.

'It would be easier with you on your side,' Tom said. 'But I don't trust you. So you'll have to put this under your stomach to allow me access between the vertebrae.'

He shoved a pillow underneath me, raising my stomach off the trolley. My mouth watered and I felt a wave of sickness. I swallowed repeatedly.

I gasped. A coldness, then a narrow needle pierced my skin, next to my spine. 'A little anaesthetic,' Tom said. 'To take the edge off.'

I took a slow breath. I couldn't afford to lose control. Out of the corner of my eye, I saw Tom lift a syringe, to which a needle was attached. The needle was about six inches long.

'It's similar to the needle you'd use for an epidural.' His tone suggested he was doing something normal. A routine medical procedure, for my benefit. He lifted the needle above him and squinted at it. 'The syringe is to help me manipulate it. That will be quite challenging when I'm doing it on myself. I'll insert the needle and move it around, to achieve paralysis. I'll need to go in at L2 to ensure that the quads are paralysed.'

My stomach gave a huge heave. I breathed in slowly and squeezed my eyes shut, feeling tears on my cheeks. I opened them again and saw Gran's trolley, pushed sideways out of the way, towards the bank of instruments.

I pictured the spinal diagrams Hannah had shown me. I'd have to let him get to the outer membrane, near the nerves. Then if I could convince him he'd gone far enough to paralyse me, he'd stop. I prayed he'd stop.

'Are you ready?' he said. 'Tell me what you feel. If you cooperate, I'll try not to harm you any more than necessary.'

My breath was coming in fast bursts, despite my desperate attempts to control it.

I felt the needle. I gasped. A sharp stab. It was going in.

'A little deeper,' Tom said. 'We're going towards the spine now.'

My heart bashed my ribs. Stars and colours flashed in front of my eyes. I couldn't afford to faint.

'You're a little plump,' Tom said. 'It would have been much easier to feel the membrane if I'd done this on your grandmother. She's skin and bone. Are you feeling anything?'

'Just pain . . . ' I gasped. If I screamed too soon, he'd know I was trying to fool him. If I left it too long, I might never walk again. I waited. I could feel the needle, but not exactly where it was.

'Yes! Pins and needles,' I shouted. What had Hannah said? 'Pins and needles down my left leg . . . Both legs now.'

'A little more then,' Tom said.

I waited a second. The longest second of my life.

What would my life be like if he did this? I thought of all the things I'd no longer be able to do. Things I took for granted, despite my friendship with Hannah, and watching *Extraordinary People* on the TV, and trying so hard to appreciate my body in all its imperfect plumpness. Until now I hadn't properly grasped what I had.

I screamed. 'Fuck, Tom, stop! That hurts!' I yanked my arms against the straps, trying to keep my back still.

'Stop moving!'

'I can't move my legs.' I pulled my arms against the restraints but kept my legs still. Completely still. 'Tom, I can't move my legs!'

'No, you can.' Tom stepped back, leaving the needle in my back. 'You're not paralysed. I've only nicked the edge of the membrane. You *can* move your legs.'

I sobbed. 'I fucking can't. You bastard!'

I pictured Hannah when she was struggling with her legs, and I put on a performance like I never had in my life before, pulling my wrists against the straps, sobbing, keeping my legs still and lifeless.

Tom took another step back so he was next to Gran's trolley. He was about a foot away from me. Shaking his head repeatedly. 'Must have gone in deeper than I thought . . . '

Gran's eyes opened.

I yanked my bad foot out of the strap, twisted my hips and booted Tom sideways with all my strength. He knocked into Gran's trolley, then crashed into the shelves of surgical instruments.

The needle was still in my back. I could feel it, millimetres away from my spinal nerves.

I caught Gran's eye. 'It's okay,' I whispered. Possibly the biggest lie of my life.

Gran heaved herself into a sitting position.

Tom scrabbled to his feet and grabbed a large scalpel from the shelves behind him. He took a step towards me. He looked dazed, holding the scalpel above him as if he was about to bring it down onto me. Onto my neck.

The moment seemed to elongate and then freeze. Tom with his arm raised, scalpel gleaming, Gran sitting on her trolley, blinking and swaying, looking like she was about to faint. There was nothing I could do. I couldn't get free. Couldn't get my leg to the right angle to kick him. Tom was poised with the knife ready to stab me. I felt a scream building inside me.

Something shoved into Tom. He spun round, his face red with fury. It was Gran. She'd collapsed sideways into him, with just enough weight to shift him sideways and knock his arm off course. He was now within kicking distance. I booted him in the shoulder. He toppled to the ground, his head crashing into the concrete floor. He lay still.

'Gran, it's going to be okay,' I said. 'We'll be okay. Can you get this needle out of my back?'

Gran looked stunned, confused, terrified. But she lowered herself down and stood unsteadily, leaning on my trolley and reaching over my back towards the needle. I lay still, trying not to picture her shaky hands spilling tea at Mum's house.

A tiny stab of pain and the needle crashed to the floor.

I let out a huge breath. 'Can you undo that strap? The one round my hand.'

Tom shifted.

Gran reached for the strap. It had a buckle, thankfully – she'd never have untied a knot. She gave it a tug but it wasn't releasing. She had so little strength in her fingers now.

Tom groaned. He was coming round.

'A bit harder, Gran,' I begged. 'Pull harder.'

Gran took a huge breath, and tugged at the strap again.

It popped free.

I let out a sob, reached over my back and undid the strap around my other hand, then reached down and freed my leg.

I jumped from the trolley. My legs collapsed and I ended up on the floor. I grabbed the needle and syringe and dragged myself to my feet, legs quivering.

Tom rose to a sitting position. He swung round, arms reaching towards me.

I lunged for him and stabbed him in the neck with the needle. He screamed and fell back on to the floor.

There was no spurt. That wasn't going to be enough.

I frantically scanned the room for a weapon. Tom was too close to the surgical instruments, but his wheelchair was in the corner.

I dashed over and yanked one of the footplates free, again thanking Hannah for my education. I turned to see Tom crawling across the floor towards me, the syringe still sticking from his neck.

I raised the footplate and smashed it down on his skull. And then again. Harder.

He dropped to the floor and lay still, blood seeping from his head.

'Come on, Gran.' I grabbed her hand and tried to pull her towards the door, but she collapsed. I dragged her to her feet, helped her onto the trolley again, and shoved the trolley towards the door, manoeuvring it around Tom's still body. I pushed her through and slammed the door shut behind us, looking for something to wedge it with. There was nothing.

Even though he was lying unconscious on the floor, I was frantic with my need to run from Tom, to put distance between him and me. I pushed Gran's trolley along the corridor towards a door which seemed to lead to outside.

The door was closed. And there was no handle. I pushed it with all my strength but it wouldn't shift. If it was the one I'd come through, it opened inwards, but the hinge looked as if it would go both ways.

I tried to get my fingers around the edge to pull it towards me, but it seemed stuck fast.

'Shit, shit.' I was panting and on the edge of a panic attack. I shoved the door again. Nothing.

The door was smooth apart from a small indentation near the floor.

I flicked my eyes desperately over its entire surface. There had to be some way to get it to open. Panic was rising up inside me. I wanted to scream.

It had to be magnetic. There was no other way it could have worked.

I remembered Hannah's tales of wheelchairs flying at MRI machines. Wheelchairs were ferrous. Maybe Tom had designed it specially so he could get through easily without a key, just by bringing his wheelchair up to it.

I shoved Gran's trolley against the door. Nothing.

If it was magnetic, I needed Tom's wheelchair to get us out.

The thought of going back towards Tom's operating theatre made me weak with terror. I let out a desperate sob and pushed past Gran's trolley. Tears streamed down my cheeks. I sprinted back down the corridor and gave the door to Tom's room a little nudge. I peered in. He was still lying on the floor.

I ran in, grabbed his wheelchair, and dashed from the room, pushing the door shut behind me.

As I shot towards the external door, I could see that the indentation was designed to receive the footplate of the wheelchair. The one that was missing.

'Oh, Jesus.' I leant and grabbed the other footplate, and shoved it into the indentation.

Nothing.

A scratching from behind me.

I'd been wrong. It wasn't magnetic.

Tom was waking. We were going to die in this place. Why hadn't I taken a knife when Tom was on the floor? Why hadn't I hit him again – harder? It always drove me nuts in films when the hero didn't give the villain an extra smack for good measure, and now I'd done the same.

I shifted the position of the footplate.

A click.

I pushed against the door.

It opened.

I grabbed Gran's trolley and thrust her out of the clinic. I glanced back and saw Tom staggering from the operating theatre clutching his head. He was holding the scalpel. I kept the footplate, got Gran out and slammed the door behind us. If Tom had to go back for the other footplate, maybe we'd have time to get away.

I dragged Gran's trolley across the slushy car-park and towards the road. My legs felt leaden like in a dream. I wanted to sob with the effort of making them move.

A shout. 'Meg?'

That sounded like Jai.

I looked up to see him running across the car-park towards us. 'Jesus Christ, Meg. What the hell happened? Why's your gran here?'

Gran and I juddered to a halt. 'I'm going to faint.' I leant forward, hands on knees, head dangling down.

Jai touched me on the shoulder. 'Come on. Let's get you out of here.'

Gran sat up on her trolley. 'Get us away from that man,' she said, with surprising force.

'Come on.' Jai grabbed Gran's trolley.

I followed Jai towards a police van in the corner of the car park. 'Is Abbie okay?'

'She's back with Rachel. Dr Li's confessed to it all.'

'It wasn't her,' I said. 'It was her son.'

# 35.

Dr Fen Li grasped her hands together, fingers interlocked, knuckles white. 'It all started in China,' she said.

She'd had the caution. She knew we might use anything she said against her. But she hadn't asked for a solicitor and she seemed desperate to share her story. Unconcerned about what would happen to her, but determined to make us understand why she'd tried to protect her son, even though he'd killed two people.

'I was born in China,' she said. 'But I went to school in the UK. I'd lived here for years. Tom was born here. And his sister, Lily. Tom studied medicine and qualified here. I thought he was happy. But then one day he told me about his . . . condition. About wanting to be paralysed.' She looked down at her clenched fists. 'He'd told Lily years earlier – he'd always felt that way ever since he was a little child. He didn't want legs that worked. It was awful. I couldn't make sense of it. I was so upset . . . and angry . . . He told me he'd had ideas about trying to actually paralyse himself. It was terrible.'

'It must have been,' I said.

'I was convinced it should be curable. I mean, JCB drivers develop mental maps that include the digger arms, for goodness' sake. Our mental maps are flexible. So I researched it and found out about a practitioner who'd had a lot of success helping people with the condition. He used a mixture of Traditional Chinese Medicine and Buddhist philosophy, plus he taught specific exercises with mirrors, like the ones they do with amputees. The Buddhism helped his patients see that the human body is just a temporary vessel and isn't within our control. And the exercises helped them to accept their bodies as they were. It seemed to work for people with BIID, when nothing else had. But he was in China and he didn't travel.

'I persuaded Tom to see him, and we went out there, planning to stay a few months.'

'Did this doctor introduce Tom to Falun Gong?'

'Yes. He was a practitioner. It really helped Tom. Lily became interested too. I didn't see a problem. It's peaceful. No one should be offended by it.' She shook her head. 'I still find it hard to believe. Having lived so long here. I don't think we understood . . . '

'And the Communist Party banned it?'

'They said it was a cult – a menace to society. Our doctor was arrested, and he must have given them names. They came for Tom, and Lily too.'

'And put them in prison? Just for being interested in Falun Gong?'

'They put them into a detention centre for "re-education".' She wiped her forehead. 'It was terrible. I didn't know where they were. I'm sorry.'

I gently prompted her to carry on.

'Tom told me they were tortured. I know you won't understand, but Falun Gong . . . they are peaceful and tolerant. But they don't renounce their views. They even claim not to hate their torturers – they say the torturers are victims too. I can't be like that. I have a lot of hatred in me. You can't imagine how it feels to know your own children have gone through something like that, and that you put them in harm's way. Electric shocks, beatings, the "death board", the – '

'The "death board"?'

Fen's face was grey in the cold light of the interview room. She wiped her mouth with a tissue. 'Yes. The "death board". Tom told me they strap you to an iron or wood board, so your four limbs are stretched out. They leave you there for at least seven days. You can't move, can't go to the toilet . . . can you imagine? The muscle cramps make you scream. They sometimes strip you naked to make it easier for them to clean up afterwards. Tom said someone was held on there for eighteen days. *Eighteen days.* When they let her off, she was paralysed from the waist down and she never recovered.'

I felt like I couldn't breathe properly. 'You don't have to tell us all this.'

'I want to.' She raised her head and looked out of the window that overlooked the cold grey car park. 'Tom capitulated. But Lily didn't . . . We were told she'd offered to donate her organs. She would have been alive when they took them. So that the organs were viable. They would have taken her heart, kidneys, liver, corneas . . . ' She swallowed and wiped her eyes roughly with a tissue. 'It would never have happened if I hadn't persuaded them to go to China, and made Tom see the doctor – if only I'd been able to accept him as he was, like Lily did.'

I looked across at her haggard face, not knowing what to say, or even what to think. 'After Tom was released, you came back to England?'

'We decided to try to make a new life. But you don't just get over something like that. Tom's BIID got much worse. All the progress he'd made before being in prison, it all came to nothing. He was so devastated about what had happened . . . he blamed himself, me, Falun Gong. He was a mess. He didn't have the energy to work against his feelings any more. I know it makes no sense . . . '

'It's clearly a real condition. I understand that.'

'He decided to return to England as a paralysed person. I tried to help him. Harry Gibson was a specialist in BIID and Tom agreed to talk to him but nothing worked. And when you've lost a daughter . . . other things don't matter so much. I agreed to go along with the pretence, and told people he'd had a car accident. I imagined the accident so many times, I almost came to believe it. When I told you in the gorge, it didn't feel like a lie. I did lose patience sometimes, but only occasionally. Anyway, I thought he was happy being a "pretender". But then he tried to jump into the gorge to paralyse himself.'

'I see now. It must have been hard for you, coping with that.'

'I thought it was. I didn't think it could get any worse. But now he's killed people.'

'Did you know what he was doing?'

'Of course not. But it's my fault. I gave him access to my computer. That was the trigger.'

'Tom got to listen to the recordings of Dr Gibson's sessions with Abbie?'

Fen sighed. 'He's the technical one. He helped me set up LogMeIn for Harry when he couldn't get onto my webinars. He had access to everything on my computer and Harry's too, I suppose, so all the notes and recordings from Abbie's sessions. I trusted him.'

'And he realised Abbie's nightmares related to her father's transplant?'

'Yes. Screaming that her father was a murderer, that he'd taken someone's heart when they were still alive. He didn't know for sure what it meant, but he suspected.'

'But why did Tom realise that it was about Phil's heart transplant, and you and Dr Gibson didn't?'

'I suppose Tom was the one who'd been in prison. When he heard Abbie talking about someone taking a heart when a person was still alive, it would have brought his sister to mind. Whereas Harry and I were thinking of the donor child for Abbie, because that's what Rachel had said. We missed the connection.'

'But why didn't you tell us you were Dr Gibson's supervisor?'

'I'm sorry.' She sighed. 'Tom asked me not to. He said he'd seen some child pornography on Harry's computer when he was helping him get onto the webinars. He said he'd told a friend who was thinking of taking his child to see Harry, and then he'd realised he shouldn't have done that, and I could be in trouble for giving him access to Dr Gibson's computer. I didn't know Harry was dead at that point. I was just doing what my son asked me. Then when poor Harry killed himself, Tom said it was even more important I didn't say anything, because it was our fault people had found out about the pornography. I'm sorry.'

'But at some point, you realised what he'd done, and you still protected him? Let us believe Abbie had killed her father? And then ran off with her to let your son get away?'

Why was I was even shocked? Mothers would do anything to protect their children. I'd once read about a thought experiment where parents had to say how many other children they would let die to protect their own child. One woman said she'd let every other child on the planet die to protect her own. Until she realised her daughter needed another child to play with. So every child on the planet minus one.

'I know I shouldn't have done that,' Dr Li said. 'But he's my son. The only child I have left. He's been through so much. I couldn't cope with him going to prison again. I'd never have let Abbie go to prison though. I'd have told you the truth once Tom was out of the country.'

★

'I don't regret any of it.' Tom spat the words across the fake-wood table. 'I don't care that you caught me.'

It was too hot in the small interview room, and there was a faint smell of something sharp and poisonous. Craig sat next to me, and even he seemed muted.

Tom's anger felt overwhelming – a huge, acid sea of it seething and swirling around us. I pictured a protective bubble around myself, and spoke into the recording apparatus. Calming myself by going through the familiar set-up routine.

Tom bored into me with his almond eyes, giving me a quiver of fear, a momentary flashback to that operating theatre.

I waited a moment, feeling his anger dissipate.

'Would you like to tell us what happened?' I said.

'Would I? Why should I tell you anything?'

I waited. I sensed he wanted to share. He wanted us to be impressed.

'It wasn't so hard,' he said. 'Once I'd had the idea. Blame my mother – if she'd been capable of dealing with the technology herself, I wouldn't have had access to Gibson's computer. But if Phil Thornton had just agreed to be honest about what he'd done, none of this would have been necessary.'

In Tom's mind, it has all been justified. Necessary. 'And you framed Abbie?' There was no judgement in my voice. I wanted information – it was a dangerous indulgence to let suspects know how you felt about their behaviour.

'I'd been in their house before, of course, to see the layout. How silly they were to leave a key outside, in the most obvious place. It was so easy to find. I'd seen from their calendar that she'd be away, the mother. And I knew from Gibson's notes that the child and her father would be drugged into oblivion on Sombunol. It wasn't hard to inject her with a little more, in one of her existing needle sites.' He was talking freely, with pride in his voice. The anger had gone because he was pleased about what he'd done and was relishing telling us about it.

I swallowed and indicated that he should carry on.

Tom tipped his head to one side. 'I did wonder about bringing Abbie through and stabbing Phil Thornton with her in front of me and the knife in her hand. But I decided it was too risky, so I took her nightdress, taped it on to myself, sorted out Phil Thornton with the nightdress in front of me, and then brought Abbie through and put the nightdress on her. There was enough blood around, and I thought his wife would mess up the scene anyway. I wasn't expecting her to do quite such a good job of confusing matters, of course.'

'Were you wearing protective clothing?'

'Two suits and three sets of overshoes. You can buy them on eBay, you know. I knew it would make a terrible mess when I stabbed him, so I took the outer suit and shoes off and put them in my rucksack, then I brought Abbie through and put the nightdress on her, and left her on the floor in all the blood, with the knife, smeared it around a bit so I didn't give your people too much help. I put the third set of overshoes on, being careful not to tread in the blood of course, and I left wearing the second suit and the third set of overshoes. It all went as I'd planned. There was a difficult moment before I stabbed him when I thought he was waking up, but of course he didn't. And I put a few rocks in my rucksack and chucked all my gear into the lake at the quarry. Easy-peasy.'

'But Phil Thornton didn't get your sister's heart.'

'What difference does that make? He got the heart of an innocent person, and some other monster got my sister's.'

I looked into his empty eyes. He didn't seem to have any regrets about what he'd done. 'And Harry Gibson?'

Tom laughed. 'He *gave* me access to his computer. It's amazing what information people will give you. Once I was in, it was easy to find all his passwords. People are stupid.'

'You changed Abbie's notes after you killed Dr Gibson?'

'Maybe I did, maybe I didn't.' Tom smiled. 'Yes of course I did. But why am I telling you all this? I should make you work harder. Although I've decided I'm not too concerned about going to prison here. I suspect it will be quite pleasant in comparison to my experiences in China. I read in the paper that prisons here are like holiday camps.'

Something flicked across his face and I wondered if it was a memory from his time in prison. What kind of man would he have been without that experience? Possibly a good man, a good doctor. He had an unusual condition in wanting to be paralysed, but that wouldn't have harmed anyone, if only he'd been left alone. He'd been getting better before the Chinese locked him up. The ripple effect of their violence had spread across the globe.

'I suppose it was you who emailed your mother's CV to DCI Richard Atkins last week.'

'Of course. It wouldn't have mattered if he hadn't used her, but I thought it could be fun if he did. It made it easier for me to feed my scientific papers into the equation, and convince you Abbie could be remembering the donor child's death.'

And Richard had fallen for it, like a little kid taking sweets from a paedophile.

'But me?' I said. 'How did you know so much about me? And why did you hate me so much?'

'Obviously I was going to check out the lead detective, wasn't I? I didn't realise there'd be such a lot about you online. You seem to have upset a group of bible-bashers, which I don't have a problem with. And it turned out they were surprisingly enthusiastic bloggers. But when I found out you'd been responsible for your sister's death . . . '

'I'm no more responsible for my sister's death than you are for yours,' I snapped, before I thought it through.

A tiny jolt went through him and he looked right into my eyes. 'You're probably right,' he said. 'If it hadn't been for me, my sister wouldn't have even been in China, let alone involved with Falun Gong.'

'It's not your fault,' I said. 'And it's not my fault my sister died.'

The air in the room thickened and my skin felt prickly, like I wanted to scratch, or be sick, or go somewhere cold, or anywhere away from there.

'We didn't understand why they were carrying out health checks,' Tom said abruptly. 'They had no regard for our lives, but they kept taking blood samples. They took blood from my arms and earlobes, and they took urine samples and X-rays.

One time, they were beating me – they'd pinned me down and were hitting me with sticks – when another official warned them not to damage my organs. I didn't understand. And always, always, I worried for my sister. She was stronger than me. I knew she wouldn't give in.

'And at first I didn't believe it about the organ harvesting – there were rumours they would take our organs one by one, whilst we were still alive.' He paused and touched his cheek. 'One day, my sister was pulled from her cell and never returned. I gave up after that. I told them whatever they wanted to hear. I didn't care if I lived or died. I didn't care what I believed. Only the thought that I might one day get revenge – only that thought kept me alive.'

# 36.

I turned to look through the frost-covered trees. Mum had fallen behind. I waited for her to catch up. She was breathing heavily. 'You're fast,' she said. 'Despite your ankle.'

'That ankle may have saved my life. It's still a bit sore though.' I reached and gave it an affectionate rub.

We carried on, and arrived at the statues.

Mum stepped forward towards the screaming child. 'Terrible. To think that really happened only a few hundred years ago.'

'You know the story, then.' I led Mum to the bench and we sat down. The wood was damp and I could feel the cold even through my thick coat. 'And what if it's still going on, Mum? I know what Tom did was appalling, but for God's sake, what if his sister really was murdered for her organs and they got away with it?'

Mum touched my arm. 'You have to focus on the things you can change,' she said. 'Or you'll go mad. The world's full of terrible things. Horrific things. But you work hard here and you right some wrongs and you do your best.'

'I suppose I try. But I am going to see if there's anything I can do to help with the campaign for the Falun Gong. Everyone's talking about it now. Maybe something good can come out of Tom's horrific behaviour.'

'What'll happen to him?'

'He'll be locked up for a long time. Probably in a psychiatric unit. They'll go for insanity. We're okay with that.' I stared into the trees. Wisps of mist touched their tops. 'I understand why he was so angry though. Imagine if Carrie had been killed so someone could have her organs. How can people let that happen? How could Phil Thornton let it happen? He knew they were going to kill someone to get him a heart and he went ahead with it anyway.'

'People can be good at deluding themselves,' Mum said. 'And don't we make these decisions all the time? Children on the other side of the world are dying for want of cheap antibiotics. And yes, we send them money from time to time, but not enough to significantly disrupt our lives. Phil Thornton just took that a step further.'

'I see what you're saying, but I still think it's different. And look how poor Abbie suffered. All she went through, because of this. All the misery.'

'How is she now?'

'She's okay. Her mother explained everything to her. It was hard for her to understand what her dad did. But she'll be alright. And I'm pretty confident she didn't kill her sister. It seems the sister fell and Abbie pretended she'd pushed her because she thought it would make her dad happy.'

'Good heavens. The poor child.'

'At least she knows now that she's not going mad, and there's nothing wrong with her heart.'

'Thank goodness. And I'm very glad you're not paralysed. I wouldn't want to be looking after you as well as Gran.'

I put my hands on my knees and said a few silent words of thanks for my legs. I turned to Mum. 'Actually, what Tom said made sense. Gran would have suffered less if she'd never come round. But I couldn't seem to let that happen. Bloody stupid really. A bit like that thought experiment where you have to chuck a fat man off a railway bridge to save ten workers on the line below and you can't do it.'

'You were very brave,' Mum said. 'And a little silly.'

I sank back against the freezing bench. 'Are you okay about Gran's decision not to go to Switzerland?'

Mum nodded. 'Relieved actually. It would have been such a difficult trip. And we'll just have to manage it. I know it won't be easy. But she's so happy that she was able to help you, it seems to be making it easier for her to cope.'

'She was fab,' I said. 'The way she pushed Tom's hand out of the way. To be honest, I think she just keeled over, but it did the trick. She's in all the papers. *SuperGran.*'

'It's going on her gravestone.'

I looked up to see Jai walking towards us through the trees. 'You came,' I said.

'Wanted a look at these statues I've heard so much about.' He stepped over and read the plaque. 'Nice. It was Thornton's biggest charitable donation in his will, you know. To the Falun Gong.'

'He was tormented by what he'd done,' I said. 'It saved his life, but it also destroyed him and ultimately got him killed.'

The breeze dropped and I felt the silent presence of the statues.

'Rachel Thornton got in touch,' Jai said. 'She finally heard back from Abbie's real donor.'

I jerked my head up. 'Oh? Who was it?'

'A little boy. No similarities to Abbie's dreams. There was one weird thing though.'

'Oh yes?'

'He was very artistic – absolutely loved to draw and paint. Horses and dogs mainly. Apparently he was pretty good.'

A tiny shiver went down the back of my neck. 'Abbie started drawing horses and dogs, after her transplant.'

'I know,' Jai said. 'Not that it matters now, but I thought you might be interested. Anyway, do you both fancy a drink? There's a pub on the main road. My round.'

I grabbed Mum's hand and pulled her up off the bench. 'Come on. Quick. The statues have put a spell on Jai.'

Mum jumped up with uncharacteristic sprightliness, and set off for the main road with Jai. I waited a moment in the cold gaze of the statues before following them through the trees.

# Acknowledgements

Writing the acknowledgements plunges me into a state of extreme anxiety, and I'd first like to thank anyone I've forgotten to thank. You know who you are – please don't hate me too much.

Huge thanks to my fantastic agent, Diana Beaumont – as happy dancing to the Fun Lovin' Crime Writers as she is negotiating a deal. I feel very fortunate to have her on my side.

Thank you to my brilliant previous editor, Sally Williamson, and my equally brilliant new editor, Emily Kitchin, my excellent copy-editor, Jamie Groves, and proof-reader, Anne O'Brien, and to the whole HQ team, including Lisa Milton, Lucy Richardson, Lily Capewell, Joe Thomas, and all the others who work tirelessly to support our books.

Again, Jo and Ducky Mallard were indispensable and coped admirably with my disturbing questions about arterial spurt and blood spatter, and other gunky things that are lovely to chat about over a drink or two.

Since I wrote my first book, something wonderful has been created – the Doomsbury writing group, including Sophie Draper, Fran Dorricott, Jo Jakeman, and Louise Trevatt. Thanks guys for all your support and general loveliness. Other critiquers for this book included Gemma Allen, Fay Gordon,

Katherine Armstrong, Alice Hill, Robyn Arend, and Hjordis Fischer. Thank you so very much.

All my friends have been brilliantly supportive, including Ali Clarke and all the Alderwasley crowd, Sally Randall, Sarah Breeden, Ruth Grady, Emma Goodchild, Catherine Hodgetts, Susan Fraser, Estelle Read, Lucy Padfield, Keren Hill, Helen Chapman, Beccy Bagnall, and the members of White Peak Writers, including Tina, Pam, Isobel, Angela, Rachel, Mary, Tom, and Alex, plus Alex Davis and the people I met on his course, including Glenda, Peter, Ray and Carl. Also the patent attorney community, who have been very enthusiastic, despite (or possibly because of) me killing one of them early in proceedings. The crime writing community is also incredibly supportive and generally wonderful (and a little bit drunk). Thank you to all the writers who took the time to read and comment on my first book – there are too many to mention but I hope you know who you are. I was overwhelmed by the support I received. Likewise, the book bloggers and those who run book groups on Facebook, and those who take the time to post reviews – it really does make a huge difference. Also, my local bookshops, especially Waterstones Derby, Sheffield and Chesterfield, and Scarthin Books – I love you all. (This is becoming too much – I'm almost making myself cry. I can hear the cat saying, 'Get over yourself – it's just a book and it sent me to sleep'.)

Thank you to Rob, my mum (who has the eyes of a hawk when it comes to proof-reading) and dad, and Julian and Marina, for putting up with all this author stuff, and to Katia and Maxim for periodic sidewaysing of my book.

Finally, thank you to my readers, who've been so enthusiastic and encouraging. As a debut author, that means the world. Thank you for choosing to read this book – I really hope you enjoyed it.